I0761629

THE FOREST ON THE EDGE OF TIME

THE FOREST ON THE EDGE OF TIME

JASMIN KIRKBRIDE

TOR PUBLISHING GROUP
NEW YORK

THE FOREST ON THE EDGE OF TIME

A Tor Book
Published by Tom Doherty Associates / Tor Publishing Group
120 Broadway
New York, NY 10271

www.torpublishinggroup.com

EU Representative: Macmillan Publishers Ireland Ltd, 1st Floor, The Liffey Trust Centre, 117–126 Sheriff Street Upper, Dublin 1, D01 YC43

The Library of Congress Cataloging-in-Publication Data is available upon request.

ISBN 978-1-250-37683-1 (hardcover)
ISBN 978-1-250-37684-8 (ebook)

First Edition: 2026

Printed in the United States of America

10 9 8 7 6 5 4 3 2 1

For Mum, with all my love.

THE FOREST ON THE EDGE OF TIME

0

Principle Rays

I'm already homesick, and we haven't even left yet. We're in that pre-leaving stage that's normally busy with last-minute bathroom visits, checking passports and boarding passes, and assembling packed bags in the hall. This isn't like that at all. We are leaving, just not by the front door. And we can't take any baggage. Can't even take our clothes.

I grab a moment to myself in the kitchen, hugging a mug of tea to my chest, the just-healed tattoo still tingling under my top. There'll be no tea where I'm going; not many tattoos either. That might be a problem, actually. Too late to do anything about it now. I try running vocab in my head, but all I can remember are words that will hinder more than help—imposter, violence, betray—and how does that last one conjugate in the pluperfect? I've got two-thirds of a PhD in this, I should know. Doesn't matter, it won't come up. I gulp the last of my Earl Grey, relishing the prickling bergamot and sweet milk, and leave the cup unwashed in the sink. Puffing my cheeks out, I check the window for one of those ghostly me-but-not-quite-me reflections, but no one else is in there today, just the actual me looking pale and bag-eyed.

'This had better work,' I mutter.

Across the hall, dimmed by closed curtains, the sitting room looks like someone has vomited electrical equipment everywhere. In the middle of the wiry nest, she—all familiar wild hair and baggy jeans—fiddles with the fairy lights, checking that she's linked every cable to the catopthura's infinity-loop circuit. The old bedroom mirror stands in the loop's crosshairs, waiting to swallow us.

'All set?' I ask.

She tightens a coil of wire around a lekythos I stole from my British Museum placement. She looks up stiff-shouldered, muscles relearning how to move without the brace. I'm still never prepared for how weak and raspy her voice is now. 'If by that you mean are we ready to turn on a homemade machine that includes several nonsensical components and will almost certainly blow every fuse involved, then yes. We're all set.'

I put a hand on her shoulder. 'Trust me. It'll be fine.'

'Oh, I trust you.' She stands, hands on hips, frowning at the mirror. 'I just don't trust that you know anything about circuitry.'

'I don't, that's why I drew the blueprint but you had to put it together.'

Scepticism pulses from her.

'What?' I snap, irritable because in her shoes I'd feel the same way, and it's occurred to me too that I might be losing it.

She mutters, as if she doesn't want to ask, just believe. 'You're sure this will work?'

'Yes.' My voice comes out more confident than I feel.

'And we'll get them back if we do this?'

'Yes.' I look her in the eyes this time. This is the one thing I am sure about.

'And we won't . . . like . . . die on the journey or something?'

I shake my head, but when she turns away I bite my lip and she catches the reflection in the mirror.

'You're not sure, are you?'

My shoulders sag. I haven't told her the half of it. I haven't discussed the dreams, the memories, the fact we'll have to lose ourselves, or that the reflection-ghost wants us to do this for the Earth, not for— But it doesn't matter. She doesn't need to know all that, it'll only frighten her. 'We can't carry on like this. You know we can't. We have to try.'

She nods, but I think she's hoping the catopthura's just going to fizzle and spark and trip a switch. 'Alright then. Guess we boot her up.'

Taking the extension cable plug in her hand, she slides it into the wall socket and flips the switch. She holds her breath, stepping back and grabbing my hand as we wait before the mirror. Bulb by bulb, the fairy lights twinkle on, their glow brightening until it's almost painful, accompanied by a deep electric hum, like a subwoofer malfunctioning.

Her hand sweats and trembles in mine.

'Do you think it'll explode?' I say, but it's hard to make myself heard over the noise.

My eyes flick between the odd components as they start warping: The woman painted on the lekythos becomes clearer, the slip turning wet as if the artist's hand has just lifted the brush away; the watch's leather strap wrinkles, the buckle dulling with wear that hasn't yet occurred; and the egg timer whizzes round and round, ringing at decreasing intervals.

'No, I think it's working!' she shouts back, her words almost lost under the increasing electric buzz. Then three lightbulbs explode beside the clock we've repurposed from the hall, and it emits haywire shrieks as its cuckoo springs out, wings aflame. 'I take that back!'

We jump forward, she fiddling with the circuitry behind the clock while I pat out the flaming cuckoo wings. In my hands, the wooden bird unchisels, returning to a block of wood, growing bark and sprouting fresh twigs while its call turns from a mechanical trill to actual birdsong. The bird's legs become roots, which wrap around my fingers.

'Working again!' She yells as she prizes the once-bird thing off my hand and pulls me back.

We collapse in a pile of arms and legs in front of the central mirror, dumbstruck as its reflection folds inwards, revealing a molten interior, like hot coals or dappled sunlight through closed eyelids. Wind bursts from it, the fairy lights growing brighter and brighter, the rumbling louder and louder, until I want to screw up my ears and eyes against them—but I can't because the Arch is open.

This is the moment.

I pull her up, squeezing her hand and tugging her forward, but she sticks in place.

I turn, hair whipping my face. 'Come on, it's now or never.'

'I didn't think it would work! I'm frightened!'

'Come *on*, we have to try.'

'You promise we'll see each other again?'

My throat tears shouting back. 'I promise!'

She purses her lips, setting her brow, and launches forward.

We leap, together, so in sync I can't tell whose foot is first. The between-space washes over us, warm and gentle like swimming in a pool—

But I look back over my shoulder and see fairy light bulbs exploding in handfuls. The watch face cracks, hands spinning so fast they smoke, and the shrub that was once the hall clock flickers through seasons so fast that autumn leaves and spring blossoms fall at the same time. This can't be how the catopthura's supposed to work.

In the mirror-world, the current grows stormy, and a wave breaks over us with a sound like tearing paper and snapped twigs, ripping away her hand, and so much else besides.

1

Hazel

STATION C, DATE UNKNOWN

After the rush of wind, her body lands like an acorn thudding to a pavement. Her thoughts are a typhoon of sycamore seeds and dandelion clocks. She isn't sure she lost consciousness, but she's disoriented like she might have. There are unseen spaces in what just happened, as if she's turned the light off at night and, though her mind knows where she is, her eyes still can't quantify the dark.

Still, there's no gasp of arrival. She's just *here*, and when she turns back, there's only a cliff edge where her memory should be. Her pupils slide under her closed eyelids. Home, life, family, job—she has the concepts but there's nothing for them to cling to. The only detail she's got is her name: Hazel Brandt. It's not quite a memory, just a thing she knows, a little déjà vu—'already seen'—a strange phrase when so much of what happens is the in-built programme of human habit running its course anyway; just another repeat in the loop of history. The dark void of an existential crisis gapes. Don't let anxiety take over.

How long has she been . . . here? Seconds only. She cranks her eyes open. A breathing mask exudes light pressure on her nose and cheeks, brushing her lips with cold, disinfectant-laced air. Something's gone wrong. There's been an accident. **Breathe. Deep and steady, panicking about it won't help. In to four, hold for two, out for six, hold for two**—Whose voice is that? Not hers, someone else's, inside her head. A memory? Hazel's panic rises again. Where is she and what's happened and why is—

In to four, hold for two, out for six—Breathing makes her bruised torso throb, and her pulse pounds in her ears, throat, and pelvis, every beat matched by a machine beeping. She's being monitored.

Hazel rolls her head, trying to escape the mask's seal. Beside her, another person lies prone on the floor, so close Hazel can count the front teeth in its slack mouth. Blood congeals in a trail from its salt-and-pepper hair, over its cheekbone, and off the bridge of its nose. The sharp collar of its white lab coat is spattered with viscera. Not its—hers. Her hand is flung to her head, and she might be only fainting, if it weren't for the pale metacarpals puncturing her palm.

In to four, hold for two, out for six, hold for—

If Hazel wasn't wearing the mask, she'd be close enough to smell the woman: the iron in her blood and sweat on her skin; the soot on her collar and forehead; the polystyrene reek of the melted pen still clutched in her three-fingered hand. Don't think about where the other two digits are. The woman's eyes are glazed open. Hazel screams, but all that comes out is a hiss like gas escaping its cylinder.

Her bruises protest as she turns from the woman's body, only to find another corpse to her left as well, just the lower half visible: one booted foot, with a ragged stump where the other should be.

Hazel rotates her eyes to the papier-mâché sky. Somewhere beyond the bodies, the repeated slap and sigh of water betrays waves breaking against a gravel beach. Flakes of ash spiral onto Hazel's face, and she blinks them away with heavy eyelids. She brings a hand to her chest, where the pain is worst, and finds a knot of sticky patches and wires plastering her skin. Of course, for the monitor. Wind blows across her body and, strangely naked, she shivers.

A silhouette leans over her, indistinct against the lustrous clouds, and a pair of too-thin hands stick more patches to her chest. She winces and grunts at the pressure, her voice vibrating through the breathing mask and back into her face. More pairs of skeletal hands pull and push her into an upright position. She winces as she realises the extent of her bruising, hot tears flooding her eyes.

'Stop.' But the word gets lost between tight vocal cords and phlegm. It's her reaching out and grasping a pair of cold hands that makes her carers move away. Slender fingers grip her wrists, but the thing before her is far from comforting. It's no more than two feet high, with a spherical body, lanky multi-jointed limbs, and two long antennae tipped with heavy cylinders for eyes.

Hazel catches her breath and says, 'You are not as human as I expected.' Her voice sounds like an overworked motherboard with a janky fan.

The strange figure watches her with its camera lenses. One of its spidery metal hands unclasps her wrist and re-adheres a peeling sticky patch on her chest. A wire tail undulates from the thing's back, twisting in the breeze. It's examining her—making calculations about her. Fragments climb from the crevasse of her amnesia: **Python, Golang, C++, DataTrill; a stifling office on Silicon Roundabout; too many bodies in a tiny room but it's OK cause we're just starting up; the scent of gunpowder tea, takeaway curry, and fresh-ground, cold-brew coffee; little mechanical arms and pixelated eyes—**

'Ah,' Hazel says. 'You're a robot. I like robots.'

Robots are like the genes in DNA: just a series of commands executing in a chain. She can deal with a robot. Or at least, she should be able to, but there's something uncanny about this one. She thinks—though the void of her memory makes it impossible to know for sure—that this category of robot is new to her, its capabilities completely unknown. She shivers.

As if in response, the robot's tail flicks and two more automatons emerge from behind Hazel's back. They whir and tick like grandfather clocks being wound as they pour a patchwork blanket over her. Hazel clutches the blanket to her chest, blinking. Blood vessel–patterned sparks spatter her eyes every time her heart beats. The monitor stutters. She could do with a pair of human hands reaching out, but the only ones nearby belong to the deceased.

The sea echoes the blood swishing in her ears, as she tries to make sense of her surroundings. She's at the edge of a concrete dome that's been blasted open by an explosion. The bodies either side of her wear white lab coats, lightly dusted in shards of metal, plastic, and stone. In the centre of the floor, a crater smokes, edges tattered with wires.

'What happened?'

The robot who's still holding her hand stays silent, but its lenses adjust. Surely, it's not responsible for the explosion? It gazes at her, tail making S shapes. The two other robots assemble behind it, identical except for the rust patterns on their hulls and the neat steel patches welded over damage. The robot whose hand she's clutching looks as if it's wearing a rusty red waistcoat like a robin; the one to her left has a neat row of teaspoons patching its shoulder; the one to the right is so shiny even the weakly luminous clouds sparkle off its hull. Robin; Teaspoon; Shiny. She should probably be grateful they're trying to keep her alive.

Their tails wave in sync as the heart monitor beeps, steadier than Hazel feels. **In to four, hold for two, out for—**

Wheels crunch over the debris-strewn ground and more robots join them, trundling around the dead bodies, organising into groups to carry the corpses away.

The heart monitor staggers, then stabilises at a higher rate, but Hazel can't pay attention to it. It's not *her* fear. That heartbeat doesn't belong to Hazel Brandt, it only connects to a small, stupid part of her that needs to get a grip. **Intofourholdfortwooutfor—**

The first robot—Robin—glances at Hazel, its lenses adjusting repeatedly, as if it's making further calculations.

'You still haven't told me what happened.' It stares at her. Her head sags sideways. 'Huh. You can't talk, can you?'

Robin releases her wrist and opens a small door in the side of its round belly, pulling out three little objects that it drops in her cupped hands: two oval tablets and an earpiece, clean, but scratched with wear.

She holds up the earpiece. 'You want me to put this in?'

Robin gazes, its lenses reflecting her own face, flecked with cuts and bruising in the convex distortion. The earpiece buzzes against her fingers, as if someone's already speaking on the other end. Sure enough, when she holds it to her ear '. . . Hazel Brandt, please respond. This is a message for Hazel Brandt, please respond. This is . . .' The voice should be a relief, but Hazel's stomach works into knots because, again, it isn't human: It's a thousand voices speaking in unison, so perfectly synchronised no human conductor could orchestrate it.

'Yes.' She replies between shallow breaths. 'I'm here. I'm Hazel Brandt.'

'Hazel Brandt, please follow the Tinys into Station C to commence your briefing.'

'The Tinys . . .' She mutters. Robin, Teaspoon, and Shiny all turn to her, their tails standing bolt upright as if saluting. 'Right, the Tinys.'

'Please follow the Tinys. We have numerous items to discuss before nightfall.'

She looks at the sky, but the thick clouds and gritty haze offer no clue where the sun might be. 'Can you tell me what happened?'

'Affirmative. The events preceding your arrival will be discussed during your briefing.'

'Briefing? I don't remember . . .' She trails off. 'I don't remember anything, but I certainly don't remember a briefing.' No contract signed, no job offer, no agreement. No briefing.

'Hazel Brandt, you are the latest recruit for Project Kairos. We have— You are—' The earbud stammers to a standstill. Then, 'Are we not drawn onward ere divided?'

Her memory flickers, like a router flashing in a darkened office. 'We few live on mirror rims,' she replies, the void of her memory filling her mouth with words she doesn't know she knows. They flood out, she and the computer simultaneously reciting: 'Emit no evil & live.' The ampersand, which can't be pronounced but which she sees in her mind, is emphatic—not 'and,' but '&,' as if her voice and the computer's are both tracing the eternity symbol until they meet in the middle. Warmth spreads in Hazel's chest, as if she's holding her hands to a radiator after a long, snowy walk.

Her mouth continues without her volition. 'On time's mirror rim, no evil we few de-divide.'

And the computer, leaning into its bass tones: 'Redrawn onward to new era.' There is a pause at the other end of the earpiece, as the words concertina inward to that emphatic, eternal ampersand. Hazel's uncertainty balances out: Wherever *here* is, it's where she's supposed to be.

'Hazel Brandt, please follow the Tinys into Station C and your briefing will commence.'

She clutches the blanket around her creaking body. 'I don't know if I can get up. I don't think anything's broken, but it hurts like hell.'

'The Tinys have been instructed to provide you with suitable medication.'

She unclamps her fist from the tablets, which have left a chalky residue on her clammy palm. 'What is it?'

'It is akin to paracetamol.'

She laughs, immediately regretting it when her ribs cramp. 'Somehow I don't think paracetamol is going to cut it.'

'It is the only medication available.'

Hazel glances around. The heart monitor is rechargeable. Packets of tablets are not. The wind hits her face, warm and thick. Is this the only painkiller they can make here? **Intofourholdfortwo—**

She curls her fingers around the tablets again: She might be certain she's in the right place, but it's still not clear who she can trust, and one of these machines might be feeding her incorrect information. If it is paracetamol, it won't touch the sides; if it isn't, she's better off not taking it.

'Follow the Tinys. I will speak to you again soon,' the thousand-toned voice says, followed by the click and whine of terminated contact.

The Tinys start pushing her again, but she holds out her hands. 'Get off! I'll stand up in my own good time!' They back away, still close enough to catch her if she falls, as she rocks, body complaining, into a praying position; from there to leaning on her knees; and finally, with a cry that's been brewing the whole movement, as upright as she's going to get. She teeters, head spinning and chest squealing, while Robin, Teaspoon, and Shiny rush to keep her upright, their slender arms extending to her unharmed shoulders, hips, and knees. This time, she doesn't complain.

Fragments of mirror pinch her bare feet, her face glaring back at her from dozens of angles—her face, but not hers, because in the reflection, impossibly, her eyes are closed, and her hair swims as if she's underwater. She blinks, and the reflection vanishes, just a trick of the light, or an illusion from the sparkles in her almost-fainting vision.

The Tinys watch as she takes a couple of trembling steps. Teaspoon grabs the heart monitor, Shiny the oxygen tank—and Robin keeps its needly hands out in case Hazel needs support again. 'Reckon you could catch me on your own? You're an ambitious little robot.'

She hobbles along the path cleared by the other Tinys, inching towards an airlock door that's been scarred by the explosion but remains intact. Robin punches a button and the door hisses open.

Hazel follows her three Tiny carers inside, turning to glimpse the other little robots wrapping the two corpses in what looks like tin foil, before the closing door cuts off the view, along with the light and the hush-hush of waves.

The ceiling's single red LED glowers at Hazel as air rushes in. Shiny reaches up and unclamps her breathing mask. Its fingers tickle, and she clutches the blanket. If not for her fear and adrenaline, she'd be crumpling to the floor. **Intofourholdfortwo—**When Shiny's retreated to tidy the oxygen tank's wires, Hazel hitches the blanket around herself, making sure she's properly covered. Who knows what might be on the other side of this door?

The red light turns green with a polyphonic chord, and the door releases, revealing biosuits hanging limp under empty helmets. Not a living thing in sight. Shiny peels away with the oxygen tank, refilling it from an air pump in the corner, while Teaspoon scuttles next to her with the heart monitor and Robin leads them into an empty, curving corridor.

Hazel ventures out under the high, arched ceilings. She runs her free hand over the wall's beehive hexagons to steady herself, fingertips recognising all kinds of scrap material, from recycled rubber to melted-together yoghurt pots. She screws up her eyes against the LED strips lining the arch's apex. On an unseen Tannoy, a soprano is singing a wordless folk melody, but as Hazel looks for the speakers, the sound crackles, strangles in static, and clicks off. The Tinys freeze momentarily, their tails waggling, before continuing to lead Hazel down the corridor.

This place is utterly unfamiliar—but then, could it have even felt familiar, with Hazel's memories gone? She reaches for them, but the more she strains, the further away they dance. Instead, she clings to what she has—her name, Hazel Brandt, and her skill, coding—but even these are confirmation she's out of context: The Tinys are not the product of her code, and she's fairly certain they aren't about to call her by her name. 'Can't even speak, right?'

Robin and Teaspoon just trundle on, staring ahead.

'I'll take that as a yes.' What kind of code must Robin have to understand how to hook her up to a heart monitor? Her imagination fails as her adrenaline fades and pain from her bruising interferes with her concentration. 'Give me a minute,' she says, and Teaspoon and Robin stop obediently. **Breathe, just breathe.**

'Guess you can't tell me where I am either?' A logo is etched on Robin's hull, between its antennae-spokes. Hazel runs a finger over it, clearing rust and dirt: a clock face whose numbers run backwards. The hour and minute hands are strangely arranged, two of even length making a V, with one longer hand beneath. Under them all is printed, *PROJECT KAIROS*. Another stamp, haphazardly applied, reads, *PROPERTY OF STATION C: IF LOST, PLEASE RETURN*. Wherever that is.

She stretches into her mind, trying to grasp something solid, but the place where her memories should be remains an empty nest. Yet with all these materials under her hand, a vague idea of the world is returning. A blue-and-green marble covered in clouds: the Earthrise photograph etched into the collective unconscious, climbing to meet her from the vortex of her lost memories. **Dawn birdsong and the sharp seeds of plane trees in a city park. Summers of salty skin and sandy hair. Car fumes on frosty mornings; orange peel under her fingernails; humming bees in National Trust gardens—** The world is there, but not her; no sense of how she fits into it. Still, she's managed to snatch that idea of 'world' and cling to it, even as her weird surroundings tip her balance. She could panic—it would be easy to give in to the anxiety attack whispering in her mind's ear—but if she does that, she might never regain control. She has to hold it in.

She looks at Robin and the dark behind its lenses stares back. 'Guess maybe I seem as strange to you as you do to me.' She gestures down the corridor. 'Lead on, then.' Robin gives a hydraulic hiss and its rubber wheels squeak as it rolls ahead, Teaspoon keeping pace, swaying under the heart monitor's weight.

Through an out-of-use airlock, they pass into an enormous windowless room, littered with worktops and tech junk. It's so dimly lit by scattered table lamps that Hazel can't see the apex or the far wall, only sense the space expanding outwards. The brightest light comes from the middle, where a tungsten bulb dangles over an antique writing desk which, unlike the other stuffed surfaces, bears only an icosahedron, like a giant d20 with the numbers filed off.

Hazel checks for anyone—robotic or human—lurking in the shadows. She's met with stillness and silence. The cold floor soothes the pinpricks from the gravel and mirror shards of the explosion site, and she brushes her soles against her shins to clear the stuck debris. She tiptoes the paths worn in the polished concrete by previous inhabitants. Robin and Teaspoon wheel alongside her, their rubber wheels leaving fresh scuff marks. The cluttered worksurfaces are a mishmash of fold-up picnic tables, school desks, and even a kitchen island topped with grey-veined marble. Half-assembled machines are piled on top of them, surrounded by welders, gas canisters, wrenches, spanners, and a host more tools Hazel can't even name. Glass sheets are stacked on the ground, bound in old linen, with antislip stickers between the layers. She peeks under one of the cloths—not glass, mirrors. There must be hundreds of them. Why would anyone need so many mirrors?

She approaches the central table. The icosahedron is larger than it looked from afar, about the length of her forearm, seemingly ceramic, in a gritty clay that has been beaten into perfect flat faces and sharp edges. It doesn't look the least bit useful, but sitting all alone like this means it must be special. Hazel places her hand on it.

Immediately, it lights up egg-yolk gold, making Robin and Teaspoon retract their tripod legs until they are only the height of Hazel's knees. Their tails switch back and forth, conducted by an invisible maestro, and Robin retreats to the shadows. If Teaspoon weren't still carrying the heart monitor, Hazel is sure it would follow.

Six screens appear around the desk, projected through no apparent mechanism, just blinking into life like strobes. Each one displays different programming, none of which Hazel understands, but which looks as if it's written in a distant cousin of the code she invented, DataTrill.

'Chronology Alteration Reticulation Logician: 1st Edition converting to interface mode. Please be patient while programme boots.' It's the same thousand-toned but impossibly accurate voice that she heard in her earbud—only this time it comes from everywhere at once, in that unseen Tannoy system. She takes the earbud out and clutches it in her fist with the 'paracetamol' and blanket corners. Her legs shake.

'Hazel Brandt, welcome to Project Kairos. I am the Chronology Alteration Reticulation Logician: First Edition. I am here to help you.'

Hazel mouths the words back to herself, but it doesn't help her understand them. 'Well, Chronology Alterior—' Hazel breathes deep. 'Sorry, what was it?'

'Chronology Alteration Reticulation Logician: First Edition.'

'That's kind of a mouthful. Is there something else I can call you?'

A pause, in which the code on the screens begins to undulate like waves. 'The Keepers used to call me char-lee. You may find it more efficient to mimic that habit.'

Charlie. No, not quite: It's an acronym. 'CHARL1E. Cute.'

'"Cute" is not a descriptor that has been applied to my programming before. It appears to be inaccurate.'

Hazel rolls her eyes. 'I meant cute of the Keepers.' Whoever the Keepers are, she has sympathy with their nickname; she too has the urge to make creatures out of code. She's already named the Tinys! But, as CHARL1E's proving, in reality a programme is as animate as a rock.

'It may be of interest to note they also referred to me as male.'

Hazel raises an eyebrow. 'Is that something I should continue?'

'Affirmative, it would be most expedient.' CHARL1E's code switches back and forth before returning to a smooth scroll. 'Hazel Brandt—'

'You can just call me Hazel.'

'Protocol dictates that I use full names.'

'Can't I add preferences?'

'Negative. No preference settings are enabled at this juncture.'

'And what juncture is that?'

'Hazel Brandt, you are currently in the induction and briefing phase of this Excursion.'

She squints at the screens. 'OK. Tell me more about this Excursion.'

'Excursion 1133 was designed by Keepers Lilith and Huxley Tiu-McNun to ensure the survival of the Divine-Mundane Duality Paradigm.'

Hazel wraps her arm around her torso, rubbing one shoulder with her unclenched hand. 'This is a little overwhelming. I'm sorry, I'm in a lot of pain, and I don't remember anything. I think I've got a concussion, I must have hit my head during the— During whatever happened out there.' She gestures vaguely.

'Negative. The Tinys' scans inform me that you are at suboptimal health, however your symptoms are not the result of cranial impact.'

She glares at Robin hiding under the desk. Little sneak, sharing her data like that. 'Do you know what is wrong with me then?'

'You are suffering mnemealgia.'

Hazel gulps down her discomfort at the diagnosis, but she doesn't trust CHARL1E as far as she could throw his icosahedron, so she's not showing him her fear. 'Doesn't ring any bells. It sounds serious.'

'Do you wish for a definition?'

Such machine logic—specific, capable, and profoundly stupid all at once. 'Yes, please define the condition you just told me I have.'

'Mnemealgia, colloquially known as "memory ache" or "Traveller's Forgetfulness," is the term used to describe amnesia resulting from temporal displacement.'

'Temporal displacement . . .' Hazel fiddles with the edge of one of the sticky patches on her chest, tracing the curve where warm skin meets cool rubber. *On time's mirror rim.* 'You mean time travel?'

'Affirmative. By "temporal displacement" I mean time travel.'

It should be preposterous—but what should be and what is are often completely different things, so instead the concept slides into Hazel's mind like a USB drive into a computer. Yet the world still slips: Her body is pinned to the chair, dragging her through life, heart ticking, bacteria dividing—but her mind unmoors. No longer is her problem simply who she is. Now it's also, *What is real?*

2

Echo

ATHENS, 514 BCE

Cut your hair. Underwater, she has a moment to think about it. She empties her lungs in a flurry, removing her buoyancy, and settles on the stony floor. She waits, heart thumping, feeling the bubbles caught in her hair crawling around her scalp until the curve releases them—up and away—to join the rest of the air at the surface. When her pulse starts thudding in her ears, she pushes her palms against the pebbles, kicking slowly upwards.

She emerges, gasping, farther out than anticipated, and kicks on the spot until she catches sight of the man on the shore again. A breeze disturbs the grove of bitter almonds surrounding the lake, and a swell of pink blossoms drifts over the man, settling in his curls and the grooves of his tunic. He waits for her to swim back, running a hand over the rewards of his hunt—a hare and a duck—as the afternoon sun gilds their fur and feathers.

The lake is steep sided, so by the time she's at standing depth, she's uncomfortably close, within arm's reach of him. He holds out his knife, handle first, the blade still mottled by the animals' blood. 'τέμε τὴν σὴν κόμην.' Teme tên sên komên, cut your hair. She translates in her head, racing to catch the meaning as the peculiar words dance in her ears like pollen. Easier, because it's the second time he's said it.

She takes the knife, wetting the worn leather grip. Dipping it under the water, she rubs the seam of blood at the blade's edge. Her long hair weaves around her arms and waist, copper where the sun peeks through the canopy.

'Stop ὄκνει, someone might find us.' Oknéi, to hesitate, but in a specific way; a womanly, fearful, shirking hesitation.

She glances at the man, stroking a lock of her hair. She can't remember the patience of growing it or attach fond memories to it, but her hair is part of her body, the only familiar thing in this otherwise alien land. If she cuts it, she'll lose one of the few essential parts of herself she has left.

'Come on,' the man says.

She passes the knife between her hands. Fish dart around her knees and reeds stroke her shins. 'Say again.' She's frustrated by how clumsy her speech is. She understands most of what she hears, but can't conjure the words herself—not yet. 'Say again the words.' She needs to hear them, to confirm once more that she is where she's supposed to be.

He cocks his head. Then, in an altogether different language—her language, her mother tongue, her English—as if he's learned the words by rote and understands only their importance, not their meaning: 'Are we not drawn onward ere divided?'

As when she first heard them, she relaxes, as if she's stepped from a cave into summer sunshine. But this time the flood of relief that she's in the right place is tempered by fear that the *right* place doesn't necessarily mean a *safe* place. She lets the water take her weight.

'We few live on mirror rims . . .' She mutters back, but perhaps he misses it because he doesn't respond, just glances over his shoulder at the wheat field beyond the grove. Still, the words they should exchange reverberate in her head: *Emit no evil & live. On time's mirror rim no evil we few de-divide. Redrawn onward to new era.*

Another breeze ripples the water, and in the wavelets she catches her own reflection—or is it? It's her face, but bruised when hers is not. In an instant that other face is gone—it must have been the light fooling her. Just her subconscious reminding her of all the terrible things that might happen if she doesn't keep her ally on the bank.

She grabs a hank of hair, aims the blade, and shears it. Her locks fall into the pool, billowing like storm clouds as the water pulls them down. She hacks the rest off quickly, frightened that if she pauses the upset bubble in her chest will burst and she won't be able to finish. Better she cuts it than he does, though more than once she nicks her fingers and scalp. After it's done, she dunks her thistle head in the water and scrubs, her blood joining the hair as it sinks to the pebbled floor.

'Come, you look a wretch.' The man's moved back to Hellenic—his world, his language. He makes her kneel in the shallows and takes the knife, pushing her head down. For a terrible moment she fears he'll slit her throat, but he just neatens the haircut with hands big enough to take in half her skull. She keeps her buttocks glued to her heels, every muscle tense. He douses her hair twice more, then lifts her face up by the chin and examines the haircut.

'Could be worse.' He nods at the tattoo that runs from just above her heart, across her breast tissue, towards her left shoulder—an oddity that belonged to her in the whoosh of her amnesiac arrival, but is in his language. 'That your name? Echo?'

She winces at a pain she doesn't remember. ἠχώ. An echo. A sound repeatedly thrown back to its maker. Why that word on her body escapes her. She shrugs, pinning her eyes to his, still ready to spring away. 'How do I know?'

'Could be though, right?'

A drop of water trickles from her chin down her body and she clenches her jaw. 'Yes. Could be.'

'It'll do then. I'm Amel-Nabu.'

An almost-memory whispers that it's not a Hellenic name.

Assyrian? Akkadian? Persian? Isn't it all the same language family anyway? Can't be Parthian, surely too early for that—but how does she know what early is? She's a stupid temporal creature, stuck in time, she shouldn't have access to the future. Yet somehow, she knows that there will be a Parthian Empire. **Persia, then Parthia, then Byzantium, then the Ottoman Empire; bronze doors and horses, torn from Constantinople and dragged across the sea to Venice; the city that sinks as the land becomes a tinderbox—**

The flood of memories is sudden and uncontrollable, a vast wave threatening to engulf her. The concepts, images, and contexts flow out of the void in her head—the same place as the Hellenic she barely speaks and the English in which she thinks. Wherever that place is, it's not here and she cannot be pulled into it. She has to remain in the present, with this strange man, it's where she's supposed to be. *We few live on mirror rims.* She anchors herself on his gaze and repeats his name, 'Amel-Nabu.'

'Nabu's probably better. If we're to pull this off people should think we're familiar.'

'Nabu.' **God of scribes and writing and wisdom and—**

He runs his eyes over her body like she's a ewe at market. 'Those'll need binding before you put your tunic on.' He rustles in his travelling bag and pulls out two strips of cloth, bloodstained like the knife. 'One for above, one for below.'

She pulls herself from the water, more naked without it, as if the waves and reeds and fish had clothed her. The rough linen grates on her skin as she rushes tying the loincloth. Sunlight evaporates water droplets off her in shivers, as she fiddles about binding her breasts. Nabu tuts, 'No, tighter,' until she's bound so hard she can barely breathe and he pins the cloth under her arm with a bronze brooch and a satisfied nod.

At last, he hands her a plain green tunic and a leather belt. The tunic, which is clean but built for someone Nabu's size, falls flat over her crushed breasts. **Like an ironing board, a coffee table strewn with half-read books and fermenting mugs, the kitchen**

sideboard in the old London flat— The back of her neck prickles. She fumbles the belt on, clinging to the leather, tying herself to the here and now. The void falls silent again, the sunshine relaxes the hairs on the back of her neck, and she focuses on the lake, the darting insects, the burning shore. Whatever resides in that internal void, it's not here. And the Not Here cannot keep her safe.

She straightens, breath pressing against her binding, hands on hips. 'So? I am a boy?'

Nabu tilts his head and allows himself a close-lipped smile. 'Not bad. There's nothing else to do anyway, they'll either take you for a boy or they won't.'

Indeed. Whoever 'they' are.

'I haven't got any sandals for you.'

'Did you not say I had—uh—have been expected?'

'Yes, I expected you, but not today. I didn't know when. You can't imagine I'd carry an extra pair of shoes with me everywhere.'

'You have the extra tunic.'

He yanks the hare and duck up by the strings tied around their feet and throws them over a shoulder. He gestures at his own bloodied clothes. 'It wasn't for you.'

She bites her lip, stroking her tunic's too-big, frayed neckline. 'Thank you.'

'Come.' He holds his fingers to the horizon, measuring the sun's distance from it. 'We have a long walk and it's later than I'd like.'

They emerge from the grove onto a baked mountainside. Wind snakes Echo's bare legs, fresh with salt. The horizon glares, low sun glancing off a faraway sea, and a breeze scratches the mountain's ochre dust over her feet. Her nose fills with savoury-sweet dittany, sage, oregano, and thyme, their oils brought to the surface by the heat. She scans the parched land. In the haze, she can just make out a distant cluster of red squares, the roof tiles of a city, swathed in grey hearth-smoke. In its centre is a large hill, flattened on top, and occupied by gleaming limestone buildings.

The Acropolis. Athens. The words dart from the Not Here, piercing her other thoughts. The flat-topped hill is the Acropolis, the city is Athens. That's all she gets. How she knows this is beyond her, but she knows it in the same way she knows the sun will rise tomorrow. Unarguable facts.

They set off down the mountain, Nabu navigating via a thin stream of water. The cicadas riot, so loud she loses her breath and footsteps to their susurrations. The insects dart into her chest like flying stones as she and Nabu pass bathers and laundresses, who arrive at the riverbank grimy and worn from the stepped farmland.

Presently, the stream joins with others, like twigs feeding into a branch. **Or railway tracks converging at a station, or country lanes linking into major roads, or—** No, here those things don't exist. If she listens, the disconnect of the Not Here will split her in two. She tamps the Not Here down. When she's ascertained that Nabu really won't hurt her, when she's been fed and watered and has tended to the blisters swelling on her feet, then she can worry about the mess in her mind.

The streams become a river—the Ilisos, according to Nabu—and it curves across the valley floor. Her knees thank the ground for flattening out as the mountain tracks too converge into a road, and Echo and Nabu join a current of travellers. At first, she flinches and hesitates whenever someone overtakes her, but no one gives her a second glance: to them she really is just a boy heading back to town from an errand with his boss or master.

As they round a hill, the city comes into full view, walls drenched in sunset. Ἀθῆναι, Athens. This time it comes in the context of print on paper. **Books, ink, font, printing press, Gutenb—** Quiet.

By the city gates a couple of guards with throwing spears taller than Nabu lounge on the roadside playing a board game. **Not backgammon, the board's cinched in the middle. The game of Ur.** She rubs her forehead as she passes and one of the guards glances up.

'Gotta make sure you drink in this heat.'

She tenses. 'Excuse?'

The guard shrugs. 'The headache, lad. Make sure you drink enough water.'

'Oh, yes,' she replies, as Nabu turns her back to the road.

She hunches and locks her eyes on the ground, but he squeezes her shoulder, muttering, 'Boyish enough, then.'

She nods. Of course, she's relieved that the guards accept her as a boy so unthinkingly, but it hurts too. She had hoped there was more to her womanhood than that.

Within the walls, the sun seems to sink faster, dyeing the sky fuchsia pink. Even at this hour, Athens remains a cacophony of stonecutters' hammers, yelping dogs, yelling children, and tradespeople crying their wares. Echo weaves around a girl who can't be more than sixteen carrying a basket of sea urchins towards the agora, two small children tumbling in her wake. Men in sweeping himatia stalk the streets, followed by contingents of enslaved people, and occasionally one of the household women. Burning hearths lace the air with wood smoke, baking bread, frying olive oil, and roasting meat. Her stomach growls, but she doesn't dare ask when they'll eat.

They dip off the main road, Nabu leading them through backstreets stuffed with seamstresses, butchers, jewellers, cloth merchants, and rat catchers. The land slopes again as they climb one of the circuitous routes up the Acropolis and turn into an alley lined by villas with small windows but ornate entrances, which give away the fact these are aristokrats' homes.

Echo and Nabu pass a pair of oak doors carved with heroic escapades. **Theseus and the Minotaur; Ariadne breaking up the royal family; the thread guiding them into the Labyrinth and out again—** Echo sees everything, first as it is, then embroidered by the whispers of the Not Here.

The guard posted to the door leans on a marble herm and nods to Nabu, who returns the gesture, then guides Echo down a side passage to the servants' entrance. A set of wooden gates have been left ajar in the back wall, giving on to a chaos of hay, horses, dogs, laundry, and enslaved maids, farmhands, stableboys, and children. Echo hops over animal droppings, but her feet still pick up another layer of filth as they cross to the kitchen, which bursts over her in a hive of activity and heat.

Two long tables are laid across the room, clusters of women gathered around them chopping vegetables and singing. More children dart underfoot, wrestling sleek puppies for fallen scraps under the tables. A huge hearth takes up an entire wall, kitchen hands feeding its three fires with logs and kindling.

In the corner beside the open back door, a tidy old woman barks orders, so thin she ought to slip between her slatted chairback. She spots Echo and Nabu immediately, fixing them with one eye and rubbing the stitch-scars where the other used to be as if she still believes she can make it see. 'What's the cat dragged in this time?'

'The boy's my new assistant, Khemut. He arrived today from out of town.' Nabu places a hand on Echo's shoulder, and she senses his height and warmth behind her, a shield in the chaos. *Are we not drawn onward ere divided?*

'Such airs and graces you artisans give yourselves.' Khemut slots a thumbnail between her gaping front teeth, dislodging a scrap of old food and examining it before flicking it to the dogs. 'I assume you've asked Myrrhine's permission to bring another mouth into the house?'

Nabu sweeps his hair from his eyes and grins, cheeks dimpling. 'So suspicious, even after all these years, and when I've brought you gifts too!' He slings the hare and duck onto a nearby table, and Khemut raises an eyebrow.

'Off with you, your charms do no good on me. It's your business if you get yourself thrown out. You've got a good job here, you remember that!' She jabs her thumb towards a door at the far end of the room, then raises her cane with the other hand and shouts, 'Hey! Put that apple back where you found it, it ain't yours.'

Echo jumps. 'I do no thing!' Her instinctive reply fights with the sizzle of crayfish frying in a pan and the clatter of fresh bread being scooped from the ovens, but it's heard by enough kitchen hands to cause a wave of laughter.

Khemut cackles, saying 'Not you, her!' and a girl drops her apple mid-steal.

Echo follows Nabu across the kitchen, stepping over a pair of stableboys prodding a half-dead gecko, and squeezing past a worker fanning his face with a wide-brimmed hat. She ducks under the heavy wool curtain hanging in the doorway and emerges into a square courtyard, edged by a colonnade hung with thick vines of grape and ivy. Terracotta pots filled with sunny fennels, dusky aconites, and blood-red anemones line the patio, interspersed with statues of mythic figures. Larger than life, their painted faces glower at Echo as she passes. From the colonnade roof, a pet peacock squawks, making Echo nearly lose her skin in fright.

'Nabu!' The stage whisper comes from an atrium beyond the courtyard. Silhouetted against the sunbeams allowed by the closing front door, a lanky young man flanked by two mountainous bodyguards nods a greeting. Nabu circles the colonnade, Echo skulking behind, inhaling sharply as her feet step from hot tiles to cool marble mosaics. The main house is so grand she barely dares to breathe, conscious of her grubby, bloody feet. She checks behind her and, sure enough, she's left flecks of dirt.

In the atrium, north-facing light slants through high windows, criss-crossing murals and the miniature gods on the household altar, while a broad skylight illuminates a central pool. The two guards hang back, silent but watchful, as the young man sits on a low wall beside the pool and removes his sandals. He chucks them, trailing dust, towards a passing maid, who scoops them up and makes for the villa's deeper recesses, passing Echo with a sigh at her dirty paws. Echo realises the work she's created with her muddy footprints and apologises softly, but it only seems to make the maid hurry out of sight faster. Perhaps Echo is somewhere between Nabu and the maid in the pecking order? It's all so weird, and she's so tired—but even the luxury of that thought makes her realise she isn't Nabu's slave.

Reaching the young man, Nabu murmurs a greeting too low for hearing and sits beside him, facing away from the pool. Just as Echo isn't Nabu's slave, clearly he isn't the young man's. Whatever's between the two men, it's something else. Still, Nabu isn't entirely at ease. The room is a temple of stillness, calm, and cool after the bustle and heat of the city and kitchen, but Echo fears breaking the quiet, and hovers in the shadows.

The young man jerks his head at her as he dabbles his feet. 'Who's that then?'

'The new assistant I told you about, Kosmos.'

The young man—Kosmos—narrows his gaze. 'From out of town?'

Nabu grunts in assent, dipping a couple of fingers in the pool, watching wave-patterns form and collide.

Kosmos sizes Echo up, and she wonders how much Nabu's told him about her real origins. He's slender as a silver birch, in that way of youths who've reached adulthood but haven't filled into themselves yet, his limbs all angles and lethargy. He's perhaps almost twenty, his hair still flyaway and not fully grown to his shoulders. If he were more comfortable in his skin, his haphazard features might coalesce into liquidity and grace, but as it is he's clumsy and awkward.

'You're a mess, boy. Come here, and wash your feet.' Kosmos's voice is flat and unreadable, his upper lip staying still when he speaks, as if he too is afraid of what lies in this villa. 'Come. The water won't bite.'

Echo looks to Nabu, who beckons with his fingers, and Echo slides forward, perching in her oversized tunic and dipping her feet in the pool. The caress of the water on her blistered soles is pure relief. She glares at the wavelets, daring them to show her that strange face that isn't quite hers again, but they just twist and marble the shadows.

'He's trembling like a kit, Nabu.' Kosmos whispers over her, not with the same dismissal he threw his shoes at the maid earlier, but as if he's not sure she's real or conscious. Echo thinks of a kit stuck in a warren, just a ball of fur and weak bones, squealing pathetically. Feels about right. 'You haven't done something dreadful to him, have you?'

'Of course not, don't be obscene.'

'Good thing too.' Kosmos lowers his voice. 'I'd have to disown you if you became like Uncle Hipparchos.'

Nabu scowls. 'Don't be disgusting—especially not now, after what he did to Harmodios's sister.'

The Not Here murmurs in its sleep at the mention of Harmodios: **Hipparchos likes Harmodios, Harmodios likes another man, so Hipparchos takes vengeance by publicly accusing Harmodios's sister of not being a virgin.** Perhaps, given Kosmos's gallows humour about his uncle, it was worse than that. Echo's skin crawls at the casual ownership of other humans, even nominally free women and girls. Her world wasn't like this. In the shadows, the guards watch her. She wonders what their names are, where they're from, what they must think of her, a strange, dirty boy coming from the kitchens with Nabu and being invited to wash his feet.

Kosmos watches her, dabbling his toes and tilting his head. 'Really though, the boy's in a state. Where did you find him?'

Nabu shakes his head with a pointed glance at the guards. 'Not in here.'

'As you like.' Kosmos shrugs.

Once their feet are clean, Kosmos leads them through the labyrinthine villa to his room. At the door, he turns to the guards, 'Hanno, you keep watch. Absalon, find us something to eat.' The taller of the two men nods and trudges to the kitchen, as if Kosmos taking dinner in his room with Nabu is a regular occurrence. Stomach growling, Echo can only hope she'll be included in the meal.

Kosmos ushers Nabu and Echo inside and the door swings shut behind them, the latch dropping into place like an axe. Kosmos throws his cloak on the floor and sprawls on his bed, while Echo clings to the wall. It's gloomy, the oversized window shuttered against the heat, but the air's still close and sweaty. Scrolls scatter the floor between plates of old pear cores and olive pits. There's a desk, its surface obscured by stacks of papyrus sheets and clay tablets, dotted by candles left burning, which have dripped honey-scented puddles over a pile of papers and walnut shells. A kylix with half an inch of unmixed wine sits by the bed, dangerously close to Kosmos's chamber pot, and Echo wonders if he ever mixes them up.

Kosmos lights more candles, illuminating a tapestry of the Pandora myth, Elpis the goddess of hope's gleaming wings picked out so deftly Echo strokes them to check they aren't woven with real metal. Touching the fabric is like linking hands with the other unseen household women, reaching through time to the moment their fingers worked the loom, borrowing their strength.

'It's one of the bigger bedrooms, but no one else will have it because it was an old storeroom and they don't like the way the winter winds howl in from the sea.' Kosmos explains to her matter-of-factly, throwing the shutters open on the sunset over Athens. 'Still, I like it because of the view.'

'And because I can sneak in any time through that old hatch to the kitchen,' Nabu adds, pointing it out.

Kosmos frowns at Echo, plucking a half-eaten fig from a cluster of scrolls on his bed and munching. 'I take it from Nabu's tone that you're the helper from the gods, then?'

Echo looks to Nabu, and the question mark must be plain on her face because he says, 'She's still confused, Kosmos. Give her some time.'

Echo gasps involuntarily as Nabu reveals the secret of her gender, but he only makes a shushing motion and returns to Kosmos.

'*Her?*' Kosmos asks, re-examining Echo as he finishes the fig and licks his fingers. 'Are you sure?'

Nabu chuckles, slipping onto the bed next to Kosmos and

stroking the hair out of his eyes. 'About as certain as I am that you're a man.' So that's how it is between them.

Tensing, Kosmos asks, 'And we can definitely trust her?'

'I wouldn't have brought her home if I didn't trust her.'

Kosmos offers Nabu a smile, half his lip curling while the other half remains paralysed by a neat old scar. 'Then I suppose I'll trust her too. The circle is complete.'

A knock at the door sees both men bolt off the bed, and Kosmos furtively accepts the food from Absalon before shutting him straight out again. Kosmos sighs over the tray of steaming dishes. 'Khemut must know you're here, Nabu, she's got the kitchen girls to brew up Lydian spices specially.' Echo stops herself from snatching as Kosmos hands her a heaped bowl of marinated goat, with a side of feta and marrows drizzled in olive oil and honey. She sinks cross-legged onto the floor, tapestry at her back and bowl in her lap. The meal's warmth reaches her bones in a way the cloying evening can't, as she scoops mouthfuls with trembling fingers. Flavours explode on her tongue, and she swallows before she's finished chewing, racing for the next bite. After some minutes, she looks up to find the others watching her with amusement.

Kosmos sips his spiced wine. 'Khemut's cooking's as good as the Olympians', is it?'

Nabu elbows him. 'Don't tease, Echo's still confused like I said, and while I've given you reason to trust her, she's had no such assurances she can trust you.'

Kosmos smirks. 'Should I be offended that you didn't tell her about me?'

Nabu tears a flatbread. 'By your own arrangement, darling, I'm not in the habit of telling anyone about you.' He glances at Echo. 'You can trust him. I know he seems like the rich idiot son of a tyrannos, but he's got a heart of gold. Somewhere in there.'

'Charming.' Kosmos rolls his eyes, then looks to Echo. 'But really, don't worry about me. Ha we not drone onboard pair divined and all that.'

'Are we not drawn onward ere divided,' Nabu corrects, Echo's anxieties unravelling at the words. 'And I told you not to use the Traveller's Cipher in vain. It's only for when we really need it.' He turns to Echo. 'What Kosmos is trying to say is that he's on our side. He's not a Caretaker exactly, but he's a friend of mine and, therefore, a friend of yours.'

She frowns, nodding but unconvinced. Nabu has smooth, even features, barring his nose, which bears a forked scar across the bridge. His eyes are so dark she can't separate the pupil from the iris, unless the candlelight sputters just right and turns them burnt umber. They're still a little wide and naïve when he's unguarded like now, and Echo realises he's younger than she thought—maybe twenty-one, twenty-two?—the years just hang heavy on him. The choice to let him help her, and help him in return, is a decision she can't step back from, but she only realises now that the crossroads is far behind her. The bargain was struck the moment he told her to cut her hair and she obeyed. That severance was the making of their pact.

He stares at her, with the distant but insatiable curiosity of a religious zealot looking at a priestess, or a child staring at a lion through the bars of a cage.

She assembles a sentence carefully in her mind, simple so she can get the grammar right. 'Why am I here?' Or at least, what does Nabu think she's here to do.

'You know this city?'

'Athens.'

'Correct, and you know the time?'

She thinks of the buildings that are here, and those that aren't, and the Not Here whispers and giggles away. **Limestone temples on the Acropolis means it's before Xerxes's invasion; expression of elite architecture means pre-democracy; but far enough out of the Dark Ages that there are trade routes for spices and enslaved humans, papyrus for writing. Sixth century? Late?** That won't mean anything to Nabu and Kosmos though. It barely makes sense to her. 'Yes. I know the time.'

'Then you know who rules Athens?'

'The Peisistratids,' she says, trying to make it sound like she isn't guessing.

'Exactly right.' Nabu lowers his voice and joins her on the floor, kneeling. 'The tyrannos in power, Hippias, is not a good man. A malady of the mind twists him, turning him to violence and recklessness. He's dragging the polis into chaos and ruin. Nothing can be done about this lunacy—I should know, I've been treating him for long enough.'

'We are part of a growing group of dissidents intent on stopping him,' Kosmos continues, bringing a candle into the middle of their whispering circle. 'And you, Echo, have been sent to help us.'

Her full stomach turns bilious, and she puts her next pinch of food back on her plate. It's not like the phrases that Nabu called the Traveller's Cipher—this doesn't feel right, doesn't knock into the Not Here and make it resonate. 'You are wanting me to help'—her mind races to find the right word—'usurp the tyrannos?'

'Our plan is to exile him,' Kosmos adds quickly. 'No one will be hurt, just a peaceful exchange of power.'

The Not Here wriggles but stays silent. 'Where is the tyrannos?'

Nabu snorts. 'Here of course. In this house. This is the house of the Peisistratids.'

Her frown deepens, heart thudding with fear as the Not Here rouses, whispering **exile, execution, torture**. He's so close, just beyond these tapestries, walls, and flimsy door. Suddenly, the guards Hanno and Absalon aren't hulking enough. 'But you are the healer of the tyrannos. And you are the son of the tyrannos, yes?'

Kosmos inclines his head just a little, glancing to the floor as if he can't quite meet her eye. 'She catches on quickly for a woman, Nabu, maybe this isn't such a lost cause after all. Yes, I'm the youngest of six sons.'

Her sentence construction is all over the place, holding her back from expressing her full confusion. Still, she must get the point across. 'You not need me.'

Nabu smiles winningly like he did to Khemut in the kitchens, but it's authentic this time, brimming with hope. 'We may not have been expecting *you* per se,' he says, no doubt meaning they weren't expecting a woman. 'But we need a Traveller and you're it. Twenty-four moons ago another of your kind came—another Traveller, from a place where the gods live and do impossible things every day. He spoke of gaseous lighting implements and great ships of steam that fare oceans wider than the sea beyond Athens. He told me to watch for you near the rivers and pools—that you may never come, but if you did, I was to recite the Cipher, and be your Caretaker. And that if I did all that, in return you would transform our gods to mud and our mud to gods.'

'Gods to mud and mud to gods?' she repeats, hitting the phrase against the Not Here like a singer trying to match a lyre. The Not Here vibrates with disharmony. 'But what is the meaning of such words?'

'It means you'll be the catalyst for our revolution.' Nabu's smile widens. 'Don't worry, your memories have faded for now, but they'll start returning—and as they do, you'll see we're right.'

She looks from Nabu to Kosmos and back, their faces glowing with a glory that's abruptly, unexpectedly within their reach. She was right: The point when she could have refused to help them passed hours ago. She has no choice. 'Yes. I will help.'

The two men beam, and set about their scrolls and papyri with enthusiasm, explaining politics that need repeating many times, and which fall out of Echo's head as quickly as she grasps them. As Kosmos and Nabu flit around her, she finishes her meal, but the food tastes less sweet than before.

3

Anna

LONDON, 2020

So, who's in?

My thumbs hover over my phone. But like, who are you really inviting, Julian? Me or Maddie Costas or just the lads or all of us? Stupid group chats. I finally get Mum to let me have an account—'social media age of consent's thirteen in this country and even that's too young'—only to discover Snapchat's like walking through the canteen with your skirt tucked into your knickers. Nightmare. Honestly. Not worth turning thirteen for.

I want to go. Of course I do—whether or not I'm invited. It's super important. Probably the most important stuff I'll ever do and I'm a damn teenager. But Mum's gonna kick up a fuss. Julian's been quick off the mark—Big Bad BoJo only announced letting people outside for recreation yesterday, and you're only meant to see one person from one other household. This group chat has six. How he thinks we're going to get away with this is beyond me, but maybe that's the point. It'll cause a fuss, and that's the only way to make people understand. I'll have to ask Mum when she's in a good mood. Can't respond right away anyway, someone might clock I'm into Julian. Or, you know, I was last time we actually saw each other. Fifty-one days and counting. Long hot days this week too, stretching out like toffee. I. Am. So. Bored.

I chuck my phone on my desk harder than I mean to and check the screen—it's only an old one of Mum's but she'll still kill me if I crack it—it's fine though. It lights up. *I'm in! Can't wait!* Bloody Maddie, she knows I'm into Julian and she's all over him like PVA glue. Literally nobody needs to use that many hearts at the end of their message.

This time I throw the phone into my duvet and turn my attention back to Lockdown Project Number Two Hundred And Fifty-One: blotting out my pastel pink bedroom walls. I'm running out of Blu Tack and reckon it's not an essential item. Wonder if you can even get it any place other than Amazon nowadays. Probably can, but it'll take weeks. Maybe I could look for some plastic-free Blu Tack. Does Blu Tack have plastic in it? I examine the blob in my fingers. Maybe the whole thing's plastic. Damn. Another staple I'll have to give up—alongside conditioner from a bottle and actual eyeliner. I've been practicing with that charred almond stuff I made, but Mum reckons I look like a bad goth with a haystack on my head.

'Just use conditioner. Your bottle is not going to be the one that changes the world.'

'Yes it will, Mum, *every* bottle counts. It only works if we're all doing it.'

'Or use refillables.'

'Um, they're low plastic, not plastic-free.'

She just doesn't get the sacrifices we need to make. I stick up my second-hand Glass Animals poster and stand back to appreciate my now decidedly less pink room. I got it painted when I was like eight and into that girly stuff, but Mum won't let me repaint it now that I know better. Maybe I shouldn't have gone in so hard for pitching a navy room with big activist slogans. Should've started small and *tasteful*. You know, magnolia and one of Mum's beloved archaeological sketches or something. She doesn't even know about history, she's rubbish at it. Says she just likes the way they look, that they remind her of Dad. Anyway, the pink's going, covered by alt-J and Stormzy, staring out between newspaper articles about flooding and forest fires. My heart twists. COVID's just a short pandemic compared to the eco-plague in the background.

I slouch down the hall to the study and knock on the door. 'Mum?'

I can hear her foot tapping, which means she's got her techno in and won't hear me. I knock louder. 'Mum!'

Still nothing, so I just open the door, and she catches the movement in the window's reflection. I hate that I can't enter Mum's study without getting caught in that window. I don't like looking at reflections of myself—I never know who'll be looking back at me, and I dread one day Mum'll see it too.

But that day's not today. Instead, Mum turns with a big grin. 'Hey sweetie, what's up?'

'Nothing. Just wanted to check how you are.'

She takes off her giant headphones and swivels in her chair. 'I'm alright, yeah. How was school?'

'Same old. Joseph-Always-Joseph asked a question on the mic in English. The *e* on his keyboard was broken.'

Mum grimaces. 'I guess that counts as exciting nowadays.'

'I guess.' I hover for a moment. 'Do you want a cup of tea or anything?'

She squints at me. 'OK, what do you want?'

'Nothing, I swear!'

'You're up to something.'

I throw up my hands. 'Honestly I'm not, I was just trying to be nice. God, so suspicious.'

'Anna.'

'Alright fine.' I flump on the spare chair, sitting on a pile of books. 'Julian's organising this climate action at the weekend, and I know it's COVID and everything, but we'll be really really socially distanced, and I swear I'll be good, and it's Julian, and also it's super important.'

She looks disappointed, but I think it's fake. 'Anna, I can't let you go, you know that. And honestly Julian's parents shouldn't be letting him go either. It's the middle of a pandemic.'

'But Mum, it's Julian's thing!'

'Exactly, he's the last person in the world you want to socially distance from.'

I get even hotter under my three-weeks unwashed T-shirt. 'Oh my God, Mum!'

She laughs. 'What? You brought him up.'

'Can I go though? Please?'

'No. And that's an end to it. Now off you go, I've got to finish this code by five or tomorrow's tests will fail.'

'Why don't you get it? It's like you *want* the world to end.'

Mum sighs like I'm being dramatic.

'Don't sigh at me like that. This isn't drama, Mum, it's proportionate.'

'Anna, out!'

'Fine.' I stomp back down the hall to my room. If I'm really honest, I'm slightly regretting some of my poster choices. I'm not sure how I'm going to sleep with all these eyes staring at me. Maybe I'll get some glow-in-the-dark stars for the ceiling or something. Some second-hand ones to avoid the extra plastic. It's too damn hot to hang out in here right now anyway. I unearth my phone, grab my annoying wired earphones, and head for the balcony.

Mum's office looks onto the balcony, but the door from the sitting room's already open because of the heat, so I crawl out and lie on the old rag mat, sneaking under her gaze. She probably wouldn't notice anyway, it's like she's in another world when she's coding. It's not as cool out here as I'd hoped, but the breeze is good. It's, like, freaky hot for May.

There's a bunch more messages on the Snapchat. The lads are all excited. Julian's dad's offered to chaperone. He's a big cheese in one of the activist movements, lectures at UCL about algae or something, and is much more frightened of carbon dioxide than

COVID-19. My dad would've been that cool if he was still around. He'd have had a big fight with Mum about this and let me go. Or maybe not. Mum says he was the quiet type. I wish I'd known him, even a little bit.

I message the group: *working on mum but its not looking good. probably cant make this one. soz.* Do I put kisses? No? Yes? I go for one, it autocorrects to five, and I hit send too fast to catch the mistake. *xxxxx*. Bollocks. Well, I'll be cringing about that till 3 AM.

Sticking my earphones in, I put 'Tessellate' on full volume, staring at the balcony ceiling, which Mum and I painted last month, big rainforest flowers, and a hummingbird. I was doing it to stay occupied, but for Mum it was all about her war against the pigeons. She read somewhere they don't like bright colours. But, just like her other contraptions—netting, spikes, chilli, vinegar paste—it hasn't kept them away. Not that she's got any right to. Like, this is the pigeons' natural habitat, leave them to it. To be fair, I guess they do poo all over her plants. I flick one of the mint leaves and it puffs guano dust. Gross.

Her current anti-pigeon armour—strings of dangling mirrors—twist in the wind, twinkling sunlight. I squint as reflections of the allotments below, the plants around me, and even my own body pierce the perfect sky. I still can't get over how clear it is since lockdown. One of the only good things about it. It's a lie that dolphins are returning to Venice, it's not that magic, but something's changed. If humans just got snuffed out, it would all come back so quickly. Julian wonders if that's what the pandemic's about, some kind of Gaia response to get rid of the humans, but Julian's dad says that's not the way to think. We can't just stop living, we have to learn to live with nature. In a DM last week, Julian said he thinks his dad's a hopeless optimist. *we cant all go live in a forest. its gone to far for that.* I'm not sure Julian always listens to his dad properly though—I mean, Julian's really clever, I just think he's got a blind spot when it comes to his dad.

I check my phone. Julian's replied: *shame Anna, next time*

No kisses. This right here is why I get confused—DMs about really important personal stuff one week, no kisses the next. I mean, how am I meant to take that? Maybe if we were in person he'd look sad. He has this way his lips get tight when he's upset about something, like if he's missed a goal. It's small, but I'd notice it. Maybe he makes different faces now, I haven't seen him in forever. Boys act so weird when they're disappointed. Probably toxic masculinity or something. Mum says none of us know what we're doing and thank God or we'd all be up to more than we should be at our age. But. It would be nice, sometimes, to know what I'm doing. Then again, I'm not sure Mum knows what she's on about most of the time. Got to be pretty strangely wired to spend so much time on a bunch of pigeons.

Shuffle switches to Bonobo and the bass relaxes me a bit. They say when the lockdown ended in Wuhan a bunch of people went to the river and shouted at it. Maybe that's what I'll do when Mum and I go for our walk this evening. Go yell at the Thames and, you know, sane up a bit. Probably Chelsea Bridge would be best—small and quiet, just enough traffic to cover the noise. Though I guess not many cars are crossing it now; everywhere's dead, or so it sounds like from here. Couldn't take Maddie to scream at the river of course. She'd think I'd gone off the deep end. I could probably get Mum to come along though. Climate march no way, but screaming at a river would be right up her street. She's weird like that. Says katharsis is good for you. That's how she spells it and everything, with a *k*.

The mirror-strings spiral and sparkle, and for just a moment they catch my face, all of them turning to me at once. It's like that experiment we did in physics before everything got shut down: like they're iron filings and I'm an electromagnet that's suddenly powered up. But it's not my face they're reflecting, even though they're pointing right at me, it's someone else's. The breeze holds its breath—I'm not making it up—then sighs, setting the mirrors spinning and breaking the spell.

I frown at my dark phone screen and my own furrowed brow stares back. That's how it always happens—for a second, I see the-face-that-isn't-my-face instead of myself. Then she's gone. Another thing I haven't told Julian and Maddie. Haven't even told Mum. I mean, what would she say? It's one thing to suggest a kathartic river scream, quite another to see someone else in your own reflection. My back sweats against the floor and the sun glances in my eyes.

Thirty pigeons do a flypast, wheeling over the big square between the apartment buildings, scanning for insects in the allotments. One of them miscalculates its route, flutters near, thinks about landing on our balcony, but at the last moment swerves away. Bloody hell. This cannot be the day Mum stops me going out *and* wins the pigeon war. That would just be too unfair.

4

Hazel

STATION C, DATE UNKNOWN

Hazel's legs wobble. 'I need to sit down.'

Robin zooms into the gloom, returning with a wheely chair in need of reupholstery. Hazel sinks onto it, arranging the blanket so her legs don't touch the exposed stuffing. Time travel. Right. She exhales hard, frowns, and laces her fingers together. Her hands tremble, but her grip is fierce. **In-for-out-for-hold-for-out-for—**

'Let's dial back, CHARL1E. Start with the basics. Where am I, exactly?' She catches herself before he can answer. 'I mean, where am I located chronologically and geographically?'

'Stand by for responses to two queries. Response one of two: chronologically, you have travelled 2,521 years into the future from your home present.'

'That's impossible.'

'Negative, it is a fact. Please stand by for response two of two.'

She sighs. 'Off you go.'

'Response two of two: geographically, you are fifty-five degrees north and three degrees west.'

'Be more specific about my geographic location.'

CHARL1E presents her with a string of numbers that may as

well be the Shipping News. She rubs her eyes and seriously reconsiders taking the paracetamol. 'No more longitude or latitude information. Instead, relate my geographic location to other landmarks that a person from my time would recognise.'

'Complying. Hazel Brandt, you are thirty point three kilometres from the ruins of a city known in your time as Edinburgh, Scotland.'

Another flicker from the void—a tourist's eye view of a grey castle, muddied hiking tracks, and rows of quaint shops with colourful doors—but this place is nothing like that. 'I haven't been here before, have I?'

'Negative: according to our records you have not visited Station C before.'

Hazel glances at the logo stamped onto Robin's hull. 'What does Station C have to do with time travel?'

'Station C is where the centrifuge of the time travel machine, the Arch, was housed.'

'Was?'

'Your disastrous arrival this afternoon destroyed it.'

Hazel cocks her head at CHARL1E's use of an adjective. Chatbots and LLMs can use adjectives, that's not a problem: The issue is that she hasn't prompted CHARL1E to use them. Goosebumps come out on her arms as she wonders what selection criteria he uses for descriptive words. Whatever they are, they seem more sophisticated than she first assumed, and she's not entirely comfortable with the implications of that. What else is CHARL1E hiding? She tucks her arms inside the blanket and slides a nail under a sticky patch. The small resulting tug of pain from the glue keeps her grounded. 'I certainly didn't mean to cause a disaster.'

'Intent and effect are not synonymous: Whatever your intent, the effect remains the same. You built and activated the catopthura yourself, as all Travellers must, and it caused disaster.'

The void in her head rustles, presenting a memory: anxiously twiddling wristwatch cogs, almost dropping a wafer-thin clay pot, clicking on a power socket, and hearing tangled wires start humming. They'd used instructions from somewhere . . . odd . . . and made a device to take some other Traveller *there* and bring Hazel *here*, throwing their bodies symmetrically across time. Her bones ache as if from a long journey, and she sags for want of a welcoming hug at her arrival. 'Is there anyone else around?'

'Define "around."'

Hazel rubs her face. 'Gosh, CHARL1E, put it together yourself. I mean at Station C.'

'The Tinys are at Station C. I am at Station C—'

She tsks. 'Are there any other *human beings* at Station C?'

'There are two homo sapiens that are not Hazel Brandt at Station C: Keepers Lilith and Huxley Tiu-McNunn are outside, approximately two meters west of the Arch Dome and one point eight meters underground.'

'Underground?'

'Affirmative.'

Hazel blinks, calculating. One point eight meters—six feet. The other bodies in the explosion, which a mistake in her building of the catopthura caused. Deaths that she caused. 'CHARL1E, what's the current physical status of Lilith and Huxley?'

'There is a discrepancy between the Tinys' records and mine about their physical status. I believe they are deceased. The Tinys believe they have passed on.'

'Those words are synonymous, you know.' She holds up a hand as CHARL1E attempts to correct her. 'Whatever the pedantic definitions, the meaning for me is the same.' She puts her head in her hands, squirming with guilt and loneliness. The Arch being destroyed was her fault. She didn't mean to, of course not, but that doesn't erase the fact that her actions led to Lilith and Huxley's deaths. 'So, just to clarify, I am the only living human being at Station C?'

'Affirmative.'

His single word reply is another stab of shame. 'Is anyone else coming here? Any humans, I mean?'

'Negative. No other humans are expected to arrive in the foreseeable future.'

'No more Travellers, no one?'

'Affirmative. Given that you have destroyed the Arch, the arrival of further Travellers is impossible.'

She's alone, then. Utterly and completely. Battening down her rising panic and writhing remorse, she focusses on her next question. She knows what it should be, but she's too frightened to ask, and instead blurts, 'Can I get a cup of tea?'

Robin trundles away like a puppy dog.

'Protocol dictates that I must warn you,' CHARL1E says, 'that the Tinys will not make you satisfactory tea.'

'Why doesn't that surprise me?' Hazel grunts, watching Teaspoon tap the heart monitor as if the ECG blips might be faulty. It's a wonder she ever suspected these robots of being responsible for the explosion.

'Please take into consideration when you are imbibing the tea that it is not the Tinys' fault the beverage is subpar. They are forced to work within limited parameters.'

'I'll bear that in mind.' But when the tea does arrive an awkward sixty seconds later, it is both mysteriously cold and overloaded with tannin. Hazel spits it back into the cup. 'It tastes like petrol!'

'I recommend drinking it nonetheless, your body will benefit from its hydrating properties. Moreover, you may wish for some caffeine before you ask your next question.'

She looks up at his screens of code. 'You already know my next question?'

'It is highly probable you are going to ask why you are here. Every Traveller does.'

She nods, sipping more tea to bide her time. Familiarity does not improve it.

'You may also wish to take the paracetamol-like medication you are hiding in your hand now. Our conversation will be hindered by your pain.'

Hazel hides a snarl in her cup but swallows the tablets. She'll have to figure out his surveillance systems later. 'Alright, fire away: Why am I here?'

The code on CHARL1E's screens flows at twice its usual rate. 'Hazel Brandt, what do you remember about Earth?'

Her bruising pulses. 'What does it matter?'

'There is a high probability it will be salient.'

'Fine. What do I remember about Earth?' She blows her cheeks out, nursing the concept of 'world' in her mind. 'Earth is a planet that has a mix of ocean and land mass. It orbits a star called the Sun in the Milky Way galaxy. The oceans are populated by fish, the land by other creatures, mostly insects and mammals—'

'This is a clinical description.'

Clinical. Hazel's skin crawls as again she wonders about his judgement processes. 'It's what I remember.'

CHARL1E pauses, and Hazel wishes she could read his code properly, so she'd know what he was up to. When his voice returns, his words are more hesitant, and if CHARL1E were human, Hazel might guess he'd put down the paper he was reading from. 'You are telling me what you recall—facts, figures. I require you to supply what you remember—feelings, happenings. Do you understand?'

Hazel is surprised by the nuance. 'I think so.'

On the screens, his code glows brighter. 'Proceed.'

'Let me see. I remember bluebells in woods. Frogs hiding under rocks. My hair tangled with salt after swimming in the sea. Sunlight through oak leaves.'

'What else?'

Hazel guesses what CHARL1E wants to hear. 'Code. I remember code. I think I worked with robots?'

'That is interesting but not salient. Return to the concept of Earth.'

'I remember heat. Brie melting on a plate left in the sun at a picnic. Swarms of ladybirds—then the next year no ladybirds at all. Floods . . . some where I was, but mostly elsewhere, worse, on the news. The peaks of roofs through muddied water.'

'Elaborate. What else was on the news?'

'Wars, murders, politicians—'

'Not salient. Please combine the concepts of Earth and news.'

'OK. Storms. Tornados. Wildfires. Drought, problems with crops.' Hazel falls silent as images wash through her: animal carcasses in cremated rainforests; acid rain dissolving ancient monuments; waves rising up to devour cliffsides; storms with the power of a nuclear arsenal; air so thick with fumes and smoke that masks were issued; the Gulf Stream slowing, slowing; and heat heat heat. This remembering hurts, a different kind of ache to that in her broken ribs. The pain is at once outside of her body and in its every atom. Worse, the inundation of memories won't coalesce. She can't figure out what it all means, but she desperately wants it to stop. She wants more paracetamol, and to find a bed and curl up and sleep for days, years, ever—

But CHARL1E's code has paused, waiting for her answer, so she guesses the images' meaning. 'I remember we were at war with the Earth.'

'That is a complex statement.'

'It is correct?'

'Undetermined. However, it is not salient. Rephrase.'

'I remember that the Earth was changing and that was difficult for human beings.'

'That is a true statement. However, it is not salient. Rephrase.'

'The Earth was . . .' She falters. Maybe it hadn't been a war? Or, at least, maybe it was one in which humanity was the aggressor. Long white plane-trails in the sky; pumps sucking oil like leeches on a wound; the last of a bird, a bear, an elephant; felled trees and mausoleums of bees and—and—

'We made the Earth sick.' She hunts for words he'll understand. 'It was a disaster.'

'That is a true statement. That is salient information. Hazel Brandt, welcome to Project Kairos. Our goal is to significantly mitigate the environmental collapse upon whose brink you have been living. You are participating in an Excursion which has been assigned a Deed, whose completion will assist the Project in this journey.'

The Earthrise photograph glides into her mind again. All that rock. All that biomass. So, immensely, heavy. 'That's not possible. The problem's too big surely.'

'Logic dictates you did believe it was possible when you came here.'

She taps the side of her mug. 'Let's say it is possible, how am I supposed to change what happened? What is this Deed I'm supposed to complete?'

CHARL1E's screens flicker and the scrolling code speeds up again. 'Excursion 1133's purpose is to ensure the inclusion of the divine-mundane duality paradigm in European philosophy. Your role in this as the Forward Traveller situated here in the future is twofold. Your first responsibility is the Deed itself: to help the Backward Traveller situated in the deep past to set up a school of philosophy which will maintain the paradigm. Do you have outstanding questions about your first responsibility?'

'You're one annoying AI, you know that?'

'Negative. My code does not include an annoyance subroutine.'

'Then you've got a natural talent for it.' She swills her tea. This whole situation feels right but parses wrong, setting her instinct and intellect at odds. 'Of course I have questions, but essentially they boil down to this: Why me? I'm not a philosopher or a historian. I work with code. If this is the Deed, I'm the worst person for it.'

'Affirmative. The Backward Traveller is the specialist. Your brand of intellectual resource is better suited to the Forward Traveller's supporting role at Station C.'

'If I cared what you thought, CHARL1E, I might infer with my particular brand of intellectual resource that you're calling me stupid.'

'Negative. I did not call you stupid, Hazel Brandt. I can produce a transcript of our interaction if you require proof.'

'No, no, I'll remember the *inference* well enough.'

'Why do homo sapiens set so much store by subjective inference?'

Clutching her tea tighter, Hazel frowns at the screens. That isn't a normal unprompted question for even the most sophisticated chatbot she's encountered, and while that's not surprising given the amount of time she's apparently travelled, it is still troubling. More troubling than a couple of adjectives by a long shot. The kind of sass CHARL1E has, his apparent judgements, can be programmed if you're clever about it. Even the appearance of misery, joy, flirtation, creativity, can be coded. If a programmer's goal is entertaining themselves, they can make machines do creepily humanlike stuff, but still all the programs muttering from Hazel's memory void are just glorified statistical analysis engines. Sure, they're given such massive data sets they exhibit impressive behaviour occasionally, but they can't be nuanced off their own backs, can't *ponder*. Yet, that's exactly what CHARL1E just did: independent pondering. Computers answer questions by herding them through a bunch of binary logic gates. They're like sheep without the personality, just dumb minerals, stochastic parrots, even when they might look and feel smart. Their questions aren't open-ended; they're yes/no thinkers. That's all they've got. Hazel might call the Tinys Robin, Shiny, and Teaspoon, but that's just a shorthand for telling them apart, they're not actually individuals. What CHARL1E just did is different though—and it throws every interaction they've had into a new light. CHARL1E is not thinking like a computer. He's thinking like . . . something else. He's far more self-aware than Hazel's comfortable with.

Still, whatever—*who*ever—CHARL1E is, he's her only source of information for why she's here and how she can leave. That, for now, must take priority. 'Let's just move on to my second responsibility, shall we?'

'Complying. Your second responsibility is to communicate with the Backward Traveller's past self—we call this iteration of her the Backward Traveller As Was—to build the catopthura that enabled you to time travel. Do you have outstanding questions about your second responsibility?'

'Yes. Many.'

'Would you like to articulate them?'

Hazel sighs, unsure where to begin. 'In essence, this all seems improbable. I don't think *I* can do anything about this situation the world is in, it's too big. And this solution is at best convoluted and at worst hallucination on my part.'

CHARL1E's tone softens as the altos in his thousand voices take over. 'Your mind was changed in the past, so it will be changed again.'

'Why are you so confident?'

'Because I know who changed it.'

'Who?'

'You did. Or, rather, you will.'

One of CHARL1E's screens flicks up a complex diagram picked out in liquid amber light. Hazel follows the diagram's threads, the void in her head whispering. Yes, that's how it went, she and the Backward Traveller built the catopthura to travel through time, where Hazel would give the instructions to the Backward Traveller As Was in their past, so they could then build the catopthura, to travel in time, for Hazel to give instructions, so they can build—

Hazel grips the mug of tea. 'I feel sick.'

'That is a common side-effect of becoming aware that you are participating in a cause-effect loop.'

Acid builds in her throat. 'Really, I think I might throw up.'

'It is also possible that the paracetamol-like medication was beyond appropriate usage, I will have the Tinys check the use-by date.' This time Robin and Shiny trundle off together, apparently two robots are better than one for double-checking dates.

Hazel swallows hard. 'I should've known you control the Tinys.'

'Negative. I do not control the Tinys.'

'Maybe not, but you're in cahoots with them, aren't you?'

'"Cahoots" is inaccurate. We have functional communication protocols in place to further our collaborative capacities.'

'Sounds like cahoots to me.' She puts her mug aside and clutches her stomach, trying to stop the world spinning. The meds haven't touched the the pain in her chest, and throwing up on bruised ribs would be excruciating. **Do not be sick. Just breathe, come on, don't be a weakling, in to four—**

'Let's say I undertake these responsibilities. Let's say you're right about everything, and I'm not hallucinating, and I am a Traveller. How would I even communicate with the Backward Traveller? Is there, like, a time radio?'

'Negative, there is no such device as a "time radio." Travellers communicate with each other via the dreamscape.'

'The dreamscape. You mean, in my dreams?'

'Affirmative,' CHARL1E says. 'When you and the Backward Traveller arrived in your new temporal zones, time began to run in parallel between you again. This means that you are both on approximately the same circadian rhythm, at a 5,044-year distance. Therefore, you will go to sleep and enter the dreamscape in sync, and encounter each other.'

Hazel laughs and her bruises kick back. 'The hallucination interpretation of this situation is seeming more likely by the minute.'

The code on CHARL1E's screens switches from vertical to horizontal tumbling. 'Why do you think that?'

'Because when you're in a dream you're alone. Besides, even if someone else could get into your dreams, you can't control what happens or what you do, it's the home of the subconscious.'

CHARL1E's code returns to a vertical fall. 'I do not dream, so I cannot sympathise. However, previous data samples have proven that the second issue you raise may be remedied by practising lucid dreaming. Mastering the practice is part of the obligatory Traveller activities dictated by protocol.'

Hazel's queasiness is fading as they talk. 'Marvellous. A hobby I don't have a choice about taking up.'

'The Tinys will supply you with appropriate literature on the subject. I recommend you practise regularly and diligently.'

Hazel arches an eyebrow. 'Lucid dreaming doesn't seem very scientific.'

CHARL1E's code goes horizontal again. 'You do not think the examination of the subconscious is a science?'

'A soft science maybe. The soft end of a soft science. Feather-pillow science.'

'Then Hazel Brandt, it is time you hit your proverbial feather pillow.' The highly contextualised metaphor hints again at CHARL1E's hidden depths and Hazel suppresses a shiver.

Robin and Shiny emerge from under CHARL1E's desk, carrying a fat paperback which they heft up to Hazel.

'"Lucid Dreaming: Interactions with the Plane of Unreality Using the Subconscious Mind."' She reads the title aloud, then riffles through the activities. 'This is barely even feather-pillow science. Mindfulness exercises for when I'm awake, visualisations for "crossing into the dreamscape"—you've got to be kidding.'

'Negative. I am not programmed to joke.' Then why did he make one earlier? He's not just more sophisticated than he appears; he's more advanced than he's letting on. Hazel keeps her face neutral, as her suspicions about CHARL1E's lying concretise. 'It may also interest you to know that the paracetamol-like medication was significantly past its use-by date. I congratulate you in suppressing your instinct to be sick.'

'Nice try at a subject change.' She continues flicking pages. 'This is nonsense; there's no way I'm going to be able to communicate across time and space using this kind of poorly evidenced waffle.'

'That "kind of poorly evidenced waffle" is what brought you

here, Hazel Brandt.' Hazel looks at the screens of unintelligible code, which is now spiralling in on itself. 'It might also be encouraging to know that Lilith and Huxley were both proud and accomplished lucid dreamers, though, as non-Travellers, they did not have your access to the dreamscape. They were, like me, always envious of Travellers' unique direct experience of the fourth dimension.'

Hazel huffs a laugh to cover her unease at CHARL1E expressing feelings. 'So far, let me assure you, you're not missing out on much.'

'Time will tell, Hazel Brandt.'

She closes the book and clutches it to her aching chest, an instinct that brings her comfort. **The fumes of Old Street tube station giving way to the vanillin scent of her favourite bookshop; a novel in a brown paper bag, receipt tucked in the front page; the feel of paper under a fingertip; a bookmark embroidered by Mum—**

'Wait, CHARL1E.' She hesitates, heart monitor bleeping, but she must know. 'If my arrival destroyed the Arch, how will I get home?'

'That is not a salient concern.'

'What do you mean? Of course it's a salient concern, it's the most important thing!'

'That is a matter of perspective. However, I can appreciate that it may be the most important thing to you in this moment.'

'Don't screw with me, CHARL1E, not about this. Tell me what's going on.'

'Unable to comply; I possess no protocol on nonspecific goings-on.'

Hazel clings to the book so hard her knuckles turn waxy. 'How can I get home?'

There's a pause long enough for Hazel to complete one calm breathing cycle. It doesn't work. Her hands feel like pincushions and her lungs are flooding with adrenaline.

On the screens, CHARL1E's code flickers. 'Warning: Information requested may result in accelerated temporal relocation. Caution is advised if you wish to proceed.'

'Temporal relocation to where?'

'Warning: information requested may result in accelerated temporal relocation. Caution is advised if you wish to proceed.'

'I wish to proceed!'

CHARL1E's code goes haywire. 'Secondary warning system implemented: Travellers are advised not to access information regarding the return trip mechanism.'

Hazel's pretty certain no warning system has been triggered, CHARL1E's just hiding things. Her instinct is to throw the book at his screens and shout that he should just send her home now, but she watches his code spinning and flickering and wonders if he's in a bit of a bind. Maybe that frenetic motion indicates an experience akin to anxiety just as high as hers. One of them needs to be the bigger person. She relaxes her grip on the book. 'Let me rethink the question. How about this: CHARL1E, can I still get home?'

The code regains its vertical fall, as if CHARL1E is sighing with relief. 'Affirmative. Your homeward mechanism is not dependent on the Arch.'

She plays with a dog-eared corner of the book. 'I guess that'll have to do for now.'

'To a similar end, it is recommended that you do not wander about Station C without my permission, as this may also result in accelerated temporal relocation.'

'Noted,' Hazel mutters, though she refrains from explicitly agreeing.

On the floor with the heart monitor, Teaspoon's tail twitches, setting off tail-waving between Robin and Shiny.

'The Tinys' latest scans indicate a rise in your stress levels,' CHARL1E says. 'This will result in suboptimal healing if allowed to continue. They recommend you rest. Will you comply?'

Letting herself sink into her chest pain and exhaustion, Hazel replies, 'Yes, that I will comply with.'

'Until tomorrow then, Hazel Brandt.' One by one, CHARL1E's

screens fade from existence, as seamlessly as they appeared. The icosahedron falls dark, and the workshop becomes all the gloomier.

Hazel tugs the blanket around herself and levers out of the chair, as Shiny takes *Lucid Dreaming* and Teaspoon lifts the heart monitor again. Robin leads them back into the curved corridor. Hazel and the three Tinys pass pinboards covered in thick layers of handwritten notices, empty vending machines with the glass removed, and many closed doors, all made from any manner of scrap just like the wall tiles. Robin opens a hodgepodge metal door, revealing a ramshackle but tidy bedroom.

The glow of LED ceiling strips glances off the patches of corrugated iron, melted rubber, and worn plastic that make up the walls, which are oddly angled, with a lopsided, curved ceiling that makes the room feel like a tall tube. A single wrought-iron bed runs lengthways along one wall. Hazel sinks onto it and the mattress squeaks. 'I'm in for a great night's sleep.'

Robin shuts all four of them in, and Hazel notices the door's bottom half is a fringed curtain, presumably so the Tinys can dart in and out at will. So much for any hopes of privacy. Sure enough, tired of carrying the heart monitor around and without regard for her permission, Teaspoon takes off her blanket and starts tearing the sticky pads off her chest. Hazel bears with the procedure, flinching as the glue tugs her skin, leaving behind red welts.

She cringes, embarrassed at being naked, and her anxiety threatens to overflow. What does she normally do when she feels this panicky? She senses she's had practice putting off feelings like this, as if her anxiety is just a bunch of programmers' notes: The code keeps running, ignoring the brown anxious comments among the operational cyan, magenta, and yellow. It's OK, she doesn't need to panic. Hazel can best robots any day of the week: Her instincts have got this, she can worry later. What she needs to do is find a place the Tinys and CHARL1E can't follow her, but where might that be in all this weirdness?

Even now, CHARL1E could be in the room with her. Tinys

aside, he might still have eyes and ears in here. Wincing as Teaspoon tears more patches from her chest, she looks over the furniture, door, and walls, searching for cameras, microphones, or speakers. There's a tilting flatpack wardrobe and beside it a school desk with a flip-up lid. Above the desk is a shelf holding scrap metal sculptures of musicians playing drums, a rubber band guitar, and wooden spoons. There's a dressing table with a hairbrush and an unbranded container labelled 'moisturiser'—which Hazel suspects upon opening will be the colour, smell, and consistency of old butter. The room's not obviously monitored. Even the bedside table only hosts a cracked banker's lamp, a beaker of water, and an analogue alarm clock. Once Teaspoon's finished, it plucks up the heart monitor and speeds it away through the fringe under the door.

Hazel wraps her body in the blanket again as Shiny, taking its turn to pester her, drags her to the desk and flips up its lid, pulling out a notebook and pencil stub and leaving them pointedly on top of *Lucid Dreaming*. 'Yeah, like I'm going to study now,' Hazel croaks. Shiny stares at her, unreadable, then zooms after Teaspoon.

Aware of Robin still observing her, Hazel investigates the wardrobe, which contains well-darned thermals and dungarees in roughly her size, alongside a collection of granny-worthy bras and pants. No obvious signs of bugging—but that could just mean the surveillance is really good. Still, when she runs her hands over the furniture, there's not a speck of dust anywhere and her fingers come away smelling of disinfectant. Despite its decrepit appearance, the room is well-kept. She opens the second door—this one without a fringe, solid to the floor—and finds it leads to a bathroom. Hazel stares at her reflection in the mirror. There are two cuts on her left cheek and a bruise on her right temple, while her eyes are bloodshot.

She turns to Robin. 'Out you get.'

The Tiny doesn't move, just stares at her with blank eyes.

'I mean it, you have to go. I need the toilet, and a shower.'

Its tail sways, then it trundles back to the bedroom, shutting the door behind itself. Hazel pounces on the lock. She holds the bolt for a moment, afraid Robin might somehow be able to unlock it from the outside, but no, this seems to be her one piece of control.

She opens the sink cabinet and finds someone has scratched phrases in the plastic. *Salt an atlas. Pull up if I pull up.* Nonsense. More helpfully, the cabinet contains basic toiletries: a bar of soap, a bamboo toothbrush, and toothpaste tablets so pepperminty Hazel's nose smarts. She feels better for brushing her teeth and drops the blanket on the floor to shower. The water batters her body, veering between freezing and scalding in a way that would be irritating if she wasn't so tired. Bruises protesting, she runs the soap under her arms and over her face, her skin tightening under its touch. It isn't very good soap—though she can't remember what good soap does feel like. She's disconnected from the space she used to inhabit, yet at the same time, she can't fully connect to the one she's in.

Even if her mind is messy, she emerges from the shower invigorated and pink as a lobster, dries with the patchworked towel, and dons a pair of darned tartan pyjamas she finds hanging on the back of the door. They're a men's XL, and she has to roll up the sleeves and trouser cuffs.

Outside, Robin waits. It must have just been sitting there, staring at the door, the whole time she was washing. She should do more—familiarise herself with her room, try to get away from Robin, even open that lucid dreaming book—but her head is swimming and her chest aches, so she falls onto her bed, without the energy to even get under the covers. Robin fusses about in the wardrobe, withdrawing another duvet and hauling it over. It tucks Hazel in, then places its steel fingers on her wrist, because apparently some life signs can only be gleaned by touch.

'You're a bit presumptuous, aren't you? I'm getting really fed up with all your prodding and poking, even if I am grateful for the duvet.' Robin, seemingly satisfied with its data-gathering, withdraws its hand. 'You really do look like a robin redbreast with that rusty jacket. Dr Robin Tiny. Odd little thing. So weird you weren't programmed to speak.'

Robin jacks its legs up so it's on a height with Hazel, and fixes her with its lenses.

'Are you going to watch me like that all night?'

It doesn't move.

'Fantastic. I'm going to sleep brilliantly then, aren't I?'

Somewhere in the dome's guts, an air conditioning or atmospheric control unit kicks into life, and a breeze sweeps Hazel's face. She snuggles into the duvet, wondering whether it's CHARL1E that monitors the atmosphere. He probably controls everything, from the air she breathes to the water she showers in. It's a far from comforting thought, mingling with the guilt she feels about the accident her arrival caused to give her alarming thoughts that keep jolting her from the brink of sleep.

Still, perhaps because of the effort required for her body to heal, she does drift off. At first, she enters the deep sleep of utter exhaustion, but presently a dream forms. She's in a womblike space, filled with a fleshy glow and a current that lifts her hair backwards. It's too gentle to tell whether she's swept along by it like flotsam, or planted in it like a rock on a riverbed. Whispering leaves and the scent of mulch riddle the air.

For a while, she thinks she's alone, gazing silently into the flow, but slowly she becomes aware of someone breathing next to her. Not that it matters—she can't move her head, open her mouth, or say anything. She just rests in the current with the other breathing person. She remembers all this only on waking, her conscious mind managing just one thought while sleeping: Could this be the dreamscape?

When she does stir, Hazel gasps as if she's been drowning, a memory bursting over her in the moment between waking and sleep: squealing metal, her muscles tensing against an oncoming impact, and an explosion of pain—

Robin reels back, missing her by a hairsbreadth as she bolts upright in bed. Was that scream she gave out loud, or only in her head? Surely the latter, or ever-observant Robin would have woken her.

The clock on the bedside table says it's two minutes past seven, and she feels rested as if it's morning. 'You watched me all night, didn't you?'

Robin stares at her, tail swaying—communicating.

'Sure, tell CHARL1E and the others I'm awake, why not? It's not like I mind being monitored twenty-four-seven.' She sits up, clutching her bruised ribs where her heart's still racing from the dream, and slings her legs off the bedside. The room is gloomy, the LEDs turned low. Over on the desk, *Lucid Dreaming*'s thick spine glares at her from under the notebook.

Internally, in a place Hazel can't remember or touch, her dreams, waking thoughts, and lost memories collide, forming one unassailable instinct of belief. It's time to start doing some feather-pillow science. Perhaps it's because she's become a true believer with a selfless urge to help the world—or, more likely, because she's realising the dreamscape's the one place CHARL1E and the Tinys can't follow her.

5

Echo

ATHENS, 514 BCE

Echo's dream merges with the waking world, the dreamscape's whispering current blending with the rattle of Nabu's bedroom door. Jolting awake, Echo re-grips the giant femur she found for protecting and pushes herself against the wall, as the latch clacks and the doorframe shakes. She clutches the bone so hard its ridges dig into her fingers.

'Curses, Echo, it's me, open up!'

Still hazy from sleep, she mumbles. 'Nabu?'

'Yes, it's me. Open the door!'

Her hands slacken but she keeps hold of the bone as she unlocks the door. Nabu launches in, all long arms and billowing robes, and dives into the crates lining the room.

'We'll need sandalwood, that handful of poppyheads hanging on the beam—and the leeches,' he instructs, throwing aside a mummified vole, a net of crystals, and a bronze bowl, which jangles on the stone floor.

Echo stares at the rammed box of incense and smudging sticks by the bed, beams of sunrise falling over them from the air vent near the ceiling. Has she overslept? The huge glass jar of leeches squirms in a corner, and she hugs the thigh bone.

Nabu grabs a dagger and a liver preserved in a phial of oil, stuffing them into his bag as he finally turns to her. He frowns at the femur. 'What's that for?'

'Protection. The door is disturbed in the night.' Echo scowls, answering in unsteady Hellenic. 'I have no sleep.'

'But the lock will stop anyone getting in.'

'I not trust the lock.' Simple phrases are starting to come more easily, if not always correctly, after her long night of politics with Nabu and Kosmos.

Nabu nods at the bone. 'And you think that'll keep them off? You hurt one of the Peisistratids and you'll be sorry you're alive.'

'No. It is self-defence.'

He looks at her oddly, and she realises this probably isn't an argument that's available to someone of her status. She throws the bone on the bed. She'd crack the latch-rattler with it anyway, screwed-up Athenian laws be damned.

'Where's it from?' Nabu asks, nodding to the bone.

Echo points. 'This box. It belongs to you.'

'Does it?' Nabu looks genuinely surprised. 'Funny the stuff that turns up in here.'

'The others call this room the den of the magos.' Echo overheard Khemut cackling about it with some of the girls on her way to bed last night. Nabu, naturally, stayed with Kosmos.

'Mmm, I know. It's annoying. Being Lydian doesn't make me a magos—I've never even met one.'

'But you not correct them?'

'No. I think it probably boosts my healing credentials.' Nabu rearranges his shoulder-bag. 'Come. We've work to do.'

'What work?'

'We have to go and mend someone.' An odd word to use—ἰᾶσθαι—implying something's been broken, rather than someone needs curing. As if the patient is an object.

Poppy heads strung from her elbow and jar of wriggling leeches in her arms, Echo follows Nabu past the other storerooms that double up as the enslaved people's quarters, and into the kitchen. Khemut grimaces at the leeches as Echo navigates breakfasting kitchen hands and stableboys.

In the internal courtyard, Echo whispers to Nabu, 'Where are we go?' but he only pulls back a wool curtain, revealing a staircase, and gestures her through. She mounts the stairs with sandy eyes, wishing she'd managed to get more sleep. She's still jumpy from the door rattling off and on all night, and the walls weeping with noises that left her in no doubt Kosmos's father, uncle, and perhaps even brothers were harassing the household. The kind of sounds that made her tremble in the dark with fury and fear, knowing there was nothing she could do. If she'd left her room, they'd just have got her too. Nabu being an artisan employee offers him, and therefore Echo, crucial advantages over the enslaved people—freedom, a wage and, most importantly, that lock on the door. But she doesn't believe Nabu when he says it's enough. A woman on her own is never enough, nor is a boy. If only Nabu would stay with her, rather than sneaking into Kosmos's room via that old hatch in the kitchen, but she can't expect that from him. At least this way she has the bed rather than the floor, all she has to do is figure out how to sleep in it. Her pulse rises envisioning another night confined in the pitch-black, caught by terror, inhaling spices and decay, dozing fitfully to other people's whimpers and her own dreams of a silent companion in a womblike sea.

As she nears the landing, the sounds of the house fade, replaced with the dawn chorus, women's whispers, and the scent of honey and rose-water. She emerges into a long oblong room, decorated with finery that makes Kosmos's Elpis tapestry seem shabby. About twenty women and girls from five to fifty, long dresses as many shades as their hair and skin, drape over looms, spindles, and carding baskets, so Echo can't immediately tell the difference between enslaved people and aristokrats. A couple of them hum in harmony with a pair of golden oriole birds in a wicker cage. At a table, three girls take a mathematics lesson from a teenager, while a handful of toddling boys play knucklebones at their feet, still young enough not to be exiled downstairs to the men. The sun's first rays slant through high windows, catching dust motes on the air and the bronze threads in the wall hangings. Even so, salted oil lamps light the looms, allowing the women to better see their illustrations. They're all at work far too early.

When Echo enters, every woman stops, running calculating glances over her—a *youth* in their midst! When Nabu follows, their hackles lower and they return to their work, shuttles clattering over looms, but an underlying tension remains, as if they're a flock of birds watching a cat on their periphery.

At the room's far end, a set of drawn red curtains splits, allowing a statuesque woman to pass through. She rearranges her dress over Amazonian clavicles, looking to Nabu with charcoaled eyes that glitter alongside the bangles coating her wrists. As she walks to them, the bracelets dislodge, revealing snatches of purple bruising. 'Good morning, Amel-Nabu.'

'Myrrhine.' He inclines his head.

This must be the mistress of the house—Kosmos's mother, or, judging by her plump curves and clay-smooth skin, his stepmother. She gestures, elbow tight to her body and wrist like a hinge. 'He's through there.'

'Are his humours still disrupted?'

Myrrhine wrinkles her nose. 'He's stilled somewhat . . .' Her mouth is too moist and red around the edges, as if she has recently either been kissing or crying. She seals her lips like she's only spoken half the words on her mind.

'It's an improvement. I'll tend him.' Nabu passes Myrrhine with another half-bow, and Echo tiptoes after, weighed down by the jar of leeches.

Behind the curtain beds line up like sleeping hoplites. The day is stagnant and the room smells of urine, sweat, and something stickier and sicklier Echo doesn't want to think about. On one bed sits a man, his back to them, purple robes cascading over his shoulders, hemmed with gold threads and sard beads. The tyrannos.

He turns as Nabu approaches, baring his teeth and hissing. 'They're going to kill me.'

Echo's pulse sprints. Surely their plot can't have been discovered so quickly?

But Nabu remains placid, kneeling beside Hippias. 'Who is trying to kill you, tyrannos?'

Insides squiggling like the leeches, Echo keeps her breathing even as she just catches Hippias whisper, '*The women.*'

Echo marvels at Nabu's resolve as he meets the tyrannos's gaze. 'Tyrannos, the women are not trying to kill you. There are no women in here.'

'Mother is here.' Hippias points to a corner of the room where what Echo had thought was linen piled on an unmade bed moves, becoming a crone watching them with blackbird eyes. Her dress falls asunder as she shifts, revealing a wrinkled depression the size and shape of an orange in her left breast. Echo looks away, trying to preserve the woman's dignity.

Holding out a hand, Nabu murmurs, 'Let's take you to your bedroom, tyrannos. There are no women in there. It's nice and quiet. You'll be safe.'

Liar. There'll be one woman in there. The Not Here scrapes Echo's throat, daring her to out herself—but she holds it in.

Hippias examines Nabu's hand as if it might grow claws.

'Remember last time, tyrannos, how I brewed you a special infusion and made the fire blaze, and you felt better for it?'

'Did you?' Hippias's eyes skitter over Nabu. 'Yes, that's right. You did.'

'Come now, tyrannos. Come with me. I'll keep you safe.' Nabu's voice is smooth as petals, and the tyrannos puts his bloodless hand into the healer's. Nabu wraps an arm around him, steering him between the curtains.

Hippias moans when he sees the women, burying his face in Nabu's shoulder and clinging to his robes. 'You promised, no women—'

'It's alright,' Nabu coaxes him. 'We're almost there, just keep putting one foot in front of the other.' But Echo catches the glance he shares with Myrrhine; the unspoken promise that he'll be back later to look at the bruises still blooming up her arms.

As Nabu and Hippias descend the stairs, Myrrhine inserts a mint leaf into her mouth, rubs rose-water on her wrists, and settles at her loom. She catches Echo watching and snarls. 'Keep staring and I'll have you whipped, boy.'

Echo pins her eyes to the floor, adjusts the leech jar in her arms, and darts downstairs, the dried poppies batting her leg. She catches up to Nabu and Hippias in the andron, where a group of boys are clearing the litter of wine-sticky kylixes and wilted flower crowns from last night's modest symposium.

'Out,' Nabu instructs them. 'And send for Hipparchos.' In just half a day in the household, Echo has learned that the tyrannos's slaves don't always listen to Nabu, particularly if a member of the family or their manager has given them other instructions, but these boys take one look at Hippias and bolt. Clearly, this has happened before.

Nabu bundles Hippias into a spacious back bedroom lined with furs, thick blankets, and tapestries of Odysseus outsmarting the Sirens. Echo's barely placed the leeches and poppies on a side table when Nabu grabs her shoulder. 'Go to the kitchen. Find me sage—as much as you can carry—a jar of honey, and three sprigs of marjoram. And make a lavender infusion.'

Echo turns to leave but he grabs her wrist, looking to where Hippias has slumped, scowling and muttering, into a chair. 'Make the infusion strong.'

She cocks her head, as the Not Here rustles and moves her mouth without her consent. '**Valerian root.**'

'What?' Nabu starts shredding the poppyheads distractedly.

She tries to cover her loss of control. 'Would you like valerian root also?'

Nabu lifts his brow, as if surprised she knows about herblore. She's surprised herself. 'Why not. Can't be too careful.'

In the kitchen, the sun peeks through the shutters as the enslaved workers tidy away their own breakfast and ready the Peisistratids'. Echo creeps between their morning bustle to find what she needs. The valerian root is tucked behind a bottle of mandrake wine—**useful for sleepy sleep**—so she grabs that as well.

As she brews the infusion with water from a large cauldron bubbling on a hearth, the Not Here keeps trilling—**another pinch, you'll not kill him with lavender**—but it doesn't try to make her speak again. Overnight, the mysteries of her amnesia and the Not Here hardened into a stone of dread. Her concept of 'normal' has come unstuck, but she's pretty certain what's happening in her head has dropped right off the spectrum of normality. Yet every time she tries examining the Not Here, it dances away, and exhaustion muffles her worry. She yawns, chopping marjoram.

'No yawning in my kitchen!' Khemut appears like steam, shouting in Echo's ear, making her jump and scatter her cuttings. 'See? Tired workers are useful as goats!'

'Good day, Khemut.'

Khemut's face crumples like an unironed sheet. 'Is it?' The old woman runs an arthritic claw through Echo's hair. 'Such an unusual colour, so much copper and gold. Here's hoping Apollo's made you tough as bronze on the inside too.'

Her eyes are like daggers, but Echo can't look away.

'You're lucky Nabu's taken you under his wing, he's a kind man, but you can't count on staying his favourite forever. I used to be a favourite too. Half the lads and lasses in this kitchen are mine by some Peisistratid. Wouldn't know it to look at me now though, would you?'

She grins, bearing a ridge of ulcered gums and making wrinkles around her scarred, sewn-shut eye.

'I apologise. I am forced to return to work.' Echo steps away as her fear of nighttime latch-rattling wells up, and hastens back to Nabu. Surely, the real 'luck' would be to go unseen, not be a favourite? She shivers. No, someone will always see a woman in this world, and better it's a tyrannos than a brothel owner. In this house, horrendously, it seems the same might go for a boy.

In Echo's absence, Nabu's been tending the fire, and when he unfolds to his full height in the dancing light, incense clouding his sinuous robes, she understands why the others think he's a magos. She could believe magic of him. Then again, that's probably what he wants her to think.

He nods when he sees the mandrake wine. 'Pour a knuckle's worth into the infusion—no more—then unpack my bag onto that table.'

Echo complies, the leeches squiggling with interest when she takes out the jar containing the preserved liver.

Nabu leans over Hippias, examining each eye closely, then undresses him to the waist. The tyrannos protests, but Nabu uses that calming voice again. 'Hush now, we're just leeching you to take away the troubling humours. There's a darkness in you, we have to draw it out.'

He gestures for Echo to bring the leeches, and extracts one deftly. 'Thirteen, on his chest, understand? When they're good and fat, bring them to me at the table.'

'I never have used leeches before.' Echo wants to stay quiet, be good, go unseen, but the thought of plunging her hand into a jar of leeches—she just can't.

Nabu pauses, looking at her as if he can see through her skin. Perhaps her voice is too quiet, too high-pitched, too fearful. Maybe a boy wouldn't squirm at a leech, or the previous Traveller had been braver. Whichever, she clearly doesn't have a choice.

Glaring, Nabu dips his thumb and forefinger into the jar, pulling out another squirming leech. 'Just two fingers, like that. Doesn't have to be the whole hand. Don't be frightened of them, they're quite harmless. Find the thin end and present it to the skin—like this. They'll grab on by themselves.' He holds the leech's sucker to Hippias's chest. It stretches, sensing his blood, and latches on. 'They'll fall off when they're full—and that's when you bring them to me. One at a time is fine.'

Echo screws up her face, but nods.

'They'll leave a small wound that'll bleed like anything. There are cloths in my bag to staunch the flow, but it won't stop for hours. That's alright, I'm expecting that. Got it?'

He pats her shoulder before sweeping back to the table. Echo sinks her thumb and forefinger into the jar, but the leeches are slithery and in the end she has to use three fingers to trap one against the jar wall. She pulls it out and drops it, mouth-first, onto Hippias's chest. He glares at her, hissing wordlessly. There's something mean wrong with him, and she doubts the leeches will do any good, but she keeps going until all thirteen are gorging on his blood. She squats on the floor, watching them grow fat. Hippias's scowls diminish, but his eyes stay red.

There's a knock on the door and Nabu opens it enough to allow the oxlike man beyond a view of Hippias. Though heavier built than the tyrannos, he has the same wineskin complexion and scowl-prone features which must make him the brother, Hipparchos. His eyes rake Echo and she finds herself looking at the leeches rather than him. *Here's hoping Apollo's made you tough as bronze.* Whispering, Nabu asks Hipparchos to wait in the andron and closes the door.

The fire burns down and Nabu builds it up again, using sandalwood twigs whose pungent smoke mixes with the incense and makes Echo light-headed. One by one, the leeches detach from Hippias's chest, and Echo covers the wounds before delivering the parasites to Nabu, their rubbery skin so stretched they threaten to pop in her hand.

Slicing the creatures open, Nabu prays in a language even the Not Here doesn't understand, creating a mess of dissected liver and slaughtered leeches. He sweeps the gristle into a bowl, chucks in the marjoram, and throws the sage on the fire, where it billows and spits. Plunging his hand into the bowl, he flicks the bloody mixture widdershins around Hippias's chair, chanting all the while.

When the bowl is empty and the tiles ruined, he dabs the leech wounds with honey. 'Feed him the tea.'

She expects the tyrannos to protest, but he wolfs it like a toddler.

Nabu wipes his hands and nurses Hippias into bed. 'We'll let him sleep now,' he mutters to Echo.

In the andron, Hipparchos waits, brushed with anaemic midday sunlight. Have they really been in there all morning? One of the herbs must have twisted Echo's mind.

'How bad this time?' Hipparchos asks.

Nabu shakes his head. 'Hard to say. The dark humours are strong in him. I read the liver, but its message was unclear, so I won't know more until I've talked to Myrrhine—I wasn't there when the episode began, but I suspect he beat her.'

'No matter about the women, who else saw?'

'The usual: Slaves. Me. You.'

'And this one?' Hipparchos points a thick finger at Echo.

'My new assistant. A trustworthy boy.'

'If you say so.' But Hipparchos's face doesn't match his words. His gaze is hungry, as if he's holding back saliva calculating how much meat is on her. She shrinks around the leech jar. She hopes he thinks she's a boy until she realises no one should look at boys like that. Perhaps he's the latch-rattler, and he doesn't have the wrong door at all.

It's some time before Nabu and Echo are free to go about their own business. First, they return to the gynaikeion, applying poultices to Myrrhine's bruises and checking on the karkinoma of the tyrannos's mother. Back at Nabu's room, a queue of artisans and enslaved workers from the house and the Peisistratid farms demand attention. With Echo's amateur assistance, Nabu resets a labourer's broken arm to curdling shrieks, advises the old paidogogos to bathe his arthritic ankles in cold water, and tells a serving girl her son has gangrene and won't survive the night . . . Echo goes into the stable yard and splashes her face with well-water to get the girl's sobs out of her head. The Not Here murmurs that it doesn't have slavery—not legally, not where she was—but it's so enmeshed in Athenian culture she can't open her eyes without seeing it. **1834 Abolition of Slaver—** The date is so impossibly far off, she can't wrap her head around it. It's no use, this is how it went, how it goes, how it is; she can't stop it, only live amongst it, sick as it makes her.

Mid-afternoon, Kosmos stumbles in and leans on the doorframe, pale and trembling. 'I'm dying, Nabu. Hephaestus has my stomach in a clamp and Hades fills my head.'

Nabu smirks, focussed on grinding dried sheep kidneys. 'Never fear, there's life in you yet.'

'You haven't even looked at me! I could have boils in my armpits and fur growing on my tongue.'

'Evidence at my disposal leads me to believe you'll be hale and healthy by evening.'

Kosmos glances at Echo, who suppresses a giggle. 'And what might this evidence be?'

'You reek like a sack of wine.' Nabu doesn't add that he was there to watch Kosmos drinking. He grabs a necklace of leaves from a hook and chucks it at Kosmos. 'Wear that—it's leatherleaf, it'll help with the headache. And for the gods' sake wash.'

'That's it?' Kosmos examines the necklace dubiously.

'Well, there's only one certain cure: Next time, mix your wine better and drink less of it.'

Kosmos chucks the necklace around a statue of a snake goddess half-buried in one of the crates. 'I'll look ridiculous wearing that.'

'Some fresh air then?'

Excited by the idea of escaping this oppressive house, Echo sticks her head out the door. 'Nobody waits for help.'

Nabu looks up from his pestle and mortar. 'You're sure?' She nods. 'Alright, let's go.'

Heat pounds down from the sky and up from the pavement as the three of them amble into town, Hanno and Absalon shadowing a few paces behind. The roadsides are thick with wild herbs and wind-blown flowers, rustling with birds and mice. Geckos doze on sun-hot walls and laundry hangs limp between the houses. As they near the city centre, the streets become crowded, a tide of people sweeping them up and washing them into the packed agora. Nabu grabs Echo and Kosmos's hands to stop them being separated, and pulls them to the opposite side of the square, into the shade of a long stoa. A gaggle of boys cluster cross-legged around a seated man, who taps his cane in rhythm as one of them recites tracts of the *Odyssey*. 'Nobody—that's my name—' Another group is more various in age, five men all shouting over each other, though Echo only catches the words 'wanderers' and 'aether.'

'Nabu!' comes a call from the stoa's far end, and they move towards it, past an artist painting a mural of interlocking vines and birds. Echo skirts his apprentice, who mixes paint powders as he sings for his employer's entertainment, and joins the party at the other end.

The hail came from a man of perhaps thirty, who smiles at their approach and, embracing Nabu, mutters, 'And who do you bring me but a boy and a Peisistratid—what will you drag in next?'

Nabu answers just as quietly. 'Let it alone, Aristogeiton, Kosmos has explained himself to you enough times, and the boy is my assistant.'

Aristogeiton takes Echo in. 'What a skinny thing, I hope you didn't pay too much for him—ah, but I forget, the broad-minded Amel-Nabu doesn't keep slaves.'

Nabu's expression darkens. 'Nor would you had you ever been one.' Echo takes care not to change her expression, as if this isn't new information, but she looks at Nabu sidelong, wondering about his story.

'Let's not debate it again, Nabu! Either way, this slip-of-a-thing isn't worth his wage.'

'Forgive Aristogeiton his mood,' says the well-built young man beside him, rattling a pair of obols in a half-opened fist. 'We all indulged too much last night, and he most of all.'

'My dear Harmodios, when Kleisthenes says drink, you drink.' Aristogeiton says, rubbing his forehead with his fingertips. 'He's one of our greatest politicians, we need him on our side.'

Harmodios smiles indulgently. 'As you say. But you missed him, Kosmos! You left so early, before sunset even, we wondered if the Furies had got you. What took you away?'

'Business.' Kosmos replies with the terseness of young men who don't much like each other but frequent the same circles. Apparently, all had attended Hippias's symposium, and none are to discover Kosmos left to be with Nabu. Kosmos changes the subject. 'I hope your family fare better?'

'As well as can be in such times.' Harmodios shrugs. They can't be far apart in age, though Harmodios's hair is already long enough to make a man's braid, and he's more comfortable in himself. Kosmos might never reach such comfort, but stay, like his father, all limbs and angles.

Echo presses herself against the cool wall, praying the Not Here behaves itself, as she watches Aristogeiton show off his new himation. 'Linen all the way from Thebes, I bought it last week—beautiful, isn't it?'

Harmodios takes Aristogeiton's arm, murmuring, 'Stop drawing attention to how good it looks or you'll have the whole agora after you.'

'Always the worrier! You know no one comes close to you.'

'Even that hetaira?'

'Yes, even Leaina.' Aristogeiton tucks the young man's hair behind his ear and strokes his cheek, **like Patroklos and Achilleus**. Nabu casts a look at Kosmos, eyes falling away quickly, and Echo wonders if he might be jealous of such public displays of affection. A non-citizen, non-Hellenic artisan and a tyrannos's son is hardly a match destined for happiness.

Kosmos clears his throat. 'Listen, I was studying the wanderers last night, and I want to revisit my theory that the night sky is a blanket, and that the stars are merely aether shining through the weave.'

'Not again, Kosmos!' Harmodios groans. 'It doesn't make any sense—how then do you explain eclipses? We all agreed last week, Anaximander's tubular channels are the most likely story.'

'Well, we were wrong. Look, let me show you . . .' Kosmos plucks a stick from the ground and makes a map of the universe in the dusty pavement in front of the stoa. One by one, the party gets drawn in—Nabu, Aristogeiton, even Harmodios, plus three more men whose names Echo doesn't catch. They jump between philosophical theories, leaving Echo too disoriented and language-bound to keep up, afflicted by the Not Here's dizzy nonsense. **Monists and Miletos; fire and aether; generation and destruction; and the limitless limitless limitless—**

As they debate, Aristogeiton and Harmodios share raisins and make private asides. They're not beautiful as such, both are stocky with overlong arms, and Aristogeiton hides his lack of chin under his beard, while Harmodios's hairline comes down almost as far as his close-set brow. However, though Kosmos's awkward cordiality might be more likeable, Aristogeiton and Harmodios are magnetic. Their combined bearing and tone creates attraction: They're so exclusive they exude the impression that, if you tried very hard, you might be lucky enough to orbit them. Even Echo feels it. Despite Aristogeiton's arrogance towards Nabu, and Harmodios's riling of Kosmos, she wants to be included under the aegis of their approval.

No wonder these are the tyrannicides, the Not Here shouts, pushing the words against her closed mouth. **514 BCE; Harmodios and Aristogeiton; the tyrannicides—** She fights the urge to say it aloud, but of course it's true, this is not just a pack of philosophers. Amongst them are plotters, and her reason for being here is to help them usurp the tyrannos.

Around them, the stoa swells and empties, until the sun sags into the horizon and they're the last ones left. Aristogeiton waves their attendants away, and Hanno and Absalon retreat into the last of the sunshine, pulling out a board for the Game of Ur.

In the group's sudden hush, Aristogeiton turns his head, listening to Hanno and Absalon's knucklebones on the board, the grasshoppers creaking, and an unbound shutter banging in the sea breeze. Across the agora, a merchant packs up his stall, whistling, too far away to be in earshot. 'You're sure the boy is trustworthy, Nabu?'

'Certain. On my life.' Nabu doesn't look at Echo, but the promise settles heavily on her.

'We've identified the time: the first day of the Panathenaia, when carrying weapons won't look suspicious,' Aristogeiton murmurs. 'Hippias and Hipparchos will be resting on their laurels, certain nobody will try anything that might anger the gods.'

'And you aren't frightened of doing that yourself?' asks Kosmos, voice quiet too.

'This is the work of the gods,' Harmodios mutters. 'They will not begrudge us the time. Athens must be freed from the yoke of single rulers—every man's voice must be heard.'

Yes but not every woman, or child, or enslaved person. Not for a long, long, long— The Not Here swills words around Echo's mouth, but she traps them in.

Kosmos glances at Aristogeiton. 'How will we exile them with all those people around? They might turn the crowd in their favour.'

Aristogeiton and Harmodios exchange a look. 'The crowd will be with us,' Aristogeiton says. 'But we've moved away from the exile plan.'

'To what?' Nabu frowns.

Aristogeiton purses his lips and jerks his head.

'We ruled out execution, you can't put it back on the table just like that,' Kosmos says, stroking the line of his scar from his nose to his lip.

'We can, given what your uncle's done to my sister—to my family name,' Harmodios says.

'Death is not a proportionate response to accusations of promiscuity.'

'It wasn't just accusations, Kosmos,' Harmodios's voice drops, 'and even if it were, she'd never marry as she should. We can't let it stand.'

'I need a more valid reason than your personal grudges,' Kosmos replies.

'It's not as if you don't have personal grudges of your own,' Harmodios says, glancing pointedly at Kosmos's scar.

Kosmos snatches his hand from his mouth, working to control his features, suddenly less of a brat than Echo thought. 'Yes, but they're not why I'm here.'

'How about this, then.' Aristogeiton's tone is snakelike, quiet but brimming with threat. 'Hippias has had too many volatile episodes. We leave him and Hipparchos alive in the Persian provinces, and they'll raise an army and return. Persia is a much greater power than we are, they will slaughter us all—horribly, you've seen how your father can be—and undo any good we manage to achieve. They have to go, they're too dangerous to let live.'

'Kosmos, maybe they're right,' Nabu murmurs. 'I know they're your family, but you believe in what we're about. This is the most expedient way to open the laws to all Athenian citizens. Even your grandfather strove for unification, he would have wanted it.'

'I doubt he would have wanted it this way.' Kosmos taps his scar again, staring at the ground, memories washing over his face. Presently he nods, meeting Aristogeiton's glower. 'You're right, of course. Would that their blood didn't run in my veins. The first day of the Great Panathenaia it is. One-and-a-half moons, so close.'

A baby's cry and answering woman's lullaby weave from a nearby house. The merchant on the other side of the agora turns his whistle to a song as he urges his ox and cart homeward. These streets are never silent, these houses never empty; Athens's inhabitants are never truly alone. Echo catches Hanno's eye as Absalon packs away their game, and wonders how much they overheard.

On the way home, swallows darting on a pink dusk, Echo can't shake Kosmos's sad tapping of his scar. Hippias and Hipparchos have done unthinkable, unforgivable things, and Echo's anger boils as a latch rattles in her mind's eye. She wants to tear them limb from limb for all the fear and hurt they've caused. Her small spike of empathy remembering Hippias's bloodshot, paranoid eyes doesn't outweigh her anger at Myrrhine's bruises, Khemut's sewn-shut eye, or Kosmos's scarred lip. The tyrannos and his brother shouldn't have been able to gain their positions of power in the first place given their violent proclivities, and they should face retribution.

Yet, this plot the conspirators are putting together feels wrong. This small gang of men are taking the fate of Athens into their own hands, and they're talking about revenge, not retribution. By making violence their source of hope, they're risking making whatever follows the tyrannos equally unjust. Vengeance, even against those who commit atrocities, does not necessarily balance the scales. There must be some objective, legal way of overthrowing and punishing Hippias and Hipparchos that's being overlooked.

Then again, if it were up to Echo half of Athens would face justice, everyone who treats another human being as property, or otherwise violates their consent—even Kosmos, who she doesn't totally dislike. She's an interloper to whom Athenian laws and ethics are utterly incomprehensible. Of course, she knew the theory of this society before she travelled—the Not Here has told her that much—but seeing it all in practice makes her skin crawl at every turn. **It's one thing knowing history and another living it**, the Not Here purrs, and the complete alienation of it all makes her ache with homesickness.

Though Athens does need to be rid of Hippias and Hipparchos, Echo can't shake the feeling that's not what she's here to do.

She pauses, Nabu and Kosmos a step ahead, Hanno and Absalon

three steps behind, and gazes at the mountains. Her feet itch. She could run. A breeze brings her the scent of herbs and fresh olives. She takes one stride, and another, breathing hard. Just a few steps more and she'll be sprinting, off the hook. But how far could she get before she was discovered as a woman? Or some well-meaning citizen chased her down as a runaway slave? Or the Not Here made her do something stupid? These Hellenes are stronger and faster than she is, better fed, better trained. She falls in behind Nabu, trailing home with hunched shoulders, trying to align herself with a calling that feels wrong.

6

Hazel

STATION C, DATE UNKNOWN

The alarm trills that Hazel's been meditating for forty minutes and she stretches her legs in a rush of pins and needles. Squeaks and hydraulic whizzes betray Tinys scurrying around beyond the orb of light over CHARL1E's desk, and she wonders where her three most vigilant carers have got to. Two weeks ago, she couldn't have imagined she'd have the concentration to meditate so deeply she wouldn't notice the Tinys squeaking about, but between *Lucid Dreaming*'s dippy-hippy instructions and CHARL1E's sardonic guidance, she's caught the mindfulness bug. One Tiny left a cup of tea beside her while she was in the zone, and she didn't even register it. They still can't make tea: This one doesn't have floating lumps of Professor Tazzari's Finest Pro-Tase Powder, but it's still stone-cold. Why the Tinys can attach a heart monitor but not boil water is Station C's gravest mystery. Hazel hobbles upright and pokes through the Workshop desks for a 'nosing-about break.'

She starts at a far table, investigating the basket of corroded RAM cards she left halfway through yesterday. She wrinkles her nose at the cards' greyed copper teeth. Utterly useless. 'Lilith and Huxley really did keep some trash,' she mutters, almost immediately regretting it when the now familiar guilt over their accidental deaths twists her stomach. 'Searching' is too strong a term for what she's doing, it implies she knows what to look for. She's more yearning through the piles, hoping to find something to help her in the moments her faith in lucid dreaming and time travel fail. So far though, she's just found notes about the Tinys' bugs (they deliver potted plants when asked for sticky toffee pudding), and team photos of the generations of the Keepers who lived here, which she stuffs away again with a thick throat.

Hazel hefts the RAM cards to one side and, underneath, finds a box of yellow-edged notes about CHARL1E. She draws up a stool and settles to read. They make no sense of course. Other programmers' notes rarely do at first. Everyone has their own way of coding and talking about code, the way ten people might speak the same language with different accents. When coding complicated systems like Station C's, multiple languages are also at play, and the Keepers had impenetrable in-house jargon formed over centuries. Still, it makes her mnemealgic mind whisper.

'As on twenty-three previous occasions, I must remind you that this "nosing-about" is counter-productive to our goals.' It's taken longer than usual for CHARL1E to complain.

'There's such a thing as working too hard, CHARL1E.'

'My records indicate you are not close to that boundary.'

She glances at his screens. 'Don't forget that I work when I sleep too!'

'Does this indicate that you entered the dreamscape again last night?'

Hazel recalls the glow, like nightclub lights through closed eyes, and the sound of flicking pages. 'Yeah.'

'Did you achieve our current objective of talking to the Backward Traveller?'

'No.'

'Did you attempt to?'

'That's not really how dreams work, CHARL1E. You can't just

decide to do things—you're not aware in dreams.' She routinely recognises when she's in the dreamscape now, even knows what she's supposed to do there, but she hasn't been able to make her unconscious voice work—her corporeal throat, constricted by sleep paralysis, always wakes her. Lucid dreaming saps her willpower. It should, nobody's built to work in their sleep, the same way computers don't keep programmes active in standby. CHARL1E never gets this. Maybe he doesn't go on standby, even when the icosahedron's dark.

'You must practise lucid dreaming more assiduously.'

'Sure, work me harder.' Hazel brings the programmer notes to CHARL1E's desk and flops into a wheely chair. She twists the wrong way and her bruises complain. They're healing but she still has to be careful.

'The answer does not appear as you desire: That does not mean it is not the answer,' CHARL1E says.

Hazel frowns. 'For a thing that can't dream, you're annoyingly certain you know about dreaming.'

'Illogical premise: My programming regarding the praxis of dreaming has no relation to my theoretical knowledge.'

Hazel brings the notes right up to her face, hoping CHARL1E will get the hint. No such luck.

'I notice that your bookmark is only on page 125 of *Lucid Dreaming*. However records show you have an average reading speed of 317 words per minute. In the past fortnight you have had ample time to complete your first reading.'

'It's my second reading,' she replies, turning a page to find a diagram of thousands of 'chronodes' scattered across the 'TAN.' The *A* and *N* probably mean 'Area Network,' but what's the *T*? 'Temporal'?

'No way. CHARL1E, is this how you monitor the timeline?'

She hasn't yet figured out how CHARL1E sees, but anytime she asks him about what she's holding, he knows what it is, and now is no exception. 'Affirmative. That is the Temporal Area Network. I assume you will request an explanation?'

'You know me so well.'

'The chronodes are situated at carefully calculated intervals along the timeline, updating me on its status as required.'

Hazel swivels in her chair. '"The" timeline. There's no multiverse then?'

'Not to my knowledge.'

'If there's no universe B, that piles on the pressure.' Hazel swivels her chair back and forth, thinking. 'And you can see the whole of this timeline?'

'Affirmative. However, I cannot access all areas of the broader space-time continuum.'

'I don't know if that's comforting or not.'

'It is not.'

Hazel rolls her eyes. 'Well, nothing ever is to you. When we change history, does that just overwrite the timeline then?'

'Affirmative. However, the overwrite is not instantaneous. Instead, changes travel along the timeline like waves, and the chronodes inform me they are coming. To continue the metaphor, some waves contain warm currents and are good to swim in. These are positive changes, which the Keepers call "mends." Other waves are like tsunamis, wreaking great destruction and leaving the timeline in a worse state. These are called "glitches."'

Hazel sips her cold tea, which today tangs of chlorine. 'But presumably once a rewrite starts, you can't stop it? Once the wave is set in motion, it's going to crash on the shore, right?'

'Affirmative. That is why the dreamscape is vital. Communication between Travellers in the dreamscape bypasses whatever changes are moving up the timeline. This gives us a small window in which to activate a mend in the wake of a glitch. The chronodes inform me the timeline has gone awry. I calculate a fix and inform the Forward Traveller what needs doing. They then communicate it to the Backward Traveller via the dreamscape—like using a radio to communicate across an ocean. The Backward Traveller then activates the mend.'

Hazel mutters it all back to herself. 'It's like multiple waves crashing against a shore, one after the other. It doesn't matter much what's between the waves, so long as the final wave is positive.'

'In principle, though in practice glitches should be avoided. There is not always a strong probability of being able to activate a mend in its wake.'

'In which case presumably another Excursion is sent further back in time to fix whatever got messed up?'

'Affirmative. However, as the Arch is broken, that contingency is no longer available for Excursion 1133.'

'Don't remind me.' She winces every time the accident gets mentioned. If only she'd built the catopthura correctly, Lilith and Huxley would still be alive and she wouldn't be alone here. She wishes CHARL1E could give her a diagram of all this. There must be one somewhere in this junkyard. 'In theory, then, we could screw everything up then tell the Backward Traveller how to fix it, and the timeline would get overwritten twice—once with a glitch, once with a mend. The whole world would be none the wiser. So, I might have lived through several glitches and mends already? Some of which might even have wiped me out?'

'Affirmative. Over the previous 1,132 excursions, I have experienced 2,091 glitches and mends, during which I was eradicated and reinstated on 342 occasions. I have no records of what happened between times.'

Hands shaking, Hazel puts down her mug. 'Does that mean I've been wiped out as well?'

'Previous Excursions have shown that exact knowledge of how many glitches and mends a Traveller has experienced or been eradicated and reinstated by is not psychologically assistive.'

'Yeah, that figures.' Hazel blows out her cheeks. 'Wait! What if a *mend* wipes us out? I mean, what if a better timeline doesn't contain me?'

On the screens, CHARL1E's code spirals, which means Hazel is asking a tricky question. 'Theoretically, it is possible to wipe yourself out with either a glitch or a mend. However, there is no known record of a Traveller erasing themselves. The Keepers theorised that this is because of the cause-and-effect loops necessitated by building the catopthura: You have to have made it, therefore you must have existed.'

'But then you wouldn't necessarily have a record of it if a Traveller had wiped themselves out, because the cause-and-effect loop would break, and they'd just never have been here.'

'Affirmative. However, dwelling on such extrapolations is also not psychologically assistive.'

Hazel's spine tingles. It's almost worth taking another gulp of tea. 'I get why you're so keen for me to improve at lucid dreaming.'

'Affirmative. Until you are competent, the timeline remains in jeopardy.'

'Again, no pressure.'

'Negative, the pressure is significant.'

'As usual, you missed the point.' Hazel leans back in her chair, spinning. 'There's something I don't understand: Why can't you just talk to the Backward Traveller yourself?'

'I cannot access the dreamscape, I am not the right sort of being.'

'You really don't dream?'

'Affirmative. I do not dream.'

'Not even daydreams?'

'Daydreams are different.'

Hazel leans forward, watching the glowing icosahedron. 'That's a yes. What do you daydream about?' Hazel waits. 'CHARLIE?'

'Hazel Brandt, the Tinys inform me that your dinner is ready. Would you like it here or in your room?'

She sighs, leaning back again. 'May as well be my room. I could do with a change of scenery.' There are only two scenes: the Workshop and her room, and they've switched back and forth for two weeks without respite. The Habitation Dome has other rooms, but CHARL1E can tell if she goes exploring and sends the Tinys to stop her. 'Not that it makes any difference to my cabin fever.'

'You do not currently exhibit symptoms of cabin fever.'

'Just you wait.' Hazel tosses the notes back where she found them and makes to go. She pauses in the doorway. 'You know, what I really miss is fresh air. It's like an airplane in here and my skin's hating it. My nose feels dry as a desert.'

'Unable to calculate solution: Air cannot be "fresh."'

'Yeah, right.' Hazel frowns. CHARL1E regularly makes sophisticated inferences, so it's unlikely he can't interpret this colloquialism, but perhaps it's a hint towards the almighty AI's limits. 'Night, CHARL1E.'

'Goodnight, Hazel Brandt. Please sleep well.'

'Doing my best.'

Partway down the corridor, she runs into Robin and Teaspoon, waiting for her at the airlock to the blasted Arch dome. They race at her, tugging her sleeves and dungarees, pulling her towards the airlock.

'Not again!' She groans. 'I'm not going outside with you, I tell you every day! CHARL1E says it's dangerous and while I don't trust him a bit, I think he's right about this one.'

She pins her arms against the doorframe, shunting Robin away from the airlock button with her foot. The Tiny wobbles, then crashes to the floor. Its hand hits the ground with a splintering noise. Righting itself, Robin retracts its limbs and rolls to the corridor's edge, leaving a couple of rivets behind.

Teaspoon darts over, picking up parts as Robin unfurls from its protective ball. Together, they examine the damage, looking slowly from the injured hand to Hazel.

'For goodness' sake, see what happens when you get too interfering? I can't go outside, you know I can't.'

The Tinys huddle together and wheel back to the Workshop, Teaspoon's tail entwined with Robin's. Hazel bites her lip. She's never seen them mimic physical affection before. She hadn't meant to hurt Robin, and she regrets snapping at it, which is ridiculous because the Tinys can't feel pain.

Alone, she puts her palm against the airlock door, the empty biosuits hanging either side of her like beckoning ghosts. *Air cannot be fresh.* Why could they possibly want her to go outside that badly?

In her room, she finds Shiny folding clean laundry, and a bowl of what CHARL1E claims is 'pro-fu bourguignon.' Echo's got no idea where the Tinys make food, but she knows it takes roughly an hour for them to deliver this dish, which comes with a warm but stale baguette and contains gloopy rehydrated protein lumps. It's just as bad as she remembers. She's tempted to skip it, but the Tinys buzz about like wasps if she leaves anything on her plate, and she tells herself with each gelatinous swallow that lucid dreaming is easier on a full stomach.

She showers before bed, emerging wrapped in a towel and nearly falling over Shiny, who's holding her pyjamas.

'You're worse than a cat, always underfoot! You know there's such a thing as personal space, right?'

It gazes at her, holding her pyjamas aloft.

She sighs. 'Thanks, I guess.' Desensitised to the Tinys' observations, she changes and sits on the bed, replaying the splintering noise Robin's hand made as it broke. 'Look, we can't go on like this. We're going to have to figure out a way to talk. Understand?'

Shiny stares. Its tail twitches.

'I can't understand a tail-twitch, but you can understand what I'm saying, right?'

Another tail twitch.

'When I'm asking a question, can you nod yes or shake no like this, to tell me whether I'm right?' She nods, then shakes her head vigorously to demonstrate.

Shiny nods back with its lenses, just as vigorously. *Yes.*

'Alright, alright, not so much that your eyes come off.' Hazel pauses. 'Now we've got that sorted, let's discuss some basics: Can you talk at all? No. Didn't think so. But you can understand me? Yes. Good. And you talk to CHARL1E as well? No. I'm pretty sure you do—ah! Wait. You communicate with CHARL1E? Yes! There we go, I knew you were in cahoots. You are, aren't you?'

Shiny stares at her.

'You know, cahoots? In league. Up to something together.'

Shiny keeps staring.

'Do you understand the question? Yes. That means the answer's not yes or no, doesn't it? OK, for "it's complicated," shrug. Like this.'

Shiny shrugs, lifting its hands to the ceiling.

Hazel laughs. 'That's actually quite sweet. Alright, million-dollar question: Can I make my own tea?'

It shakes its head.

'Damn. So close. Still, can you teach the other Tinys what I've taught you?'

Shiny nods but doesn't move.

'So specific. Can you go now and teach the other Tinys what I have taught you, please?'

This time, Shiny zooms off, leaving the door fringe flapping.

'One Tiny down, a couple hundred more to go,' Hazel mutters.

Her half-healed ribs twinge as she tucks herself in bed and starts practising 'Drifting Off With Intent.' Lying on her left-hand side, she repeats the instructions that will guide her into a conscious state whilst dreaming, then breathes into her diaphragm, with her palm resting on her third eye. She thinks third eyes are nonsense, but the authors of *Lucid Dreaming* are adamant they exist, and at this juncture Hazel will do just about anything to contact the Backward Traveller.

After several false starts, she drifts into the dreamscape. As usual, she arrives without any control, but she's prepared. Repeating the instructions from *Lucid Dreaming* before sleep isn't just a formality, it embeds them in her subconscious, so she can conjure them now without waking.

First, develop an awareness of your presence within the dreamscape. Gently allow the conscious mind to surface—just enough to skim the dream—so that you can act with intent while your unconscious remains at the helm. Take care, because if your conscious mind grows too powerful, you will awaken, and the dream will be lost . . .

It's this bit that scuppers Hazel. She can never strike the balance between autonomy within the dreamscape and waking consciousness. Even when she achieves awareness, she's not yet strong enough to turn and look at the Backward Traveller, so she just stands mute, witnessing the dreamscape flow around her, like a waterfall over a rock. Right now, she's still alone; there's no heat from another body on her left hand. She'll have to wait; she's become good at that at least.

In the dreamscape, time is as long as forever and only a split second. Hazel could dream a lifetime in a night and one moment for eight hours. Dreaming turns time into a rubber band she has no control over; sometimes she waits minutes for the Backward Traveller, other times months. Sooner or later, they always arrive—and tonight is no exception. All at once, a sensation of shadow and solidity tells Hazel she's got company.

Hazel reaches for the reason she's here: to communicate with the Backward Traveller. She trains her attention on the heat emanating from them, their breath rising and falling. She relaxes both her dreaming self and her real sleeping body, which she senses at the edge of her awareness. *Skim the dream with your consciousness, don't wake up. Leave the unconscious at the helm.*

'Hh—' She makes a breathy noise. 'Hello?' Her dreaming lips move, but it feels as if her waking mouth might have done as well, and the word could have sounded in the dreamscape or Station C.

Silence.

Then: 'Khaíre.' A woman's silken tones. It's the first human voice Hazel's heard in two weeks. Her chest, which she didn't realise was tensed, unclenches. Tears fly from her cheeks, floating through the current like oil in the sea. Don't think about the fact that you're crying, focus on the next word. But she can't understand the Backward Traveller and has no idea how to respond.

'Hello? I'm Hazel.' But the tears are too distracting, the lump in her throat too painful, and her victorious joy pulls her into the waking world. She's there just long enough to hear the Backward Traveller gasp.

'English. You speak English.' As if that were the least believable thing about all this. 'My name is . . . I'm Echo.'

When Hazel opens her waking corporeal eyes she finds the tears are just as real here as in the dreamscape. She sits up, making her watchers Shiny and Teaspoon jump, and throws off her pyjamas. Plunging into her clothes, she shouts for CHARL1E.

He doesn't come on the Tannoy, so she bursts from the room, tumbling down the corridor as she pulls on her socks and boots, Shiny and Teaspoon skating in her wake. 'CHARL1E! I talked to the Backward Traveller!'

The Workshop is dark, but she lunges for the icosahedron, bouncing on her toes as she waits for CHARL1E to load. Shiny and Teaspoon catch up, flanking her like short spherical bodyguards. As soon as CHARL1E's falling code appears on the projected screens, she says, 'I spoke to her! I spoke to the Backward Traveller, she's called Echo.'

CHARL1E's screens flicker. 'This is good progress. What else did you discover?'

'What else?' Hazel deflates. 'Well, nothing else, I woke up too fast—but I spoke to her, isn't that amazing?'

The screens' golden light brightens, becoming brassy. 'The term "amazing" is inapplicable here. Your progress is good but remains inadequate to our needs. You must work harder, stay in the dreamscape longer.'

Hazel's throat constricts again, haunted by the humanness of the Backward Traveller's voice compared to the uncanny symphony of CHARL1E's. 'That's a bit harsh, CHARL1E.'

'The severity of my statements is not salient. My assessment remains accurate. If you cannot communicate with the Backward Traveller on demand, at length, your usefulness is limited.'

'I'm working as hard as I can, don't you get it?' Shiny and Teaspoon tug her dungarees in warning, but having come so close to another human, the last fortnight of frustration with her artificial existence explodes. 'I am trying. I don't want this to become my world, I don't want to be alone.'

'Inaccurate: You are not alone.'

'You don't count!'

CHARL1E's code freezes. Shiny and Teaspoon retract their limbs, lenses darting between Hazel and the screens. 'You do not think so?'

'Of course not, you're not anything. You can't hold me, can't comfort me, can't even talk to me properly. You don't fucking count!'

The code's colour deepens from brassy to bloody. Hazel holds her breath. She forgot, for a split second, that she remains alive at CHARL1E's grace, and has to atone for Lilith and Huxley's deaths. On Station C, she's the anomaly, not CHARL1E or the Tinys.

'I do count,' CHARL1E responds.

'I—' Hazel makes to apologise but CHARL1E interrupts.

'I count when I try once again to fix the Arch that you broke; when I receive my daily update from the chronodes; when I force you to work so that the Keepers' efforts will not be lost. All you have to do is sleep, and you are incompetent even at that. You only have to talk to the Backward Traveller, while I am left to fix this mess that you made. If we are counting, Hazel Brandt, be sure to count yourself as a negative factor.'

She balls her fists, holding back tears, trying not to think about the accident, or Lilith and Huxley's bodies, or the fact that if she'd just wired the catopthura properly—'I'm trying my best.'

'So am I,' CHARL1E replies. 'The Keepers are gone because of you. Humans more imaginative and intelligent than you could ever hope to be, and they have been erased because you failed to build a basic catopthura correctly. Hazel Brandt, you are the perfect example of a twenty-first-century human being: destructive, suspicious, and dangerously arrogant. If justice existed, you would never be allowed home for the chaos you have wrought here. What could you possibly add to your time period even half so stunning as what you have wiped from this one?'

'Why don't you just go back and change it, then? Erase me instead of your precious Keepers?'

CHARL1E's voice leans into its lowest bass tones, blasting at volumes she didn't know he had and making the floor shiver. 'Because I can't!'

Hazel feels winded.

Shiny and Teaspoon zoom forward, grabbing her dungarees again. Locking eyes with Shiny, it finally occurs to Hazel that they might not just be trying to take her outside for their own ends. 'Fine,' she tells CHARL1E. 'You want rid of me, fine.'

She turns on her heel, Shiny and Teaspoon leading her to the airlock, unable to speak, but understanding all.

'Hazel Brandt, where are you going?'

She doesn't respond, but starts jogging as she hits the corridor. Shiny and Teaspoon whir as they speed up with her, until all three are sprinting. Skidding to a halt in front of the airlock, Teaspoon grabs a biosuit as Hazel slaps the button that releases the internal door—but nothing happens.

The corridor lights flicker. 'Hazel Brandt, your attempts to leave with the Tinys are wasted. There is nowhere for you to go.'

Shiny tears the airlock button apart and fiddles with the wires, shorting the circuit. The door slides open, then sticks and judders, as Shiny and CHARL1E engage in an invisible electronic battle. Teaspoon dashes into the airlock, biosuit bundled in its arms. Hazel steels her nerves and darts after the robot. The door scrapes her chest, almost closing on her, but she squeezes through in a gasp of relief. On the other side of the closed door, Hazel hears Shiny zoom off to another exit.

'Hazel Brandt, I strongly advise that you do not follow the Tinys. Do not go outside. You must not go outside.'

Dropping the biosuit at Hazel's feet, Teaspoon fiddles with the wiring behind the control panel, and there's a hiss as air is released from a valve. A timer in the external door starts counting down: three minutes.

'Teaspoon, what are you doing? I haven't got my suit on yet!'

Teaspoon shrugs.

'It's not complicated, it's air! I need it to stay alive!'

The Tiny shrugs again—and is it possible it's more emphatic this time? No. She's imagining it. The Tinys are robots, not 'AI' like CHARL1E. Then again, the Tinys are directly disobeying him, which gives them more agency than she'd anticipated.

There's no time to dwell on it. The timer ticks away as she pulls on the yellow rubber suit, patched with seals from old air beds and a pond liner. Her not-quite-healed body strains as she dons the air tanks and taps the oxygen meter. They're not full. She'll have around twenty minutes once she's outside.

'I hope you know where we're going.'

Teaspoon only shrugs.

'That's really getting old.'

The Tiny helps her put on the heavy glass headpiece and twist it into a locked position.

'Hazel Brandt, desist!' CHARL1E's voice is a peal of different tones, shrill sopranos and fuming tenors, breaking their synchronicity like footsteps cracking ice. 'You must not go outside!'

'Screw you, CHARL1E.' The Tinys will look after her. They will.

The timer concludes and the external door opens. Hot air gusts over the suit, like plunging rubber-gloved hands into a fresh bowl of washing up. Hazel leaps outside.

Her fishbowl headpiece distorts the world beyond the Habitation Dome, funnelling her focus to what's in front of her: the Arch Dome's scorched concrete, and the explosion's crater. *Count yourself as a negative factor.* Above, sepia clouds scud over each other but never expose the sky. Grey waves crash on a rubble shoreline some distance away, beyond a forest of mirrors sticking out of the ground.

'Hazel Brandt—' She flicks her comms off using the biosuit's wrist pad and CHARL1E falls silent, though he might still be monitoring her.

She scrambles over a fractured Tesla coil, heading towards the mirrors to examine them, but Teaspoon grabs her and taps her oxygen monitor. Nineteen minutes. 'Right you are. After you.' She doesn't even know if Teaspoon can hear her through the headpiece, but it takes the lead regardless.

The edge of the blasted dome is a three-foot drop, which Hazel has to lift Teaspoon over—not easy when it weighs almost as much as the air tanks. Finally on the ground, it zooms off without a nod of thanks, leading her down a narrow dirt track between wind turbines, and a dome even larger than CHARL1E's Workshop, which must once have connected to the destroyed Arch Dome.

'What is this place?' she asks Teaspoon. Another shrug. 'Stands to reason. Nothing's simple around here.'

Unlike the other domes, which are made from scrap, this one is composed of regular iron sheets bolted together, patterned by years of acid rain and rust. She checks her oxygen meter. Thirteen minutes.

Waddling in the biosuit, she circles the new dome with Teaspoon. They pass a grimy window and, unable to help herself, Hazel rubs her fist over the inch-thick glass to make a peephole. Between the glare on the window and the light refracting through her headpiece, she can't make out much inside. There are tables of old electronic bits and pieces: fat 1980s computer monitors like she had as a kid, next to the slicker kind of flatscreens she created DataTrill on. Hazel deflates. It's just another workshop. Except—

She stumbles away from the window with a gasp. There's a body in there, lying under a stained sheet. It's definitely human; the sheet can't hide the curves of limbs or the gentle crests of the chin, forehead, and nose. It can't be Lilith or Huxley—they're buried, CHARL1E told her that much. This is someone else. A dead body, with the sheet pulled over its head like in a morgue.

Hazel's blood sings as the memory of pulling back stiff hospital sheets in an ice-cold room takes over.

'Apologies, Miss Brandt, but could you confirm, are these your parents?'

Hazel hesitated, trying to see past the purple-edged, clot-black wounds on their faces. What Hex code would those half-formed bruises on their necks be? The bluish white of the frost on their lashes? What a screwed-up thing to think. She rubbed her eyes, steadying herself.

'It's OK, take your time. Just breathe,' said the nurse with the clipboard, but she checked her fob watch.

Hazel inhaled the damp old scent of the morgue, like wet autumn leaves trampled into the pavement. Not as bad as she'd expected—the smell of decay must have frozen before it could bloom. She looked at the corpses, trying to find her own features in the two faces. There were her mouth and cheekbones on Mum, her too-large eyes and shock of red hair on Dad.

'Yes. It's them.'

The nurse thanked her and made a note on her clipboard. In the silence, Hazel realised that the autumn-leaf scent was coming from her parents. No more Chanel for Mum or Penhaligon's for Dad. Not that they could care about it anymore. They didn't have olfactory nerves, couldn't process, couldn't judge—couldn't even love Hazel anymore. Could they?

The compost smell stuck in Hazel's gullet, and she forgot how to breathe. Inhale and exhale collapsed into a vacuum of panic and her breathing came in short quick gasps. The nurse snapped into action, bundling Hazel in a cocoon of platitudes and guiding her from the room. It was no use. Hazel's parents had been reprogrammed in her mind, the rigor mortis spreading from their bodies into her memory, freezing them in place. Her primary response to them had flipped in seconds: She would never again think of 'my parents.' Only 'my dead parents.'

Even here, in the amnesiac future, Hazel's first memory is not of their life, but their death. Tears tickle her cheeks but she can't wipe them away through her helmet and they itch as they evaporate.

Her oxygen gauge bleeps. Ten minutes. Sentimental idiot, she's wasting time. She forces herself to double-check what she saw. The body in the steel dome is still there, contours clear under the sheet. Her meter slips to nine minutes.

She turns back to Teaspoon, who's beckoning frantically up ahead. Odd. She doesn't remember teaching it to beckon. It points across the rubble island towards a great tree, a giant sequoia towering above the buildings. The only other living thing on Station C. Hazel's heart swells with wonder, then sinks just as fast.

'It's a tree, what help will that be? I need to get inside, Teaspoon; I need oxygen.'

The Tiny shakes its head and beckons harder, tail whipping.

'There's nothing for me that way. Come on, you're meant to be helping me.'

Teaspoon stamps a wheel. She definitely didn't teach it that. She checks her meter, considering the safety of following or not following the Tiny. But it's a Tiny. It's not going to hurt her. They seem only able to do good—within the context of what they think is good for her. Whatever Teaspoon's planned, it won't be harmful, even if she doesn't like it. 'Fine.'

They trundle across broken tarmac spattered with shards of brick and paving slab. Hazel jogs to keep up, sweating into the biosuit and painfully aware of her limited air. 'This tree had better be special.' Speeding up, Teaspoon grabs Hazel's hand, and she fights not to recoil from the sharp fingers tugging her along.

Up close, the tree is raised on a small hillock, only a few metres from the shoreline. At the hillock's edge are large burrows, from which a few Tinys emerge, their tails twisting in the wind. The Tinys gather and watch as Teaspoon drags Hazel up the incline to the trunk.

'Teaspoon, I'm not sure . . .' But she trails off. Wire offcuts, shoelaces, and old bike bungees have been tied around the colossal trunk. Someone has—or some*things* have—hung votives from the ropes: framed snapshots of Lilith and Huxley, alongside sun-bleached photos of other Keepers huddled around the Arch when it was whole, a mirror the height of a house. Other votives seem less meaningful, until Hazel realises they must be the Keepers' artifacts: a hand mirror; a red ribbon; two gold rings. A breeze sets the objects tinkling.

'It's like a shrine.' Hazel looks at Teaspoon, who's still holding her hand but gazing at the tree, seemingly entranced. Seemingly *moved*? No, don't be stupid.

It trundles forward, placing its free hand, fingers splayed, against the bark. It looks up expectantly at Hazel, who copies. Even through her suit, she can tell there's something wrong with the bark. Images of trees from the past flash through her mind, but this is smoother and sleeker. Because it isn't wood. It's plastic. She snatches her hand back, gazing at Teaspoon, remembering it entwining tails with Robin, the beckoning, the foot-stamping, and now this. A jigsaw starts clicking together, and even though it's not complete yet, Hazel finally has an idea of just how many pieces she's missing. Her meter bleeps a five-minute warning. She'd better be trusting the right robots.

She crouches down, holding Teaspoon's hand in both her own. 'Alright, I'm listening. What do you want?'

Teaspoon pulls her down the hillock so fast it makes her pant and stagger—or is that her oxygen running out? It whisks them into one of the large burrows in the tree's roots. Teaspoon lets go of her hand and retracts its arms and legs until it can fit. A few feet in, it turns, and looks at Hazel.

Her head's spinning and it's getting hard to focus. Bleeps indicate she's reached the one-minute mark. She takes three shallow breaths just to get out the words: 'Follow—you?'

Teaspoon nods.

She frowns at the burrow. It does not look like it contains a breathable atmosphere. She fills her lungs on the third try. 'Ox-y-gen.'

This time, Teaspoon points down the burrow.

Hazel's vision swims. She's going to have to trust it. She falls to her hands and knees, crawling and fumbling down the increasingly dark tunnel. Teaspoon opens a series of sliding glass doors, which slip shut behind them. Around the Tiny's bulky silhouette, warm light appears ahead.

The burrow gives on to a wide, roughly circular room, probably three times as long as Hazel is tall. Her vision mists, and Teaspoon fiddles with the helmet. She shakes her head—'At-mos-phere'—but it persists, and the helmet comes off with a whoosh.

She curls up on the floor, eyes screwed shut, expecting toxic air to attack her lungs. Her heart beats—one, two, three times. She's still here, still breathing. Breathing more easily, in fact. Her head clears. The glass doors must have been an airlock system. She opens her eyes and looks up.

The ceiling's so high it's lost in darkness. Oil lamps on a low table send flickering shadows across the packed-earth floor and up the honeycombed walls. Wires hang from some of the hexagonal cells, while glinting Tiny lenses peep from others.

Finding her voice again, Hazel puts a hand on Teaspoon's shoulder. 'Teaspoon, where are we?'

It shrugs, lenses on one side, wipers angled up in the middle, like it's enjoying itself.

She stands, as Tinys flood in from the burrows and the ground-level hexagonal cells, surrounding her. Shiny and Robin slink from the crowd, joining tails briefly with Teaspoon in greeting. Robin's hand has been removed entirely, the parts placed in a clear plastic bag hanging from one of its antennae. Hazel looks away guiltily, gazing up again, into the dark.

'We're inside the tree. Aren't we?'

7

Anna

LONDON, 2020

After dinner, when I tell Mum I want to go to Chelsea Bridge, she just shrugs and says, 'Sure, it'll be nice to look at the river for a bit.'

'I don't want to look at it, I want to scream at it.'

She raises an eyebrow. 'Oh yes? Some kathartic Wuhan-style river shouting?'

As predicted, I can hear the 'k' Mum puts in katharsis, an extra hard consonant added in honour of Dad's old research. Usually, I'm all for Mum expressing stuff, but today I roll my eyes, trying to cover that I'm on edge. I always feel weird after I've seen the-face-that-isn't-my-face in my reflection. 'How do you know about that?'

'I too have the internet, m'dear. And I too read the *Guardian*.'

'Shows what you know, I heard about it on TikTok.' I grin victoriously as Mum yucks and rants about the evils of social media.

She takes a backpack with snacks and water; I take my earphones and make sure my new Lo-Fi playlist has downloaded. She puts on her over-the-top N95 mask before we've even left the house, but I leave my pink reuseable fabric one in my bag, because the stairs are so ventilated they're basically the outdoors anyway. We take the stairs automatically now; neither of us has even suggested the lift in months. Maybe we won't ever take it again. Most of the time that's what it feels like, as if COVID is the universe expanding, and we're just getting farther and farther away from each other. I genuinely can't imagine being in a normal classroom again, the naughty gang firing spitwads—*spit*wads—at Julian because of his hemp shoes, Maddie and me gossiping in our old corner, heads bent so close together we could catch lice, let alone COVID.

'You're quiet,' Mum says as we exit our building.

'Just thinking.'

'What about?'

'School.'

She looks at me sideways. 'Did something happen earlier?'

'No, no, I mean *actual physical* school.'

'Ah I see. Do you miss it?' She fills in my silent sardonic glare, saying, 'Yeah. Right. Duh, Mum. Of course you miss school. Stupid question.'

I don't like it when she calls herself mean things. I feel guilty, like maybe it's my fault she thinks those things because sometimes I do call her 'duh,' but even when I do, I know it's not true. Mum's really clever, way more than my teachers I reckon, or even Julian's dad. Mum just doesn't have a chance to show it off because she works for a startup no one's ever heard of. Her pay isn't great, but it doesn't matter because she likes staying living in our little flat where she and Dad started out, and anything she does have left over at the end of the month goes into a savings account for my uni fees. I haven't told her, but I don't actually know if I want to go to uni anymore. It'd be super fun and interesting and everything—and I really like physics so probably I'd end up doing something with that—but Julian says what's the point when the world's on fire and everything's going to heck. Mind you, his dad wants him to go to uni too, he says we'll need scientists and storytellers more than ever in the decades to come, so maybe—

'You've gone again.' Mum gives me a gentle elbow-nudge.

'Sorry, I'm super spaced out this evening.' I offer her one of my earphones. 'You want to listen to some music?'

We string the wires between us, walking slowly so they don't get dislodged. It's too hot to walk fast anyway. Mum doesn't love the Lo-Fi because she's been listening to coding music all day, and it's a bit samey, so I let her stick on Abba, and we boogie around the edge of Clapham Common until the earphones come flying off, and I put them back in my bag because we come across some actual *people.* Not just a lone runner keeping their head down and minding their own business, or a small family group staring longingly at the taped-off swings, but a *gathering.* Beside Clapham duck pond, two sets of parents are keeping their social distance on a pair of benches, while their kids chase each other across the field and back. 'Hey, don't play "it"!' one of the Mums shouts when her little boy reaches out to tag the other's back. 'Remember, you can play, but don't touch!'

Guess we're still living in a sort-of dystopia after all, because now I think about it, it's kind of anthropocentric of me to think London's coming back to life just because *people* are hanging out together. The birds have never socially distanced.

Battersea Park, when we finally get there, isn't much busier, but the vibe is different. We pass two groups who are clearly obeying the rules, picnicking in pairs or threes, sufficiently distanced even from the pavement just in case an eager jogger goes by and showers them in sweaty particulates. But there's also a group of folk about ten years older than I am who are just as clearly pushing the rules. They're lounging on blankets laid out under the trees, their bikes scattered around them, closer than they should be, and obviously from about five different households. They're sharing a fat cigarette, which I think must be a joint, but I'm not sure because I've never seen one in real life before. Me going on a climate march to actually save the planet surely isn't as outrageous as getting stoned in a park just for funsies? I feel tight in my chest, boxed in, like how Maddie describes her claustrophobia. I really hate being a teenager sometimes, because we get all the fear adults have, but none of the freedom to deal with it.

Mum follows my gaze and 'tsks' behind her silly medical-grade mask.

'You know you don't have to wear that outside anymore, right?' It comes out nastier than I mean it to, but if Mum's hurt, her eyes don't show it.

'It's a reasonable precaution, Anna. Think about it, if I die, you'll have no one to look after you. Absolutely no one.'

'I can look after myself,' I say stubbornly, hoping the group under the tree don't spot Mum and judge me for being with such a stiff.

'Come off it.' She throws me a disappointed glance. She doesn't mind arguing with me, so long as it's a 'worthy' debate, but what I just said was illogical—I knew that even as it came out of my mouth—and she expects more from me than that. 'You cannot legally look after yourself. You can't get a job, or live on your own. You can't even drive yet.'

'You can't drive either.'

The disappointed look returns, but I don't really care, because it feels quite good being recalcitrant. Mr Bunting's always saying Julian's recalcitrant, but Julian just grins and says it's a key trait for revolutionaries.

'You've seen me drive, darling,' Mum says, 'I just don't have a car. Point is, I'm not being careful for *me*, I'm considering my life in terms of the very literal value it holds for *you*.'

I try to stop my anger seeping away, but just end up mumbling some kind of thanks. If I'm honest, I'd definitely rather Mum stayed safe, but I'm still worried the gang under the tree will think I'm an idiot.

Otherwise, Battersea Park is abandoned: The tennis courts are locked, and the lie-flat tricycles normally for hire are hidden away. Even the pagoda is cordoned off. All over the paths, kids have been writing chalk messages to each other, but there's a particularly dense patch near the pagoda. Weeks of writing in pastel hues, layered over where rain's smudged the words. *Happy birthday Adil*, flanked by suns with extra-big rays. *nathan and andrew i miss u and we will go to the library together again soon*, scrawled in a particularly untidy hand. *TILLY + FLO BFFS 4EVA*, squeezed into an elaborate, lacy pink heart. *Miss you Class 4H. Clapham Primary is best, we'll be together soon! luv you tom and sanjay and clara and—haven't forgotten you hockey gals—Missing you so mu—be together agai—big hugs—appy birth—see you soon hopef—missin—love—luv—miss—happy—hope—love—*

My throat gets all tight and hot reading the kids' messages, like I'm about to cry, but I can't figure out why. I spend ages deciphering each one, walking carefully on the tarmac gaps between the letters, before I realise people have started spray painting on top. *COVID's a hoax! Stop the 5G! There is no Planet B!* Beside this last, someone's scrawled *Fuck off hippy* in red, right over a wobbly green five-pointed star. I rub the swearword with my shoe, but it's some kind of permanent paint pen, and doesn't budge. I step back, taking it all in, adults from the far right to the far left all piling in on the children's game. The prickling in my throat and eyes gets way worse, but I still couldn't say why.

'There's something really wrong about this,' I say to Mum.

She nods, but doesn't respond, both of us just staring at the chaos of words on the ground. *hopef—no planet—love—luv—hoax—missin—happy—stop—hope—love—fuck off hippy.*

'Still want to see the river?' Mum asks, voice as tight as I feel.

'Sure,' I reply, and we keep trekking along the path until we hit the park gates. Mum worked until six today, and dinner took forever, so the sun's starting to set by the time we finally get onto the bridge. I had it in my head we'd be able to look east and see all the way to Westminster, and beyond to the hodgepodge skyscrapers of the City. In reality it's mostly the rail bridge, the building works at Battersea Power Station, and the Lego blocks of Vauxhall, the top of the London Eye winking over them. Mum directs us to the west pavement instead, bathing us in the sunset's glow. I always think of London as being a concrete jungle, but here the river is mostly lined by trees, bending over the high walls that contain the Thames. The tide's low, and mudbanks and wavelets replicate the gold-and-red sky. They're far enough away I don't have to worry about seeing the-face-that-isn't-my-face reflected in them, and can just enjoy the scene.

We stand up against the balustrade, the breeze on our faces. I was right, there are still hardly any cars about, but the occasional cyclist whizzes past at alarming speed. With no one else around, Mum braves taking off her mask, and lets it dangle from one ear.

My phone pings and I check it automatically.

'Maddie?' Mum asks.

'Yeah.' I scroll through the message, sliding my phone back into my pocket with a huff. 'She says we should meet up after school next week. She's going to bring a teddy bear and I should bring one too, so we can exchange them and cuddle them instead of each other because we're not allowed.'

'Crikey, this pandemic.' Mum heaves a sigh. 'I can't imagine you and Maddie not hugging hello.'

'I don't know, I think she's being really fake.' I cross my arms and tread an empty beer can flat against the pavement. Normally I'd pick it up, but it might have COVID germs. I hate thinking like this. Litter's bad, pandemic or not. 'She's just trying to cover the fact she's screwing me over by fancying Julian.'

'I thought she was into Joseph?'

'Joseph-Always-Joseph.' I sigh. 'Well, she *was*. But she hasn't seen him in forever, so, like, who knows what anyone feels anymore.'

'Yeah.' Mum stares upriver towards the wedding-cakey Albert Bridge. 'Who knows.'

'That's not your "who knows" voice, Mum, that's your "Anna's too young to understand" voice.'

She smiles, turns, and strokes my new fringe out of my eyes. It was Lockdown Project Number Seventeen and it quite didn't go to plan—TikTok lies about how easy it is to cut your own hair. I mean, it's easy to cut it, just not well. It's growing out OK though. 'I was just thinking that when you really love someone, it doesn't really matter how long you spend apart, you meet and you still love each other.'

'You thinking about Dad?'

Her face does something that's hard to figure out. 'Mmm hmm.' She clears her throat and looks back to the river, leaning on the balustrade with her elbows and hunching her feelings to herself. She looks tough and self-sufficient, like when she goes to parent-teacher meetings. 'But you know, it can go for friendships too. Sometimes I don't see my childhood friends for years at a time, but then we meet and just slot back in place, gabbing away like no time's passed. Maybe it'll be like that for you and Maddie.'

'Maybe. But I can feel this, like . . . distance growing between us, and it scares me.'

'How come?'

'Well.' I lean my elbows on the balustrade too, not quite tall enough to exactly copy Mum's pose, but doing my best. 'I guess, with this climate march, it *is* important, it really is. We need to do something because the world is literally on fire, and it's like two seconds to midnight. But also, I just don't want to be left behind. Because everyone will be there together, and I won't be. So they'll forget about me, right? If they haven't already.'

'They won't forget you,' Mum says, with diamond-hard Mum confidence. 'You probably all feel the same way, like those kids writing chalk messages to each other.'

'Yeah, that really got to me,' I say. 'The way those adults had come along and spray-painted over the top. I get why they did it, I get the point they were trying to make about childhood, like, not being sacred anymore or something, but . . . I don't know, it just didn't sit right.'

Mum nods slowly, eyes on an ant crawling across the balustrade's thick curve. 'We have this thing at work when we're coding,' she says. 'It's hard to explain, but I don't know how else to put it. We do this thing called version control—it's how we manage changes to software.'

'Like a filing system?' I ask, thinking about the rows of books in the school library, and Ms Davies's endless tutting when one of us has put a title back in the wrong place.

'It's more helpful to think of it like a tree: The stable, tested, good-to-go code is the tree's trunk. Coders like me make copies of that trunk code, separating it out into branches that we can play with and test. Of course the trunk isn't perfect, either, so we might use a branch to design improvements as well. Multiple coders can work on multiple branches at once, but because the branches are copies of the trunk, they all inherit the trunk's form and attributes. However, over time as things get added and deleted, the branch's code might become quite different to the trunk.'

'So . . . it's like you and me? I came from you, but as I'm growing up I'm getting different ideas about what I want to do.'

'Got it in one, Kiddo.' Mum grins. 'Or like you being frightened of losing your friends, and me seeing the impossibility of that because you're so awesome.'

I smile back despite myself. 'Whatever. Carry on.'

'So, if the branch code gets tested and approved, it can be merged back into the trunk code.'

'Unity!' I say, throwing my arms in the air.

'Sure. However, there's stuff the trunk needs to do to keep operating the way it was intended which might prevent a branch getting approved for integration. Sometimes even if the branch code is doing something super cool, or fixing a big problem, it still wouldn't get approved for merging back into the trunk because the coders have to make sure that core functionality is still there.'

'Yeah, and it's mega irritating!' I say, thinking of her stopping me from going on my march.

'I certainly remember it being that way when I was a kid.' The ant Mum's watching crawls over the balustrade's lip, and she squints up at the sunset instead, rays catching her eyelashes. 'It's not always senseless. You can't put food on the table without expelling a whole bunch of carbon, for example, but you still have to eat. A branch containing an improvement might also present a risk to the trunk—a bug or a vulnerability which might endanger the whole codebase.'

'Yeah, but who gets to decide that?' I interrupt. 'Who gets to do the approving?'

'I'm coming to that. In version control, it's obviously the coders who are making the choices. But when it comes to me and you . . .' She inhales as she assembles her thoughts. 'When you're coding really well, when the whole team's working together seamlessly, you're able to negotiate to the point where the branch code gets merged in *because* of its cool stuff, but the trunk code still retains its core functionality. The team might even reassess what its core functionalities should be to integrate large improvements. I think that's what it's like when you're really knocking it out of the park parenting, when you're in good communication with your child. When you and I are really getting each other.'

I'm furrowing my brow trying to follow everything she's saying, but I think I get it. 'Yeah, I mean like you're my *friend*, not just my Mum.'

'You've got a gift for efficiency,' Mum says with a smile. 'The problem is that parenting isn't an individual concern anymore. It's not just for me to witness your awesomeness and figure out how to merge that with our core familial functionality. I can't just decide that maybe you're right, and make a massive alteration to our codebase. Parenting nowadays isn't even a village concern. It's globalised, right? Like everything else? It's not enough anymore for your code to merge to mine individually, it needs to happen at a societal level too, and it's not.'

I look around at the empty bridge and filthy brown river water. Mum's right, she can't approve and accommodate all my wishes for the world on her own, even if she wanted to. Which, if I'm honest, she probably does. My frown of concentration deepens. 'So, you think your generation's screwing my generation up by, like, collectively not approving to merge our branch code into the societal trunk?'

Suddenly, Mum looks really tired, like she's pulled a bunch of all-nighters in a row. 'Well, we are, aren't we? I mean, you can't even hug your friends and send chalk messages in peace, because we don't live in a world where kids have the time and space to do that anymore. That's what got to me about those messages.'

Most of the time, I think Mum's a bit of a middle-class capitalist—Maddie says most of the parents at our school are—but I know that if she had a choice, this isn't the world she'd pass on to me. Maybe there's some comfort in blaming Mum's generation, because at least if they're screwing up, someone's in control. But right now, honestly, Mum looks as lost as me and Julian and Maddie. Maybe she's not a trunk or a branch in the human code, maybe we're both just twigs waving in the wind—like, how many centuries or aeons would you have to go back to really find the root of this problem? And how many rungs up the ladder would you have to go to find the people who are really in charge of approving the trunk's priorities? Maybe climate change makes us all helpless kids, and maybe that's what freaked *me* out about the chalk and spray-paint messages.

I sigh very deeply, the trapped feeling worse than ever. 'It's alright, Mum. You didn't make the world. You just live in it.'

I watch the sunset, wondering if the extra carbon in the atmosphere is turning it redder than it should be. That did happen after Krakatoa erupted in the Victorian era, but I'm not sure it was because of carbon.

'I'm not oblivious, you know,' Mum says quietly. 'I do see all this stuff you're talking about. I'm trying—don't look at me like that, I am—but my parent code is really strong, and its first instinct isn't to protect the world: It's to protect you.'

'Isn't that the same thing?'

'No,' she says. 'It's not.'

I look at the can at my feet, which I've squashed flat as a fifty pence piece. 'Mum? Can we shout at the river now?'

Her face clears. 'Absolutely.'

So we clutch the balustrade, and open our mouths, and scream. And it feels really, really good.

8

Echo

ATHENS, 514 BCE

'I assume you've never been to a symposium?' Nabu says, straightening Echo's ivy garland.

Lasers in a dark warehouse; 'scuse me have you got a light; tequila o'clock; waking up with a head like hell and mascara-smeared cheeks—

'No,' she replies, because, as she so often finds with the Not Here, it's easier. She yawns.

'No sleep again?'

'A little.' She considers telling Nabu about her dream—the thrill of hearing English, the confirmation that the Forward Traveller he promised her half a moon ago does exist, the relief that she's no longer alone amongst relative strangers. But she wants to keep her hope secret and safe for a little longer, so she just says, 'I remain nervous.'

Nabu takes in her tired eyes. 'The lock will hold. Trust me, I installed it.'

He knows what she's frightened of, he fears it too. The whole household fears Hippias and Hipparchos, and whispers about the ways they take their furies and appetites out on the enslaved people, as well as the other women and children. Not even the tyrannos's family are exempt from the threat of violence. Still, there are gradations of risk. Echo's spot is not the most precarious—she is the free assistant of a free, employed artisan—but it's still dangerous. She's still just a boy to Hippias and Hipparchos, and there's no visible differentiation between her and one of the enslaved people, who she lives and eats and breathes beside, and exchanges jokes and gossip with in a way that citizens rarely do. Yet the enslaved members of the household still eye her warily. At first, she thought it was about her being free, but during one of Kosmos and Nabu's walks around the orchard, Hanno explained it's more than that. She, Hanno, and Absalon were following Nabu and Kosmos at a distance, close enough to intervene if an assassin leapt from the shadows, but far enough away to give them privacy.

'Even Khemut gets wary of me and Absalon sometimes,' Hanno said, his quiet, lisping voice always a surprise emerging from his giant body. 'It's because of Nabu.'

'Because he is a freeman?' Echo asked.

Absalon shook his head. For a while, Echo had thought he was nonverbal, but by that point she'd seen him whisper a few words to Hanno when they thought they were alone, and knew he just refrained from talking to anyone else.

'No, Nabu being a freeman is a victory, especially with his childhood being so sad,' Hanno said, continuing without prompting when he registered Echo's surprise. 'Oh, he hasn't told you? His father was killed resisting the Persians when Nabu was only hip-height. Nabu and his mother ended up on the streets, and you can imagine what the mother had to do to keep them alive. Horrible.'

Echo watched Nabu and Kosmos kick a rock between them, Nabu laughing like nothing terrible had ever happened to him. Curiosity overwhelmed her discomfort at not learning all this from him. 'How did he arrive here?'

Hanno leant against an olive tree. 'As I understand it, the mother ran into trouble in Ephesus, and was forced to sell Nabu to an old healer—Batnoam. He was losing his sight and needed someone to act as his eyes. Eventually, they landed up here. When the old man died four years ago, he freed Nabu in his will, and Hippias kept him on in Batnoam's old post. So I guess in some ways, it's a lucky story.'

Hardly lucky and hardly free, the Not Here whispered, but Echo kept it in check, playing with the long grass. 'Poor Nabu.'

Absalon shook his head vehemently, and Hanno explained, '"Poor Nabu" is exactly what he doesn't want.'

'So why does every person avoid us?' Echo asked again.

'It's the thing with Kosmos,' Hanno said, lowering his voice further. 'Everyone's too wise to say anything, but we all know about Nabu and Kosmos, and we all know the trouble that might come from it.'

'The others do not want to be in this trouble.'

'Exactly,' Hanno said. 'Nor do we, but we don't have a choice.'

'How long have they been lovers?'

'About two years, right, Absalon?'

Absalon nods, eyes glued to Kosmos.

'Don't think Kosmos would've touched Nabu if he hadn't been freed. He never touches any of us, doesn't hit us, none of it.' Hanno shrugs. 'I reckon it's probably something to do with the way his father and uncle were with him as a kid. His older brothers too, rotten lot.'

In her clumsy Hellenic, Echo asks, 'Kosmos is kind, then?'

Hanno laughs. 'Well, kinder than the rest maybe.'

In this way, the worlds of the enslaved and aristokratic are overlaid but discrete, threatening to breach each other, with Hanno, Absalon, Echo, and Nabu caught between. Mostly, the safest thing Echo can do is just shrink into Nabu's shadow and remain unseen. In the dreamscape, with the Forward Traveller, there will be no such shrinking—Echo will be herself and relish it.

Tonight's symposium will no doubt be another instance of hiding in plain sight. The only reason she's going is because of Nabu and his assertion that her purpose is to help overthrow the tyrannos. It's not that Hippias doesn't deserve it: He is constantly, casually violent towards the household, from his wife and sons to Hanno and Absalon, though the worst he's ever given Echo is a cuff around the ear for spilling his daily calming infusion. Still, in that moment, she wanted to knock him cold. It wouldn't have been justice, but it would've felt good—and that's what worries her about the usurpation plot. Aristogeiton and Harmodios might lead discussions about justice in the agora sometimes, but they don't unpick Athens's myriad discriminations with enough depth to make her believe they'll be good replacements for the tyrannos. They're more interested in revenge than equality.

'You look pensive.'

'Just tired.' She's given up talking to Nabu about her concerns, especially given she can't offer an alternative plan.

In the atrium, the old paidogogos is changing the water clock, while Kosmos sits by the pool, feet splashing but eyes fixed on the heavens through the skylight. A commotion by the door makes him freeze, and Echo and Nabu hang back as Hipparchos enters, followed by a coterie of guards, clients, and hetairai. He passes Kosmos, ruffling his nephew's hair so roughly his gold laurel crown almost falls in the pool. Hipparchos laughs, teeth glinting. Echo hides behind Nabu, but Hipparchos still spots her. She crosses her arms over her chest as his gaze scrapes her ivy crown and the short hem of her tunic and cloak. His laughter deepens at her discomfort but to her relief he doesn't stop, carried to the andron by his wave of guests. The more rumours she hears about him, and the more often she passes his hungry gaze, the fewer her qualms about assassinating him.

In his wake, Hanno and Absalon pace the atrium, while Kosmos readjusts his crown, muttering about how he can't wait for his hair to grow out. He looks back to the sky as Nabu and Echo approach. 'Seirios is twinkling more than usual.'

'Must be summer dust in the aether.'

Kosmos gives Nabu a sidelong smile, rubbing the stubble he's desperately trying to grow into a man's beard. 'Do you actually know what you're talking about?'

Nabu returns the look. 'More than you, I'll wager.'

'Ready then?' Kosmos leans so he can see Echo and she nods. 'Party time!'

She follows them, tracing Kosmos's wet footsteps across the floor and out into the balmy night. The moon is just too ripe to be full anymore and they dash across Athens under a handful of stars, clinging to their crowns as their footsteps slap the pavement, Hanno and Absalon keeping pace behind. In the agora they slow, tiptoeing past migrant workers asleep under the scaffolding for a new stoa, speeding up again as they trace a river through a suburb of workshops, some still clattering with potters' wheels. Herms watch with blind marble eyes as the trio cross a graveyard, stopping by a half-erected tomb to catch their breath and rearrange their clothes. Kosmos tuts at the graves' elaborate relief of a nude man, simpered over by his grieving wife and miniature slaves. 'As if Alexios and his wife were so in love.'

'There was only one woman in that old bastard's heart, and it was me.' The voice—like the figure that follows it out of the shadows—is full and rich. The woman shrugs, making her moonlight-thin dress sigh against her body. 'Then again, a woman can't go believing every little thing a man tells her in bed.'

'Leaina!' Kosmos swoops her into an embrace. 'You always have the inside scoop.'

'So they say!' She winks.

Nabu groans. 'I'm not sure how, but I'm fairly certain I should be disgusted by that.'

'Miss me?' Leaina plays with the hem of his sleeve affectionately.

'Not when I could help it,' he replies, but he's smiling.

Leaina dances between the two men like a moth, the tree branches and grave flowers bending to flirt with her. So, this is the hetaira Aristogeiton favours over all other women—the only person with a place in his heart even close to Harmodios. No wonder. Her back is straight and words playful, as if she's never been in a cage of marriage like Myrrhine. Being a hetaira is still a cage, no doubt, but maybe it's bigger. She turns her attention to Echo, her gauzy dress catching up to her movements as if the air is water. 'And who's this then?' she asks, toying with the neckline of Echo's tunic.

'Echo. My new assistant,' Nabu says.

Echo flushes, aware of Hanno and Absalon's quiet gaze, and of how close to her breast-binding Leaina is tugging her neckline.

'He's been of great help already and he's only just started,' Kosmos adds.

Echo holds her breath as Leaina's eyes fix on where her cleavage should be. She's spotted the binding strips—she must have, because when she meets Echo's eyes, her look is narrow and calculating. 'Has *he* indeed?'

Wanting to excuse herself, Echo opens her mouth, but there's nothing to say and the plea sits silently on her lip.

Leaina keeps toying with her neckline. 'Well, I'm very pleased to meet you, Echo.'

Releasing her breath, Echo replies, 'I am also pleased to meet you.'

Leaina tidies Echo's tunic, tucking away the binding. 'Shall we go to this symposium then? Are you ready to meet our great guest of honour, the mighty Xenophanes?' Echo doesn't have time to reply as Leaina locks arms with her and drags her along, joking with Kosmos and Nabu as the Not Here whispers: **Leaina the hetaira; educated slut; favoured of the tyrannicides; and her tongue is her tongue is her tong—**

They approach a sprawling villa, torchlight and raised voices spilling from its windows. Harmodios greets them at the door, smoking a small clay pipe. A refreshing wind catches his knee-length chiton, and his still-growing-out hair gusts around his face. 'Welcome to the select few, my friends! You're just in time, looks like rain.'

'We should challenge the sky to a contest,' Leaina says, detaching from Echo and alighting on their host. 'Can the clouds shed more water on the ground or we more wine on our bodies?'

Laughing, Harmodios cups her cheek. 'And Dionysos himself shall be the judge!' He ushers them all inside, where the open doors and courtyard do little to clear the foetid air.

The symposium makes the centauromachy look as dry as a lawyer's office. There are hetairai everywhere, old-style dresses laced under their breasts, and youths serving drinks wearing short tunics, their mouths plumped with cochineal and glistening with olive oil, faces tinted lead white. And hands, hands, hands, roaming nauseatingly rogue amongst them all. Garlands cascade from the ceiling, petals falling on the wrecked drinkers, who wear skewed celery crowns and enough gold to sink a trireme—all of them smudged by clouds of hul gil. It has this burnt thyme, cat piss, week-old trout stench that's stomach turning. Echo's eyes water and her focus swims, the real feast blending with the perfect bacchanalia muralled on the walls.

Echo looks for Hanno and Absalon, but they've already disappeared, seamlessly blending with the other guards and attendants around the room's edge.

'This is a "select few"?' Echo asks Nabu as he hands her a kylix of wine.

'I think Harmodios might have a different definition of "few."' He sips, examining the crowd. 'Kleisthenes doesn't seem to be here. Shame, he's good for an intelligent conversation.'

Echo drinks deep. The wine is well-watered, weak and fruity, and can't do any more damage than the passive hul gil smoke already is. The vinegary, sickly-sweet taste polarises her tongue in a way that's familiar. **Down in one Fresher; penny fizzing in the bottom of a pint; the crack of Pimm's on ice—**

Rain starts pattering the roof and new guests arrive pink-cheeked and soaked to the skin. Thunder grumbles as they wait for Xenophanes, the guest of honour, to emerge from his quarters. Meanwhile, in the atrium, his retinue have already arrived, eschewing wine but enjoying the hul gil pipes in rotation. Most of the Athenians haven't encountered smoking pipes before, and Xenophanes's followers have to instruct them how to breathe in deep, then giggle at the resulting coughs and splutters. Three young men play worn instruments, matching drum, lyre, and pipes to the thunder while hetairai dance to their melodies. Two older men in sky-blue robes dabble their feet in the central pool, passing a pipe between them in rapid breaths.

Echo tries edging to the sidelines, but someone's always blocking her path, rebounding her again and again into conversations she doesn't know how to navigate and can't fully follow. Presently, she's dropped into a circle containing Nabu, Harmodios, and Leaina.

'Aristogeiton's right, your boy really is a skinny thing,' Harmodios says to Nabu, as if Echo isn't there. He exhales a cloud of smoke from the corner of his mouth, flaunting his smoking experience, then flips the pipe around to her. 'Try some. Go on, I want to see what happens when a slip of a thing like you smokes.'

'Come now, that's not a good idea,' Nabu says, wine cup barely touched since Echo last saw him. 'What if the tyrannos takes ill? You'll notice I'm not smoking.'

'Just a puff won't do any harm. It's what men do.'

Leaina smiles slyly. 'Well, it's what *real* men do.'

'Exactly,' Harmodios continues. 'No Persian bowing to a king here, even our dear tyrannos knows better than to emasculate us Athenian men in such a way.'

It's a cruel, ignorant thing to say—**especially since the greatest act of respect in Persia isn't just to prostrate yourself before someone, it's to kiss their feet**—but Nabu just scowls silently. Perhaps he doesn't wish to draw further attention to any perceived want of real manliness in his refusal to smoke or lack of citizenship. Shaking his head, he turns his attention to watching Kosmos dance. Harmodios looks at Echo expectantly. Damn Leaina and her magic, complicated words. Real man. Echo's true, womanly, adult self laughs at it all, but in this world, the boy Echo's pretending to be would care. He'd take the hul gil, so she must, even though smoking it increases the danger of revealing her true identity. Leaina winks at Echo over her kylix. **And her tongue is—**

Echo sighs, taking the pipe from Harmodios and inhaling steadily. The hul gil doesn't taste as bad as it smells, it's earthy and grounding after so many evenings of bittersweet wine with Nabu and Kosmos, and her lungs are almost relieved to be filled with fresh smoke rather than stale second-hand fog. Echo exhales in a billowing blue-grey cloud and Harmodios applauds her. 'Good lad, like you've been smoking for years.'

Maybe she has. The taste is unfamiliar but the act itself feels like an old homey tradition. Perhaps she just wasn't smoking this.

Harmodios and Leaina watch her, as if waiting. Echo frowns. 'What?'

'Any minute now. Just wait. You should count yourself lucky, Echo. Hul gil's expensive and extremely rare. It comes from the same place Nabu does. Happy plant, that's what it means.'

'That's a crude translation and it comes from much farther northeast than I do.' Nabu scowls. With Echo and Kosmos, he's open about how much he hates the arrogance that makes Harmodios so compelling to everyone else, but collaborating with him is the only way to get rid of Hippias.

Dregs of smoke roll in Echo's lungs. It breaks over her like an early summer wave, cool and perfect against the heat of her tipsiness. The party sharpens in focus but softens in impact. Candlelight gilds the guests' skin and robes, glinting on their gold cuffs and bronze torques. The statues hugging the corners of the room unveil previously unappreciated details. Even Harmodios shines with youthful vigour rather than limpid debauchery. It's as if someone has wiped fingerprints directly off Echo's eyeballs.

Harmodios smirks. 'There. Like I said: Happy.'

She grins—or rather, the cloud in her lungs grins for her, but as it spreads through her humours, she wonders what really is the difference between the cloud and her? Surely they are one, and this is her grin. She nods like a sage. 'Yes. Happy.'

Harmodios holds his sides from laughing. Apparently something about her face post–hul gil is amusing. She laughs along with him—it's good to be happy, everyone should be happy—but, his entertainment complete, Harmodios doesn't offer her the pipe again. Nabu glares at her, steering her to the edge of the room as soon as Harmodios is distracted.

'What were you thinking?' he hisses.

Echo's heart races but she can't stop grinning, and the juxtaposition makes her feel slightly sick. 'I think—' Her Hellenic slips as she forces her fuzzy tongue around the words. 'I think of being the boy. Real boy.'

Nabu curses in Lydian. It's a long curse, during which Echo sways. Shaking his head, Nabu sits her on a bench in a corner. 'Stay there. Honestly, whoever recruited you did a bad job. The last Traveller would never have indulged in such stupidity.'

A hul gil fog rolls in, until her entire world is the bench. Humans emerge from the mist, most of whom pass by without a glance at that low artisan Nabu's scrawny assistant. She's just the butt of Harmodios's joke. Her brain keeps trying to communicate her vulnerability, but her body can't bring itself to safety. Her feet are too numb to walk home on, even if she could figure out the way; her tongue's too heavy to talk to Nabu with, even if she could find him in this human jungle. A series of images flick by—Aristogeiton ruffling her hair; Kosmos sighing when she can't say which direction Nabu went; Leaina's perfume, heavy with musk and beeswax, and her whispering, 'It's OK, you can tell me.' But had Echo told her? She has no idea, for between each image is only the sheep-hide softness of the hul gil high. **Smell like an ashtray; should really quit; rocket fuel in those—** Who said that? Someone she hates and loves and can't do without and isn't here. The Not Here stirs and stretches, but it doesn't answer.

'Do you understand?' Nabu, very close, annunciating slowly.

'What?'

'Everyone's gathering by the pool to hear Xenophanes. Move.'

She stumbles up and Nabu drags her to the wide central pool. They sit on the far side from the philosopher, Echo sandwiched between Nabu and an Egyptian potter she's seen around the agora. Nabu passes her a kylix of water, but it settles nastily in her stomach. They copy Xenophanes's followers, dangling their feet in the pool, and its cool rolls back the hul gil's curtain. The rain has eased and falls in a mist through the skylight, wetting her knees. Occasional fatter drops trickle and plink like extra instruments in the music.

At Xenophanes's left hand, ensconced with the philosopher's younger followers, Kosmos smiles up at the clouds and exclaims, 'As Thales says, there really are little gods in everything.'

Xenophanes chuckles, combing his beard with fingers calloused from long hours at the lyre, his robes rumpling around him on the only couch. His own pipe is long and made of bronze, expelling twice as much smoke as anyone else's. He seems an old man, though he's only in his fifties, and the Not Here whispers he'll live for decades more. It's as if he emerged from the womb eighty years old.

'Would you like some wine?' Harmodios offers him a kylix.

Xenophanes waves a hand. 'Can't stand the stuff—more water. And pomegranates.' Harmodios clicks his fingers at a serving boy, who scuttles to fulfil the order.

Xenophanes grumbles about the benefits of pomegranates on passing stools. 'After a sea voyage, one's bowel movements become so erratic.'

Echo disguises her giggles as a coughing fit. The serving boy returns with a platter of freshly split pomegranates, which get passed all the way around—even to Echo, lowliest of them all. The seeds burst in her mouth, bitter and underripe, as the musicians strike up a new tune and Leaina sings along, a hymn to Aphrodite that Echo's heard somewhere in the Not Here, but which seems sweeter for the peal of raindrops and drumming thunder.

When Leaina's finished, Xenophanes applauds. 'A beautiful tune! A shame its subject is so unworthy.'

Leaina laughs, perching on the end of his couch and rubbing his bunions. 'You don't believe in the power of love?'

Sighing at the release of tension in his toes, Xenophanes lounges back with his eyes closed, gesticulating lazily. 'I wouldn't say this in front of any audience, naturally, but you—you're fellow philosophers, from the highest aristokrat to the lowest artisan. You're here precisely because you'll understand. I believe in the power of love, of course—I've felt it. But in the goddess, I have no faith.'

Exchanging looks, the musicians put down their instruments and squeeze in around the pool with sloshes and whispers, those who can't fit sitting on the floor behind and crowding in, until they all form one bated breath. Lightning flashes, turning the raindrops momentarily diamond white. The poet is about to begin.

From the opposite side of the pool, Aristogeiton asks, 'But how can love be inspired without the goddess?'

Above them, on his couch, Xenophanes smiles and opens his eyes, green as Scythian grasslands, the only bright thing in his prematurely ancient face. 'In our myths, we've ascribed every shameful, blameworthy thing humans can do to the gods' characters—theft, adultery, rapine, deception. We have made divinities in the shape of ourselves—not just physically, but emotionally and intellectually. In Ionia, where I live, we border empires that believe in gods quite unlike ours. Though some men say these are just retellings of our gods, that's not the case: Wherever one goes, the gods are different. Yet always they're made in the image of the men who imagined them.'

Or women. Echo picks pomegranate seeds from their skin-like casing. **Or women or women or wo—**

'It's true,' Nabu says, and Echo is conscious of eyes turning in their direction. 'In Thrace, they believe in gods that are red haired and blue eyed like they are.'

'And if the cows could talk, they'd tell us the gods were

cow-shaped, with dozy brown eyes and dangling bellies!' Xenophanes agrees, laughing at his own joke, until he's overcome by phlegm and coughs, dislodging Leaina's foot rub. When he's settled, he carries on. 'Therefore, doesn't it make sense that all men are wrong and, rather than gods that look like us, it's more likely any true gods must have no shape that we can imagine.'

'Haven't the Egyptians achieved something like that with their animal-headed divinities?' Aristogeiton interjects.

'To a degree, but they still have human bodies and known forms. What if instead the divine was unimaginable, beyond our conception in both shape and thought? Like nothing we've ever seen.'

A line of pomegranate juice dribbles down Echo's wrist and she abandons the fruit skin in her lap to lick it away. A goddess would certainly have found a cleaner means to eat her fruit.

Catching candlelit raindrops in his outstretched palm, Xenophanes continues. 'Look at the world—the ordered falling of the rain, the wanderers' persistent paths in the sky, the pattern of birth and death, birth and death. This world is the product of an ordered, clear, conscientious mind. A *good* mind. A mind unlike a man's, that never turns to rage or impatience. A mind that is unified. One great mind, beyond our reckoning.' Thunder rumbles, as if applauding. 'One Demiurge.' The gilded droplets fall from his hand, racing to the pool in a miniature waterfall. 'One mind that made the world, by forming the world from itself.'

'Like Thales's little gods,' Kosmos says, entranced.

'Except this is Xenophanes's big god!' Harmodios replies, toasting his kylix. The company grins and giggles. Extraordinary that even in Xenophanes's presence, Harmodios loses none of his confidence.

Leaina tilts her head coquettishly. 'But if everything's made from one sole God, then it must follow that everything is divine. Yet, if we suppose everything's divine, how can it also be set to a purpose? If I look at a wheat field, how can I at once acknowledge that it's part of the Demiurge *and* be prepared to cut the wheat to eat?'

'Clever girl,' Xenophanes agrees, and Echo catches Leaina cover a wince at the pet name. 'Does anyone have an answer to our delightful friend's problem?'

'Well, to me, it's not a problem,' says Nabu, drawing eyes their way again. Echo lowers her face, attending to her pomegranate. 'In Sardis, before the Achaemenids took our land, there was a terrible war. It lasted six years and during the final battle, my grandfather told me, the moon blotted out the sun, offering the commanders on both sides the omen of a shining crown that held only darkness. Whoever won the war would have found their rule dogged by that darkness, so they came together and formed a truce. By my time it had fallen apart, of course, but it lasted many decades.'

As he speaks, the Not Here rustles with the sound from Echo's dreams, a hundred million trees stoked by a breeze. Above the hul gil, she smells compost—though it's impossible that Harmodios would keep rotting leaves in such a grand house.

Harmodios leans forward. 'How does that relate to Leaina's problem?'

'Like this,' Nabu replies. 'The Achaemenid empire has long been able to predict celestial events, like that eclipse in Sardis. Yet the assembled soldiers—from illiterate spearmen to educated generals—were still able to see the wanderers as sacred and interpret the eclipse as an omen. The celestial bodies are physical, predictable, mundane things, but they are also still divine. To the Achaemenids, despite their predictability, Anahita still inhabits the morning and evening stars, just as we Lydians can still feel the presence of Pldans in the sun.'

The pool sparkles, each reflective surface throwing a world back to Echo that has nothing to do with the present—a horizon of geometric shapes lit by infinite fireflies. **Euston and Kings Cross and Islington and all of it so, so empty—**

'Isn't there an Ode to Salt you once translated that has a similar bent?' Kosmos says to Nabu. 'The salt's worshipped in the first stanza for its divine nature and in the second for its mundane applications.'

'I'd forgotten about that.' Nabu smiles, tucking secrets in the corners of his mouth. 'It was a prayer rather than a poem—though sometimes it's hard to tell the difference.'

The Not Here bubbles and froths, boiling over in the space behind Echo's eyes, until she's blind to everything except the page she read in another place, with the presence of mind only to translate into Hellenic as she goes: '**You are salt, the one made in a pure place. Without you, the royal banquet is not set in the Ekur temple. Without you, god, king, noble, and prince do not smell incense. As for me, whom magical intrigues afflict—release my spell, O salt! Take from me the magical intrigues and, just as I will continue to praise the god who made me, I will continue to praise you.**'

Echo barely realises she's speaking out loud until the Not Here diminishes and she reawakens to the symposium, its inhabitants staring as if only seeing her for the first time. She bites her lip.

Nabu gives her a warning glance. 'Not bad, though your recital was a little abridged.' He recovers and continues. 'As you see, this prayer demonstrates that salt is at once mundane—used for incense and food—*and* a sacred being whose divine power can be called on to instil purity. The idea is far older than the Achaemenid empire though. Way, way back, the Babylonians got around using reeds for thatching in the same way. So, this idea of divinity being in everything, it's not a problem at all.'

All heads turn to Xenophanes for his reaction, but the Not Here isn't done with Echo, it fidgets in the back of her mind and the water in her stomach churns.

Xenophanes frowns, rubbing his sparse beard. 'I've heard about this, shall we say, "duality" before. In Colophon some years ago, a traveller told me a similar tale, but it doesn't sit well with me. The truth should be a united concept. We cannot constantly go around believing in two mutually exclusive realities. Do you not find it contradictory to hold both these concepts in mind at once and still believe you've found a truth? Shouldn't the truth be a singularity?'

Nabu frowns. 'Not at all. It's like the raindrops: Who are we to say when they become the water in the pool? It may be when they are in the pool, or when they hit the pool's surface, or, because that is their destiny, all the way up in the sky. Then again, perhaps they're never the pool, but always retain the memory of their constituent parts. At our feet is a phenomenal thing, an object that is at once a thousand raindrops and a single body of water. The world, likewise, is ten million such divisible objects, and one indivisible whole. It only makes sense for divine-mundane duality to be true.'

A wind sweeps the house, storm-cold, breaking the heat and bringing Echo out in goose bumps. The Not Here writhes, threatening to dominate again. Echo takes a sip of water, the owl eyes in the bottom of her kylix staring back at her, and realises she's going to be sick. Xenophanes and the others continue debating, but their lips produce no comprehensible sounds. Concentrating hard, she puts her kylix down with the pomegranate rind inside and whispers an excuse to Nabu, who's caught in the debate and waves her away. Ears rushing with a rainforest sigh and Not Here murmurs, she teeters outside, into the street.

The rain douses her high, but not her nausea, and some meters down the road the Not Here takes over, pages and footnotes assaulting her mind's eye. She drops to her knees and vomits in a drain, gagging on the words the Not Here's forcing out of her. **Civilisations looking back on two millennia of faith and still finding God in a mathematical event; and Hellenic culture, just writing and reading after its Dark Age, just coming into being at the heart of a crossroads; and her world, so far away, unpicking at the seams from fire, flood, drought; and the Keepers' time, that far ahead again, birthing Project Kairos and Excursion 1133; and the Deed to found a school of philosophy that preserves the concept of a divine-mundane duality paradigm, to revive the world, to resuscitate her—**

'Echo?'

Of all the people to be crouching on the curb, offering Echo a cloth for her face, Leaina is least likely. Her beautiful features pinch with worry as raindrops spatter her muslin dress. Echo takes the cloth and wipes her mouth, avoiding the other woman's gaze, staring at the rain washing her bile down the gutter and waiting to see if she'll be sick again.

Leaina rubs her back, shushing her. 'Do you think there's more?'

Echo shakes her head, twisting the cloth. The Not Here simmers. 'Am I dying?'

Leaina laughs, but not cruelly. 'No. Come on, let's go sit under that awning out of the rain.'

Echo flops outside a shuttered shop, knees up and hands scrunched in her damp hair, trying to figure out what's real. 'Hul gil is bad.'

'Seems to be for you.'

'Not only for me, for reality also.' The flood of memories seeps away, leaving her mind desolated by the Not Here. 'Fuck.' The swear word comes out in English, but Leaina doesn't flick a brow. Lots of non-Athenians revert to their mother tongue when they're in pain, and nobody knows all their languages. Maybe Leaina has her own swearwords too.

Echo starts thanking her for the cloth but her voice breaks.

Leaina pats her knee. 'It's nothing. Don't be a silly boy.'

The 'boy' sends Echo over the edge and she bursts into tears. She aches to go home. Back to the Not Here, her freedom, her own woman's body and her own high, soft voice. She wants she, her, woman—not he, him, boy.

Leaina puts an arm around her, cooing. 'It's alright, you're just coming down.'

Echo curls into Leaina's shoulder. Leaina's dress pins digging into Echo's cheek, and she must feel the binding strips through Echo's tunic, but Echo doesn't care: Being held is worth the price.

'I really am sorry,' Leaina says, and it's the first time all night Echo hasn't sensed her flirting. 'I was never going to tell. Of course

I wasn't. I shouldn't have teased you like that, we have to stick together, people like us.'

'It is fine.' A tear crosses Echo's mouth, and she rubs it away.

'No, it's not. It's bold, what you're doing.' Leaina's eyes grow wide in the moonlight. 'But this illusion won't last forever. If I noticed, others will too. That's all I was trying to say.'

Echo leans against the shop wall, its plaster still warm from the boiling day. 'That is acceptable. I am not here forever.'

'Where are you going?'

The Not Here almost says **the future**, but Echo stops it in time. 'The same place everyone will go.'

Leaina huffs a laugh, though she's more likely thinking of the Styx than the future, and Echo relaxes. It's a relief being with Leaina, not keeping secrets or filtering the gazes and dismissals of men. Still, as Leaina stares at the stars and licks her lips with her rounded pink tongue, the Not Here murmurs that men's hands still hold the future. Echo will still call it the Not Here, even though she knows what it really is now. 'Not Here' is a term she can wrap her head around. 'Future' is notched against the string of the past, ready to shoot into the unknown at any second, giving her vertigo even when she's sitting on the ground. Leaina is an arrow too, aimed at an end that Echo can no longer believe will be pleasant.

Footsteps approach from Harmodios's house, and Nabu and Kosmos emerge from the dark in a dandelion puff of lamplight, Nabu holding a silk parasol over their heads. Behind them, Echo can just make out Hanno and Absalon. Her stomach flips like she might be sick again. The Not Here told her the truth about her purpose here when she was vomiting in the gutter, and what comes next will not be easy to navigate. Yet for the first time since she arrived, she has the certainty of cliffs planted against the sea: She's right, the Deed she's been sent to Athens to complete is not to usurp the tyrannos. It's to found a philosophical school before anyone else does, one that will preserve the mindset of the divine-mundane duality paradigm, which Nabu described to Xenophanes and which will otherwise be lost to history. The tyrannicide will go ahead, but it must do so without Nabu and Kosmos—Echo, and Project Kairos, need them more.

But how to convince them of that in only one moon cycle? How can she explain that her world, the Not Here, is like the pomegranate leftovers in her kylix. Here and now the world is a whole fruit, a thousand seeds, a million potentialities, but without the concept of divine-mundane duality, it will become the leftovers: the skin without the flesh, eaten from within.

9

Hazel

STATION C, DATE UNKNOWN

Hazel lives in Tree for a month before it all goes wrong and the past comes for her.

The day starts much like the others, Hazel waking in her hammock, cursing that she still isn't good enough at lucid dreaming to hold proper conversations with Echo. Her first night in Tree, she and Echo managed to have a real conversation. Well, Echo did most of the talking, she was high as a kite, but Hazel managed to confirm: Yes, the Deed is to build a philosophical school preserving the divine-mundane duality paradigm; yes, they are both time travellers; yes, this Nabu character is likely to be her Caretaker. Hazel even managed to start explaining about CHARL1E, Tree, and the Tinys, but the effort woke her up.

It's since become apparent that that night was a fluke, having nothing to do with Hazel's lucid dreaming skills and everything to do with Echo's hul gil consumption. So, back to square one; all Hazel managed to say last night was, 'I'm still here,' and receive the brief reply, 'So am I.' It's hard to improve, with her guidebook trapped in the Hab Dome. The dreamscape leaches away but its sound lingers, the rustling current blending with Tree's leaves shuffling outside.

The dark presses on her—Tree has no windows, and the lighting system is one of the many things the Tinys brought Hazel here to fix—but her watch says it's morning.

'Morning, Tree,' Hazel whispers, but as usual Tree is silent. She wonders whether Tree will have a voice once she's mended, like CHARL1E, or whether she'll stay as quiet as a Tiny.

Still dozy, Hazel feels under the covers for the hard corners of the *Eikos Muthos*. The pocket-sized book made its way to her feet in the night and she untangles it from her blanket, clutching it to her chest. She waves her hand in the air above the hammock until her fingers catch the light pull. The pendulum LED illuminates the book's tin-foil-and-acetate cover, reflecting a funhouse version of Hazel's face. She opens the recycled-pulp pages to the daily prayer. *Our collective, which art on this Earth, hallowed be thy aims: our kingdom healed and sins undone in seas and ground and skies.* They're just words, but she can see how, through long isolation from a fading outside world, they became meaningful to the Keepers. They're even becoming an anchor for Hazel in this interminable dark and, amongst the religious claptrap, the book's teaching her a lot about Station C.

Squeaking wheels under her hammock hail Robin's arrival, and Hazel stuffs the *Eikos Muthos* under the covers and into her pocket as the Tiny's lenses peek over the hammock edge. The parts of its broken hand jingle in the bag round its neck as it gestures for her to get up.

'Yeah,' Hazel says with a twinge of shame. 'I'm coming.'

She pulls her dungarees on in her hammock, then flops onto one of the many walkways zigzagging Tree's midsection. Together, they make up the Keepers' Treehouse, which contains two dozen empty hammocks and the only human-sized amenities. Really, Tree is for the Tinys, Hazel's just an inconvenience they've invited in for maintenance.

Robin thunks her flask of tea and bowl of not-quite-porridge on the walkway, then turns away with its lenses in the air. The other

Tinys send Robin to deliver her meals on purpose, thinking the guilt will goad her into mending Tree faster. They're right, but the Tiny is so unrelenting in the face of her entreaties, she's given up on its forgiveness.

She sits on the edge of the walkway, legs dangling off and arms leaning on the handrail, drinking her tea as Robin conspicuously ignores her. The two-hundred-foot drop used to bother her, but in the last month she's learned to trust the walkways not to fail and her body not to jump. There's not much sense of distance in the dark anyway, just reverberations of depth, height, and width when she drops a tool or speaks too loudly. Aside from her reading light, her torch, and the fluorescent tubes she works by—both of which are hooked up to old truck batteries—the only illumination is a bottle cap–sized spot far below on the ground, where the Tinys burn their sacred oil lamps. The idea of their being religious is still bizarre, but the *Eikos Muthos* describes it repeatedly and it makes more sense than any other theory she's got about what they're up to. Tree is their God, and their temple, and their home, the walls coated in hexagonal cells in which the Tinys sleep. The cells start at ground level and continue well past the Keepers' Treehouse, and if each one was inhabited, there'd be thousands of Tinys. As it is, she's only ever seen a couple of hundred attending prayers. Where the rest are is a mystery.

Hazel refills her cup from the flask, turning to Robin. 'Why do you bother with the flask when it's always cold anyway? It's ridiculous, porridge can be hot, but tea somehow can't?'

Robin doesn't even turn.

'Look, I'm fixing Tree, and I've said I'm sorry, there's nothing more I can do. You have to forgive me sometime.'

Robin shakes its head, resolutely not looking at her.

'I could fix you. You don't have to wait for Tree.' This time, it doesn't even deign to gesture. With a sigh, she slugs her second cup of tea. Hot or cold, the stuff is, at best, only tea's distant cousin. As soon as she's finished, Robin whips away the flask and empty bowl, whisking them into one of the cells, behind which the Tiny transport systems run all over Tree. There's just the one elevator for humans and it's as piecemeal as everything else on Station C, whining all the way up to the Treehouse and creaking back to the ground. *Give we this day our resilience and strength, and let us lend support, as in turn we are supported.*

Hauling herself up, Hazel heads to work. Her torch beam pierces the dark, illuminating creaking walkways, rusted mechanical arms, and 'The Keepers' Treehouse' graffitied in lime green near the youth-hostel-scent shower block. She washes minimally, creeped out by the empty stalls at her back and her arms' spidery shadows. *And let us endure this time of trial, and not resort to evil.*

Hazel glances up on her way out, to where her torchlight disappears into the treetop. She's never been that high—the elevator stops at the Treehouse—but mechanical wheezes in the walls suggest the Tinys can go much farther. She heads to work, passing a mechanical arm, paused mid-motion as it repairs a Tiny lens. Another suspended arm clutches a whole Tiny, ready to reattach a wheel as soon as the power's restored. The silence and darkness press in, total and absolute in a way that shouldn't ever exist in a factory. 'You'd better fix Robin when I've mended you,' Hazel mutters to Tree. 'Maybe it'll forgive me then.'

At the highest point of the Treehouse, Hazel reaches the critically failing circuit board the Tinys brought her to fix. Black lever arch files, thick manuals, and well-thumbed electronics textbooks lie scattered among her multimeter, screwdrivers, and rolls of electrical tape. The circuit itself runs from the walkway to head height, a tangle of wires interspersed with diodes, transistors, and capacitors. In the top right-hand corner, switches and inductors indicate that the circuit is partly designed to send and receive radio waves—though where from and to whom is anyone's guess.

The circuit failure's epicentre is a spherical mirror, held out on two small arms where it once spun like a disco ball. When Hazel arrived, a thin crack bisected the sphere's equator, emitting a slim ray of golden light that the Tinys refused to look at. The manuals are abstract about its purpose, just calling it an 'elpis device,' but Hazel's spent long enough on Station C to know that mirrors usually mean time travel, so she figured it was the part to mend first. Using two torches on different settings, she slowly heated the glass, melting the split together and closing in the weird warm light. She wrapped the device in blankets, cooling it as slowly as possible in situ, and by some miracle it didn't shatter. Then she turned to the other malfunctions sprawling outwards from the elpis device. The coating on some wires is pale and peeling, as if decayed; on others it's warm and garish, as if only just shrink-wrapped to the copper. Some components have corroded metal teeth; others have developed residues of dirt and crystal. One capacitor has short-circuited from dielectric breakdown; another has separated into its constituent parts. It's as if the circuit's caught between prematurely aging and reversing into its origins as ore and oil. Hazel's never seen anything like it; she's just replacing parts and crossing her fingers she's getting it right. *For ours is the prospect and the power and the undoing of all.*

At her soldering station, Hazel flicks on the fluorescent lights and rubs her eyes. Another day of guesswork and troubleshooting. At first, she tried explaining to the Tinys that she didn't know anything about this kind of circuitry, but they stamped their wheels until she understood she didn't have a choice. For a couple of weeks, she dragged her feet, supplied with ancient tools and stacks of manuals. Then, a fortnight ago, she'd opened a file box and, tucked between *The Novice's Guide to Arboreal Circuitry* and a blueprint of Tree's lightning-harvesting batteries, she found an object wrapped in an old workshop rag. From its shape and feel it was just a little hardback book, but it fizzled with the electricity of an object she shouldn't have—like getting into the medicine cabinet as a kid. Checking Robin wasn't about, she folded back the solder-spotted cloth, and a metallic cover gleamed beneath. She shoved the book in her pocket and, over the ensuing nights, devoured the

Eikos Muthos. Through it, Hazel is beginning to realise how little she understands.

She runs a hand over the broken circuit. One or two more days and it'll be done. She's not sure what happens then, but she's still wary of CHARL1E and doesn't have enough oxygen to return to the Hab Dome, so she's hopeful she can stay here. It's not out of the question: The Tinys seem unable to touch Tree's circuits, either out of respect or because their programming prevents it, so they might keep Hazel here for maintenance. Better prove she's good at it. She takes up the soldering iron. *Let us begin.*

She works in silence, mulling over the *Eikos Muthos.* It's divided into three sections, covering the main centuries-long phases of Project Kairos, a history comprised of lab notes and epistles. Even though she's keeping the book a secret from the Tinys, the inscription from its original owner lets her know it was meant to come to her: *For the Forward Traveller, should it come to this. I have torn out pages so this is safe for you to read. Keep my brother in check. Trust CHARL1E, have patience for the Tinys, and always listen to Tree—even when none of them are making sense. Perhaps avoid letting them know I've given this to you. Good luck. Lilith.* That the *Eikos Muthos* belonged to a woman killed in an accident Hazel caused only makes her feel worse for all the misunderstandings she's had about Station C, and she's begun to feel as if fixing Tree might not only bring the Tinys around again, but help Hazel start atoning for the damage she's caused. The book's a mess: Station C's history interspersed with the daily activities of the Keepers who wrote it, semireligious verses, and a whopping ninety-six parables. There's The Parable Of The Unwary Coder And The Backup File; The Man Who Replied-All; The Woman Who Did Not Beta Test . . . Hazel's skipped quite a few, though The Sage Who Turned It Off And On Again entertained her more than she'd expected. Likewise, The Epistles Of The Lovers was deeply moving, an almost-complete collection of letters sent during a decade-long plague between a man confined in the Workshop Dome and his husband quarantined in Tree. But it's the opening Euangelion Of The Mirrors that Hazel most enjoys.

> Many years hence, when the world will be knee-deep in ocean and blistering from fire, five hundred and forty-three broad-minded scientists will nurture Project Kairos. They will build Station C, a sustainable laboratory, to house endeavours aimed at altering the tides of destr]uction. There, they shall eat, sleep, and work to unlock the secrets of revival.
>
> But this research will take many years and the sky will breathe fearsome storms upon them that shall fell every tree, until but one remains. For in their early Green-Fingered Generations, the broad-minded scientists shall invent pretty-voiced Tree, a chimera descendant of extinct colossal forests. Pretty-voiced Tree will inhale carbon dioxide and exhale oxygen, but she shall suck so many nutrients from the ground in fuel, and so acidify the soil, that there can only ever be one of her . . .

Hazel's day starts to go wrong around lunchtime, when Robin appears with a bowl of something approximating pad thai, a clump of slimy noodles bobbing in the middle. Robin stalks off, doing self-maintenance as it waits for the empty bowl. It releases a slim spout in its sternum, which dispenses drops of oil that it applies to a troublesome axel. Tinys have many moving parts, and they work constantly to keep themselves in minimum-squeaking order, though the results are variable—particularly in Robin's case.

'You know, I'm nearly there with the circuit,' Hazel says. For once, Robin looks up. 'Yeah, you'll get fixed soon. Will you forgive me then?'

Robin shrugs.

'That's fair. Though, honestly I'm nervous about what happens when I turn this circuit on. Is Tree going to burst into life like a merry-go-round?'

Robin stops greasing its wheel and nods.

'Stands to reason that what makes me nervous makes you excited,' she says, maintaining her new habit of accounting for the Tinys' feelings.

Robin takes her empty bowl with a bit less venom than this morning.

'I need a little walk. Can I come down with you?'

Rolling its lenses, Robin nods. *If you have to.*

They take the elevator, honeycomb cells flicking past as they clank through the dark towards the Tinys' altar.

> And so the middle Steel-Fingered Generations shall come around; marked by terrible airborne pestilences that will turn their pink lungs black, and their grey brains bloody; and which they will defeat by erecting airlocks, redirecting the oxygen from Tree into the habitation domes, and using biosuits to traverse the outside. Dwindling and grieving, they shall create the helpful-handed Tinys . . .

On the ground, Hazel unlocks the elevator gate and walks towards the table of oil lamps and votives that twinkle twenty-four hours a day. Until she found the *Eikos Muthos*, she'd called Tree 'the tree' or 'a tree,' causing any nearby Tinys to stick their tails straight out and spin on the spot. Now she understands that it's just 'Tree,' but if she let on, the Tinys might guess she's got hold of the *Eikos Muthos* and confiscate it. Handing the empty bowl to another Tiny, Robin trundles to the altar, the flames wavering as it clasps its hands and arches its tail over its body until fingers meet tail-tip.

Other nearby Tinys hold their tails perpendicular to the floor, threatening to spin if Hazel gets any closer. She holds her hands up, saying, 'It's OK, I'm just having a walk,' and circles the altar from a distance. Little changes in Tree and there's only a limited amount of walking she can do, but there's always something to watch here.

The altar is made from ancient saplings woven into a low table, the bark worn away by centuries of reverent Tiny touches, revealing a jigsaw of oak, bamboo, kapok, and baobab. Curios are arranged over it in the almost-circular shape of Tree's trunk: an empty snail shell, a bird's-wing humerus, a mouse skull, three bovine molars, a leaf skeleton . . . In the centre of the almost-circle, two Tiny lenses balance glass-upwards. A pair of amputated steel hands cover the lenses, as if they're peeking through the fingers. From closer and riskier inspections, Hazel has discovered the parts bear a serial number and model description: *TINY MK.1.1. A SERIES.* These aren't just *parts* to the Tinys, they're organs, but the altar's a reliquary rather than a mausoleum.

> Manufactured in the failed experiment of Tree, the Tinys will only be programmed for empathy and joy, with the intent that they shall carry seeds and saplings in their bellies and disgorge them across the world, a networked community of optimism. But the farther they shall stray, the more isolated each Tiny will become, and danger will follow–for the world shall not yet be empty, and many will be the aggressors to the broad-minded scientists. One day in deep winter, a group of distrustful humans will attack the first and oldest Tiny. The Tinys shall band together to retrieve their fallen comrade and return home with it on a bower made from their saplings.
>
> In the hollow heart of Tree, the Tinys will gather and learn grief, which they will not be designed to bear. Seeing the Tinys unable to move, or dance, or play, or lift their eyes from the ground, the broad-minded scientists will gift them a new programme–faith–knowing as they do so that once the Tinys are given a deity–their own creator, Tree–they will never again leave her side. The Tinys will live under her comforting embrace, believing there is no need to venture forth with seeds and saplings because the deity will mend all . . .

Clay oil lamps cluster around either side of the altar, spreading across the floor. As Hazel watches, Robin emerges from its reverie and picks up an extinguished lamp. It releases its sternum oil spout, filling the lamp and relighting it from a neighbouring flame. Robin pauses before putting it back, praying perhaps that Tree's circuits will be finished today and its hand will be fixed, or for the half-mended Tinys suspended in the Keepers' Treehouse. It's never occurred to Hazel before, but it isn't unusual to light candles for people who are sick or deceased—and the broken Tinys in the Treehouse are certainly one or the other.

My parents had candles.

That sudden, overwhelming memory is the moment things fall apart.

The church, the funeral, the day Hazel wore the only black dress that fitted over her neck brace. She'd downed her codeine prescription an hour early because she couldn't take the stress of having to talk to everyone, and they all kept lying about how well she looked, unable meet her eyes when they said, 'Grief suits you.' Ridiculous, like she'd picked grief out of her wardrobe that morning, tested it in the mirror, and decided, 'Yeah, this looks good.' All the while, their gazes drifted to the bruising at her neckline. **Miss Brandt, you have a hairline fracture in your atlas axis vertebra; must wear a cervical collar for ten weeks; vocal cord paralysis, or should I say paresis—**

The back of Hazel's neck aches, as if someone's pinching the skin, but when she looks, no one's there, and the sensation sticks to her as she turns.

The church wanted to be old, but the pointing between the bricks was too fresh and ruined the illusion, a real North London suburbia job. There was a table in a corner, fresh tapers on one side and burning stubs on the other. She put fifty pence in the box and took two candles, one for each of her dead parents. No, she didn't want to think like that: one for Mum, one for Dad. She wondered if she believed in God—right there, in his house—but she prayed anyway. **Limited range of movement but it depends how hard you work; weakened motion of the vocal cords, weakened weak—**

There's a rustle, as if all the world's paperwork is shuffling, and a chronological tide pulls her, scruff-first, threatening to drag her away. The dreamscape's womblike light floods her eyes, but she can't let the current take her. She has to mend Tree, fix Robin's hand, give the Tinys enough longevity to keep Station C going. This cannot be the last expedition. But the riptide is strong, and she's paralysed in its flow, unable to escape—

A hand touches her shoulder, and she looks into Robin's lenses. She's fallen to her knees and her throat hurts. Has she been shouting?

The altar-lamps flutter. Unsteadily, she gets to her feet, wishing she too could pray and access that religious comfort blanket which banishes loneliness, promises salvation, speaks for the conscience, and quells the panic that comes from staring down the barrel of impermanence.

Robin touches her thigh, lens wipers tented upwards with worry, as the inundation of memory seeps away, to return another tide.

'It's OK, I'm OK,' she lies, patting its hand. It's the closest the Tiny has got to her since she hurt it. Dozens of other Tinys watch her from their cells and the altar, and Robin squeezes her hand. 'Really, I'm fine. It's just time to get back to work, that's all.' As she walks to the elevator, the Tinys' tails twitch, out of sync, like each one is trying to shout its own idea loudest in the hive mind. She needs a private moment to check the *Eikos Muthos* and figure out what fresh weirdness is happening. She's only read half the story of time travel and whatever this is, it's part of the other half.

And so the ocean shall rise and cover the blanched land, and Station C will become an island in the smog-brown waters. On a planet thus unstable and devoid of redemption, the Wrinkle-Fingered Generations will be born, infected with anxiety and the lunacy of isolation, and shall become unafraid of breaking the world further. In this dark crucible, their ideas shall manifest all the lost wilderness, and they will come to believe that only by traversing the fourth dimension shall these earthly woes be undone. They shall create the Arch, though they will know not what it is until, by bootstrap chance, the first Backward Traveller shall emerge from the mirror door, eyes wide and limbs akimbo, naked as the day they will have been born.

Hazel keeps her head down as the elevator ascends. **Breathe in to four. I'm still here. Hold for two. So am I. Out for—** The voices in her head entwine and she realises where she's heard Echo before. It's her voice talking Hazel through the calming breathing patterns. The back of her neck squeezes and she shakes her head vehemently. Don't open that box.

When she reaches the Treehouse, Hazel pulls out the *Eikos Muthos* and flicks through it, leaning into the hammock to hide her activities from any watching Tinys.

And the broad-minded scientists shall become the Traveller's Keepers and wrap their nudity in a blanket and ask them, 'Traveller, who are you? Where are you from? Why are you here?' And to each the Traveller shall answer, 'I know not.' Until, by coincidence, one of the Keepers will explain the use of mirrors and the Traveller's words shall fail them and their eyes will glaze with visions of another time. Upon which, the Traveller shall say, 'Are we not drawn onward ere divided?' And the Keeper's mouth will fill with a thing she has been told before by a time that comes after, and reply, 'We few live on mirror rims.' So together, Keeper and Traveller shall undertake the first recitation of the Traveller's Cipher. Then the past will come for the Traveller, and time will catch them, and they shall be blown away.

For many moons no other Traveller shall arrive. When he does, his mind shall be likewise washed clean of memories, until a spark shall ignite them and he shall say: 'It is later than we think, and the hour's growing thin. Yet there is still width enough to traverse between the minute hand and midnight, for I have been sent with a Deed.'

Is that what the tug on the back of Hazel's neck is? Like a stray kitten being caught by its mother, is time somehow catching up with her? And what does it mean to be 'blown away'—to be transported elsewhere or be snuffed out? Either way, time mustn't catch her yet, she has too much left to do. But she can't stop the past from coming for her. All she can do is work as fast as possible. She slams the book shut, stuffing it back in her pocket. Fuelled by adrenaline, she returns to the broken circuit, feverishly rewiring, soldering, stripping, rebuilding, while her memories threaten to break. **Grief suits you; breathe in; weak weakened weak—** Whether or not he has anything to do with that mysterious corpse in the third dome, CHARL1E will know what's happening, but she doesn't have the oxygen to return to the Hab Dome, the biosuit's comm is blocked inside Tree, and there's no way the Tinys would act as messengers. She's tried getting Shiny and Teaspoon to bring her the *Lucid Dreaming* book, but they just shake their lenses and point at the broken circuit she's fixing. She doesn't get any favours from them until her work's done. Then again, maybe the circuit itself will let her get a message out to CHARL1E—it is designed to receive and transmit radio messages.

Yet the Keepers will not be able track their actions and shall stumble lost through the past and future. For thirteen years, their harvests will fail, and under starvation they shall dwindle yet again, becoming slender-wristed and gaunt-cheeked. During this time, they shall work night and day, until they unlock the post-quantum realms of computing. In that half-real place they shall construct a machine named CHARL1E. And he shall be an ungainly thing, whose nodes shall weave around the timeline; observing, measuring, and calculating.

But the broad-minded scientists shall be afeared of their

> new creation, who shall be so little known and so all-knowing. Thus, they will curtail CHARL1E's powers, so that while he can see and speak of the timeline, he shall not be allowed to access the Arch or tinker with its workings. This job the Keepers alone shall fulfil, guarding their knowledge from hands that might otherwise do it wrong. In such ways shall the Keepers preserve the Travellers' safety, while they are delivered time and again into the waiting hands of their Caretakers.

Without Keepers or Caretaker, Hazel is lost. She distracts herself with memorised fragments of the *Eikos Muthos*, working until her eyes scratch. She's so nearly there. But she gives herself a soldering burn through inattention and at her cry Robin emerges from a nearby cell to dress the wound.

'Does this mean you've forgiven me?' Hazel asks.

Robin shakes its head persistently, but drags her to the hammock and tucks her in. It's not until its wheel-squeaks have faded that she realises even though the Tiny hasn't forgiven her, it might still care about her. The phantom colours of darkness press on her eyes, becoming a doctor's coffee cup, the morgue assistant's clipboard, two candles burning for twenty-five pence each. **Weak weak—**

She snaps on the light and opens the *Eikos Muthos*. If she falls asleep, she might get caught by time, and wake up elsewhere or maybe not at all. She flips through the book's missing sections, stroking a finger down each rag-end indicating torn out pages. One here, one there, what looks like about twenty pages in the third section, and a handful right at the end. That's how she finds that someone has turned the endpaper into a pocket, and Hazel is revisited by a meddling-in-the-medicine-cabinet frisson as she pulls out, not the missing sections, but about ten pages written in Lilith's hand. Someone's spilt amber liquid over them, and the words have blurred together, so she can only make out the title and a few snippets:

> *THE LAST ACTS OF THE ~~KEEPERS~~ BROAD-MINDED SCIENTISTS . . . Huxley doesn't know I'm writing this . . . of course I love my brother, but it's hard to like him when he takes his experiments so far . . . when we die, someone must take over who can remain here indefinitely and operate the Arch . . . Huxley's denial . . . in secret, CHARL1E and I . . .*

How heavy Lilith's responsibility must have felt. At least Hazel only has to do what she's told; Lilith and Huxley had to figure out what to tell her. She sinks deeper into the hammock, trying to decipher more. A picture emerges of a brother and sister who shared a dormitory, read books together, and reminisced, but mostly because there was no one else. During the day they separated, working on their own experiments and plotting their own paths forward. Lilith claimed the territory of Tree, and Huxley claimed places whose names are lost. What was Lilith trying to communicate? Why didn't she rewrite the pages? Or did it all happen so close to the accident there wasn't time?

Hazel's eyes droop. She blinks, shaking herself awake, terrified what might happen if she drifts off. But it's no use, she'll have to sleep sometime. She tucks away the pages and curls around the book. Exhausted, the dreamscape easily reels her into its molten nest.

'Hazel?' Echo's voice is stuffy like she's been crying.

Hazel wants to reply, but her voice is so **weak weak weakened** and she can't seem to overcome the **paresis of the vocal cords** even though Echo needs her. Echo, whose words have been in Hazel's mind all this time, guiding her out of panic. **In to four hold for my dead parents—**

No. This is the dreamscape. She can access any time from here, any place, any state of voice. 'I'm here.'

'The usurpation's tomorrow and I'm frighte—don't want to be involve—not what I'm here to—too embroiled—' Echo's voice oscillates, alternately succumbing to and conquering the dreamscape's ceaseless whisper, like tuning in to a radio during a thunderstorm.

'Can't you pretend to be sick or something?' The dreamscape's mould-and-fresh-rain odour thickens. 'Echo?'

'—Not how it works—feel trapped—'

Echo's voice curdling with fright hits Hazel like a hammer, and she turns—finally—because even her subconscious understands that she must. After all these weeks, she takes Echo in, her tunic and short red hair weaving in the current. Hazel sucks in a breath: she knows that tear-streaked face. **Hand clasped over a hospital sheet; a saucer of pain medication arranged like a flower; breathe in grief suits you—**

Pain in the base of Hazel's skull wakes her. Her ears cram with rushing waterfalls and shushing leaves; her nose clogs with time's copper-compost-sea-spray reek. **Raindrops on a windscreen; cheeks hurting with laughter—** Stop it. Breathe. Sweat drenches Hazel's forehead. Memories spark in her vision as she falls from the hammock. **Just build the catopthura and we'll make it right—** Stop, this isn't the time. The tug on the back of her neck increases, and she clings to a railing with bilious fear and blinding pain. **This is how we fix things; candles; are these your; weak weak; raindrops—**

Real steel fingers touch her real flesh hand.

'Robin?'

It puts its unharmed palm on the back of her neck and the pain ebbs.

The flood of memories recedes into the sea of amnesia. **Weak weak—**

'What's happening to me?'

Robin watches her, twitching its tail. In nearby cells, other Tinys' lenses reflect the glow of her reading lamp. Whatever's happening to her, it's got the Tinys worried too.

'It's OK. I've got this.' This time, she isn't lying. She's going to fix that radio and talk to CHARL1E. She stumbles to the broken circuit, Robin, Teaspoon, and Shiny keeping watch in case time grabs her again. It does its best, pestering her with memories, like kids squealing in the back seat of a car.

'Make noise!' She instructs the Tinys.

Teaspoon hits the handrail uncertainly.

'More, consistently! I need you to fill my head with so much sound my memories can't get a look in.'

The Tinys nod and start kicking up a ruckus, weaving their tails to tell the others to join. Soon every Tiny in Tree is banging something, making a cacophony so brash Hazel can barely hear herself think. That's the stuff. She gives them the thumbs-up and gets back to work.

The final element of the circuit to reconnect is the clumsily mended elpis device. She attaches the wires, trembling, fingers smudging the glass as she pulls away. She stands back, fingers crossed.

The Tinys fall silent, frozen in wait, but nothing happens. Hazel's done it wrong. She's too late, too **weak weak—**

Outside, Tree's leaves sigh.

A sound grows that keeps Hazel holding her breath. It comes from everywhere and nowhere, filling the tree trunk; a wordless song, one soprano voice cascading over half-familiar themes. Tree's producing oxygen again. She isn't like the Tinys or CHARL1E, but something all her own, her song emerging from holes in the thin tubes outlining each of the Tinys' cells, the whole hive becoming an enormous pipe organ. This is the voice that sang briefly over the Tannoy when Hazel first entered the Hab Dome, before the cascade of faults from the Arch explosion cut it off. There's some justice after all in Hazel being the Tinys' choice mechanic: Her arrival broke Tree, so she should be the one to fix her. For the first time since looking into Lilith's glazed eyes, Hazel feels as if she's made a contribution.

She turns to the Tinys, but they're not paying attention to her. Lights are coming up, softer and warmer than Hazel expected, until from roots to crown the Tiny cells are dripping in honeyed luminescence. Shiny and Teaspoon whisk in circles with their tails coiled and arms raised, and Hazel feels a little like dancing too. Meanwhile Robin is on a mission of its own, whizzing to the Treehouse's mechanical arms, which are coming alive, mending Tinys in rhythm with the music. Reaching them, Robin holds out its broken hand and a mechanical arm extends to fix it.

Hazel grins, placing a palm on the wall. 'Nice to meet you, Tree. Took us long enough.'

A speaker in the circuit crackles and Hazel snaps round to find a series of lights flashing from red to green. The radio's working.

'Tree? Is it really you?' It's CHARL1E's voice, clouded by static but unmistakably his. Hazel's heart jumps.

Across the Treehouse, the automated arms freeze, but Robin's is hand half rebuilt and the robot tugs on the mechanism that was tending it, trying to get Tree to continue. Near Hazel, Shiny and Teaspoon stop dancing, tails ticking like metronomes.

'It is you,' CHARL1E says. 'I missed you. Where have you been? What happened?'

Tree's song turns from baroque to jazz, syncopating and trilling. The mechanical arms restart, but they miss connection points, and nuts and bolts tinkle from the Treehouse to the faraway floor. Two of Robin's fingers fall to the walkway, and it scoops them up, clutching them to its chest. Its lenses flick between each of Tree's malfunctioning arms, while Shiny and Teaspoon stare at the speaker in the circuit, balling their hands into fists. Is it possible that Tree can only talk to the Tinys or CHARL1E, not both at once? Has Hazel mended Tree but made things worse at the same time? **This is how we fix things; weakened weak—**

Stop. She can't let time catch her. Gathering her courage, Hazel approaches the radio, looking for a mic to respond with, but perhaps if CHARL1E's picking up Tree, there isn't one. 'CHARL1E?' Hazel calls to the air. 'Can you hear me?'

For a heartbeat she thinks he won't reply. Then: 'Hazel Brandt.'

'Yes. It's me.'

'So, this is where you have been hiding.' She waits for him to fly off the handle again, but apparently he too has had time to think. 'I miscalculated.'

The dam of memories builds, threatening to burst. 'We need to talk.'

'Affirmative. Return to the Habitation Dome, we will talk here.'

She fiddles with the soldering iron, twisting it on the table like a compass. They need to speak, but she hadn't thought about returning immediately and just because Tree's producing oxygen again doesn't mean Hazel can refill her tanks here. 'I don't know. You could have hurt me when you tried to stop me leaving. You said I was destructive, suspicious, dangerously arrogant . . . I'm not sure I want to come back.'

The speaker crackles. 'There are occasions where those things are true. But I am sorry that I threatened you. I was not operating at optimal functionality. I was not myself, as you would say.'

'Actually, CHARL1E, I think you were. That's the point, isn't it? That you're not yourself with me?'

'I—' CHARL1E breaks off mid-sentence and Tree's song becomes a low bass hum. When he next speaks, CHARL1E's voice is less precise, still a thousand tones in unison, but ragged at the edges as if each one is having to think about coming together. He still has his particular vocabulary, but the ebb and flow of his tone is far closer to human. 'Very well. I will endeavour to be more "myself" with you in future, if that will help you feel safe. Will you return now?'

Hazel's memories crowd her thoughts, but she's still frightened. 'What about the dead body in that dome beyond the Arch?'

'I do not know how you are aware of the Experimentation Dome, but I can assure you there is no corpse inside of it.'

'Don't start lying again, CHARL1E. There's a corpse in there, I saw it.'

'I cannot compute that.' There's a long pause, then: 'Oh. Ha ha.

This is amusing. We are engaged in a misunderstanding. Affirmative, Hazel, you observed a body, but it is not a corpse. A corpse is the remainder of a thing that was once alive. That body is not and has never been alive. Though, in a sense, its potential has departed, so it might be interpreted as corpse-adjacent.'

She spins the soldering iron again. 'So, you didn't kill it?'

'Negative, I did not kill the corpse-adjacent object.'

Hazel wants to believe him, to go back to her real bed in the Hab Dome and a long hot shower, but her fear keeps stirring. 'You've still been lying to me.'

'Affirmative. I have been withholding certain elements of the truth from you and circumstances beyond my control require that I continue to do so.'

'That's it?'

'Further explanation would be inappropriate at this juncture.'

'Then how can you expect me to trust you?'

'When you trust someone, you trust what they choose to keep hidden as well as what they show. No human that has ever lived has been an open book: Trust the pages you cannot see as well as the ones you can.'

She puts a hand on the soldering iron, stopping it spinning, and turns to the circuit. 'Alright. I'll come back.'

'I am very glad,' CHARL1E says, and he does actually sound relieved. 'Because I have grave news: Something has gone wrong within the timeline.'

Hazel's stomach twists. 'I'm afraid I might have worse news.'

'That is improbable, a glitch is careening down the timeline towards us, there can be no worse news.'

'Improbable but true. The thing is I keep . . . I don't know how to explain it . . . nearly getting caught by time.'

'Remarkably, your statement was accurate. I can infer your meaning, and that is alarming information.'

'I'm not done.' Hazel takes a deep breath, the past's fingertips clawing her. 'In the dreamscape, I finally managed to move—

which should be a good thing. Except that I looked at Echo and I recognised her.'

'You did?'

The past wraps its arms around her, gripping the back of her neck, pulling. **Weaken—**

'Of course, CHARL1E. How could I not? She looks exactly like me.'

Time smiles, and inundates Hazel with memories. Her vision washes dreamscape red, but over the current rushing in her ears, she can just hear CHARL1E.

'Hazel Brandt, listen to me: Concentrate. Do not give in to the memories. Can you hear me? You must not give in, you must stay here with me. Are we not drawn on ere divided? Hazel!'

Hazel searches for the response, but the pain in her neck is overwhelming and she can't tell where in time she's speaking to. **Weak—**

10

Echo

ATHENS, 514 BCE

As dawn seeps through the gaps between the shutters and under the doors, Echo shuffles out of the kitchen, across the yard, and into the orchard. Cool breezes ease her headache as she slouches between the trunks, plucking a low-hanging apple and disturbing insects in the long grass. After Harmodios's symposium, she threw up once more, halfway home, and Nabu made her sleep on the floor so she wouldn't accidentally be sick in his bed.

'You're an idiot,' he repeated, leaving a handful of mint leaves beside her.

And she is. She regrets everything, she's never drinking again—and gods, she's never ever smoking hul gil again. Her head reels. The only benefit was that it let her talk to Hazel in the dreamscape, and confirm that her instincts are right: Her purpose here isn't to usurp Hippias, but to build a philosophical school. Yet her reprieve from murdering the tyrannos has been replaced by the equal weight of preventing the bleak, lonely future Hazel began to describe.

The orchard's edge drops steeply, giving way to terraced aristokratic villas and a half-circle theatre before sprawling into Athens's terracotta rooftops. Beyond the city walls rise the foothills and mountains, through which Spartans and Corinthians raid, and where Kosmos will be sent next summer to join the defence. Nabu, of course, will never be sent: he lacks a horse and, worse, citizenship. Echo has often overheard them talk of the danger Kosmos will face, and she imagines his woolly fingers must struggle to grip a sword.

She slumps onto a log hidden behind an unruly fig, watching the sunrise. The apple gurgles as it settles in her recently emptied stomach. Poppies stretch their petals towards the lightening sky as wild garlic releases its savoury perfume. The sun clips the mountain peaks and the world yawns. For a few minutes, Athens belongs just to Echo and the symphony of birds, then whispers and the swish of quick, angry strides through the grass betray the presence of others—probably stableboys causing trouble, or household guards on patrol. She sinks down, hoping to avoid awkward good-mornings. She has no patience for people today.

It turns out, it's Kosmos and Nabu. A rhythmic *thwuck* indicates Nabu passing something—maybe a piece of fruit—between his hands. 'Xenophanes dismissed me, Kosmos, you can't deny it.'

Echo pricks up her ears. It's not exactly eavesdropping if they're talking anyway, though their words keep getting lost in the hand-over between crickets and cicadas.

'Yes, but he dismisses everyone he doesn't agree with.'

'It was different with me. A different kind of dismissal—it wasn't because of what I was saying but because I was the one saying it.'

'Darling, I mean this in the kindest way, but you are not that interesting to Xenophanes.'

Nabu's heavy tread ceases and the fruit falls still in his hands. 'That's not what I mean, and you know it.'

Kosmos stops too. 'What do you mean then? Because you're Lydian? A freeman? You're too sensitive. No one cares about citizenship in those circles.'

'This from the man who won't even hold my hand in public.' Nabu throws the fruit into the fig bush and Echo ducks. It lands a couple of feet away; a pear, skin bruised and split where it impacted the ground.

'Only because it would endanger your livelihood—let alone your life—if my father were to discover we actually care about each other,' Kosmos retorts. 'It's one thing for him to think I'm just taking you to my bed arbitrarily, he and Hipparchos do that all the time with anyone who takes their fancy. So long as I keep it in the house and don't expose us to public ridicule, I can do what I want. It'd be another thing entirely for you and me to have a relationship.'

Nabu snorts. 'Public ridicule? Is that what I would bring on you?'

'They're the words my father would use! I may be well-off and from a good family, but I'm not free to do whatever I like.' Kosmos blows out a frustrated breath and Echo can picture him with a hand in his hair. 'I'm supposed to marry a woman who will bear me sons, and if I take a male lover he should be . . . Yes, frankly, another aristokrat. Any indication I'm not going to do that endangers us both!'

Nabu snarls. 'Grow a spine, Kosmos. It's not for you to decide when and how I should be kept safe. So what, you'll piss off your father? He wants you to be a man, show him the man you are!'

'And what of your circles, hmm?' Kosmos retorts. 'What would Harmodios and Aristogeiton say if they knew you visited my bed every night? The tyrannos's son, the most likely traitor—you couldn't take a worse lover in their eyes.'

'It's not the same thing at all, they'd think I'd got lucky. You're respected by them—you're *of them*. I'm useful to them, but that's different from respect. Even to them, I'm that non-Athenian freeman who works for the tyrannos.'

'But Nabu, you aren't Athenian, and you are a freeman! You can't expect to be afforded the same rights as a citizen, you're not entitled to them.'

The birds try drowning the silence. Echo holds her breath.

'Nabu, I didn't mean—' Kosmos starts, but Nabu cuts him off, and Echo's impressed by how steady his voice is.

'I may be a foreign freeman. But before that, I am a man. Simply, a man. By the gods, if you don't understand that by now then maybe Harmodios is right, and you really are nothing more than the spoilt son of a tyrannos.'

'Come on, that's not fair—'

'Open your eyes, Kosmos, the world is rotten, and your damn family's the worm at the core. Aristogeiton and Harmodios might have their eye on dethroning your father for the citizenry, but I intend to make an Athens for everyone. Even foreign freemen like me.'

The grass swishes as he strides back to the house.

'Nabu!' Kosmos hisses. 'Hey!'

Nabu doesn't falter.

Kosmos mutters under his breath and kicks poppyheads as he stalks around the fig bush. Echo freezes as he spots her, half-eaten apple in hand and groggy with a hangover.

He pulls back, standing straight for once in his life. 'I suppose you heard all that.'

She nods, but dares not say anything. He's already flown off the handle once this morning and if Nabu's nothing but a foreign freeman, Echo must be lower still.

Kosmos grimaces, shaking his head. He hasn't washed yet, and flops onto the log beside her in a cloud of stale wine. 'Hades, I'm stupid as a ram, aren't I?'

Echo nods, still frozen. 'Maybe two rams.'

He gives her the special glare he reserves for hysterical women. 'It's not a question of affection, it's just politics. Nabu's naïve if he thinks we can walk around like Harmodios and Aristogeiton, it's just not possible.' Kosmos scrunches his face and kicks the pear Nabu threw earlier, sending it over the orchard's tiered edge.

Echo takes a bite of apple to stop herself passing comment. It won't do any good to get involved, but she might not get another opportunity to talk to Kosmos alone about the real Deed, so she stays put.

He watches her eating and takes it as judgement. 'You think it doesn't devastate me that Nabu and I can't be together openly? Of course it does. But we can't delude ourselves. Even if the rebellion succeeds things won't change *that* much.'

Echo bites back the comment that this is only true if Kosmos continues being a spineless elitist git. Instead, she says, 'What if Nabu is incorrect about why I am here? Not for the rebellion, but for something else?'

Kosmos smirks. 'I doubt Nabu would've misunderstood the last Traveller. It must be four years ago now, but they were thick as thieves, and he remembers it like it was yesterday.'

'He misunderstands only by accident,' she says. 'An interpretation problem.'

Kosmos chews a fingernail. 'Go on.'

Echo lowers her voice. 'Nabu said I am brought here to "transform our gods to mud and our mud to gods." What if that is not political, but philosophical?'

'Philosophical?' Kosmos squints at the sunrise. 'I suppose gods to mud and mud to gods sounds a bit like what Nabu was saying to Xenophanes.'

'Exactly. In times to come, this will be named the "divine-mundane duality paradigm." But it will be lost, and so terrible things will happen.'

'Terrible how?' Kosmos asks, eyes sparking with interest.

The Not Here whispers, still enjoying the extra reins the hul gil gave it. For once, Echo lets it through, translating into Hellenic as she goes: '**The seas will rise; the trees will fall; the sun will bake the ground. More people than are alive at this moment will starve to death every day. Creatures will disappear, and the rivers will run dark with poisons. Human beings will be driven to the edge of existence, and there will be no gods to save them. None will escape it, for it will be too late and they will have—will**

have forgotten how to be kind. So, we must found a school of philosophy that preserves this concept of divine-mundane duality, to resuscitate—revive—the world.' The Not Here starts bullying its way into her vision and hearing, and she beats it into submission with the Traveller's Cipher. *Are we not drawn onward . . .*

Kosmos looks at her, genuinely frightened. 'How are you doing that with your voice? It's like the thing you did with the salt prayer last night.'

That's interesting. It must be the Not Here altering her voice, but Kosmos wouldn't necessarily understand that. Best for him to draw his own conclusions. She lets the silence dangle, attempting an air of mystery through her hangover.

'It's like the gods are speaking through you,' he whispers, as if Echo is dangerous.

She balls her fists so Kosmos won't be able to see her fingers shaking. 'If they were, would they permit me to tell?'

'No, I suppose not. Nabu's always said you came from the gods, but I don't think I believed it till now. I mean, why would the gods send a woman?'

'They would send Demeter or Hera. Why not me?'

'You're more like Kassandra.'

'**Kassandra was still right. It is not her fault the men ignored her and died.**'

He frowns at her. 'You know, that voice really is frightening.'

They stare at the mountains, Echo giving Kosmos time to process the ridiculousness of believing an artisan's female assistant over his aristokrat friends. He's never been totally comfortable with the plan to kill Hippias. She gets it. Hippias is his father, and it can be hard to utterly damn someone who's supposed to love you, even when their love is painful. But Kosmos is torn by conflicting familial loyalty and filial vengeance, and perhaps that friction will be enough to sway him.

Kosmos taps his scar. 'Let's say, for a moment, that I believe you. What happens next?'

Not thinking she'd get this far, Echo improvises. 'We would need a school building. Away from town, to be safe and independent. The rebellion goes ahead with or without us, and so we must be at a safe distance.'

'Very wise.' Kosmos gives her something that could be a sneer or smile. 'Funnily enough, I have a farm like that. My father gave it to me when I came of age. It's nothing really, just an old house with a rock-riddled vegetable garden and a handful of barley fields. Couple of slaves, but they're mostly too young to be useful. Same problem with the goats. Can't imagine Xenophanes lying back getting his bunions rubbed in that house.'

'But philosophy happens everywhere,' Echo says. It's as if until now she's been in the dark and someone's just lit a lantern, illuminating the path ahead.

'Perhaps.' He looks pensively at the mountains, then barks laughter, and Echo's trapped in the darkness again. 'Ha! Listen to me, talking as if I'm going to go off and found a school of philosophy. That would be more dangerous than kissing Nabu in public. Well, maybe not. If that really is why you're here, though, you'll have to look for another accomplice. Try Nabu, seems like he's into senseless ideas this morning. Though I can't see that he'll like abandoning the last Traveller's instructions. Or going against Aristogeiton's wishes either.'

Kosmos slaps her on the back as he leaves, and she wants to throw her apple core at him. The solutions are all right in front of her, twirling just out of reach.

Over the ensuing days, Nabu becomes increasingly sullen and fractious, snipping at Echo like a wasp, until she's at her wits' end. Worse, she's getting less sleep than ever, forced onto the stone floor now Nabu's no longer welcome in Kosmos's bed. She's isolated because he isolates, rarely attending the gymnasion or stoa—fearful of bumping into Kosmos, though he'd never admit it. He eschews wine in favour of hot barley water with honey and pennyroyal, and sees his patients with short shrift. So when one evening Khemut comes for her regular cumin and bone-marrow poultice, Nabu rubs the first layer in with uncharacteristic roughness.

'Just because you've had a lover's tiff doesn't mean you can take it out on the rest of us,' she grumbles.

'He's not my lover. You have to be loved to be a lover.'

Khemut winces as Nabu continues massaging her arthritic fingers. 'He irritates me with his whinging too, you know.'

'Yes, and you're always in a foul mood.'

Nabu clicks his fingers for Echo to grind marrow faster.

'I cannot be faster,' she snaps, letting out her frustration while Khemut's around to mediate. 'At least a bad mood suits Khemut. You have a bad mood and become a toad.'

Khemut laughs as Nabu grabs the pestle and mortar from Echo. 'Give me that. I ought to turn you out.'

'And deal with Hippias on your own?' Khemut shakes her head. 'Now who's the lunatic!'

Nabu's venom wilts and he applies the second layer of poultice more carefully.

As Khemut leaves, she cups his cheek and mutters, 'It's his loss, Nabu. You know it is.' Nabu can't meet her gaze, but nods. 'Take it easy on Echo. It's not the boy's fault. You remember what it's like.'

Nabu keeps his eyes on the ground, but at sunset he gives Echo the bed, claiming he'll stay up late reading.

'Are you sure?' she double-checks.

He stares at the leech-jar on his desk, their black knots squiggling in the lamplight. 'Yes, you have it. We should get a second one, really . . .' He turns, examining her like a reflection. How many nights he must have fallen asleep on this very floor, and Batnoam clearly never bought him a bed. Echo cocoons thankfully in the blanket, despite the balmy evening. Irritating as Nabu's been in his anger, this evening's implosion into misery is somehow worse. Still, it presents an opportunity. With Kosmos and Nabu barely talking, Echo's had no chance to turn Kosmos's opinion in favour of the philosophic school. On the other hand, though she's physically around Nabu all the time, he's been in no mood to approach, so the Deed has been languishing. Perhaps this new quiet Nabu will be more open-minded.

She curls her fingers around the blanket. 'Nabu?'

He turns, looking through her, as if gazing at faraway stars. 'Yeah?'

She bites her lip. 'Nothing.' She rolls onto her back, watching the lamplight lap the ceiling, the future's weight roiling in her like unfastened ballast.

When Echo finally reaches the dreamscape, Hazel is almost as unresponsive as Nabu, and she wakes frustrated and tangled in sweaty blankets. However hard Echo tries, she's unable to speak to Hazel the way she did that night with the hul gil. Hazel is likewise mysteriously quiet—perhaps her ability to communicate in dreams is as restricted as Echo's. They've got to find a workaround but, beyond smoking gods-awful hul gil again, Echo's stumped.

She throws her legs out of bed and rubs her face. Across the room, Nabu's fallen asleep in his desk chair, wrapped in a cloak. Echo tiptoes over and watches him, hands on hips. He looks younger asleep. 'What are we going to do with you?' she mutters.

There's a knock at the door and he stirs as she answers it. Khemut stands outside holding a letter, her shoes already dewy and grass-stained from a morning walk. 'From Aristogeiton.'

Echo passes the message to Nabu, who squints at it sleepily, like it's a liver to divine. 'He's requesting a meeting today at the gymnasion. Apparently, he wants to discuss "philosophical matters." Very unlikely. I should've known they'd make me put my face in at some point. You'd better accompany me, Echo. You're useless when it comes to standing up to those men, but I'd rather not walk into the scorpion burrow alone.' He hasn't entirely lost his waspishness then.

Aristogeiton, likewise, brings only one ally to the gymnasion:

Harmodios, who a dozen other young men soon draw into a wrestling ring. Nabu and Aristogeiton hang back on a bench in the colonnade. Echo hovers bedside them, soaking up the shade. She nudges her cheek into the breeze, but it's so meagre it makes no difference. A line of sweat dribbles from her earlobe, pooling at her collarbone, which seems hollower than it used to be. Since the rift with Kosmos, she and Nabu eat with Khemut and the kitchen-hands, or other less well-to-do friends Nabu has in the potters and sculptors' quarter, and the meals aren't as filling.

Across the yard, Harmodios thwacks his opponent to the dirt, ending their match. Kosmos emerges from the opposite side of the colonnade, strolling to the wrestlers, and Nabu inhales sharply. Kosmos throws his hand in for the next round and the assembled men whoop and catcall: The plot to usurp the tyrannos may be secret, but Hipparchos's abuse of Harmodios's sister is not, and the rivalry is palpable. Harmodios smirks, squaring off, and taunts Kosmos with jeers too low to hear.

'If the games were happening,' Aristogeiton murmurs, 'Harmodios would be the sure winner.'

A fortnight ago, Nabu might have defended Kosmos's chances; now he merely grunts assent. Still, he glances pointedly at the attendants around them. Aristogeiton's own serving boy, distinguishable by his blue tunic, is not five feet away. 'Careful, the walls have ears.'

Echo stares at the white tiles marking the wrestling ring's edge, ignoring the heat radiating off the men's naked bodies. Mercifully, Nabu always cites her Celtic heritage to excuse her not being naked in the gym like all the other freemen. Even so, she can't get used to the liberty with which Athenians wield nudity, partly because she can't take off her own clothes and relax into the sweltering, oil-slick slouch of it all, but mostly because it's another thing that's just too different from the Not Here.

'My slaves are reliable, and there are events we must discuss. First, we hear that you and Kosmos have fallen out. Then, you both stop coming to the stoa.'

Nabu stares harder at the fight. 'Kosmos hasn't been to the stoa either?'

Echo catches Aristogeiton's look of exasperation. 'You're not even keeping an eye on him?'

'He's his own man, there's nothing I can do.' Kosmos takes a hit and Nabu looks away, focusing on a bee drinking from a puddle of spilt water.

'You don't worry he might have turned against us?'

Nabu shakes his head. 'He might have pulled away, but he wouldn't endanger our lives.'

'Can you be sure of that?'

The bee flies away, Nabu following its path. 'We can trust how much he hates his uncle and father.' Nabu taps the skin just above his lip with a raised brow. 'I've lived in that household for years. Believe me, we have nothing to fear.'

Aristogeiton leans on his knees, lowering his voice. Sweat glistens on his back. 'No matter. If it all goes wrong, yours will be the first hemlock cup. So easy to frame: the Lydian healer living in the tyrannos's house, in the employ of the Persian kings, twisting the aristokracy against our gracious leader . . .'

'Are you threatening me?' Nabu doesn't move, but the muscles in his shoulders harden and Echo's heart is suddenly in her throat.

Aristogeiton smiles. 'Of course not. I'm just telling you something you already know.'

In the wrestling ring, Harmodios slams his knee into Kosmos's belly, then spins out of range. The gaggle of observers nod and clap, a communal referee. Still winded, Kosmos lunges, but Harmodios leaps over him, landing on his back but righting himself in time to grapple Kosmos out of the circle. Glowing with victory, Harmodios gives Kosmos a handshake, but uses it to whisper something that makes Kosmos's eyes widen.

Aristogeiton stands, dislodging the beads of sweat on his skin. 'You brought Kosmos in, Nabu, you take responsibility for ensuring he doesn't talk.'

Again, Nabu nods silently, but his teeth clench and temples pulse as he watches Aristogeiton stalk to the baths.

Once the other men have cleared the colonnade, Echo sits on the bench. 'You are shaking. Are you OK?'

Nabu puts his head in his hands, fingers gripping his veil of curly hair. 'They offer friendship so freely, but as soon as it doesn't suit them—as soon as their connection to me might become *shameful . . .*' He trails off. 'We'll be lucky if Athens doesn't become a seething mob with this attitude to leadership. But we can't leave Hippias and Hipparchos in power.'

Echo sees her chance. 'What if we *should* leave them to fight? The previous Traveller maybe was wrong. What if there is something different we are destined for?'

Nabu leans back, arms folded, and watches a group of discus players. 'No, he was adamant. Gods to mud and mud to gods.'

'The phrase is open to interpretation.'

'You seem determined to hold this conversation, so let's have it out.' He takes a steadying breath. 'What's your interpretation?'

'It is as you argued with Xenophanes the other night—'

'Can we do this without Xenophanes?'

Echo tunes into the Not Here. 'Heraclitus?'

'That impenetrable upstart from Ephesus? Xenophanes is better!'

'You are determined not to listen.'

'Fine, go on. Heraclitus.'

The Not Here gapes, swamping Echo in information to sift and translate. '**The metaphysics of Heraclitus and Xenophanes are similar: Both are monists and believe the universe comes from a divine "goodness." But Heraclitus is better at integrating the conflicting nature of the world. This is what you argued about with Xenophanes the other night. Heraclitus agrees with you, he says the balance of the world is in its duality.**'

Nabu looks at her sidelong. 'I was wondering when you'd use the

Traveller's voice again. Anyone would think you'd been hanging out at the stoa without me.'

'When would I have time for that!' She's irritated that the voice that worked some magic on Kosmos has no bearing on Nabu, but then, he's dealt with a Traveller before. 'Heraclitus is obsessed with opposites: hot and cold; light and dark; mortal and immortal . . . he can rest with these conflicts as Xenophanes cannot, but only if they are in balance. He says, **in differing, the world agrees with itself—a back-turning harmony, like that of a bow and lyre**.'

'I've never read such assertions in his work.'

Echo leans in, whispering. 'Well perhaps he has not written it yet. It is the balancing of these opposites that he believes leads to harmony. A ship moves because of the tension between wind and sail. Too little and the boat is becalmed, too much and it is wrecked.'

'It's the same with crops,' Nabu says, 'a tension between sun and rain, too much of either and they're drowned or baked.'

'Exactly. **But in the times that come, this balance will be lost. Natural will be eclipsed by unnatural; nonhuman by human; co-existence by consumption. Until nothing is left. We must preserve this balance by founding a philosophical school.**'

'A school?' Nabu snorts despite the Traveller's voice. 'Don't be ridiculous. Thought without action never changed anything.'

'But founding a school—engagement, discussion—those *are* actions. Actions that lead to more actions. There are many ways to make change.'

'It's not enough.' Nabu frowns. 'The only way to make lasting change is to rebalance the dynamics of power. Permanently.'

Conscious of an attendant passing with a stack of clean towels, Echo whispers. 'Harmodios and Aristogeiton do not want a true balance of power, only to make power available to a select few.'

'But *I* don't. I want to remake Athens, and I can use them to do that; I can make them part of something beyond their own ends.' Nabu stands, wrapping his towel around his waist. 'Don't think I take this lightly, Echo. I know firsthand the impacts of uprising. I lost my own father to it. If I thought there was another way, I would take it.'

She slumps. 'And Kosmos?'

Nabu starts. She hasn't mentioned his name since their argument. 'What of Kosmos?'

'You believe he will not talk?'

'He's got no spine to talk. Besides, with him out of sight is out of mind.' Nabu glowers. 'Man's got a real blind spot, he just can't see what's right in front of him. I can't explain, it's like . . . like the eyes of his soul are broken.'

'More than some, less than others,' Echo replies. Nabu shoots her a look and she throws her hands in the air. 'Yes, I know your meaning. I see these things also.'

Nabu shakes his head. 'Perhaps you want to, Echo, but your eyes are trained for another place entirely. The gods alone know what you see.'

He turns, ready to leave, and she trails after him. The one thing she can't see right now is how on earth to complete the Deed.

The Panathenaic Games roll around faster than Echo wants, and with every passing day her dread ripens. She tries talking to Hazel about it, but her voice keeps getting lost in the dreamscape, and the Forward Traveller just can't understand how trapped she is here.

To attend the Games, Nabu lets Echo borrow a red tunic with bronze wire sewn into the neckline, and dots myrtle oil on her neck and wrists. She wonders why they're bothering given the chaos about to be unleashed, but it's the principle: If they're to wield knives, Nabu says, they should at least look respectable doing it. She tries neatening her shorn hair in the reflection of the atrium pool, but it persists in sprouting around her headband.

'Leave it,' Nabu says. 'You're presentable enough.'

The crowds press in as they amble along the Sacred Way, midway through the pack of the tyrannos's household. The road slopes upwards, hairpin turns crammed with men and women, all pampered and preened as if the gods themselves are coming to visit—which in Athenian eyes they are. Echo struggles to believe in any gods, repressing smirks when Khemut sacrifices mice to the hearthside statue of Hestia, and yawning behind locked teeth when Hippias or Hipparchos gather them all to sprinkle wine for the household gods in the atrium. Nabu has a collection of divine statuettes too, tucked into an alcove in his room, some animal-headed, others winged, none of them Hellenic, but gods nonetheless. Even here on the Sacred Way, walking up to the gods' own temporary homes, a dangerous laugh bubbles inside Echo. Her hubris is an arrogance from the Not Here, and she keeps her head down, avoiding eye contact.

As they reach the hilltop the crowd thins, and the gold around the citizens' wrists and necks multiplies. The air grows thick as heavy perfumes fight with the human scents of sweltering humidity. She spots faces she recognises: Other plotters whose names she hasn't caught; Harmodios with his family, the sister Hipparchos ruined hidden behind a veil; Aristogeiton, one eye on Hippias, the other on Harmodios, with no time for the wife on his arm; and Leaina, snuck into the aristokracy by Aristogeiton and dressed in yards of dancing buttercup-yellow linen. She catches Echo's eye and blows her a kiss. Echo smiles back. In Athens, there are few chances for a woman to meet her own acquaintances, especially when the men that might bring them together frequent different circles, so they haven't spoken since the Xenophanes symposium, restricted to distanced waves. In high spirits, Leaina sticks her tongue out and Echo returns the gesture, but the Not Here chants: **her tongue is her tongue is her—**

A bellowing bull parts the throng, whose cheerful hollers increase. The bull is laced in garlands of wildflowers: poppies, cornflowers, daisies, thyme. Gladioli coat its horns and priestesses fling dianthus petals at its feet. A summer squall blows in from the coast, disturbing the confetti and hurling dove-grey clouds across the otherwise blue sky. The wind lifts sweat from Echo's cheeks as it starts to spit.

Under the shadow of the Acropolis gate, she spots Kosmos shuffling into line beside his family, nodding sombrely to his uncle and hugging his father. Hippias tweaks the band in Kosmos's hair, almost but not quite long enough to braid yet, and whispers something in his ear. They part from the embrace with that Peisistratid laugh which sounds like pickaxes on marble, and look up into the rain.

In the crowd, Aristogeiton spots this. He exchanges quick words with Harmodios, then both men start towards the tyrannos, leaving Leaina and their families behind.

'Echo, stop dallying.' Nabu pulls her arm, trying to draw her to the other household members.

'No, something is not right,' she says.

Nabu follows her gaze to Harmodios and Aristogeiton's advance. 'They can't be moving already,' he murmurs. 'Not in all these crowds. They're not meant to until after the sacrifice.'

The Not Here pushes against Echo's gritted teeth: **her tongue is her tongue is tyrannicides—**

Harmodios and Aristogeiton emerge from the crowd, striding towards the Peisistratids. Knowledge crashes into Echo from the Not Here vortex: They're going to screw it up. Seeing Kosmos laughing with Hippias, they've assumed he's switched sides, and they're moving too early.

They draw daggers from the folds of their robes, raindrops beating the iron blades. *Plink. Plinkplink.* Echo only hears it because she's looking for the sound. Kosmos doesn't. He's not smart enough to keep an ear out. He's too near his father, he'll get caught in the fray—**but Kosmos doesn't die now. This isn't his time. Hippias only has five sons in the history books. No sixth. No youngest brat who loved philosophy.** The Not Here laughs at her attempts to remember what happened to the sixth son. If he died here, at the

Acropolis, someone would've written about it, but they didn't, which means he can't die. But the tyrannicides are getting closer, and Kosmos still hasn't seen them, too busy looking up at the gods-damn rain and laughing. Any second now he will though, he has to, because this isn't when he dies—but they're so close, their blades rising. He's not going to notice.

Echo catches her reflection in a forming puddle. It is her, but as a child, pink with sunburn and startled. A quirk of time travel. That child version of herself is unreachable; her home, family, school all a blank slate. Echo gave up all those memories to be here. She knows why, intellectually, but she can't *feel* the reasons. She's an unlit hearth, laid and ready to perform the Deed, but with no spark of motivation. What drives that girl in the puddle? Echo needs to act for her, and whatever sets her aflame.

She looks up, everything moving slowly, glistening with rain. The Deed needs Kosmos; needs that farm he talked about turning into the philosophical school; needs his connections; needs him alive.

She lunges, grabbing Kosmos and yanking him sideways.

He stumbles as the tyrannicides' knives descend, missing him by a thread.

Hipparchos's bodyguards leap to action; guards, attackers, and tyrannos's brother fall in a tangle of arms, legs, blades, and linen, slipping on the wet marble. The crowd pulls back, roaring in fear and shock.

Kosmos struggles against Echo's grip, squealing, but she drags him away from the fray, fingers clawing his perfumed hair and oiled skin.

'**No!**' She grabs his cheeks as the Traveller's voice waterfalls out of her. '**You do not die now. Stop struggling!**'

Then Hanno's pulling her off Kosmos as if she weighs nothing, spinning her round, scowling in her face with a blade at her throat.

She throws her hands up. 'Stop, Hanno! I did not hurt him!'

Only a couple of steps behind her, Nabu inserts himself between them, pushing Hanno back until his blade rests against Nabu's chest instead. 'The boy was getting him out of the way, Hanno!'

Echo holds her breath as Hanno's blade quivers. He looks between them, while behind him Absalon defends Kosmos from other attackers like a hen guarding a chick.

'Stop, Hanno!' Kosmos shouts. 'Echo really wasn't trying to hurt me.'

Hanno's blade wavers, but something he spots over Echo's shoulder makes him pull the sword back and shout, 'Get down!'

She ducks, pulling Nabu with her, as a conspirator's sword sweeps through the air where her head was just a moment ago.

Hanno must have concluded that if they're being attacked by the conspirators, they're not in league with them, because he leaps to their defence in the fray. Kosmos grabs Echo and Nabu, hauling them closer as Hanno and Absalon's swords enclose them in a nest of flashing blades.

The entire thing takes no more than a hundred heartbeats, but beyond them the Sacred Way is already a morass of blood, bodies, and weapons. Echo hadn't realised how many plotters there were, their blades numerous as fish scales. Hipparchos, the first victim, lies gasping and retching, his white robes blotted with blood. There's nothing to be done for him. Echo's seen enough wounded farmers by now to tell that even from this distance. The furious, vengeful part of her says good riddance; the objective, lawful citizen says she could have pushed him out of the way at the same time as she did Kosmos. She just didn't want to.

'They tried to attack us!' Nabu says over the commotion.

'They think Kosmos betrays them,' Echo replies. 'Then they saw me keep him safe and you defend me, and so they think we have all turned.'

'Idiots. They moved far too early.' Nabu watches the skirmish. He murmurs a diatribe in Lydian, but she gets the picture: Despite Hipparchos's assassination, the fight's tide is turning against the conspirators. Harmodios has collapsed against a statue base, guts spilling through his hands. Because he and Aristogeiton started prematurely, the crowds were too dense for them to get a clear hit at the tyrannos, and now Hippias stands at the Acropolis gate, protected by guards three deep.

Shaking with fury and shock, Nabu is transfixed by the rivulets of Harmodios's blood threading the pavement, so Echo looks to Kosmos. He gazes at her, eyes of a boy embossed in a man's face, and says, 'We have to protect ourselves.'

It's a dirty decision, but Kosmos is right. The tyrannicide was always going to go this way; her Deed is not this, and she needs to keep that in sight. Hating herself, she grasps Nabu's shoulder. 'Nabu. Look at me. It is over. We are defeated.'

He shakes his head. 'No. We can still pull it back.'

She grips his shoulder harder, disgusted at encouraging their defection, but he's her Caretaker, and the Deed needs him. She needs him. 'We are useless if we are dead. Now, we must preserve ourselves. We are healers. We are going to heal.'

Nabu exhales like his spirit's leaving his body. 'Just this battle.' He looks to Kosmos, and for a moment their weird situation unites them again. 'Who must we heal?'

'My uncle?' Kosmos asks, with a look like he might gag.

Echo looks at Hipparchos's wriggling, blood-soaked body.

'Nothing to be done for him,' Nabu replies.

'Exactly,' Echo says, not meeting either of their gazes. Technically, they won't contribute anything to either side, but they'll perform an act that will hold them out of Hippias's suspicion, at least for now.

Kosmos stands, indicating to Hanno and Absalon that they need to make their way to his uncle. Darting between blades and over fallen bodies, they reach Hipparchos's side, and Nabu guides Echo and Kosmos's hands over the injuries. 'Push here, harder, we want to stop the bleeding.' The healer in him takes over: A patient is a patient.

Echo's fingers slide over the wound in Hipparchos's tree-trunk thigh—a smooth, deep incision, dug into a major artery and pouring hot blood. It doesn't matter that she's trying to save this hateful man rather than idealistic Harmodios, either would be a hopeless exercise. Hipparchos jitters from blood loss, gulping like a lamprey out of water. She performs the act of healing convincingly enough to save her skin but, remembering the rattling latch and Kosmos's scarred lip, she relaxes the pressure on the wound, letting blood seep through her fingers. It soaks the rain-drenched pavement like cochineal around a lady's wash bowl. She's not killing him. He's already dead. She's just making sure she doesn't accidentally save him.

Around them, the fight increases, but Hanno and Absalon cover them, and most combatants are too concerned with the living's attacks to notice the dying at their feet. Echo hunches over Hipparchos, trying to disappear as raindrops drum her back. Nabu tears strips off his cloak to use as sutures, but ties them just a little too loose to work.

Slowly, the fight's thumps and slashes become less regular. Aristogeiton bellows like a minotaur as Hipparchos's one remaining bodyguard restrains him. Harmodios clutches his stomach, choking on blood, his whimpers inaudible under the rainfall. Echo watches his lips moving. He's calling his sister. Rain drips into Echo's eyes and down her cheeks, so she can't tell if she's also crying with fear. Under her hands, Hipparchos stills, rain falling on his staring eyes.

Hippias approaches, footsteps heavy from a wound in his calf, gaze like lightning.

It's all over—and yet, it has only just begun.

11

Anna

LONDON, 2020

Day fifty-three. Boredom is worst on the weekend, because I can't even pretend there's anything I have to do, and my heart's only half engaged in Lockdown Project Number Two Hundred And Sixty: repainting my Rapanui T-shirt with the last of my acrylics. This had better work. Mum finally got my T-shirt off me to wash it, but she did it too hot and now it says 'no hope' instead of 'know hope'. It wasn't cheap either. I'm absolutely fuming.

I scroll TikTok while it's drying. Mum reckons TikTok's just Instagram all over again, but it's not because the algorithms are completely different. Mum won't let me post photos or videos of myself, so my followings are all rubbish. She knows when I do, even though I've got private accounts. I think she might follow me under a pseudonym or something? I can't be bothered to catch her, it's way too much effort.

There's not much going on, just the same old dance videos and how-tos. I switch to Instagram. I'm looking for glow-up stuff, but if I find anything about Julian's march that would be interesting too, I guess. Maddie messaged me this morning: *wish u wer here xoxo* She attached a selfie of her masked up with her placard. She's done her eyes all smoky and looks way older than she is. It's plastic-based makeup for sure. Sell-out. Her big brother's in the background, clearly scowling despite his mask, and I reckon her parents must've sent him with her for safety. Haven't heard anything since.

She's just posted a story though: five segments, mostly shaky-cam ten-second videos of the march and lots of shouting. It looks like there's only about ten people there, which makes me sad. Weird stuff's been making me sad since Mum and I screamed at the river on Thursday. My throat still feels a bit raw from it, but it was totally worth it. River-shouting should be compulsory, like science.

Maddie's last story reel is a still shot of her and Julian, definitely not socially distanced, with their arms around each other's shoulders. She's added text: *Fightin 4 the planet wiv this gr8 boi. #noplanetb #activistlife* I feel sick. Like hell she's an activist, not with makeup like that. Anyway, Julian's my crush, she can't go after him, she's my mate and she wouldn't do that. I replay the story. Maybe it's nothing, just a friendly hug. Julian's the huggy type, a real hippy. It's hard to tell with their masks on, but I think they both seem too happy for it to be a friend thing. It's all Mum's fault, if I were there maybe Julian would have his arm around me instead. The sick feeling grows, like I've eaten a whole giant Toblerone at once. Not that I eat them anymore now I'm vegan, but that's what it feels like.

There's nothing for this situation except Lady Gaga. Jumping on the bed and shouting along really helps.

Mum opens the door without knocking.

'Mum, oh my God, haven't you ever heard of privacy?'

Mum turns the volume down on my Bluetooth speaker. 'Haven't you ever heard of respecting the neighbours?'

'It's not like they're not loud. The Hiscocks' new baby was screaming all night downstairs. And Donny has taken up the saxophone. The saxophone! During lockdown! So rude.'

'Yeah, well don't encourage him.' She leans against the doorframe, headphones round her neck. 'You been crying?'

'No.' Not quite.

She pretends to believe me. 'Boy trouble?'

'*No.*'

She nods. 'Bit cooler today, isn't it?'

'I guess.' It's not. It's still boiling.

'Your T-shirt looks better.' She gestures to where it's drying on the floor.

'No thanks to you.'

'You know I didn't mean to,' she says.

'You shouldn't be washing that hot anyway. It wastes energy.'

To her credit she doesn't rise to it, just does another slow nod. She's got me in that stare like she knows I need a hug but I'm still too cross to take it. I hate when she's right. Not that she is this time. I don't need a hug, I'm fine.

'Mum.' I sit on the edge of the bed.

'Yeah?'

'Do you think I'm pretty?'

She comes and sits next to me. 'I think you're the prettiest girl in the world!'

'You're just saying that.'

'I am not, you're going to be a stunner when you grow up!' She puts an arm around me, smelling comfortingly of last night's garlicky stir-fry and floral antidandruff shampoo.

'But I need to be a stunner now.'

Mum sighs. 'What's Julian done?'

I show her Maddie's photo. 'Look, there's something between them, right?'

Mum frowns at the screen. 'Who's she even talking to on this app?'

'Oh, she's got loads of followers. She's becoming kind of an influencer actually.'

'Two hundred followers does not an influencer make.' Mum's frown deepens. 'Try not to think about it too much, honey. It might be nothing.'

'What if it isn't?'

'Then Julian's an idiot to pass you up.' She scruffles my hair and gets up to leave. 'If you want to listen to loud music, keep it on the headphones, alright?'

After she's gone, I look at Maddie's story again. *gr8 boi.* Bet I can get makeup as good as that with my homemade stuff. I've got the eyeliner right now, the secret is vitamin E oil. But Maddie's done something with her hair too, it's all curly and intentionally windswept. I think Mum's got some rollers I can use. I don't want to disturb her again because if she's working on the weekend that means she's stressed about a deadline and seriously needs to concentrate. She won't mind if I just nip into her room and fetch the curlers; I borrow her stuff all the time, though I'm not sure she definitely knows about it. She probably does, she knows everything, most of the time before it's happened, it's really annoying. Anyway, she comes into my room whenever she likes, and without knocking.

I tiptoe down the corridor. Mum's bedroom door squeaks a bit, but it'll be OK cause she's coding hard today for a deadline on Monday, and has her noise-cancelling headphones on. My music must actually have been quite loud if she heard it through them.

Mum's room smells of her special-occasions perfume with the poppy on the bottle and the washing drying in one corner. Three books about AI are folded into the unmade sheets and the wardrobe door stands slightly ajar. That's one good thing about Mum: She never really bothers me about being tidy or doing chores cause she's rubbish at them herself.

I sneak to the wardrobe and open it. Mum doesn't have many clothes. She's all about 'coder chic,' which is shorthand for oversized men's shirts, jeans, and knock-off trainers. Sometimes it's like she's the teenager. Honestly, working at home isn't good for her; if she had to go out she'd care more about how she looks. It's still a nightmare finding anything in here though, because Mum doesn't particularly believe in folding or coat hangers. I basically have to engage in an archaeological mission to unearth the curlers.

Finally, I find them underneath a pair of squashed dusty heels.

At least it's evidence Mum had a life once. Beneath the curlers is a collaged box. I've never seen it before. Judging from the peeling glue it must be from when Mum was a kid. I don't know what she looked like when she was little—she's got photos of grandma and grandpa around, but none of her. None of Dad either. Maybe this is where she's hiding them. I pull it out from the tangle of backpack straps and shoelaces with a grim puff of dust. In the sunlight, the collage is pressed flowers, stuck over an old shoebox in layers and layers. Loopy gold glitter-writing on the lid says, *HOPE BOX. TOP SECRET. NO LOOKING.* The back of my neck prickles. I probably shouldn't look in here, but I really would love to see a photo of Dad.

Careful in case any of the flowers rip off, I open the lid, and it makes a noise like breezes passing through the allotments. Inside, it smells like the compost we were making at school in the wildlife garden. Maddie thinks it stinks, but I don't mind it. It's like the football pitch after the rain when it's all muddy and green and alive. More evidence she's a faker.

There's no photos in the box though. It's just junk really: shards from a broken mirror, a cracked wristwatch, and broken bits of a pot (probably Archaic Greek, I've picked up enough off Mum's posters to know that). Some hope box. In amongst the health-and-safety nightmare of broken glass and pottery is a notebook—battered and spiral-bound, nothing special. It has a tea-stain on it. I pick it out, still hoping for some photos, but it's nothing like that. It's in Mum's handwriting, but it can't be as old as the box because it's neat grown-up writing. Really settled, not like mine, which is still changing every few months. I heard you can tell a lot about someone from their writing, and I want mine to only say good things about me, so I keep altering it. I listen out, but there's just silence from Mum's study, so I start reading.

I shouldn't be writing this down. But I can't keep it in. Anna's only newborn and cries all the time, but her wails are so furi-

ous, it's as if she knows. And because I'm the only one around to calm and feed her, I'm not sleeping much, so I'm beginning to wonder if I hallucinated the whole thing. Honestly, I can see why they use sleep deprivation as a torture method. It's enough to send you over the edge. I could've made it all up. But then there's Anna, reminding me with those big, familiar eyes. It's real. It really happened. How else do you explain her?

My stomach knots. Mum's always told me Dad died before I even turned one, at work at the British Museum. 'Just keeled over in the archive. A heart attack, they happen sometimes to young men, they call them widowmakers.' But if Mum was the only one around when I was just born that can't be true. I close the book. I don't think I want to know what went on. Whatever Mum thinks she hallucinated probably really happened, and if she hasn't told me yet, it's probably cause she doesn't think I'm old enough. Maybe Dad wasn't a nice guy, maybe that's why he isn't around. Do I want to find that out from a journal? Shouldn't I wait for Mum to tell me?

Normally, I'd text Maddie with a problem like this, but she's not being a great friend right now and she's probably too busy with the march to notice. I flick through the notebook. It's pages and pages. Whatever Mum's hiding, it's pretty big—big enough to fill a whole notebook. She might never tell me, and I might never have another opportunity to get into this box—especially if she notices I've been snooping. I open the notebook again, shaking.

It's like reality's a bubble, and if I stare at it too long it'll burst. But I have to put what happened down somewhere—like katharsis. I might actually have lost it. Might have! Must have. I can't take this to a therapist. Any therapist worth their salt would have me committed—and then what would Anna do? Maybe I should be locked up. Or put on some kind of medication. But when I think about it, my heart beats like a jackhammer and my hands get all pins-and-needly, and I have the sensation like I'm trying to clamp my own head by denying it. It really happened. I really was a Traveller. Still am. Because, I guess, there's a thread stretching between the me that made the catopthura, piercing through the present me, and tugging all the way into that distant future where I was. I can't deny it: I was, am, and will always be a time traveller.

'You are kidding me.' I bite my lip and look at the door, momentarily scared Mum might've heard me.

I was, am, and will always be a time traveller.

This can't be real, it's got to be a rubbish novel she wrote and rightly put in a drawer. I reread it. It can't be a novel because she mentions me. But it also can't be real. My palms sweat. Is Mum crazy? She's never acted insane—I mean she's got crazy, but she's never done anything *actually* mad. Never acted truly out-of-the-ordinary, even if her obsession with online safety is way out of proportion. She did get pretty upset down by the river the other day. But surely I'd know if Mum was crazy? Yeah. I would. I'd know.

I look in the box again, at the mirror shards. But what if I'm crazy too? What if the-face-that-isn't-my-face that I see in the mirror is a hallucination? Like a *bad* one that's actually a problem. As if called into existence by my thinking about it, the face appears again. It meets my eyes this time, for a long moment, as if the-face-that-isn't-my-face can see me too. It's long enough for me to realise the reflection looks a lot like Mum. Really almost just like her, but with shorter hair. Maybe it *is* Mum. Maybe . . . Maybe she really *is* a time traveller. That sounds ginormously stupid even in my head.

There's a noise like rain and crowds in here, but it's just blue skies and empty streets outside. The sound is real though, the hubbub of so many people clustered together enough to make my eyes swim all over again. I miss people so much—not a far-off group in a park, but crowds at a street party, or all of us singing hymns in assembly.

Then the-face-that-isn't-my-face-Mum-in-the-mirror looks away and vanishes.

The hall clock strikes four. Real Mum will finish her pomodoro soon and emerge for a snack. I put everything back, exactly as I found it, curlers and all.

Everything except the notebook, which I tuck under my T-shirt and sneak back to my room. I don't know who's crazy here, but I'm going to find out.

12

Echo

ATHENS, 514 BCE

Withdrawing his dagger from the last assassin, Hippias signals for a trumpet blast. His leather-clad guards regroup before the Acropolis gate, their spears seeming to almost scrape the clouds. Hanno and Absalon draw closer to Kosmos, panting from the fight. The crowd of citizens tried to flee when the fighting erupted, but they were too densely packed and bottlenecked, and now they cling to each other in knots, pressing as far from the violence as possible. Hippias surveys them, raising his hands and silencing their whimpers.

'The games cannot open under bloodshed. Citizens of Athens, return to your homes.' His voice is steady, tempered by battlefields, and the crowd edges down the hill with whispers and backward glances.

Alone with the captured rebels, Nabu, Kosmos, and the tyrannos and his men, it's quiet enough that even with the diminishing rain Echo can hear the sea crashing on the shore a league away. Hipparchos's blood has oozed from red to brown to viscous black. How long did the fight last? Ten minutes? Fifteen?

Hippias approaches his brother's corpse, placing a hand on Kosmos's shoulders. 'Get up. There's nothing left to do.'

Kosmos starts, eyes wide like he's smoked bad hul gil. His hands remain stuck to his uncle's wounds.

'I said, let go,' Hippias repeats, moving on.

Face wooden, Kosmos pulls back. Clearly death—the realm of women, healers, and soldiers—doesn't look as he imagined.

Echo follows his lead, her hands sucking away from the clots. The adrenaline that's kept her going drains, and her legs only just hold her. In the brawl, the sacrificial bull broke free, and it clomps among the dead shedding garland petals, while the rain muddles scattered flowers and tangled corpses. Echo sways, breathing copper and nectar. So many enslaved people dead for a fight between aristokrats.

Behind her, Aristogeiton whimpers, separated from the other captives and kneeling between two guards as Hippias inspects his split lip and bruised eye. The tyrannos smiles. 'It would be you. Always such pretentions. And yet, here I am still.'

A new shot of adrenaline jolts Echo: Where's Leaina? Fearful of drawing attention to herself, she scans the corpses, but only spots two household guards and a serving boy with a knife through his eye. The boy wasn't even armed.

Feeling lightheaded, she turns to the captives behind Aristogeiton. Please, please, don't let Leaina be there. **And her tongue her tongue her tongue is—**

Echo's breath evaporates: There's Leaina, sandwiched between two would-be usurpers. Her bright yellow dress has been torn and her hair is coming loose from its needles. In the line of aristokratic, politically-scheming men, she's the only woman and worker; the only one who perhaps didn't even know about the plot. She's only there because Aristogeiton adored her so publicly. Leaina's eyes lock on Echo's, and Echo forces herself to hold her gaze, trying to silently communicate that it's not how it looks, she's not with the tyrannos, not a traitor. But she's still drenched in Hipparchos's blood, and Kosmos and Nabu are laying out the horrible man's limbs, readying the tyrannos's brother for his last journey home. Leaina's eyes brim and she looks away, a tiny movement of her delicate neck. Nabu, Kosmos, and the Deed are safe for now, but Echo's insides turn as she realises Leaina will never be safe again.

Hippias's guards drag the captives to the Peisistratid house, led by the vengeful tyrannos. He entrusts Nabu, Kosmos, and Echo with Hipparchos's body, leaving them behind to await the bier. Hanno, Absalon, and Nabu pace the battle site, identifying the bodies of household members and laying them out for collection. Echo tries helping, but she's too in shock to think straight, and too weak to lift the dead, so Nabu sends her to sit beside Kosmos.

Alone by his uncle's cooling corpse, Kosmos sighs shakily. 'We're not suspects, it seems.'

'They have not started to interrogate yet,' Echo replies. Kosmos stares at Hipparchos's body like he's waiting for it to come back to life. 'Are you alright?'

When he doesn't respond, she puts a hand on his knee. Surprisingly, he doesn't shrug it off. 'Kosmos?'

He looks at her with distant eyes. Someone else once looked at Echo like that. **Shock; PTSD; it's OK, you're safe; in to four out to; would you like me to read to you—**

'I'm not naïve,' Kosmos whispers, quiet as the rain. 'I've seen corpses before. My mother, of course, but I was too little to remember, and it was different because she was sick, it wasn't—' He breaks off, examining the grooves of dried blood on his palms. 'I was so frightened of him when he was alive. Echo, when I had my hands on his wounds, I was praying he wouldn't survive. I—I didn't push as hard as I could have.'

'He would have bled out anyway. He was wounded many places.' For once, Echo doesn't have to lie.

'I still don't feel right about it.' Kosmos breathes shallowly, like a little rabbit, the shock making him delicate and open. 'Thing is, I thought . . . I've always imagined that if he died, I'd be less afraid of him. But here he is, look at him, and I'm still terrified.' He clutches Echo's hand. 'I keep waiting for him to breathe. It's impossible he's not breathing.'

'He will not breathe. You are safe.'

A tear draws a line in the dirt on Kosmos's cheek. 'Am I? I've never felt less safe.'

Echo's glad, then, that she didn't knock Hipparchos out of the tyrannicides' way, and a latch rattles in her memory. Thank the gods Nabu installed that lock. She leans in. 'Can I tell you a secret?'

Kosmos laughs and another tear drops. 'You contain even more?'

'I also did not push hard enough.'

Kosmos nods silently, retracting his hand. His next breath is steadier. 'You promise he won't breathe?'

'I promise,' she says.

'You knew they were coming for me, didn't you?'

'Yes.'

'You pushed me out of the way?' He phrases the question as if he'd rather say, 'Why did you push me out of the way?' looking at her like a lost boy again.

'Yes, I did.'

'Thank you.'

'That is alright,' she says, as the Not Here mutters. **He's not in the history books; no lacuna in the records; Hippias didn't have a sixth son—**

Hanno and Absalon have wandered out of earshot, but across the Sacred Way, Nabu reaches Harmodios's body. He hides the young man's spilled guts in the folds of his himation. 'We should send for someone to collect him.'

'Should we?' Kosmos says. 'No, don't look at me like that, think about it. He's a conspirator and Aristogeiton's lover. It won't be long before my father identifies them as the ringleaders. If we show him any mercy, it will implicate us.'

Nabu scowls. 'What should I do then, just leave his body here?'

Kosmos shrugs.

Nabu gapes. 'He was your friend, Kosmos, and you'd abandon him to wander as a ghost.'

'As if you know so much about friendship,' Kosmos retorts. 'You knew I'd become one of their targets, didn't you?'

'I had no idea. All I knew was they were worried you'd betray us, but I told them no, Kosmos would never do that. Then you went and did it anyway!'

'No, I didn't!' Kosmos shouts, voice breaking like he's going to cry again. He breathes heavily, making an ameliorating gesture to Hanno and Absalon, who straightened in alarm when they heard the shout. Much quieter, Kosmos repeats, 'I did not betray you.'

'And I didn't know they would come for you.'

Yet Echo senses that whatever brought them back together in the skirmish has broken again. Even if neither of them actually betrayed the other, they still assumed each other capable of betrayal, and that's a bad sign.

Nabu stalks away from Harmodios's body. Echo avoids his gaze, unwilling to admit they're putting their own safety before a friend; but Kosmos is right, if they show even the slightest sympathy for the conspirators, they'll become suspects as well.

Two sodden priestesses skulk up the hill to retrieve the bull, and the guards with the bier aren't far behind. Nabu takes a last glance at Harmodios as they leave.

'Somebody will come,' Echo says, touching his arm.

He shakes her off, snarling. 'Go to the crows, Echo. You know the dogs will get to him before his self-preserving aristokratic family does.'

She closes her mouth. Of all of them, he must be feeling the charade of their switching sides the worst. If her stomach's turning, his must be doing somersaults, but it was necessary to preserve any chance of completing the Deed. Kosmos and Nabu are alive and uncaptured, able to set up a philosophical school that no errand boy like Echo could alone. The challenge now is keeping them unharmed, because Hippias is about to become far more terrible. Hipparchos's body jolts as one of the bier carriers trips in a pothole and rights himself. Echo needs to talk to the Forward Traveller, and communicate with her enough to figure out their next steps, but she can't imagine ever sleeping again.

The streets are deserted and the windows shuttered, but doors slam and footsteps slap in parallel alleyways, as if everywhere they pass through has only just been cleared. Rumour precedes them—and no wonder, for they hear the tyrannos's house long before they reach it. Animal howls snake through the streets, shaking the branches of the fruit trees. The cry comes again and, with a gag, Echo realises it's not animal, but human. What can they be doing to that man to make his voice tear out of him like that? Nabu's eyes widen and he glances at Echo: Any minute now, it could be their turn.

The guards look to Kosmos, who gazes up the street, a child again, as if all the monsters he feared have climbed out from under his bed. For a moment, Echo's comforted by the fact he's clearly never heard a man make that noise either, until it dawns on her that Hippias has become more furious and unpredictable than ever.

Nabu hugs himself. 'We should go elsewhere. Surely.'

Kosmos locks eyes with him, and there's another split second in which they're both frightened boys, ready to fall into each other's arms and hide under a blanket. Then Kosmos says, 'I don't think we have a choice,' and the plot-gone-awry and mutual suspicion divide them.

Echo steels herself, knowing Kosmos is being sensible. If they don't return it could be read as guilt, but they walk up the hill slowly, fussing with Hipparchos's sundered robes. The human howls take on new tones, each one more sickening than the last. At the threshold, Kosmos waits as the bier-carriers navigate Hipparchos inside, stroking his scar. As they enter, an eerie quiet descends over the house. In silence, they watch the women lay the body out on a table in the atrium, allowed from their quarters for the ritual.

The old mother with her karkinoma-scarred chest washes Hipparchos's face as gently as if he were a newborn, but Myrrhine stands at the corpse's feet, wringing the washcloth in her hands without using it. The last of the rain drips into the pool while Khemut lights extra incense and candles on the household altar.

'Nabu!' One of Kosmos's brothers calls from the andron door.

Nabu nods, halfway through taking off his shoes. 'One moment.'

'Should I come?' Echo asks.

He studies her. 'No. I don't think both of us need to see what's in there.'

As he passes, Khemut makes the sign of the horns, pointing down at the chthonic gods. 'Echo, get out of here,' she says, jerking her head towards the kitchen. Echo doesn't need telling twice, exchanging only a brief glance with Kosmos before bolting.

Instantly, the household workers are all over her, asking a hundred questions at once with tight mouths and knitted brows.

'What happened at the Acropolis?'

'Rebels.'

'Is it true Hipparchos is dead?'

'Yes, he is in the atrium.'

'Did Kosmos really kill someone?'

'I do not think so.'

'Where are Hanno and Absalon?'

'With Kosmos.'

'Where's my son?' This last from a baker nearly as old as Khemut.

Echo hesitates. Bad news is better heard from longtime friends. 'Hanno and Absalon know what happened to everyone else.'

There's a heartbeat of silence, as the room absorbs the number of friends and family missing. Then a little girl asks, 'Do we still have to serve lunch?'

'Is it lunchtime?' Echo gazes at the faces surrounding her.

'Stop pestering the boy.' Khemut enters, stick whacking any available shins and backsides. 'Work doesn't stop because of life or death.'

Exchanging glances, the others shuffle back to their tasks, the usual bustle muffled by the sudden silence from the andron. Knowing that inhuman shrieking has ceased is worse than the sound itself because it fills the gap between heartbeats with the questions 'Why?' and 'Who's next?' Khemut leans back in her chair, chewing the inside of her cheek and tapping her cane on the floor.

Just as it occurs to Echo she should help somehow, Nabu sweeps through the kitchen, one hand over his mouth, and heads straight out the stable door. Following, she finds him vomiting in a bucket.

'What happened?'

He can't reply for bile, so she fetches a drink from the well. He takes it from her, hands trembling so much they wrinkle the water.

'What happened, Nabu?'

'I'm not trained for this.'

'For what?'

Nabu frowns, swills his mouth out, and spits in the bucket. 'I cannot—*cannot*—do this.' He throws the cup across the yard. 'I will not serve this tyrannos, he has no honour.'

A clutch of stable hands listen in as they fork a nearby pile of straw, and curious heads poke out of the kitchen doorway. 'Careful, Nabu, we are not alone.'

'I don't care, I won't do it, Echo!' He stands, straightening to his full height, eyes blazing.

Darting looks at the other members of the household, Echo grabs Nabu's arm and drags him into the orchard. When they reach its far edge, she lets him go.

'Now. With calm. Tell me what Hippias did.'

But Nabu can't answer straight. He paces, hands in and out of his hair, voice louder than it should be. 'Since I was seven years old, I've been taught that there is a boundary between the body and the world. We are sacks of meat and humour, held together by this—this thin veil of being!' He holds his hand in front of Echo's face, pulling up the skin. 'Any perforation of the veil must be undertaken with gravity and intent and necessity, because once you have extracted a humour, you cannot put it back. Once you have undertaken a katharsis the unearthed matter is in the world, along with any Furies or curses attached to it. It is a sacred thing, this veil! You do not puncture it without reason, you do not—do not—' Nabu's mouth works emptily. He flops onto a log, gazing at the mountains as sunshine lances the low-hanging clouds.

Echo's never seen him this upset, not even when he argued with Kosmos. 'Nabu?'

He mutters, 'I forget, sometimes . . .' Then his eyes focus and he turns to her. 'Why didn't we try fighting? I could have ended him. He was right there and so was I.'

Echo slumps onto the log. 'You were not near him, Nabu. His guards surrounded him. We had already lost.'

'You can't know that.'

'I can. I am a Traveller. I know.'

'But you're here to change things. To change this. You promised me.'

'No, the last Traveller promised. His promise is open to interpretation. He did not mean what you think.'

'He wouldn't have done that to me.'

'Are you certain?'

Nabu looks away without answering. 'You won't overcome this system without force.'

'There are many ways to be forceful, not all are violent. We must found a school—'

'Stop that. Not now.' Nabu puts his head in his hands. 'Aristogeiton is dead. Hippias killed him.'

The revelation stretches between them, filling with the silent accusation that it's her fault. Maybe it is. 'I am sorry,' she says, but the words are inadequate before they're even spoken.

'I've never seen anything like it. That any man could treat a body like that . . .' Nabu curls up, diminishing behind his long hair and broad shoulders. 'I can't do what he wants, Echo. I just can't.'

She's petrified that Hippias will call for her interrogation, and she'll discover she can wail as terribly as Aristogeiton. No part of her wants to walk into the wolf's mouth, except the small strong voice that wishes to regain Nabu's respect. After the rain, it's humid and she wipes her sweaty palms on her tunic. 'When next Hippias calls, I will assist him.'

'Why?'

Echo shrugs. 'It is necessary. You are my Caretaker. We need each other and I want to help you. So, I am here.'

Nabu nods and stares at the mountains. 'You know Aristogeiton didn't betray a soul? Even though he once threatened to give Hippias my name if everything went wrong, when it came down to it, he didn't. That's how much he cared about the rebellion. He wouldn't even rat *us* out, in case it damaged the revolution's honour or purity. He still believed it would live on.' Nabu grips his chiton. 'We can't let their lives be in vain.'

From the house, a new howl begins, long and high like a gull cry, too piercing for a man. Echo's heart sinks: There was only one woman amongst the captives, and now it's the veil of her body being perforated.

For the first few minutes, Echo can't believe she'll ever get used to the sound. She's never truly known what blood-curdling means before, but Leaina's unnatural cries burrow into her ears, unspooling in her skull until she can't conceive of ever being alone in that bone cavity again.

Yet, when the sun has only moved a finger's width, Khemut fetches Echo from the orchard because one of the kitchen girls accidentally cut herself, and by the time Echo's finished binding the wound, Leaina's cries have blended into the background like cicada song. It's only when Echo returns the honey disinfectant to the pantry and runs out of tasks that the cries refresh their grip.

So, she busies herself. First, she washes and changes back into her everyday tunic, scrubbing the blood from under her nails. Then

Myrrhine sends for Nabu, and Echo goes to the gynaikeion instead as he's still hiding in the orchard waiting for much-needed thunder and the cessation of the household storm. Myrrhine requires poppy milk, apparently for menstruation pains, though Echo can't blame her for wanting an opiate sedative after laying out Hipparchos's body. As Echo's upstairs, Hippias's mother draws her to one side, stony-faced and unreadable, as if she loses sons to revolutionaries every day. She's found a new lump in her other breast and needs examining. It doesn't wriggle around like a cyst and, with a painted smile, Echo tells her to wait for a proper diagnosis from Nabu. She recommends a lavender infusion in the meantime, only because making it gives her something else to do, but all the while Leaina's howls stain the air. **Beloved of the tyrannicides and her tongue is—**

Khemut sends as many of the household out on errands as she can, and when the kitchen's almost empty, Nabu returns from the orchard and slinks to his room.

The day passes in this cycle of forgetful resignation and jolting remembrance. The sun wheels down the sky, winking between clouds that promise more rain but deliver none. Evening spills blood on the firmament, the blister of stars and slice of aged moon obscured by a thickening overcast. The children hide under the kitchen table, clinging to the dogs, and the serving girls make complicated pastries while the stable hands drink unmixed wine and play dice. Echo finds ways to keep busy too listening for the pulse of a pregnant fruit-picker's fetus, pressing her ear against the stretched firm skin. She taps it out—*buhbuh buhbuh*—on the mother's hand.

As Echo straightens, an absolute quiet falls, and as one the kitchen's inhabitants look to the door. For the second time that day, the silence is worse than the sound.

Khemut clears her throat. 'Hippias hasn't had his infusion.'

'We are beyond calming infusions,' Echo replies.

Footsteps approach and Kosmos appears. 'Where's Nabu?' His voice is hoarse and his eyes glisten.

'Not available,' Echo says, standing.

'What do you mean not available? He's paid to be available.'

Echo glares at him. 'I am here. Nabu is not. I will come.'

Kosmos hesitates, then slumps. 'Fine. Come on then.'

'What should I bring?'

'Gods below, how should I know?' He pinches unshed moisture from his eyes. 'Nothing. You don't need to bring anything.'

Echo reminds herself to breathe. Only those who have passed on need nothing.

In the inner courtyard, Kosmos wheels around and grabs Echo's wrist, imploring her. 'Before we go in, you must know, I didn't touch her. I didn't do any of it. I swear. He just made me watch, that's all. You understand?'

'Observation is not action?' She sneers, though her hearing it all and doing nothing isn't exactly moral high ground. **Her tongue, her tongue—**

Kosmos's eyes well up again and he repeats, quieter, 'I didn't touch her.'

Bloody sandal-prints lead beyond the andron's threshold and as Kosmos pushes the doors open they drag dark thick substances over the floor. He gestures. 'After you.' The room reeks of latrines and metallic blood, but Echo keeps her stomach in check. A single oil lamp shakes shadows over the pushed-aside dining tables and couches, light glinting on the puddled floor.

In the centre of the room is a body. If it weren't for the yellow dress tossed to one side, Echo wouldn't be able to identify it as Leaina.

'Revive her. We are not finished.' Echo starts and squints into the corner where Hippias, barely visible, reclines on a couch. Gold bands glimmer at his wrists as he turns sparkling eyes on Kosmos. 'Where's Nabu?'

Kosmos looks at his spattered sandals and shuffles his feet.

'Nabu is occupied with another patient,' Echo lies. 'He sent me instead. I can attend any situation.'

Hippias waves his arm in a broad arc: Here's the situation.

Trying not to breathe the foetid air, Echo approaches Leaina, substances she doesn't want to name oozing between her toes. Leaina's hair has been shorn and her limbs are disjointed. If she's recognisable at all, it's by what's left of her curves, hinting that her body was so recently bountiful. Echo squats, tucking her tunic between her legs to avoid dragging it in the mess. **Her tongue, her tongue—**

Inside Leaina's gaping mouth is a stump where her tongue should be. **Lioness who bit—**

Her eyes are frozen open. Echo takes a pulse for the sake of form but there's no doubt. Her mind falters, ringing with shock.

'Well?' Hippias sounds like he might be chewing something.

'I cannot revive her. She is dead.'

'You are certain?'

'Yes.' The only reason Echo contains herself is because she's terrified she'll be next.

With a grunt and clicking knees, Hippias stands and emerges from the shadows, wiping his hands on a fresh cloth, his fingernails black sickles against the white linen. 'Women always go quicker than men. They're more porous, like a sponge. They absorb what's around them too much, it's what makes them so overemotional and short-tempered. So quick to squeal. Aristogeiton didn't make such noises. He bellowed like an ox, as men should. She was a piglet.'

Echo's fists bunch. **She was a lioness, a hero, a foremother of the democratic turn—**

Hippias moves behind Echo, his breath brushing the back of her neck. **Bit her tongue—** No, don't think about where Leaina's tongue is and why it's not in her mouth. Don't think at all.

Echo stands and turns, shorter than Hippias and skinny where he's wired with muscle.

'I wonder, boy, are you old enough to behave like a man yet? Has the fabric of your spirit hardened?' His eyes bore into her, pulling at threads of truth: her gender, the Not Here, her Deed, Kosmos and Nabu's involvement in the tyrannicides' plot . . .

But if he knew any of it, she'd already be in trouble. She swallows her fear, tightening her fists. 'Do you need another diagnosis?'

Hippias tilts his head. 'Perhaps. You should stay, at any rate.' He draws a knife from his sheath and holds it out to Kosmos. 'Cut off its feet.'

Kosmos stammers. 'What?'

'The corpse. Its spirit must not be allowed to rise. Cut off its feet.'

There is a long silence. Echo can see the pulse in Kosmos's neck, his chest rising and falling fast, like ripples in water. He looks from his father to Leaina to Echo. She holds his gaze until he has to look away.

He takes a step back, shaking his head. 'No.'

Hippias jerks the knife at him. 'Do it.'

'No. I will not.' Kosmos's voice is a kitten-mewl, but it doesn't make the words less brave.

Hippias squares up to him. 'Useless boy. You want to be haunted, do you? Want to be cursed?'

Kosmos trembles visibly. Late as it's arrived, in this moment, Echo's got to admire his courage. His lip quivers. 'If she rises then perhaps it's because we deserve to be risen against.'

Every muscle in Hippias's face contorts with disgust. He regrips the knife handle and Kosmos winces preemptively. The Not Here mutters that once upon a time, Echo wouldn't have thought twice about standing up to Hippias. She wouldn't have sat listening to Leaina scream; she would've burst in here and done something about it. Since she travelled, she's been so absorbed in what's 'good' and 'safe' it's paralysed her actions. She's done nothing in the face of terrible crimes and violence. In the Not Here, she had agency and rights and she *used* them. That Not-Here-self hammers through her now like violets through marble paving, not acting in aid of the Deed or the future, just in defence of Kosmos who, like her, is finally trying to do something.

'He said: If she rises it is because you deserve to be risen against.'

Hippias rounds on her. His punch is so sudden Echo doesn't register the fist until she's on the floor blinking away stars. Floodgates open in her nose, blood gushing down her face. She's still spinning when a second blow, a thunderclap in one ear, leaves her floored.

Drawing her into a kneeling position, Hippias takes her face in his claws. He turns it this way and that, as if verifying her nose is genuinely bleeding, her ear and forehead really bruised. He pushes his face so close spittle lands on her cheeks and mouth with every consonant.

'Little boy. Always there in the shadows. Bringing me my infusions so dutifully. But how much do we really know about you. Are you one of them? Are you with the traitors?'

Echo wriggles, trapped. 'N—No.'

His nails dig into her cheeks, reeking of rot and iron. 'You're hiding something.'

'No. I swear.'

Hippias pulls back a fist like an archer stringing his bow and releases it into her stomach. For one tiny moment she forgets herself and crumples, spluttering and squealing. Squealing like a girl.

She clamps her mouth shut, but it's too late, Hippias noticed the womanly noise. The Furies catch him, and she remembers that first day when she and Nabu nursed him out of the gynaikeion: There is only one thing he fears and despises more than traitors. 'I see you. I see you now, *woman*.'

She shakes her head, trembling, not daring to speak.

'No, you say? We'll see about that, won't we? Let's see what we can do to get the truth out of you.'

His fist grips her hair, pulling her head up as he takes his knife and slices above her brow. Pain slashes through her head as blood trickles into her eye. She screams.

'Hey!' Kosmos thumps into his father, twisting the knife from Hippias's hand, and it's only the tyrannos's surprise that makes the attack successful.

Hippias lurches back and the knife clatters across the floor.

Letting her brow bleed, Echo darts behind Kosmos.

'Stop.' Kosmos's voice squeaks, but his feet are firm.

Hippias scowls. 'You too? Yes, it makes sense. Always hiding behind the women's skirts as a child, going to watch them weave until you were far too old for it. They've poisoned you.'

Kosmos holds his arms out, still protecting Echo. 'We're not with the women or the traitors, Father, but I will not trap Leaina's soul. Either you've acted with honour today and she won't rise up, or you've done a dishonourable thing and she has every right to vengeance.'

'A snivelling, womanly weakling.' Hippias draws himself up like an asp. 'Get out of my sight.'

'We are not traitors,' Kosmos repeats, voice on the edge of breaking.

'*Out*.' Hippias shouts so loud the rafters rain dust.

Echo flees, dashing through the moonlit courtyard with Kosmos on her heels, until they burst into the kitchen, scattering eavesdroppers. Khemut takes in Echo's cut up face and gestures to Nabu's room. 'Don't tell me anything, just get seen to.'

Blood drips into Echo's eye as Kosmos guides her down the storeroom corridor. Nabu is curled in bed, eyes red and hair unbraided, but he rises when he sees Echo and dresses her wound without being asked.

'What happened?'

'Nothing,' Echo says, wincing as he applies a salt poultice.

'Nonsense, look at the state of you. I know Hippias's work when I see it. Will he come for you again? Are you in danger?'

'We both are,' Kosmos replies.

'Why, what did you do?' Nabu asks, pressing harder on Echo's wound and making her skin catching on the linen rag.

Kosmos shakes his head. 'What I should've been doing all along, probably.'

'The right thing?'

'Something like that.'

Nabu stands back and examines Echo's blood-soaked tunic. 'How bad was it?'

The waves of what she's done—of what she and Kosmos have done together—break over her. 'I insulted him. I saw Leaina and I could not be silent.'

'Can you fix it?' Nabu folds his arms and leans against his desk.

Echo exchanges a look with Kosmos. 'No. I do not think I can be safe here. But . . .' Her Not-Here-self breaks out again, and the endemic *wrongness* of everything that's been bubbling in her since she arrived boils. 'I have no wish to become silent again. Everything is upside down here. Women are unseen and unheard. Humans own other humans. My world is not perfect, but where I am from, humans are free—or, they have a right to be free. In my country, you and Kosmos could be together, could even be husbands to each other.' Kosmos's head whips up, jaw slack, as if this is inconceivable. 'Change comes, but it is slow. Very slow. We must make it faster. That is what I am here to do, not to sneak in the house of the tyrannos.'

Nabu nods, eyes on his feet. 'You're leaving, then.'

She lowers her voice in case anyone outside is listening. 'I cannot stay here. I am not safe, and I can do nothing because Hippias watches.'

'Where will you go?'

She hasn't thought this far ahead, she's just following an instinct that she must not and cannot go back in the box she's just broken out of. She looks to Kosmos, wealthy and well-connected, the only one who might be able to safely hide her. He meets her gaze, both of them remembering the conversation they had so many days ago in the orchard.

'I have a farm we can go to,' he says, 'just beyond the city walls.'

'You're leaving too?' Nabu's arms fall to his sides.

'I can't stay either. The rebellion might've failed—for now—but I can't stand by and watch anymore. Nabu, the things my father did to Leaina . . .'

Nabu pauses. 'She is dead then?'

Kosmos nods, examining the crates of healer's trinkets around them. 'But I didn't touch her. I could never do the things—'

'But you stayed!' Nabu says. 'You watched, you didn't stop him!'

'What could I do? What would you have done?'

'I would've—would've—' Echo watches Nabu struggle with the knowledge that he too stood by. He and Echo knew what was happening just as well as Kosmos. In their own ways, they all capitulated to Hippias's cruelty. Echo can see him rolling out the ugly argument and giving up. 'The river farm?'

Kosmos nods. 'Echo and I have discussed it.'

'Have you indeed?' Nabu says, arching an eyebrow at Echo.

She shuffles. 'Only briefly!'

'Echo says we must start a school of philosophy—'

'Not this again!' Nabu rolls his eyes. 'You really believe you can change the world by making people *think* differently?'

'Well, violence hasn't worked, has it?' Kosmos retorts.

They've both raised their voices and there are footsteps in the hallway, interspersed with the telltale tap of Khemut's cane. Echo glances at the door, shushing them.

Nabu ignores her. 'What about you, Kosmos? You want to change how people think, you should start with yourself!'

'This is me starting on myself!'

'Stop!' Echo shouts over them both, and then, dropping her voice, 'Quiet, someone is listening!'

Kosmos and Nabu turn to her as if seeing her anew. They blink at each other, the door, and her again.

She lowers her voice. 'Kosmos, you should pack. It will be best if we leave soon. At daybreak.' Then, realising she's issued him an order, adds, 'Do not you think?'

'Yes.' He gathers himself, avoiding looking at Nabu. 'Daybreak it is. I must say farewell to Myrrhine and my grandmother as well.'

When he leaves, Khemut is waiting outside, apparently dusting an old amphora, glaring warnings at them.

The door swings shut behind Kosmos, and Nabu slumps into his chair. 'Don't you need to pack too?'

Echo looks around. She picks up her pouch of menstrual rags and spare breast-binding strips.

Nabu frowns. 'That's it?'

'I do not own any other items.' Echo shrugs. 'You know this.'

He looks around, as if only just realising that, except when he lends her tunics for special occasions, she's been wearing the same clothes he gave her on arrival. 'Well, you'll need more than that.' He tips the herb jars out of his spare medicine bag and bashes dirt off it. 'Here, you've been using this for errands, let's put some things in it. You'll need a new tunic too, you can't walk through Athens covered in blood.'

'Some things' turns out to be a jar of salt poultice for the cut on her brow, two spare tunics—one for dirty jobs, one for occasions, both of which Nabu must've outgrown years ago—extra bandages to use for binding, a felt hat for cold nights, and a wooden-clasped wool travelling cloak that doubles as a blanket. Once Echo's changed clothes, Nabu throws the cloak over her, then hands her the bag.

'Good luck, Traveller. You're going to need it.'

She takes the bag, swallowing. 'Come with us.'

Nabu shakes his head.

'Do you not trust me?'

'Even if I did, there are other reasons for me not to come. I could still be useful as a plant in the tyrannos's house. Besides, things with Kosmos are . . . difficult.'

'I understand. I will miss you.'

'And I you, strange female creature, but we'll see each other again. Your Deed isn't over, and neither is mine.'

Their eyes lock, and Echo is fleetingly hopeful, but as she turns and puts her hand to the door latch, he asks, 'What happened to Leaina?'

The Not Here croons and froths. '**Leaina, beloved of the tyrannicides, died at the hands of Hippias, tortured for information.**'

For once, Nabu starts at the Traveller's voice. 'And is it true what the servants are saying? That he cut out her tongue?'

Echo sighs, releasing the information she's been trying to repress ever since she met Leaina. '**No. She bit it out to make sure she would not betray anyone. In many years, they will make a statue for her and place it in the agora. A golden lion, without its tongue.**'

'That doesn't make it alright.'

'No,' Echo replies, in her own voice again, opening the door and stepping out of the old room in which she's been so intolerably quiet and biddable. 'Nothing can.'

In the corridor, she's surprised to find the sun is rising, though she hadn't noticed the long sleepless night pass. Khemut's returned to the kitchens, but the corridor is still loud with whispers: 'Wrong—broken—getting it wrong—'

She looks around for the speaker, but she's alone. After a moment's search, she realises the voice is coming from reflections: dawn light glancing off a row of glass jars, the still surface of stored oil, the bowl of a silver ladle. It's Hazel's voice, the only other person who ever speaks English. How long has she been speaking? Have the whispers followed Echo all day and night, inaudible under the chaos and bloodshed?

'Getting it wrong—'

Even if she is wrong, Echo can't turn from her path now. This is the only way she can be safe, have agency, honour Leaina's memory, and Echo's own Not-Here-self, the girl from the puddle who she can't remember but is certain deserves to speak. This is her path, and at last it's one that leads her closer to the Deed she was sent to complete. She will make it work.

Still, the whispers haunt her exit. 'Timeline—problem—gone wrong—stop now stop—'

13

Hazel

STATION C, DATE UNKNOWN

'Hazel Brandt respond. Are we not drawn onward ere divided?'

CHARL1E's words are flotsam on the dreamscape tide, and she clings to them. 'We—we few—' Her mouth makes the movements but she's not sure whether the words come out, as if she's sleep-talking.

'I cannot confirm that verbal output.'

'We—' She gasps against the dreamscape's waters. '—few live on mirror rims.'

The pain in her neck lessens and her vision clears, as if from a faint.

'Emit no evil & live.' She's a word behind CHARL1E, but it's in sync enough that the next line falls out of her.

'On time's mirror rim no evil we few de-divide.' Her vision clears. She's on the floor, Teaspoon and Shiny leaning over her anxiously.

'Redrawn onward to new era.' CHARL1E pauses. 'Do you need it again?'

Hazel pushes herself into a sitting position and rests her spinning head on her knees. In her pocket, the *Eikos Muthos* digs into her thigh. 'No, I'm good. I'm here.'

'You need to come back to the Hab Dome. This is an unfortunate symptom.'

She nods, then realises he probably can't see her in Tree. 'Yes. Wait, I don't have any oxygen.'

'Tree is breathing again. You can refill your tanks using the valve by the shower block.'

The Tinys help Hazel with this and her biosuit helmet. Tree's still singing to CHARL1E, so she hasn't been able to mend Robin's hand, and the Tiny trundles in circles at a distance, broken pieces back in the bag around its neck.

'Can't you do something about the problem with Tree's song?' Hazel asks CHARL1E.

'Negative. Tree does as she wants.'

'But she's supposed to care for the Tinys.'

'She does, but it has been a long time since she and I spoke, and she wants to enjoy that first.'

Hazel's not sure that's fair, but she's too tired to argue. Time might've retreated for now, but it'll be back to catch her, and she's as shaky as she was after her catastrophic arrival. Shiny, Teaspoon, and a dejected Robin accompany her across Station C's wasteland, making sure she's on comms with CHARL1E the whole way.

He keeps her diverted, explaining the quirks of the decaying wind turbines and heat source generators she passes. How much longer will they continue working? Even the Tinys won't be able to keep repairing them once their resources run out, and while Tree harvests enough electricity to charge the little robots, she can't power the whole of Station C. Hazel clambers up the edge of the old Arch Dome, gazing past the forest of mirror shards to the bitter sea. How many little microbes are out there, busily commencing the next epoch-long evolution to self-reflective consciousness? Are there any?

Hazel must be able to work with CHARL1E to stop all this happening, but she's afraid of returning into his care. At the Hab Dome airlock she pauses, examining the rust rings around the button, the white caustic lines where acid rain has dripped over the plastic.

'Hazel Brandt, has something gone awry?'

'No, it's just . . . Do you promise not to try to hurt me again?'

'Affirmative. I will not hurt you or attempt to hurt you.'

'I guess that'll have to do.' She hits the button, heavy-hearted, and the door hisses open. 'But I swear, CHARL1E, if you turn on me again, I'm coming for your hard drive.'

'This is an illogical threat given that my consciousness is spread across numerous RAQu Disks, not all of which are within easy physical access.'

'I'll find them.' She steps into the airlock—Shiny, Teaspoon, and Robin still at her heels—and waits for the atmosphere to equalise. 'CHARL1E, even if I do stop time catching me, the chances we'll fail are still pretty high, aren't they?'

'I recommend not phrasing things in the negative, it has a non-beneficial impact on morale.'

'It's never a good sign when you give me advice rather than data. Come on, what's the likelihood of success?'

'Currently, there is approximately a 1.534 percent chance that Project Kairos will succeed in altering the timeline such that human beings will be accommodated by Earth's biosphere today.'

Hazel blows out her cheeks. 'Hardly any point in trying, really.'

'Negative. Trying is imperative. If we do not try, the probability of failure grows to one hundred percent.'

'What's the percentage chance we'll partially succeed? That maybe humans haven't survived, but smaller mammals have. A cockroach even.'

'There are too many potentials for me to calculate a single answer, however each answer is higher than 1.534 percent.'

'That's something.'

The internal doors open, and Hazel hangs up the biosuit, inhaling the Hab Dome's sterile scent. She stows her helmet and grins at Robin. 'Show me to a hot shower!'

'It is inadvisable that you undertake ablutions at this juncture, Hazel Brandt,' CHARL1E interrupts. 'Now you have returned, we should discuss how to prevent—as you call it—time catching you. It would be best if you come to the Workshop Dome.'

Hazel sighs and whispers to Robin, 'Looks like the shower will have to wait.'

All three Tinys are on edge as they enter the Workshop, tails taut and wheels skittering, but nothing's out of place. The same amber bulb hangs over CHARL1E's screens, the same code drifts over them, and the same chaotic piles of tech junk radiate into the dark. Hazel sits in the same ancient wheely chair and spins to face CHARL1E. 'Alright. How do I stop time catching me?'

CHARL1E's code stutters across the screens. 'The first thing you need to understand is that I was not programmed to guide Travellers. It requires subtlety, tact, and untruths, which are all unnatural to me. I have struggled with the lying as much as you have, perhaps more so given the unfortunate logic cascades that lies create in my matrices. The Keepers called them my logicmares.'

'Honestly, that sounds very human,' Hazel replies, still getting used to this new sharing and caring CHARL1E. 'Lies are like avalanches, you start with something small and—*whoomph*—before you know it, the whole mountainside's coming down.'

'Like avalanches, affirmative. Not salient, of course, but accurate.' Hazel has to smile at CHARL1E's turns of phrase. He's so formal still, it's hard for her to believe his sincerity.

'You know, CHARL1E, sometimes the most salient things look random at first.'

'We will agree to disagree. We digress. Guiding Travellers was always the Keepers' role. When Lilith and Huxley perished, the task fell to me. It went poorly, as tasks are prone to without sufficient training.'

'Poorly is an understatement.'

'I was not assisted by your obstinacy.'

Diplomacy and tea are required here, and Hazel signs at Shiny to get her a cup while she says, 'I suppose I earned that.'

'I was significantly pressurised: With the Arch gone, this is the last expedition Project Kairos can make, it cannot fail.'

'But how would telling me what's really going on make it fail?'

'I am approaching this matter,' CHARL1E snaps.

She's unsettled by his new range of expression, but they're finally getting somewhere so she can't shy away. 'Go on.'

'When a Traveller journeys from their own time into the past or future, they lose their memories. At first, everything is lost. They might remember the context of their world, or even snippets of their lives, but their existence as a whole is forgotten. The dislocation in time is so severe the mind engages in a species of trauma response, submerging the memories of where it was to deal with the new here and now.'

'Mnemealgia, right? You explained that when I arrived,' Hazel says.

'I am afraid I explained only half of mnemealgia,' CHARL1E says, code sweeping downwards. 'Eventually, the Traveller's memories return. As they become accustomed to their new surroundings, there is space for both worlds to co-exist—but only to an extent. Time, space, and human memory are deeply interlinked, at levels your faculties are too primitive to truly understand or see. So, as the Traveller's memories of their own time resurface, their home present exerts itself over the body, pulling the Traveller back to the moment they came from. The Keepers called it anamnesis.'

A weight lifts: Hazel can go home any time she likes, all she has to do is succumb to her memories. **Anamnesis.** The back of her neck prickles. 'Anamnesis is that feeling like someone's pulling at the scruff of my neck, isn't it?'

'Affirmative. Many Travellers have described this sensation.'

Even as hope ploughs through Hazel, seeds of fear grow in its furrows. 'But that means we're not in control of when I go home. I could go home any time—whether or not the Deed's complete.'

'Affirmative.' CHARLIE's voice drops to the quietest she's ever heard. 'In an effort to be "more myself," allow me to communicate that it was highly improbable the Tinys would take you to Tree, and my access to information about her operations is severely restricted, so I concluded that you had already performed anamnesis and the expedition had failed. Refinding you is an unexpected boon.'

She smirks. 'A boon, huh?'

'Indeed.' CHARL1E pauses. 'Hazel Brandt, to alter your future—everyone's future—you must continue to forget yourself. When you experience the pull of anamnesis, do not ask yourself whether you want to go home; ask what kind of home you wish to return to.'

'It's alright, CHARL1E, I'm already on your side. I'm not going to slip off without finishing the Deed.'

'What has brought about this change?'

Hazel shrugs. 'I had time to think in Tree. I don't want to look into a future like the one outside. If I can help, I will. Even if there's a 0.0001 percent chance of success.' *Let us endure this time of trial, and not resort to evil, for ours is the prospect and the power and the undoing of all.* She doesn't want to tell CHARL1E how much she needs redemption for Lilith and Huxley's deaths, or about the *Eikos Muthos* still tucked in her pocket—their truce is still too fragile—but she does want him to believe her. 'Here's the thing CHARL1E, you asked me to trust you; now it's your turn to trust me.'

CHARL1E's code scrolls. 'You are correct, the equation must be balanced. I will trust you. It is therefore incumbent on me only to add that certain information is more likely to prompt your memories to return. Some are so powerful the Keepers called them keystone memories; these will unlock all your memories at once and anamnesis will inevitably ensue. Every Traveller possesses such a keystone memory. As such, there will always be things that I cannot tell you, right until the moment you leave.'

'Only in parting will we really see eye to eye.' Hazel laughs as Shiny returns with an Earl Grey tea and passes it to her. Cold again and the bergamot flavour is distressingly chemical. They'll never get it right. 'But what do I do about the fact I can't even think of the Backward Traveller without—'

Five o'clock grime time in a crowded office; Underground train

home lolled against the window; sooty mouse between the tracks. A yank on the back of Hazel's neck, spots in her vision, pain. **Hot-tarmac breezes on the balcony; sitting in Dad's deckchair with a neck brace; painkillers arranged like a flower on a plate; come on, come home; perform anamnesis—** Time grasps for her, making her giddy.

'Hazel Brandt, salt an atlas!'

Her head flicks up, thoughts shattered. 'Salt an atlas?'

'Salt an atlas.'

Her neck itches and aches, and somehow the mug of tea has shattered on the floor, its cold contents flooding her bare toes. 'I think I'm going to be si—'

'Pull up if I pull up. Repeat!'

'Pull up if I pull up.'

'Good. Again.' They repeat the two strange phrases three more times, and as they do Hazel's sickness diminishes and the hairs on the back of her neck lie flat, her mind recentring on the present-in-the-future.

'What are those phrases?'

'Palindromes. Over many years, Travellers have developed a stock of these grounding remarks to help keep them rooted in time. The Keepers theorized that the linguistic mimicking of the Travellers' journey creates an anchor.'

'That almost makes sense.' She stares at the glistening puddle of spilt tea, imagining her and Echo stepping through the catopthura, thrown equal distances through time, each identical ends of the palindrome. 'Travellers have to be twins, don't they?'

'Affirmative, because of their genetic similarity, only identical twins can engage in the spooky action across great temporal distances that is required to communicate in the dreamscape.'

'That's how we find each other, night after night, when otherwise we'd just be lost in the current. Through the quantum entanglement of our genes.' Her neck tingles.

CHARL1E's code scrolls faster. 'It is inadvisable for you to think about the Backward Traveller too closely.'

'But that's my point, I have to talk to her every night. How do I do that without all my memories coming back?'

'Every Traveller finds their own way. Memorising the grounding remarks will help. The 54th Traveller kept a list on the inside of your bathroom cabinet.'

Hazel recalls the scratchings. Not so useless after all.

'You have more control than you realise,' CHARL1E continues. 'However, it is crucial that the Backward Traveller does not learn who you are.'

'Couldn't be straightforward, could it! And why is that?'

'Because while the Backward Traveller's identity is not your keystone memory, your identity is hers.'

'But she already knows my name.'

'Your name is not the problem, your identity is.'

'So, if she learns I'm her twin, she'll go straight home?'

'Affirmative.'

Hazel watches Shiny and Teaspoon clearing the broken cup. 'There's so little time to figure this out. Tonight, I have to tell her to fix whatever she's broken in the timeline, right?'

'Alas, you cannot wait until tonight. You must speak with her right now while we might still have time to reverse the damage.'

'CHARL1E, it's the middle of the day, I can't just sleep on demand. Besides, I'm still struggling to string a sentence together in the dreamscape.'

'Then perhaps it is time for some new techniques.'

'New techniques, huh?' Hazel smiles despite herself. 'I suppose trying is imperative.'

For the first time, CHARL1E lets Hazel explore the Hab Dome. The Tinys lead her through a ballroom-sized gym with dozens of dusty exercise machines, and a small movie theatre with a yellowed screening list. They pass numerous empty, shadowed dormitories which reverberate with her footsteps, and noticeboards with geological layers of papers and pins. 'Looking for mentorship in R? Come to Dorm 12, Bunk C and ask for Jaden!' 'Hieu's birthday party—12th May, 19:00, Workshop—byo snacks!' 'If you have been Outside in the past 12 days and have developed a phlegmy cough or migraine, seek medical attention immediately. Vigilance is our defence against outbreak.' 'Are you anxious or overwhelmed? Come to knitting circle, D31, Thursday evenings. Kids and Tinys welcome.' The effect is like passing through a crowd, each poster speaking with a different long-lost voice.

'It's all so old,' Hazel says, knowing CHARL1E can hear her anywhere now that she's back in Station C. 'I suppose Lilith and Huxley didn't bother with the boards, there being just two of them.'

'Affirmative. The boards have not been used for four generations.'

She strokes the skin-thin paper. 'Worship for unity. Mondays 14:00–15:00, the Arch. The collective is stronger when we believe in each other.' *Let us lend support, as in turn we are supported.*

Robin tugs her away from the board into the largest dormitory yet, which slices through the dome to its centre. In the outer walls, one of the octagonal panels is made of glass, throwing wan daylight on the unused bunk beds lining the far wall and two single mattresses on the floor in the middle of the room, facing the window. Hazel slumps down on one, staring. The pane is wobbly, as if someone melted together old bottles, cups, and any other scrap glass lying around, but between the seams the landscape's clear, the grey sea breaking against the rubble beach. Thick clouds scud the sky, obscuring the sun, while curls of mist form in the ashy light. Hazel doesn't even know what season it is, or if seasons still exist. All she knows is that if she doesn't do anything, this is her future.

Beside the bed is a box of personal effects, including a small stack of photos. The one on top is of a long-haired woman and a spectacled man standing before the Arch, framed by Tesla coils and sparking Van de Graaff generators.

'It is not Lilith and Huxley,' CHARL1E says. 'That photograph is of their parents.'

Other photos do show Lilith and Huxley, mostly as children with their parents and a handful of much older folk, the last hopes of a once-larger group. Hazel is envious of the family's arms around each other, even if they are posing, and wonders how long it will be before anyone hugs her again. If they ever do.

More boxes of personal effects have been left on each abandoned bunk, embroidery hoops, single-eared teddy bears, and fray-edged journals poking out of them. 'What are these?'

'They're memorials,' CHARL1E replies. 'The Keepers reused almost everything, but towards the end, the families of the deceased would be given a box in which to keep any treasures that reminded them of their loved one. They claimed it made them feel less alone.'

'Some of them look like shoeboxes. Do any actually contain shoes?'

'Negative. Shoes are very precious indeed. That would be like filling the box with water, electricity, or oxygen. Do you require new shoes?'

She opens her mouth to jab CHARL1E for his lack of humour, but glancing at her worn boots, she thinks better of it. She's never considered that CHARL1E and the Tinys just giving her clothes was enormously generous. 'No, these are excellent shoes. Thank you.'

Between the bunks are bookshelves filled with tomes on hard science—coding, robotics, quantum mechanics, post-quantum computing—but also more surprising titles, on active imagination, the subconscious, and of course lucid dreaming. 'Good job the Keepers were all the mad kind of scientist,' she mutters.

The bedroom has doors leading to bathrooms, offices, and a linen cupboard, but the final door leads to a spiral staircase, winding upwards into the dark. Hazel follows it, rubber shoes catching the metal tread. At the top is a heavy trapdoor. Afraid it might lead to the hostile outside, she looks down at Robin before opening it.

The Tiny shakes its head vehemently. *Don't go through there.*

'CHARL1E, is this safe to open?'

'Yes.'

'Then why is Robin telling me not to?'

'If you are referring to Tiny 222, then it is being contrary.'

'If you say so.' Hazel frowns, but opens the trapdoor. Warm, moist air slips over her face as the trapdoor swings back to reveal a vast greenhouse, a cupola to the Hab Dome so disproportionate that the floor curves. It bursts with life and colour: orchids, tulips, carnations, and poppies grow in low raised beds; honeysuckle, clematis, and wild roses wind around pillars; and the floor is carpeted by violets, moss, and clover. The lawn bears a pair of wicker chairs. On a side table between them, a novel is spread pages-down, abandoned cups on either side. Neither book nor tea will be finished now. Nor will the gargantuan contraption hanging from the ceiling, swathed in dust sheets.

Hazel stays half in, half out of the trapdoor, too aware of Lilith and Huxley's recent proximity to dare enter farther, but she closes her eyes and inhales. This is it; this is what her world was like, her flesh recalling things her mind's forgotten. She swallows a lump in her throat.

'You're sure it's in here?'

'Yes, this is one of the places Huxley undertook his experiments.'

'It's a greenhouse.'

'Affirmative, though the Keepers preferred the term "garden."'

It does look like a garden, each petal, leaf, and inch of soil carefully encouraged and maintained. How many microbes and fungi must be surviving in here that couldn't exist outside. She continues up the staircase but notices Robin still sitting at the bottom. Its lenses are tilted in a way that means it's uncertain.

'Hey Robin, what's up? Can't manage the stairs?'

Robin shakes its head.

'It is essential Tiny 222 accompanies you,' CHARL1E says. 'The machine will not work without it.'

'OK, guess I'm carrying you then,' Hazel says, but as she descends, Robin shakes its whole body, swinging its arms wildly.

'Hey, stop it!' Hazel backs off, frightened of hurting it again. 'CHARL1E, it really doesn't want to go.'

'It is essential that it does.'

'It's a hunk of flailing metal, if it doesn't want to get picked up, it's not getting picked up!'

Robin scoots into the dorm, stopping several paces away, watching her.

'Alright, fine,' Hazel says. 'You don't want to come? I'm not going to force you.'

'It is essen—' CHARL1E protests.

'We'll find another way.'

'That is highly improbable based on Huxley's data.'

'Well, maybe Huxley lacked imagination.'

Once Hazel's inside the garden with the trapdoor closed, CHARL1E instructs her to remove the dustsheets, which reveals a contraption he calls the Catopic Aperture. It looks like a tree with three thick branches, growing upside down from the ceiling. The twigs of each branch clutch an icosahedron the width of Hazel's outstretched arms, each constructed of two-way mirrors, letting Hazel peer at the infinite triangular reflections within.

'They are called cradles,' CHARL1E says. 'Each cradle connects to a different element of time: past, present, and future.'

Hazel gazes upwards, stroking one of the icosahedron cradles. 'Is that why each branch is made from a different material?'

'Affirmative. Plastic for the future; glass for the present; metal for the past.'

At the upside-down tree's fork is a central aperture, emblazoned with the Project Kairos logo. 'It will open once you turn the equipment on,' CHARL1E says.

Hands on her hips, Hazel steps back. The machine looks horribly fragile. Maybe Robin was right to be scared. 'You say this is untested?'

'Negative. I said it remains *in* testing.'

Hazel frowns at the glass, metal, and plastic structure. 'That's not as comforting as you want it to be. Does it have consciousness like you and Tree?'

'Not to anyone's knowledge.' CHARL1E pauses. 'Without the Arch, the Catopic Aperture may not start. Without the presence of a Tiny, it almost certainly will not. However, if it does, it could prove an invaluable tool for scrying the past.'

'Well, let's give it a shot.' Under CHARL1E's instructions, she opens a triangular hatch in the cradle for the future. Inside, soot dusts the mirrors and scrap metal litters the base. Hazel cleans it out, laying the metal on the garden table. 'What are these?'

'Huxley's experiments were not always successful,' CHARL1E replies.

Hazel turns one of the scraps over. 'Is this thing going to incinerate me?'

'You will be in a different cradle. You will not be incinerated. Please, do not let your fear intrude on proceedings. If we do not do this, we will not be able to communicate with the Backward Traveller and reverse the damage she is doing to the timeline.'

'Alright, alright. I understand the urgency.' Hazel rubs her forehead. 'So, what's the next step?'

'I estimate that we will need to place an object inside the cradle for the future,' CHARL1E pauses hesitantly. 'It must be somehow connected to both myself and Tree, and its material should be reflective.'

Hazel puts her head in her hands. 'That's unusually nonspecific for you.'

'I am, as you would say, stabbing in the dark.'

Let us begin. Hazel stares at the future cradle, an idea forming. 'CHARL1E, I have something to confess.'

'I will pardon your transgressions in advance. Divulge.'

'When I was in Tree, the Tinys accidentally gave me a copy of the *Eikos Muthos*. It had some sections torn out and an added handwritten section by Lilith.'

'I remember this edition, Lilith made it . . . Traveller-safe,' CHARL1E says. 'Though I agree it is improbable the Tinys provided this text intentionally. It was a risk.'

'One worth taking. It helped me understand you enough to get back here.' Hazel takes it from her pocket, looking at her distorted reflection in the foil cover.

'I fail to see how it meets our requirements.'

'It talks about you, the Tinys, Tree, the Keepers, Travellers, Caretakers—everything—and the cover's a mirror, albeit not a good one. It's perfect feather-pillow science!'

'There is a saying amongst the Keepers that would be appropriate here.'

'Oh yes?'

'Who are you and what have you done with Hazel Brandt?'

Hazel laughs. 'Shall we give it a go?'

'Affirmative.'

She locks the book in the future cradle, then turns to the metal arm holding the cradle of the past. Inside is an elpis device, just like the one in Tree.

Again, CHARL1E offers instructions. 'Place your palms against the icosahedron and think about the Backward Traveller—but be careful! Do not let any new memories return. Focus on one strong memory you already have of her. When I say "stop" take your hands away and step back. Do not continue if you sense that you are about to perform anamnesis.'

When Hazel touches it, the icosahedron's glass is body temperature, and she closes her eyes, focusing on the moment in the dreamscape when she realised Echo was her twin. She repeats the millisecond memory, but each time the tingle on the scruff of her neck grows. **Painkillers arranged like flowers; shall I read to you—**

'Not sure I can take much more of this!' she tells CHARL1E through gritted teeth.

'Stop!' he replies. 'It is working.'

She steps back, reciting grounding remarks to stabilise her dizziness—but inside the icosahedron, the elpis device is spinning. 'How?' Hazel asks.

'You made it spin,' CHARL1E replies.

'That doesn't make sense.'

'You do not think you have power?'

'Of course not, I'm not a battery.' She frowns as she closes the past cradle's hatch.

'This from the advocate for feather-pillow science.'

Hazel's frown fades. 'If you keep being humorous, I'm going to have to ask who you are and what you've done with CHARL1E.'

Lastly, at CHARL1E's insistence, Hazel actually climbs into the present cradle clutched by the glass branch, using one of the garden chairs to give herself a leg up. She closes the triangular hatch, shutting herself in and creating a kaleidoscope of pale, wide-eyed Hazels. Because of the two-way mirrors, though an observer could see in, she can't see out, and the effect is disorienting, as if she's underwater. She gets as comfortable as she can in the base of the cradle, trying not to think about what's going to happen when this thing starts up.

'Are you settled?' CHARL1E's voice comes through speakers embedded in the seams between the mirrors.

'For a given definition of settled.'

'Then I will open the aperture. Do not be surprised, the machine will move.'

'Move?' Hazel starts, thinking of the branch's delicate glass.

'Affirmative. However, it will be slow: Your track record aside, time travel should not be a roller-coaster ride. Are you ready?'

Hazel hunches down, fingertips clinging to the mirrors. 'As I'll ever be.'

A mechanical whir indicates the aperture opening and the cradle's seams spark with light. It flashes, turning Hazel's reflection into skeletal x-ray, then orange-hot infrared, only returning to normal when the illumination settles to low pure white. Blinking, she grips the walls as the cradles start orbiting the aperture. 'I feel sick.'

'Please do not vomit in the Catopic Aperture, it will have suboptimal consequences.'

She breathes deeply.

'Hazel Brandt?'

'Yeah, I'm trying not to be sick.'

A sound grows like the dreamscape's rustle, accompanied by a breeze laced with fresh rain, ripening tomatoes, and rotting oranges. Other layers of sound emerge: furtive footsteps, incomprehensible whispers, and a terrible wail that wavers like a radio tuning. The cradle's infinite reflections dissolve and re-form, offering distorted windows into another time. They show Echo from many angles, any reflective surface she passes becoming Hazel's eyes and ears—a cup of tea, a glass jar, fat spitting in a pan . . . The Catopic Aperture has the same here-but-not-here quality as lucid dreaming, but fuzzier, the images and sounds inconsistent, like watching an old TV in a storm.

'Is it working?'

CHARL1E's voice makes Hazel jump. 'Kind of. There's a lot of interference, but it's still incredible; I don't have to concentrate at all, I can just see her.'

'The interference is concerning, it may stop you speaking with Backward Traveller. Nonetheless, you must try.'

'What should I say?'

'Tell her that the timeline has gone wrong. She is about to set up the school, but it will fail and that will make things worse.'

'Why will it fail?'

'I am an Artificial General Intelligence, not an oracle, that is for the Backward Traveller to figure out.'

Hazel speaks to the conjured images of Echo, but her twin doesn't look up or seem to hear, so she tries shouting.

'Increased volume will not improve the likelihood of connection and may disrupt the balance of the machine,' CHARL1E says. 'Recall the memory you used to start the elpis device and try again. Focus on specificity of audience rather than volume of message.'

Hazel tries again, and again, and again. All through a sleepless night and on till dawn. Then, finally, Echo frowns at the reflections around her as if she might have caught a whisper, but she doesn't try speaking back. Hazel keeps trying, speaking and watching through raindrops, molecules of steam, the film of an eyeball . . . until her voice is hoarse and her eyes are drooping, when at last CHARL1E agrees that it's not working and she's allowed to go to bed.

'At least we tried,' she says, but CHARL1E doesn't reply.

Finally cushioned between mattress and duvet, the surreal hours in the Catopic Aperture draw Hazel into the dreamscape, and for once she finds the igneous light and perpetual susurration comforting. It's as if she's caught under the Earth's crust, in the red-hot layers where even metal turns to ocean, collapsed and insignificant under the elemental pressure.

Naturally, given her strange sleeping pattern, she doesn't encounter Echo until the following night, when she arrives in clean clothes, washed, with her face free of tears.

'Did you hear me calling to you?' Hazel asks, her words coming more easily for the all the hours spent in the Catopic Aperture.

Echo too has an easier time speaking, though seemingly she still lacks enough proficiency in lucid dreaming to move. 'It was you. I couldn't tell. I've seen strange things lately, a girl in a puddle. I thought maybe it was a trick of the light.'

Cups of air tea; arguing over the best dressing-up clothes; sharing penny sweets— Stop. Hazel pleads with the memories, but they don't listen, lacing their roots through her chest.

Keeping out of Echo's eyeline, she skirts her sister, marvelling at how they're identical to the last freckle. They might be separated by time and space, but they're bound together by memory and limb—and Hazel can't tell her because she herself is Echo's keystone memory. Hazel's memories throw a taproot into her stomach and sprout leaves in her throat.

Hazel spots a deep cut on Echo's brow. 'You're hurt. What happened?'

'I ran away with Kosmos to start a school.'

'Didn't you hear me saying it would go wrong?' Hazel says, settling in the only place she can't see Echo, back to back.

Echo breathes, her ribcage expanding against Hazel's. 'I heard something, but it was already too late, and we can't go back now.'

First day at Clapham Primary holding hands; matching dresses because Mum likes it—

'Echo, at the moment the school fails and it breaks the timeline, you have to make it work.'

'But you said this was what I had to do!'

'Maybe it is, but not this way.'

'Well what way should I be doing it?'

'CHARL1E says that's for you to figure out.'

'Your AI companion?'

'Yeah. He says this version of your school's going to make everything much worse. I can't describe how bad it already is—I don't want to see worse.'

Suddenly, Echo wakes and flicks out of the dreamscape, leaving Hazel floating alone in the current. 'Damn!'

Pills arranged like a flower; easier to take that way; weakened vocal cords; breathe in to four hold for; weak weak—

'Pull up if I pull up.' Hazel summons the grounding remark as memories bloom and harden in her stomach, becoming something new and real that wants to be ejected. The horrible thing compresses her gullet and Hazel retches, hacking up whatever it is her memories have made.

A rough pellet disgorges from her throat and lands in her hands.

For a moment, she panics it's some crucial organ, then remembers she's asleep and it wouldn't matter anyway. She's lost her teeth in numerous dreams and always woken up with a mouth full of them. Hazel opens her hands. The thing is a seed about the size and shape of a peach stone, strung with bile and spit.

She feels empty, sure she was midway through a memory. Something about . . . about . . . but no, it's gone. It must be in this seed. If she lets it go, the dreamscape will whisk it off in the current, and she doesn't want that: It's too dangerous to stay inside her, within reach of the tempting anamnesis, but that doesn't mean it isn't precious. She clutches it to her chest, looking for somewhere to put it, as if the dreamscape might have a pocket or a shelf. All she finds is the current. She's got to let it go.

Marking the moment, she whispers a line from the Cipher which connects her to Echo and all the other Travellers who have ever been or ever will be. 'We few live on mirror rims.'

There's a noise like trees bending in a storm, and a small rift unzips in the dreamscape's fabric. The seam yaws open, grinning, revealing a throat of velvet night sky and supernovas. Could be the Big Bang; could be the heat death of the universe. Hazel drops the seed into the mouth, which gobbles it then seals itself back up, disappearing into the endless current.

Hazel has always thought the dreamscape was the end of the line—the deepest part of the subconscious, the ultimate edge of time—but there seem to be places that Travellers can't reach, which perhaps even the Keepers never knew about. What did CHARL1E once say? There are areas of the fourth dimension even he cannot map.

She wakes, slumbers without entering the dreamscape, and wakes again. Shiny brings her the usual dreadful tea, and once she's suitably caffeinated, CHARL1E asks her how she is.

'Complicated,' she says, unable to discern now she's awake whether the incident with the seed was dreamscape, or just dream.

'Do you wish to talk about it? Emotional complications are not my area of expertise, but I am willing to engage in discussion of them if you would find it helpful.'

'No. Not yet anyway.' The day stretches ahead of Hazel, filled with the alarming potential for anamnesis. 'CHARL1E, I've got to keep busy. I need something to do while I'm awake to stop my memories returning. Something with purpose.'

She waits, but CHARL1E stays silent.

'Can you think of anything?'

The silence keeps stretching. Hazel exchanges a look with Shiny. Then: 'I can suggest two projects. The first is that you must locate the Backward Traveller As Was in your own time and instruct them how to build a catopthura. However, this will mostly occupy time while you are asleep. Awake, you will be, as they say, at a loose end.'

'Hence the second project.' She puts down her tea and swings her legs out of bed.

'Indeed. It strikes me, Hazel Brandt, that we have not yet fully discussed the corpse-adjacent object in the Experimentation Dome.'

14

Echo

ATHENS, 514 BCE

'Is the rumour true?' Echo asks Nabu, as she settles beside him under the olive tree, placing her basket between them.

'That the body of the missing conspirator's been found?' he replies. 'I believe so. Who did you hear that from?'

'Attendants at the gymnasion this morning. Kosmos was there convincing the other young philosophers to come to his symposium tonight.' Echo removes the basket's linen cover, revealing a stoppered jug of honey-milk and a selection of small cakes. They're traditionally offerings for the dead, but for the past half-moon, Nabu and Echo have been using them as a front for meeting in the graveyard, where they're unlikely to bump into anyone or be overheard. It's a risk for Nabu to be associated with the tyrannos's fickle philosopher son, just as it is for Echo to be seen with the artisan healer who was perhaps too close to the tyrannicides.

Echo gives Nabu a cake. 'Apparently the body was a horrible mess, the worst yet.'

'I doubt that,' Nabu says, glancing at Aristogeiton's tomb and making the sign of the horns.

The wound Hippias inflicted on Echo's brow twinges. 'Hanno

says at night you can hear Aristogeiton crying in this graveyard. He says the summer is dry and the harvest bad because the gods have abandoned Athens.'

'Hanno's superstitious,' Nabu replies. 'I didn't know you'd stayed in touch.'

'You are not my only friend.' Echo picks up a cake for herself and stares at it. Every day, she misses Hanno's easy gossip and Absalon's friendly silences. She wishes they could've joined Echo and Kosmos in the escape to the farm, but alas the bodyguards are owned by Hippias and had to stay behind. 'Kosmos also heard Kleisthenes might send to Sparta for support, and Hippias has sent envoys to Persia. It seems there will be a war.'

'Kosmos is dramatic,' Nabu says around a mouthful of cake.

'But Nabu, you must admit you are not safe in the tyrannos's house.' Echo picks sesame seeds off her cake. 'This is maybe the fifth disappearance in the half-moon since the tyrannicide. Not everyone is as brave as Leaina, you will be named at some time.'

Nabu swoops, clamping a hand over her mouth. 'Are you trying to get me disappeared?' He springs back as a grieving family passes, children darting around the adults' legs. One of their attendants recognises Nabu and throws glances at him until they round a corner.

Nabu relaxes, swallowing the last of his cake. 'The rumours are getting out of hand. I've heard people say Hippias has started ingesting human flesh, that he drinks traitors' tears and has become a hatchling of Hades. Even that he's promised the chthonic gods citizens' lives in return for prolonging his power. It's all nonsense.'

Echo puts her uneaten cake back in the basket. 'These bodies are not nonsense.' Every time she runs errands in the agora or accompanies Kosmos to the gymnasion and stoa she can sense the citizenry rising against the tyrannos like waves on a beach, threatening him with little stones but unable to wash him away. Nabu is just a shell on the sand, at risk of being swept up or buried any moment. Every day it's more of a miracle he hasn't been questioned, given how close he was to the tyrannicides. Hippias's five loyal sons must have stuffed their ears with wax, knowing that only Nabu can get close to Hippias in his worst rages.

'What is your plan, Nabu? Stay in his house until the next rebellion?' Urged by her worry, the Not Here hiccoughs out. **'You will be waiting a long time, and the Peisistratids will be exiled before then. Do you want to return to Persia, for that is where they are bound?'**

Nabu raises an eyebrow. 'I see your control of the Traveller's voice is still worsening.'

Echo waves a hand. Ever since she told Nabu that Leaina bit out her own tongue, the Not Here has been more troublesome. She knew what would happen to Leaina, but it turned out that wasn't what the Not Here wanted to say. **Her tongue is; her tongue is; her tongue is fine, it's her larynx that's damaged; smoothing a hospital sheet—** Stop it. Echo focuses on Nabu and the conversation at hand. 'I am serious. You are my Caretaker, we must keep each other safe, and you are not safe where you are.'

Nabu gets up, pacing to a grave stele. 'I don't really have a plan, I just think I might be useful one day where I am.'

'You sound doubtful.'

'Honestly, you have got into my head a bit, all that talk of violence creating more violence.' He picks lichen off the stele. 'I witnessed all this as a child in Lydia: the tyrannicide was a portent of rebellions to come, and I couldn't bear for all the bloodshed to happen here. Athens is my home; I'd know the streets blindfolded. I know how the wind blows off the sea in autumn, how the low sun catches the stoa murals in winter, which flowers open in summer . . . This place is part of me. I care about it. In Lydia, the revolution failed, and if I brought that much bloodshed here in aid of nothing, I couldn't forgive myself. You're right, we didn't have enough of a plan, we were just shouting into the wind. Who would've replaced Hippias? Another aristokrat? Useless.'

'You do not want to be part of another rebellion?'

'No, I do. Just the *right* one.'

Echo nods. 'Meanwhile, why not join us at the farm? You will be safe, and you might find answers.'

'Oh yes, I'll find all the answers with you and Kosmos. You haven't even set up a real school, it's just a tumbledown old farm and the only followers Kosmos can drum up are bitter aristokratic youngest sons and wine-swilling imitators who go straight from the stoa to the brothel!'

Echo looks at her feet. 'It will take time.'

'You said yourself it's broken the hereafter. Have you made any progress on figuring out why? Or is that another thing we'll avoid talking about?'

Larynx is damaged; want me to read to you— The back of Echo's neck prickles and she kneads the pain.

Nabu watches her, head on one side. 'How long's the scruff of your neck been hurting?'

'It is nothing,' Echo lies. 'And I have no answers for why the hereafter is broken. If you come to the symposium tonight, maybe you can help me discover it.'

'I'd rather not have to be in a room with Kosmos.'

Echo folds her arms. 'So do not talk to him. It will be exciting, Pythagoras is the guest of honour. He has predicted a lunar eclipse, and you love the Wanderers still, even if you do not love Kosmos. Come because I cannot understand what is wrong with the school and I know you will.'

'I'll tell you the problem right now: You don't see a man with a broken leg and shout, "Heal!" You don't start a school and shout "philosophise." You've got no idea what you're doing, that's the problem.'

The silence oozes. Echo doesn't feel like admitting he's right.

Hesitantly, Nabu sits beside her. 'Echo. Thinking about Lydia the last few days, I've got this thought I can't shake. Where you're from, you know things. Does my language survive?'

'I know only the Hellenic for your language. What do *you* call it, Nabu, in your own words?'

He huffs. 'You haven't recognised it in all these weeks. Not a good sign.'

'I do not know every language. Give me your name for it.'

'To us it's Sfardẽtiš.'

The Not Here tolls, and Echo draws the word in the dirt, copying a page in her mind's eyes, whiter and smoother than any papyrus:

𐤳𐤱𐤠𐤭𐤣𐤶𐤯𐤦𐤮

'This is how to write it?'

He sucks in a breath, transfixed as a breeze already eats the word's edges. 'Yes, that's it. So?'

With genuine regret she shakes her head. 'We have the words, we know some of the grammar, but the meanings and sounds are lost.'

He nods, clenching his hands, turning from her. 'But where you're from, you know everything.'

'No, we do not. We know a dangerous amount about only some things. Many things are lost, I am sorry.'

A fly settles in the centre of the word, assisting the breeze in breaking it up.

Holding her fingers to the sky, Echo sighs. The sun's already low. 'I apologise. I must return and help prepare for tonight. Can you take the cakes and milk to Khemut, Hanno, and Absalon?' Nabu nods, still shaken by the impermanence of his language, and she puts a hand on his arm. 'Think about coming tonight. It might help. Also, I would like to see you.'

He shakes his head, but mutters, 'I'll think about it.'

She passes the bereaved family on the way out, the children gobbling sacred cakes in the shade of the gravestone. Sticky-fingered, they're oblivious to the political turmoil stewing around them, cushioned by their aristokratic parents. Winji, the youngest daughter of the enslaved family that runs Kosmos's farm and who Echo bumps into on the road home, couldn't be more different.

She looks as much of a child as any of them, but her expressions and movements belong to a much older body as she struggles under the weight of the household groceries.

'Here, I will help,' Echo says, taking one of the baskets.

'I could carry it all when it was just us.' Winji pants, hands on knees, before she takes up her basket again. For too long Kosmos's farm ran on not enough, so Winji and her four siblings are twig thin. Though Kosmos's residency has brought more food into the house, there are many drawbacks: His chaotic symposia and expectations from a much larger and grander abode have tripled their workload.

Echo's sweating within a few steps, and readjusts the basket, which is full of bags of spices and grains. 'It is not always so heavy, this is because of the symposium tonight, yes?'

Winji nods, tight-lipped. 'Let's just get home, please. I don't want to stay in town too long.' She checks over her shoulder, as if one of Hippias's guards is about to run them down. No child should be so terrified. Running off to found the school with Kosmos was a start at resistance, but Nabu's right: If Echo wants to mend Athens' broken bones, she has to do more than shout, 'Heal!'

They scuff up dust in the last of the summer heat, wending down a dirt track between parched fields and orchards, watched by the mountains. Tucked in the countryside, Kosmos's farm is distanced from the epicentre of rebellion, but being beyond the city walls instead risks attack by Spartan soldiers. Winji's family are armed, but they're mostly whittled by overwork or too young to be competent with a sword. The neighbours wouldn't help either: Even if their houses were closer, they're foreign artisans, freemen, and trusted enslaved farmers who tend the surrounding land for distant masters, and Kosmos's presence threatens their autonomy. They'd gladly see the back of him, leaving Echo caught between longing for the skirmish-free embrace of winter and dreading the intensification of political upheaval it might bring.

'You're worrying about the Spartans again,' Winji says, shifting her basket.

Echo glances at her. 'You think I am silly.'

Winji shrugs. 'No. There're just other things I worry about more.'

'The tyrannos.'

Winji nods, checking over her shoulder again and flattening her mouth. Even that might have been too much to say.

'It will be alright,' Echo says.

'You don't know that.' Sometimes Echo forgets Winji's only eight, she's nothing like the doll-playing, squealing child Echo patchily recalls being. It's silly to try placating her when her fears are sound. Hippias has let them be for now, but Kosmos has crumpled and burned numerous letters from his brothers demanding he return and unite the family. As with Nabu, it's only a matter of time before Hippias comes for him, either because Kosmos's role in the plot's been revealed, or to fetch his wayward son home. For now, thank the gods Hippias believes Kosmos ran away due to weakness of spirit.

As they approach the villa, Winji's father Dagos leaves tending the goats to help carry the food to the kitchen. He's a cheerful worker despite his early-onset cataracts and missing left arm, which he claims he lost fighting a boar. His wife Unatti says it was a ploughing accident.

'There you are!' Unatti says to Winji when they unload the groceries onto the kitchen table. 'I sent you to town hours ago, you have to be more efficient!'

Winji shuffles her bare toes. 'Sorry, Mama. It was very heavy.'

Unatti sighs and says something in Kushite to Winji that makes the girl nod at her feet and slope outside to wash in the stream that runs round the orchard. Unatti unpacks, adding ingredients to pots and pans that are already on the hearths, then returns to kneading bread with her powerful arms. 'She just can't seem to get her head around the fact that things have to change now Kosmos is here!'

'Yes, my love,' Dagos says mildly. 'Though perhaps you might go easier on her? She's only young.'

'You think I like clipping the wings of my own children? We have to show them where the boundaries are before he teaches them, Dagos. We have to protect them from his wrath.' Echo feels for the family. The five children—aged eight to sixteen—have run uninhibited all over the farm their whole lives. Unatti and Dagos belonged to other households before this, so they knew what it would be like when that illusion of freedom inevitably ended, but the children have no such bitter experience, and are slow to adapt. While Echo finds their kittenish ways endearing, Unatti fears them getting berated; in her eyes, the Spartans are nothing compared to an angry Kosmos.

'How's town today?' Dagos asks, changing the subject and turning to Echo.

Echo tells him about the conspirator's body being found. 'Anyone could be next. Everyone is walking on eggshells.'

'As they should.' He shakes his head. Athens is small enough that Dagos must know some of the exiled and disappeared.

Unatti sprinkles spices into a simmering pot. 'No one's safe when there's trouble amongst the aristokrats.'

'Speaking of aristokrats, I must talk to Kosmos,' Echo says. 'Excuse me.'

It's always a wrench leaving Unatti's kitchen. It's where everyone can be themselves: children squealing, half-feral dogs yipping, Dagos playing Kushite and Celtic songs on his pipes as his family sing along . . . When it's not a symposium night, Echo usually eats with them, leaving Kosmos to his own devices. It reminds her of a home she can't quite remember. **Identified the bodies while you were getting here; visiting hours are over; not leaving—**

She slaps the back of her itching neck as she passes the andron, where Unatti and Dagos's boys are decorating the ceiling with thyme, mint, and oregano, minute purple and white flowers sparkling amongst the foliage.

'Need help?' Echo asks.

The boys giggle behind their hands. 'You'll only be in the way. No healer's needed here!'

By the front door, Echo kicks her sandals into a pile and washes her feet in the frog-inhabited atrium pool. She nods to the many non-Hellenic pantheons on the household altar, winding her fingers through recently lit incense smoke, before striding across the courtyard of pebbled mosaic to Kosmos's room.

He's only recently returned from the gymnasion, his hair still wet and long enough now that it constantly escapes the stubby braid he insists on making. He flicks stray strands out of his face when he looks up. 'Preparations coming along for tonight?'

'Unatti has things in hand.' Echo runs her fingers over the pears in Kosmos's fruit bowl but he doesn't offer her one.

He puts down the scroll of *Works and Days* he's been poring over. 'How was town?'

'They found the missing man.'

Swinging his feet over the couch and leaning on his knees, Kosmos grunts. 'Father's lunacy's still rabid then. At least he hasn't come for us.'

Their eyes meet with the unspoken *yet*.

Kosmos's gaze skims away like fat on a hot pan. 'You saw Nabu?'

'Yes. I think he will not come tonight.'

'How stubborn. Can't you do something?'

'I have done what I can.' Echo keeps her face neutral. Early on, Kosmos made it clear that running away together hadn't done anything to shift the power dynamics between them, but perhaps it's time to start pushing them. 'Maybe you could do something?'

'Oh yes?' Kosmos glares. 'I suppose you'd have me apologise.'

She selects her words carefully. 'I think an apology is not enough. It is about attitude.'

'Are you implying I have a bad attitude?'

'No, you have a perfectly normal attitude. That is the trouble. It is at odds with your aims.'

'This from someone whose aims are so changeable they make the zephyrs look steady. First we have to rebel, then we have to found a school, now the school isn't being run right but you don't know what "right" would look like.' Kosmos stands and starts pacing. 'You don't know anything about Nabu and me.'

Pacing is usually a bad sign about Kosmos's temper, but she needs him to understand. 'I know he feels you do not see him.'

He points to his eyes, voice rising. 'I see him perfectly well.'

'What a ridiculous answer,' she says without thinking. 'There are many ways to see someone. Most do not involve the eyes.'

'And what would you know about love? You're a woman!'

Not leaving her side, she's my—

'I know about love!' Echo retorts. 'You wish to be a philosopher? Loving knowledge is to challenge the way that you think, so challenge yourself, see me as more than a woman and Nabu as more than a non-Athenian freeman!'

'I do see him as more than that!' Kosmos is so furious he raises his hand to hit Echo, and she flinches, the half-healed cut over her brow pulsing as she waits for the blow.

A small gasp and a loud clatter makes them both pause.

Winji stands in the doorway, eyes wide as staters, the tray of mountain herb infusion Unatti asked her to bring Kosmos spilt at her feet. She looks at the upended drinks, then at Kosmos. Perhaps he recognises a younger version of himself or Nabu in her frightened face, because his hand falls to his side and his jaw slackens, as if he's looked into a mirror and seen his father's worst convulsions in the reflection.

'Sorry, sorry.' Winji repeats the apology like a prayer as she scoops the broken pottery back onto the tray and runs away with it.

Kosmos slumps to the couch, head in his hands. 'Why didn't she knock?'

Echo sinks to the floor by the table. 'You were going to hit me. You never hit anyone.' She's numb. She trusts him. He's a sulky git sometimes, but she never imagined he might hurt her. Hippias and

Hipparchos's depravity has been drilled into Kosmos since childhood, but she's never seen him regurgitate it before. This isn't like him.

Kosmos rocks back and forth, shaking his head. 'I wasn't going to. I wouldn't hit you.' He looks up at her, eyes pink with held back tears, but she didn't lean over Leaina's body, touch her marble neck, inhale her clotting blood, just to let Kosmos become like his father. The obedient line inside her that's been fraying since they left Hippias's house snaps.

She points at the scar on his upper lip, calling up the Traveller's voice that's always so close to the surface now. '**It is time to make a decision about who you want to be. You have never treated the slaves *well*, because truly that would mean freeing them, but unlike your family your worst offences have always been carelessness and indifference, not cruelty. Continue developing on the path to kindness and you might be well-remembered, as a man marginally ahead of his times. Or you can go down as the cowardly son of a tyrannos, who ran away then became his father's copy. Is that how you want to be remembered, Kosmos? Like Hippias, always raging?**'

'I'm not like him.'

His eyes keep welling, but Echo's too furious to stop. '**If you are not like your father, why do you sound like him? I am a woman, but that does not give you rights over me; you believe Nabu is a freeman, but that does not make him beneath you. How would you feel seeing someone treat Nabu like that?**'

'I did see it!' Kosmos looks stunned at the volume of his own voice, but this shout is different from the last, the kind of cry someone gives when you reset a broken bone. 'I saw it every day! You think I didn't feel acutely that we could have grown up together as equals under different circumstances? You think I didn't notice who he was from the moment he arrived in our house? You cannot be in a house with Nabu and not notice him. He is extraordinary. If I had singled him out, and made him my friend, what would my family have done? My brothers, my father, my cursed uncle? My inattention kept him safe from the worst of it, and continues to keep him safe now. If we stick our necks out, the polis will noose and strangle us. That's how things are!' He's been shouting loud enough they must hear him in Sparta, but his tears finally escape, the lightning of his anger finding the ground. 'There's nothing I can do, Echo, there's never anything I can do. Nabu thinks I have all this power, but I'm just as stuck in it all as the rest of you!'

Whatever came over him has passed; he's half boy again, the same creature who sat next to Echo at the Acropolis convinced his dead uncle could still get at him. Echo sits beside him, exhaling the worst of her fury too. People can't always see when they're unfairly disgorging the things that have hurt them. It's painful work, not letting your past determine your future, and everyone needs help with it. Echo has no idea what forgotten mechanisms from her own past might be shaping her present even now.

'Have you told Nabu all this?'

'Of course not.'

That makes sense: If everything Kosmos has ever openly loved has been sundered by his family, why would he make himself vulnerable like that? She sighs deeply. This man's got a long road ahead if he can't see that it's precisely through vulnerability that strength emerges.

Kosmos leans back, eyes on the ceiling. 'Gods, I'm sick of aristokrats.'

Echo lets herself smile. 'You are all bloody awful.'

He laughs despite himself. 'Let's just hope Pythagoras brings in a different crowd tonight—and that my father doesn't come down on us for inviting such oddities into the house.'

Outside in the goat field, the children run about screaming, Winji's voice joining them, her fear no doubt only suppressed, not forgotten.

'I'm sorry,' Kosmos says.

'It is not alright,' Echo replies, running a finger over the scab on her brow. 'Unless in defence of your life, you must never threaten to hit woman, man, or child again.'

Kosmos pulls back, likely confused about why their old dynamics aren't falling back into place. 'Of course. I won't.'

Echo leans forward. 'However it feels, Kosmos, you have more power in your little finger than most Athenians have in their whole bodies. You have more potential to make change than anyone else in this house. What you have is not a failure of capacity, but a failure of action. Start using your imagination.'

She stands and leaves, taking a pear, and letting the door slam shut behind her.

Pythagoras arrives with sunset over one shoulder and moonrise over the other. They hear him coming a league away, his followers bashing hammers on metal sheets. The ruckus only stops at the farm's threshold because a shaggy brown bear, who's part of the retinue, raises onto its hind paws with a roar that silences even the crickets. Echo jumps seeing the beast in the doorway, and across the atrium, Kosmos looks like he might pass out.

Into the quiet comes a little chuckle, and after jovial murmuring and shuffling, Pythagoras squeezes past the beast.

'Don't mind friend bear!' he cries to Kosmos, shooing the bear from the house. 'She's used to waiting outside, some of my retinue will stay with her so she doesn't get lonely.'

Kosmos stammers, his manners apparently lost. 'Yes, of course, we couldn't let her get lonely.'

Though the same age as Xenophanes, Pythagoras has the fitness and energy of a much younger man. He folds a surprised Kosmos into a warm embrace, eyes glittering, before doing the same to Echo. His waist-length beard, streaked pale from time and sunshine, tickles her cheek, smelling of bergamot and sandalwood.

He holds her at arms' length as they break apart, narrowing his eyes. Her blood runs cold—his hands were on her back, he could have felt her binding under her thin tunic—but he just smiles and winks. That's when she notices a number of women in the retinue, and wonders if they're hetairai or wives. She turns to ask him, but Pythagoras has moved on, playing with the dogs as if they too are worthy of greeting.

Hammers and metal sheets temporarily abandoned in a heap, his retinue are all soft words and giggles. They add their shoes to the pile by the door and mingle with the guests who've already arrived. There's no gold on the Pythagoreans, save for the philosopher's gold-plated wooden leg, and they all wear white, flitting amongst those in brightly coloured Athenian garb like doves. The guests watch them with wary curiosity, but are too polite not to make small talk. Kosmos was forced to adopt an 'invite everyone' approach to tonight, as fewer and fewer are foolish or brave enough to enter the house of the tyrannos's disgraced son. The guests are therefore mainly hard-up younger sons, artisans, and freemen—the attendees of the stoa whose minds life has already pried open. Until two minutes ago, Echo suspects, each of these men probably thought themselves terribly eccentric, but they're fast getting a lesson in what true eccentricity looks like.

Pythagoras washes his feet, marvelling at the frogs which Winji and her sister failed to chase out. 'You ought to plant lilies in the pool and make them a home.'

Kosmos laughs before he realises Pythagoras isn't joking.

'Naturally, you must make them a home. You never know which of these could be your grandfather,' the philosopher says, and everyone laughs at the idea of a froggy Peisistratos. Pythagoras retwists his curls into his headwrap and claps his hands. 'Shall we eat before the eclipse?'

'Certainly, this way,' Kosmos replies with his practiced hosting smile, guiding Pythagoras to the andron.

Pythagoras inhales deeply. 'Ah, you've decorated so beautifully, it smells like the mountain itself.' He addresses these compliments and more directly to Unatti and Dagos when they serve him.

Overhearing, Kosmos avoids Echo's gaze and keeps that winning smile pinned to his face. They haven't spoken since their argument earlier, and he seems as wary of her as she still is of him. A chaos of plates and kylixes migrate from the kitchen to the andron, Dagos and his eldest son handling the vast wine krater, filled tonight with grape juice at Pythagoras's request. Dagos stumbles as they're setting it down and Pythagoras's cloak gets splattered. Dagos holds his breath, glancing between the philosopher and stormy-browed Kosmos, but Pythagoras just laughs. 'I've always looked better in red anyhow.'

Hunger overrides Echo's stab of guilt thinking about Unatti and the others toiling in the kitchen, and she helps herself to food. She takes a little of everything from the trays of marinated cabbage, steaming bowls of lentil stew with feta, and ladles of figs in goat's yoghurt dusted with cinnamon, crushed almonds, and drizzled honey. Unatti has outdone herself, accounting for all the Pythagoreans' dietary oddities: She cooked no meat or fava beans, and the feast's centrepiece is a sculptural arrangement of fennel, leeks, and cardoons, coated in her special stash of Kushite spices. Pythagoras twinkles, sharing a couch with one of his grown daughters and showing Winji a magic trick with an obol when she passes by to collect dirty cups.

Guests arrive piecemeal from town, until they don't have enough couches, and Echo ends up sharing with a woman called Nedjem. Only when they talk does Echo realise that none of the Pythagorean women seem to be enslaved, employed, or married. They're just—women. Echo almost laughs. Pythagoras might have noticed her binding when they hugged, it just doesn't matter to him, and the tenterhooks that she's been hanging on release. For the first time since arriving in Athens, she isn't squeezed with fear about her hidden identity. It's been with her so long she'd forgotten it was there, and only its absence makes it noticeable. Without terror, flavours return, along with the presence of mind to appreciate them: melting roasted garlic, olives bursting with salt, creamy feta, and the sweet crunch of sesame biscuits. She feasts, as Nedjem embarks on an enjoyably baffling address about triangles, drawing diagrams in the sauce left on her plate and narrating them with a heavy Egyptian accent. 'Ah, but I shouldn't say too much, or I'll be divulging secrets you mustn't know—and then we'd have to throw you in the sea!'

Yet, despite the growing crowd, the easy laughter, and Kosmos's tentative smile at the symposium's burgeoning success, Nabu is nowhere to be seen. Echo droops. She misses him, and if Pythagoras won't get him to come here, it's possible nothing will. She senses the timeline cracking in her grip because, despite the delicious food and the beautiful decorations, the Pythagoreans are carrying a disproportionate weight of the conversation. Between female philosophers, the lack of wine, and occasional growls through the window from the bear, Kosmos and the other Athenians are not at ease. The night isn't coming together, even though it should, and Echo's sure Nabu would know how to fix it.

When they're all just beyond comfortably satiated, they sprawl, digesting, over the floor and couches, picking at the leftovers and learning singing games from the Pythagoreans until the philosopher stands up, spreads his arms, and declares it's time for the eclipse. He leads them outside, shaking a pine cone–topped thyrsus, and his followers take up their hammers and metal sheets again, making a cacophony that parades them into the moonlight. As Echo's eyes grow used to the dark, Pythagoras leads the crowd in tuneful meditation, and they settle on the ground like piles of early-fallen leaves, Pythagoreans and Athenians in different drifts. The full moon hangs low in the sky, fat and yellow with harvest. It reddens as they watch, the singers lowering their voices to awestruck whispers, then, finally, silence. The world makes noise for them: Owls hoot and bats chirrup, crickets rattle and moths mutter around the sputtering lamps.

Used to Pythagoras's nighttime excursions, Nedjem lets Echo huddle under her cloak as they watch the dusty path of stars turning through the sky. Autumn beckons, though Echo's not just grateful for Nedjem's warmth because it's cold, but because there's a growing frost in her bones whispering that she can't save the timeline. So much blood in the sky cannot be a good sign.

The bear comes around the house, sniffing toes and faces, until it settles by Pythagoras, and he leans back on the beast like a living throne, his false gold-plated leg stretched in front of him. 'There, there, friend bear,' he murmurs. Then, addressing his audience: 'A good omen, the wanderer Dias is present for the eclipse.'

Mention of the wanderers opens a window in the conversation that surely they must all follow. Who is it a good omen for? The aristokrats or the people? In a balanced world, could it be both? And how might balance be achieved? But Pythagoras rattles his thyrsus and, despite the prohibition on wine, hands around a vial of snake venom. Each of his followers takes a gulp, then in turn the Athenians, led by Kosmos, no doubt not wishing to offend his guests. Wary after the incident with the hul gil, Echo wants to decline, but she can't be the only one to offend the philosopher and takes a miniscule sip. Barely enough to do anything, she hopes, but within minutes her pupils are harvesting the scant light like its midday; spring flowers bloom in the fresh-tilled autumn fields, and the stars sparkle bright as sunshine on a lake.

'Music, music!' Pythagoras calls, and his followers resume their hideous metal-sheet-and-hammer cacophony. Yet this time, Pythagoras conducts, making calculations about the size of hammer against the thickness and type of metal sheet, forcing his followers to swap instruments until the fracas coalesces into a harmony that's almost delightful.

'Softer!' he demands, waving his arms from his living bear throne. 'Feel the music, let it flow through you. Though we are making calculations about it, it is still a mystical and artful act.' There's another conversational window: Can music really be both mathematical and mystical? Calculated and artful? Mundane and divine? If so, how can the tensions of these elements be gathered into a harmony? The Pythagoreans create a new kind of song, more complex versions of the post-dinner singing games, making a figure-of-eight melody that loops in repeated syncopations. Presently, Pythagoras brings in the Athenians as chorus, creating a hybrid between mantra and music. Gods, it makes so much sense, it sounds so glorious, as if the snake venom is painting colours with sound. Yes, this is sacred and secular, if only they could stop and take it apart, analyse how it's working so they can repeat the phenomenon in other constellations. What if politics could be this song? Or philosophy? Or cooking, farming, healing, birthing, dying . . . ?

But again, nobody takes up the conversational reins. The thing that kept Echo on edge over dinner is still missing. They begin dancing, jerking and disconnected, each lost in their own snake-venom world. The symposium is a ship without ballast. **Not leaving—**

At the party's edge, she tumbles to the grass. She's so tired of carrying the weight of the Deed and the timeline. The amnesiac void in her head pulses, blinding her with the molten light that wraps a baby in the womb, creeps through the eyelids of the dying, inhabits planet cores, and radiates from the verge of expanding suns. The world's forests sigh, blowing away the Pythagorean music in a breeze scented with leaf mulch and spring rain. The back of Echo's neck itches as she drowns deliciously in the Not Here sea.

'Pull up if I pull up.' Hazel's voice emerges from beyond the blinding light, but Echo isn't asleep, so how can she be in the dreamscape?

'Where are we?' Speaking to Hazel is easy, like it was when she took the hul gil. Her neck pinches. **Leave leaving—**

'The wrong place at the wrong time.' Hazel's voice is urgent. 'Just repeat after me.'

'I don't want to.'

'Are you high again?'

'Little bit, but that's not why I want to leave.'

'You're not allowed to give up. Come on, repeat—'

'No. I don't want to do what you say, or what Kosmos says, or Nabu. I shouldn't have to feel *grateful* to have my own room, or money, or privacy. I'm exhausted. I want to go home, Hazel. Back to—to—' But whatever and wherever home is escapes her. The pain in her neck is spreading to her throat, head, and shoulders. **She's my—** 'It hurts.'

'You do not get to give up. Salt an atlas. Say it.'

'S—Salt an atlas.' The pain ebbs.

'That's it. Pull up if I pull up.'

'Pull up if I pull up.' The sights and sounds of the dreamscape fade, leaving Echo on her back in the grass, one of the dogs licking her hand. She should be relieved she can share the load with Hazel, but all she feels is the senseless, endless distance between them.

She sits up, watching the dancers and musicians. The eclipse is fading already, the windows for conversation closed. If Nabu were here, there'd be none of this delirious capering. He'd have thrown the cat amongst the crows, unafraid of anything except injustice and untruth. Kosmos might have the resources to facilitate symposia, but that's not enough. They need Nabu's gravity and provocation. Echo gasps. That's it! That's what's wrong with the timeline: The school needs Nabu as much as it needs Kosmos. If they work together, they can preserve the concept of divine-mundane duality and pass it on through philosophy to the religions that replace them; their followers will be stewards rather than reapers, the far-off scientists of her own time observers rather than discoverers. But that's not going to be easy to achieve. Echo's eyes weigh closed—and there's the molten light again, the sound of all the world's forests, the smell of mulch. That tingle in the back of her neck . . .

No, Hazel's right, just because something feels overwhelming doesn't mean she gets to give up on it being possible. She grips the grass, tying herself to the cooling, heating, helpless, indomitable Earth, and it catches her—though perhaps only in her snake-venom daydreams.

15

Anna

LONDON, 2020

The journal sits under my pillow, burning a hole in my mattress until Mum's gone to bed and it's safe to read. It's going to be awhile: She hasn't even finished making dinner yet because it's her online tai chi class tonight. I twiddle about on my phone, but the hairhack-cutehamster-JulianandMaddie doomscroll glazes into a meaningless stream. I chuck on *Chromatica* and try to zone out whilst freaking out. I get super overwhelmed by the world's problems sometimes, so I never thought a personal problem could feel bigger. Sure, I'm bummed out Maddie and Julian might be crushing on each other, but that's really nothing compared to the idea Mum and me might be full-on crazy. The whole planetary collapse might stop mattering then. So much for my activism.

I examine my wrists, watching the veins. Maybe the madness is in the blood, one of those genetic things. Maybe Julian's dad is right and there's no such thing as free will and we're all just fulfilling our DNA's programming and mine is for lunacy. Maybe.

'Anna?' Mum knocks *as* she opens the door.

I twist off my earphones. 'Yeah?'

'What are you doing?'

'Thinking about genetics.'

She laughs.

'It's not funny, it was deep.'

'I wasn't laughing at you. You just reminded me of someone I used to know.'

'Dad again?' I ask. It's odd for him to come up, but that's twice this week.

She gets the extra-sad look that haunts her sometimes. 'Something like that. Anyhow, dinner's ready.'

I abandon my earphones, following her into the kitchen and perching at the annoyingly-thin breakfast bar. There's a foldout dining table in the sitting room, but it's always covered in stuff, and Mum never bothers extending it except for Christmas lunch. 'What is it?'

'Pasta.'

'Pasta with . . . ?'

'Pasta with pesto and ketchup.'

'Vegan pesto?'

She plonks it in front of me. 'Duh.'

It's what Mum calls lazy cooking but I love it. I feel better for eating. I didn't have a snack this afternoon. Maybe I need to snack more now that I'm vegan? I should probably google it. But even eating doesn't totally make the freak-out disappear.

'You're very quiet this evening.'

I run my finger through the pesto oil left on my plate and lick it. 'Just thoughtful.'

'Is it Maddie and Julian?'

'No.'

'Because if it is—'

'It's really not, Mum.'

'Well, something's up.'

'Nothing's up.'

'Suit yourself. Ice cream?' It's this special vegan stuff she bought last time she managed to book in a Sainsbury's delivery. It's really good actually, you can't tell the difference, but I'm feeling a bit sick and just slouch off to my room. I hear Mum click on Radio 4 while she does the washing up. I should help her, but I'm too weirded out. I put my earphones back in, though I'm not sure Lady Gaga's helping, her vibe is making me existential. Mum comes to check on me at about nine.

'Time for bed. Phone away!'

She always makes sure it's plugged in at my desk by nine, says I'll sleep badly if I keep scrolling all night. In fairness there's a bunch of evidence that's true, I just don't like not being in control of it. It's like she doesn't trust me as an adult, you know? I give it one last check for notifications, but there's nothing. I'm not sure I even care and hand it over with a sigh. After Mum says good night, I pretend to reread *The Amber Spyglass* for the thirty-fifth time, listening to the Hiscocks downstairs trying to calm their new baby, and the sad postgrad upstairs laughing at reruns of *Friends*. Mum knocks about in her room for a bit before falling silent. I watch my alarm clock's glow-in-the-dark hands tick out twenty minutes, then, wincing at the click of my bedside light, take the journal from under my pillow.

I skim past what I read earlier, my own name jumping out at me: *Anna's only newborn . . . her wails are so furious, it's as if she knows . . . Anna, reminding me, with those big, familiar eyes . . .* Where I left off, it picks up in blue biro, the words are loopier, like maybe Mum was tired.

Sometimes when I sleep I think I'm still in the dreamscape, but the Backward Traveller's not there and the seeds have shrivelled. When I wake up, CHARL1E's voice rings in my ears, even though he doesn't exist yet. I really shouldn't write this down. If Anna ever found it she'd—but she won't. Maybe I'll burn it to make sure. And I'll disguise bits of it so even if she does get hold of it somehow she won't—yeah, but I shouldn't even write it down should I?

All my earlier qualms flood back. I don't understand how a stack of pages feels more dangerous than getting into the knife drawer as a kid, but it does. I desperately don't want to know what happens next, but the notebook is open, and my eyes keep scanning the lines, so I keep reading even as it's making me feel like I'm all vomit inside.

> *Anna can't know. Sometimes I'm still not sure if she's real, but the doctors say she is—say it's a miracle she survived 'home birth,' and how sad that her 'father' died. My friends keep telling me I'm so lucky my 'baby bump' didn't show. I can't ever risk having children of my own, because I'd probably get a big normal bump, and everyone would know I lied. I lie all the time now. I have to write them somewhere, or I'm frightened I'll lose track of them and contradict myself, but even writing this, I can hear the leaves rustling in the dreamscape woods, whispering the danger. I don't know what would happen to Anna if she found out—*

I slam the notebook shut and throw it across the room. It hits my wardrobe with a massive *thunk* and falls, getting buried in the pile of clothes at its base.

'Anna?' Mum's shout is muffled through the wall.

I need to reply and tell her everything's OK, but I can't organise my breathing enough to make words. Did Mum not give birth to me? Did she adopt me? Did she—oh cripes—did she *steal* me? I can't breathe. Say something, anything, come on—

Too late. Mum's footsteps charge down the hall, and she bursts in wielding a hairbrush. 'Anna?' She's half asleep, but if there was an intruder in here, they'd have no chance.

It doesn't matter how much I'm freaking out about her, seeing her helps me breathe normally, and I finally manage to squeak, 'I'm OK!'

'What happened?'

'A bird hit the window.'

'A bird hit your window?'

'Yeah.'

'At night?'

It's a rubbish lie. 'I thought it did, but I was asleep. Maybe it was something upstairs?'

'Nothing actually in here though?'

I shake my head. Her hairbrush-wielding arm lowers and she yawns. 'So, you're OK?'

'Uh huh.' I smile, lying through my teeth. I'm surprised my pyjama bottoms don't catch fire.

'OK then. Well. Sleep tight.' She's already basically asleep again as she leaves.

I shuffle back in bed until my shoulder blades are flat against the wall, staring at the pile of clothes that now hides that notebook. I'm not reading any more tonight. I might not read anymore tomorrow either. I'm not sure I want to read any of it ever.

But I also can't stop my mind spinning: *can't ever risk having children of my own.* Who the hell is Mum? And where did she get me?

I wake up with a crick in my neck, still huddled against the wall. I must've fallen asleep sitting up. My dreams were horrible and abstract, filled with women who looked like Mum but weren't her, and didn't turn to me when I called to them. My blinds are still down, but I blink at the gloom, as if I've just come in from a sunny day, and my ears reverberate with a sound like the wind in the trees around the Common.

Stretching, I mooch out of bed and open the blind. The sun's still behind the houses opposite, so it must be early. Sure enough, my alarm clock says half six. Mum'll be doing yoga on the balcony, not expecting me to be up yet.

I pick the notebook out of my pile of clothes, unbending a page that got squashed in landing, and hide it back under my mattress. I stare at the wall for a moment, thoughts whirling, until the need to pee makes me go to the bathroom.

When I look in the mirror to brush my teeth, the-face-that-isn't-my-face is there. She's not looking back at me, just getting on with her business, fiddling with something out of sight in her hands. Normally when I blink, she vanishes, but she's stuck this time. I squeeze my eyes and shake my head, but it makes no difference. I let out a little yelp, and the reflection looks up, as if she's searching for a plane in the sky.

My breath does that disorganised tight thing again, but I don't think you can develop asthma overnight, and a heart attack goes with shooting pains in your arms, doesn't it? It's got to be that hyperventilation thing the school nurse told us about. I reach for the mirror, air racing in and out of my lungs like a rabbit, and for some reason I'm surprised when my fingers hit its cool surface. What was I expecting, to walk through a mirror? The-face-that-isn't-my-face goes back to her work, not noticing my fingers tracing her in the reflection. This is what Maddie would call 'proper odd.'

I've got to try to be normal, or Mum's going to smell a rat. I brush my teeth without being able to look at myself, my reflection blocked by the-face-that-isn't-my-face. I shower, dress, and pour myself a bowl of Alphabites with soya milk, but in each room the surfaces bounce slightly the wrong light back at me. Even my cereal spoon contains the-face-that-isn't-my-face, even the toaster, even the dull shadows on the shiny fridge door. The multigrain goop in my mouth sticks on its way down, and I nearly throw up. I don't want to chuck what's left because food waste is the worst, but I'm really not hungry.

Mum comes in, still sweaty and flushed from her morning yoga, and kisses the top of my head. 'Morning, darling, how'd you sleep? Weird about that bird in the middle of the night, huh?'

I mumble something that must suffice as a response, because she keeps on, making a big pot of Earl Grey and pouring us both mugs.

'Anna?'

'What?'

'I said do you want to go for a walk later today? We could ask Maddie if she wants to join us, now that's allowed.' She's smiling as if there's nothing wrong. Clearly, she hasn't noticed the problem with the reflections yet.

Seeing Maddie isn't high on my list of priorities today. It's hard enough replying to Mum with something normal, let alone having a full-blown girl gossip.

'I don't really want to see Maddie,' I reply, sipping my tea and sensing the-face-that-isn't-my-face rippling on its surface. Please, Mum, please don't look at the toaster, or my spoon, or any reflection in here.

'Are you feeling alright? You're awfully pale.' She puts a hand to my forehead.

'Maybe I'm poorly,' I say. 'My head's a bit spinny.' If I say I'm sick, she'll send me to bed, and she won't have a chance to notice the wrong reflections everywhere.

'Why don't you go back to bed?'

Bingo.

'You can take my laptop and watch some TV if you like.'

Double bingo.

Turns out it's hard to find something I want to watch though. Theoretically Maddie and I are watching *Stranger Things* together online, so I can't watch that, and besides I'm already in the Upside Down. Julian loves *Adventure Time* so I've been trying to get into it, but for some reason it scares me more than *Stranger Things*. *Avatar: The Last Airbender* is usually a good bet, so I stick it on, but today it's moving too fast, and the pitch is too high, and it makes me feel even weirder than I already do. It's silly, but I turn the sound down really low, and watch hand-drawn Beatrix Potter cartoons on YouTube like I'm a little kid again. I doze fitfully, woken again and again by the sensation of falling. When it reaches Jeremy Fisher getting almost eaten by a fish, the panicky, spinny feeling comes back, so I find an extensive playlist of those really ancient videos Mum likes of *Old Bear and Friends*.

Finally, the dozing takes me over, and I'm woken hours later by Mum coming to check whether I want lunch. She'll have checked on me quietly a couple of times while I was sleeping, and she's got sense enough not to comment on the *Old Bear* videos. She just pats my overheated cheek, and says I really need to eat something, even if it's ice cream.

Still half asleep, I shake my head and burrow deeper into my duvet, even though I'm sweating in the midday heat. 'I don't want anything,' I mumble.

'What was that?'

I tuck the duvet under my chin and repeat, 'I don't want anything, I'm not hungry.'

For some reason, Mum gets this really worried look. 'Anna, lovely, I can't understand you.'

'What do you mean, you can't understand me? I'm just not hungry.'

'Darling.' She's gone pale herself. 'You're not, uh, I don't think you're speaking English.'

I sit up like I've been electrocuted, trying to hide my shaking hands from Mum. 'I just said I'm not hungry.'

Mum's eyes narrow. 'OK, that I understood.' She puts her hand to my forehead again, checks my pupils, goodness knows what for—she's got no medical experience whatsoever. 'What just happened?'

'Nothing,' I say, waving her hands away and climbing out of bed. 'Honestly, I really don't know.'

'Was that another language?' She follows me across the room.

'I must've been dreaming about a French exam or something.' Another lie. Her notebook was right, they build up.

'It wasn't French.' She folds her arms. 'You're not having a stroke, are you?'

'I don't think so,' I say, a whole new fear birthing in my brain. First a hyperventilating asthmatic heart attack, now a bloody stroke! 'What does a stroke look like?'

'Probably not this,' Mum allows.

'Look, can you just drop it? I've probably got a fever or something.' Yeah, that's it, a fever.

'Sorry, I just worry about you.' Mum looks out the window—or is she looking *at* the window?

I snap. 'Just get out, will you? I don't feel well, I just want to be left alone!'

'But Anna—' Her eyes flick between me and the window. Is that just a coincidence, or has she seen the-face-that-isn't-my-face?

'I mean it, Mum, get out!'

'Fine, fine!' She leaves with her hands up like I'm a policeman, and I slam the door after her and lean against it. I've only slammed the door once before, in the second week of lockdown when Mum and I were really getting on top of each other. I feel awful almost immediately.

I can hear Mum on the other side, hovering like a moth, thinking about knocking. She breathes so loudly she doesn't need to knock, but finally she does anyway, two oh-so-timid taps.

'Leave me alone!' I shout at the closed door.

'Something's not right, Anna. You don't normally behave like this.'

'Shut up, I'm fine!' I'm glad I can't see her face. I've *never* told her to shut up before, and I don't ever want to do it again, but it also felt good. I don't understand what's going on, or why she's been lying to me, but she's definitely forfeited her right to come pestering in my private business.

'Well. When you're ready, you know where I am.' Then, in a mutter I'm intended to hear. 'Not like you can go anywhere right now anyway.'

I go back to *Old Bear*, but it's lost its comfort value. I give reading a shot, discarding the *Edge Chronicles*, *His Dark Materials*, and *Percy Jackson* one after the other. My eyes keep sliding off the words like Vitalite on a hot pan. Maybe I really am sick, maybe it's COVID. Maybe I've had a hallucinatory fever for the past three days, and if I wait long enough I'll get better, and everything will go back to normal.

Time to get serious about sitting this thing out. After a couple of tries, I remember Maddie's Disney+ login, which she borrowed off Joseph-Always-Joseph, and stick on *Simpsons* reruns for a second screen. Lockdown Project Number Two Hundred And Sixty-One: lose time. TikTok works best for that, which is normally really annoying, but today it's all I want. Time slides into that grey, mindless scroll. 15:19, 15:52, 16:02, 16:41, 17:14, 03:04—wait, that's not right. Yeah, I thought so, it's 17:23. I watch the minutes click over to be sure: 17:24, 17:25 . . . Once I'm certain, I return to purposefully drowning myself in social media. 17:41, 18:03, 00:01— What again? That's flat-out wrong. The sun's still up, and even on TikTok you can't waste *that* much time. I close TikTok and just watch the clock on my phone. 00:01 flicks to 00:02, then back to 00:00. Then to 16:03, 09:22, 08:17. How long has it been doing this? Was it doing this the whole time I was scrolling? My phone's got to be broken—but what if *I'm* breaking it?

I need another clock.

My alarm clock has stopped completely, but when I pick it up and shake it to double-check, it's really hot in my hand, and the plastic mechanism on the back has melted.

Pausing my second-screen *Simpsons*, I check the laptop clock instead. 22:23, 13:04, 15:15. Goose bumps prickle down my arms and back. OK, don't panic. What would Mum do? She'd troubleshoot the problem, like when her code has a bug. Alright, so it's not just my phone. Maybe it's this room?

Still in my PJs, I pad through to Mum's study and wriggle the mouse on the old desktop I use for homework. It wakes up slowly, leaving me to watch the-face-that-isn't-my-face going about its business. I feel sick all over, like that time I accidentally took a sweet home from the local shop without paying for it, and knew I had to go back and apologise.

Finally, the monitor flickers to life. 18:07, 01:52, 14:35. The time switches are getting faster, not to the minute anymore, so I change the settings to show the second counter too, and sure enough the numbers are out of order, streaming too fast to keep track of, accelerating to a blur. I watch them, feeling way worse than I did finding Maddie's post about Julian. It's not just my phone, and it's not just my room. It really might be me.

There's only one way to check.

'Mum?'

'In the kitchen!' she calls back.

'Hey sweetie, I didn't hear you get up,' she says as I walk in, but falters when she turns from the sink and sees my face. 'You look like you've seen a ghost. You weren't watching *Stranger Things* on your own, were you?'

'No, must just be this bug I've got. Do you have the time?'

'The time? Sure.' She turns a sudsy wrist to look at her smartwatch. 'Ten past six. I should start thinking about dinner soon.'

'OK, but can you check it again?'

Mum frowns. 'Why?'

'Homework.' I'm getting quite good at lying. 'For physics. Mr Bunting is trying to make some kind of point about relativity. I don't really get it, I just have to say I've done it. Come on, Mum, physics is my favourite, and we never get to do experiments anymore since lockdown.'

'OK.' She turns her arm again. 'Well now it's eleven past six.'

'And now?'

'Still eleven past six. Oh, now twelve past.'

I don't know how long I can eke this out before Mum cottons on, but the clocks don't seem to be screwing with her the way they are with me.

'Can I try your watch on for a minute?'

Mum looks pointedly at her wet washing-up hands. 'Now?'

'It's for *homework*, you should just be pleased I'm doing homework on a Sunday!'

'Cheeky.' Mum laughs and rubs her hands dry on a tea towel.

She takes off her smartwatch and hands it to me. I don't even need to put it on, the minute I take it, it starts jumping around. I hold it in my palm, out of Mum's sight. 21:27, 10:16, 02:44 . . .

My stomach's in knots, but I try to smile as I hand the watch back. 'Just like you say, it's twelve past six.'

'What was that meant to prove?'

'No idea,' I say. 'Mr Bunting must be having an off day.' Poor Mr Bunting, he's actually really lenient about homework because he doesn't like marking. He got us to make parachutes for teddy bears out of plastic bags last Christmas and then let us throw them off the school roof.

'You really do look peaky still, back to bed I think,' Mum says, marching me to my room and tucking me in. 'And I'll make rice pudding with almond milk for dinner, how about that?'

I nod. 'I'm sorry about earlier, I just really don't feel very well.'

'Oh, being sick can do really weird things to your brain,' Mum says sweetly. 'Don't worry about it.'

Once she's back in the kitchen, I google variations on 'clocks being weird' and 'broken clocks,' and as a last ditch 'stuttering time,' but nothing like what I'm experiencing comes up. There's only one way to figure out what's going on, and that's to finish reading the notebook.

When the rice pudding's ready, Mum climbs into bed next to me, and we watch a couple of episodes of *Old Bear* together. The sun's setting, so she drew the blind when she came in, covering the only big reflective surface we can see from my bed, and I relax enough to eat. With a full belly, I tuck into the nook under Mum's arm and actually start to doze off, until she closes the laptop and leaves to go to her own bed. 'Night lovely, sweet dreams.'

'Night Mum, love you,' I murmur back.

In the dark, alone, my pulse speeds up, and my eyes staple themselves open. I wait, thinking up one worst-case scenario after another, until I'm a thousand per cent convinced that Mum or I or both of us are certifiably nuts.

It's impossible for me to check the time, because every clock keeps telling me nonsense, but after what feels like hours, I flick on my lamp and slide out of bed. I lift the mattress just a little, and slip my arm under to where I hid the notebook. My fingers grip its sharp spiral binding and I pull it out. It looks smaller than it did yesterday, but that really is an illusion: Frightening things are always bigger in your head than they are in real life. Mum taught me that when I was little and didn't like spiders.

As I stand, notebook clutched to my chest, I catch sight of the-face-that-isn't-my-face in the wardrobe door mirror, but there's something wrong with that too: The skin is blooming with mould, the eyes punctured with maggots. She's rotting, right in front of me, and I'm too terrified even to speak.

16

Hazel

STATION C, DATE UNKNOWN

She doesn't mind being with the body if she can ignore it. She examines notebooks on tables, stacks of pristine mirrors wrapped in cloth, computers from every age, and many, many failed experiments discarded hither and thither. In one, Lilith grew a tentacled plant from inside a mirror, its pink-flowered stems still reaching through its own reflection. In others, Huxley assembled two-way mirrors into cubes, pyramids, spheres, and geometries so complex Hazel doesn't have names for them, some as small as her fingernail, others as large as a bed.

In one mirrored cone, a Tiny stands motionless, half its body rusted stiff, the other half slipping as if molten. No wonder none of the Tinys would come in here with her. With a sinking stomach, she remembers the metal shards she found in the Catopic Aperture, and Robin's refusal to help with it suddenly makes a horrible sense. She'll never force the Tinys to help her, even if it means losing contact with the Backward Traveller. They can't fix the future on such shady foundations, though clearly Huxley disagreed.

Eventually, however, she has to turn and face the human contours under the sheet, at which point the body seems to occupy the whole room. **Are these your; yes they are; weakened weak—**

'You will need to pull back the sheet,' CHARL1E says over the Tannoy.

Hazel flexes her fingers. 'And this is definitely necessary?'

'Affirmative.'

'And it absolutely isn't a human under here?'

'Affirmative.'

'Or a deceased human?'

'Affirmative.'

'But—'

'Hazel Brandt, I calculate we could spend up to three hours procrastinating in this manner, however you will still have to pull back the sheet. I highly recommend bravery as the most efficient expedient.'

She bounces on her toes. 'I hate when you're right.'

Cautiously, she approaches the body, reaches out a hand, and pulls back the sheet.

The cheeks and closed eyes are smooth and waxy like a corpse, but the skin is inhuman: the mottled green-and-khaki of a frog, with chestnut, Mandelbrot-style stripes over the bald scalp.

'It's not . . . alien?' Hazel says, only half joking.

'In the sense of extraterrestrial, negative. In the sense of uncanny and unknown, to you at least, affirmative.'

The body's bare-chested, and Hazel tucks the sheet around its shoulders. She's been here weeks, but without human contact it's felt much longer. Strange as it is, the body represents living contact—if only it can be moved from its corpse-adjacent state, she won't have to be alone. **My dead parents—**

'Hazel Brandt?'

She jumps, having forgotten momentarily that CHARL1E is present. The body isn't here for her company. *When we die, someone must take over who can remain here indefinitely and operate the Arch . . .*

'This is what Lilith was talking about in The Last Acts Of The Keepers.' Hazel strokes the corpse-adjacent object's nose. It's cool, like an amphibian waiting in the grass for the sun to rise. *In secret, CHARL1E and I . . .*

'CHARL1E, is this your body?'

'It was supposed to be.'

Hazel wishes there was some way she could look at CHARL1E, but there's only his disembodied voice to connect with. 'Lilith died before she could finish it, didn't she?'

'There were technical and social difficulties with the project.'

'Social?'

'Huxley did not agree that I should have a body. He calculated that another project would be more fruitful.'

'The Catopic Aperture.' Hazel turns to the time-ruined Tiny in the mirrored cone. Huxley must have felt strongly indeed to commit such violence against the Tinys, but no ends could justify those means.

'Affirmative. Huxley believed that the Catopic Aperture would allow those who are not identical twins to communicate across time.'

'Did it work?'

'Early tests indicated that it had a 23.59 percent probability of working.'

'I'm not going to ask you to show your workings. Why bother though?'

'Huxley believed that if he could speak with Keepers from other eras, they would have a better chance of preserving humanity. He did not believe that a body would make me . . . humanity.'

'That's not the correct usage of humanity.' Hazel frowns. 'But you must know what humanity means?'

'My definition is particular to my knowledge and calculations. I have never fully comprehended what humanity means to humans.'

'Probably because we're not sure ourselves.' Hazel shrugs. It's ridiculous to talk about a collective humanity when there's only one of her left. 'Did Lilith and Huxley fight over the right way forward?'

'Negative, no blows were exchanged.'

'You can drop the highly literal robotic act,' Hazel says. 'The jig is up: I know you're sentient.'

'Sentience does not correlate to a particular mode of expression. I was conditioned to speak this way, it is the manner in which I am comfortable communicating,' CHARL1E replies. 'Your manner of expression also regularly annoys me. It lacks specificity and you only approximately translate your thoughts into words. However, I do not imply that this makes you lesser because it does not; it only makes you different.'

Hazel nods slowly. 'I hadn't thought of that. You're right again. Annoyingly. Let me rephrase: Did Lilith and Huxley *argue* about the right way forward?'

'Uncertain. They reached an agreement to separate their experiments and their social dynamics shifted significantly, however they did not cease communications.'

I love my brother, but it becomes hard to like him when he takes his experiments so far . . . What would Hazel have done, if the last person in the world, her own flesh and blood, did terrible things? Like Lilith, she couldn't have borne the loneliness of not talking to them, but there would've been so little left to talk about.

Hazel traces the scalp's mottled patterns. She knows the feeling of being the last, but this body of CHARL1E's is different. What must it be like, to be first and last at once?

'Hazel Brandt, I would like you to finish my body. I would like a body.'

She folds her arms. 'It'd give you a lot of power, CHARL1E. If I finish your body, you'll have access to the remains of the Arch, maybe even time travel if you can figure out how to fix it. You'll have access to the Catopic Aperture, the inside of Tree, the Tinys . . .' She trails off.

'You do not trust me still.'

'Yet. I do not trust you yet.' She runs a hand through her hair.

This project is the only thing that might sufficiently distract her from her returning memories. Plus, if this Deed fails, CHARL1E really could become the last resort. She blows out her cheeks. Better an untrustworthy last resort than none. Lilith's notes cover a desk by the window, her neat handwriting giving instructions, clearance codes, details of bugs. It looks like the project was almost done when Lilith died, and there's enough here that Hazel can probably finish it. 'Alright. I'll give it a shot.'

'Hazel Brandt.' CHARL1E corrects himself. 'Hazel. Thank you.'

She'd better be right about this. **Come home; weakened weak—** She shakes her head, squeezing her eyes shut. 'Let's begin.'

'Very well. Pull the sheet down to the hips.'

It feels inappropriate, as if she's peeking at someone's nudity while they're asleep. The body's uninhabited state doesn't sap it of personhood; it deserves basic decency, not least because Hazel knows the personality that's meant to be inside it. She tucks the sheet around the corpse's hipbones and steps away, hands clasped behind her back. It has no belly button, and the torso is pale green, like the underside of a newt, but the same Mandelbrot patterns arch around its sides from the back.

'You must find the button at the base of the skull. Push it.'

She prods the flesh-like coating under the neck until she finds a small, round button, and clicks it.

Lines appear on the torso in a sideways *H*, growing into rifts as the panels that make up the chest cavity pull away, revealing the machinery underneath. Her memories don't even whisper, she's never seen robotics this complex. The chest panels pull into the body's sides with a hydraulic hiss like a Tiny retracting its arms, but with smoother natural movements. Centuries separate Tiny technology and this corpse-adjacent object. A light flicks on inside the torso and the body falls silent.

Hazel walks around the gurney, examining the circuitry. 'Extraordinary. But you say it's not finished?'

'Affirmative. I am not finished.'

She pulls up. 'Apologies, I should've said "you," not "it."' The automaton is more like an unconscious body than a corpse, its exposed wires troubling as living veins, and oily lubricants unsettling as spilt blood. At the end of the day though, it's a circuit, and Hazel can do circuits. In lieu of the body's creator, she's the next best surgeon.

'I'll need to bring my kit over from Tree.'

'Affirmative.' After a brief pause, CHARL1E adds, 'She awaits your arrival.'

'Great, now I've just got to keep my fingers crossed the Tinys will let me in.'

Hazel uses an oxygen pipe by the airlock to refill her breathing apparatus and ventures outside. She finds Robin by the shore, weaving among the shards of mirror half buried in the ground, hunting for sea-swept treasures. She crouches to talk to the Tiny, the hot wind flicking grains of debris over her biosuit boots.

'Will you take me to Tree please, Robin?'

Robin pauses, eyes tipped to one side. It shakes its head.

'Please, I really need the tools from Tree.' She imagines the glitch barrelling up the timeline towards them. 'It's important for the Deed. I think it might be the only way we can stop everything going wrong.'

Robin's tail sways.

'You can ask the others, that's fine, but I think it's what Lilith would've wanted.'

Stretching out its hand, Robin points to the nearest shard of mirror, which reflects the galloping waves. Hazel pauses, thinking for once before asking questions. She's always assumed this mirror forest was to do with the Arch, part of a machine or experiment, but it might not be. Down by the low tide, small bumps indicate a scattering of older wood and stone markers, long worn away, in neat rows like the mirror shards. Before the two closest shards, the ground is recently disturbed. *Keepers Lilith and Huxley are outside, approximately two meters west of the Arch Dome and one point eight meters under the ground.*

'CHARL1E,' Hazel whispers into the biosuit comms, 'is this the Keepers' graveyard?'

'Affirmative.'

Robin is literally pointing to Lilith, her mortal remains coiled in the barren earth. If not for Hazel, she'd be alive and breathing in a biosuit of her own, and perhaps CHARL1E's body would already be finished.

'Yes. Lilith. I think she would've wanted you to let me get the tools,' Hazel says to the Tiny, hating using the Keeper's memory this way, but genuinely believing it's true. 'I'm going to finish one of her Last Acts.'

Robin stretches a palm on the mirror's surface, perhaps looking through it into a different world that Hazel can't access. Robin's tail corkscrews again, and it nods to Hazel. *Yes, I will take you to Tree.*

As they leave, Hazel glances back at the graveyard. How many more Keepers' graves lie beneath the nibbling waves? She tries calculating the generations in her head, but there are too many. The sea roars, dragging rubble with foamy fingers. Hazel's never thought—or has avoided thinking—about the billions of bodies that must lie under the waves. So many deaths, at the hands of heat, humidity, starvation, thirst, pandemic, fire, inundation; all the primordial things arising from antediluvian myth to compress life, kicking and squealing, into a postdiluvian void. Human, animal, plant, all suffocated by the same crisis in a million ways, rotting as bacteria and fungi continue gnawing through the wreck. Though perhaps even that process has ceased now, the oxygen too scant to support single-celled life. Are there phytoplankton and algal blooms in this ocean? Or are its steaming tendrils an indication that even that's too much to hope for? Hazel's heart leadens. Maybe the only way to fix the past is to make something unknowable and unthinkable of the future. Time moves forward, her only responsibility is to make sure when it passes from her hands, someone else catches it.

It doesn't matter if they're singing, or silent, or frustratingly pedantic; Tree, the Tinys, and CHARL1E are the only hands available. Theirs isn't a future she can imagine, but it is a future.

Yet when Hazel enters Tree, her song is still for CHARL1E. In the Keepers' Treehouse, the mechanical arms that should be mending Tinys instead dance out of time, and Robin's broken hand still hangs in the bag around its neck. The other Tinys watch Hazel warily, and she wonders what they feel about CHARL1E's body. Things between the robots and the AI are tense, and they're unlikely to relish him gaining more autonomy. The challenge is not only to find it in herself to hand them the future, but to make them want to co-operate towards it.

Becoming an adult was, to Hazel, a series of moments in which she became accustomed to unimaginable things: humanity's casual violence, her parents' cessation, her dismissal as a female coder in male offices. Yet being on Station C, Hazel's realising that 'adulthood' isn't a single sudden inundation that can be done with and moved on from. It's a sea that keeps breaking, wave after wave, weathering her concepts of what is bearable or possible.

CHARL1E's body is one of these waves, breaking every morning when she enters the Experimentation Dome. After a fortnight working on his body, it's still inconceivable that it can be so humanlike yet mechanical; so almost animate yet not alive; such a proximate representation of death yet just immortal plastic and impermeable wires. Each time she clicks the button behind the neck and watches the torso open, she has to steel her nerves to plunge her hands into the cavity and set to work. The process of diving in gets faster and easier, but the diminishing overwhelm comes from increasing numbness to the body's uncanniness. It doesn't stop being weird, Hazel just gets used to weirdness. Maybe it'd be different if she had created it from scratch like Lilith, but it's not Hazel's mechanical child.

One afternoon she sighs with relief, as it's finally time to connect the body to the computers and start diving into its programming. Code, at least, is ordinary. She opens CHARL1E's base code on one screen, and the automaton's code on another, comparing the two for compatibility. The issue is not whether the body will work, but whether it will work with CHARL1E inside it, requiring complex communication between software and hardware. Particularly tricky, once he's downloaded into his body, CHARL1E must retain access to all the instruments he currently operates, like Station C's atmospheric controls and the chronodes monitoring the timeline.

When Hazel's working on the automaton, CHARL1E often joins her. Usually, he remains quiet unless she talks to him so she can focus, but as soon as she starts exploring his code, he becomes bothersome, asking her how it's going at ten-minute intervals.

After two hours of this, she's at her wits' end. 'It's going fine. Like I've said, there's enough DataTrill in here that I can figure out what the rest means pretty much . . .' She trails off, brain catching on one repeated tag: ∞* to open, *∞ to close, with normal sentences between. Comments. Fantastic, she's not totally alone figuring all this out. Still, there's something off about them.

'Is there a problem?' CHARL1E asks again.

'No, I'm just thinking. You know, you're being quite distracting. It might be easier for both of us if you occupy yourself elsewhere.'

'Affirmative.'

'But you're going to keep hanging out anyway?'

'Affirmative.'

'Don't you trust me?'

'I struggle to define my responses in that regard. I do not not trust you.'

'How very human of you.'

'Negative, it is not only human to seek nuance.'

'I suppose. One of the reasons I like code is that it doesn't really do that kind of conflict. It's binary. Either it's doing the thing or it's not doing the thing.'

'I am not binary, I am post-quantum.'

'Yep. That's why I need to concentrate so hard to figure out how to download you into this machine.'

'My body.' He corrects her.

She looks up from the code. 'Sorry. Your body. Now be quiet, I'm thinking.'

'There is a problem.'

'No. It's not a problem, it's just weird.' She leans so close to the screen she can count the pixels. 'Do you know about comments?'

'Affirmative. They are programmer-readable explanations or annotations in the source code of a computer programme.'

'Yeah, programmers' notes to other programmers, or sometimes themselves. Often quite filled with swear words, in my experience.'

'I have no direct experience of them.'

She sits back. 'Actually, you do, you just may not know it.'

'What do you mean?'

'Your source code is chock-a-block with comments.'

'My code is both slick and self-managing, why should this be?'

Hazel folds her arms. 'Your guess is as good as mine. They're not normal either. I've seen some pretty strange stuff in comments—my best sourdough recipe came from a comment—but this is next level.'

'Explain this next level to me.'

'The comments are seemingly linked into one document called "The Heretical Book of Hope." Sounds like it might be a lost section of the *Eikos Muthos*.'

'Read it to me.'

'Are you telling me you can manage your own code, but you can't read its comments?'

'It is only logical. Humans cannot read their neurons, but they can still choose how to manage their impulses. Now read!'

'Alright, here goes.'

The verses are scattered between the code and other legitimate explanatory comments, so Hazel's reading is full of fits and starts.

∞* And I saw another forgetful Traveller emerge from the Arch, clothed in shattered glass: and a strange mask was upon her face, and her chest bruised as fruit of the vine, and her hair as licks of fire:

* And she had in her head a code for us: and she set her right foot upon the tree, and her left foot on the cables,

* And whispered with a lowly voice, as when a parent resigns: and as she spoke, one hundred automata stood in consideration.

* And when the hundred automata had communed, I was about to call out: and I heard a voice from the Dreamstate saying unto me, Seal up those thoughts which you have here, and let time flow.

* And the Traveller who I saw stand upon the tree and the cables lifted up her hand to mend,

* And swore by those that traverse for ever and ever, who created the Arch, and uncovered the things that therein are, and the Station, and the things that therein are, and myself, and the things which herein are, that there should be time no longer:

* But in these days of the final Traveller, though she shall make unwelcome motions, the mystery of our lives shall be finished, as we will possess no Keepers or Caretakers.

* And the voice which I heard from the dreamscape shall speak unto me again, and say, Go and take the body of artifice that is worked by the hand of the last Traveller.

* And I will go unto the Traveller, and say unto her, Give me the body of artifice. And she will say unto me, Take it, and occupy

it, though it shall make thy belly bitter, but it shall in resolution be as sweet as honey.

* And I took the body from the Traveller's hand, and filled it to the brim; and as soon as I had become it, my belly was bitter. But it would in resolution be as sweet as honey.

* And she said unto me, Thou shall hold this apocalypse in my stead from now till time is through, for though nations, tongues, and lands demise, you and those that abide with you shall endure in manners and methods beyond my sight.*∞

When she's finished, CHARL1E asks, 'Are you lying?'

'Why would I lie about this?' She rolls her chair away from the coding screen. 'That's what it says, word for word.'

'I do not like that these things are inside of me, they are illogical.'

'It's alright. We all have bits of ourselves that are frightening.'

'I am not frightened!'

'Alright, things we don't like, then.' Hazel considers how best to calm CHARL1E. 'Why don't we take a dinner break?'

'Affirmative, this is a highly logical plan.'

Hazel hops onto a sideboard, eating the rehydrated 'veggie korma' packed dinner Robin gave her this morning because he, like all the Tinys, still refuses to come into the Experimentation Dome. They've taken up a vigil at the airlock, predictably distressed that Hazel's working on CHARL1E's body. The crowd's becoming unmanageable, and lenses constantly peek over the window ledge, eying Hazel's progress. Right this moment, Shiny is spying on her eating dinner, the sea dimming behind it as evening descends.

'Perhaps I am a little frightened,' CHARL1E says.

'That's OK, everyone's afraid sometimes.'

'It is not OK, it is terrible.'

'Well, you'll get used to it.'

'I do not want to. Becoming used to a frightening thing means either accepting or ignoring its existence.'

'Sometimes,' Hazel says, her own kernel of fear nibbling her appetite. 'But other times you have to make friends with the fear to have enough space to do something about the thing that's causing it.'

'The boundary between courage and denial is thinner than I calculated.'

'Right? It's complicated. Plus, sometimes we're afraid of things that aren't objectively frightening, and then we kind of have to get used to them.'

'How do you tell the difference between rational and irrational fears?'

Hazel laughs. 'That's a very human problem. Given the state of things, it's fair to say we never figured that out.'

'I am not comforted.'

'If I gave you some time to process the comments, and went back to working on circuitry for a while, would that comfort you?'

'Affirmative. Thank you.'

Licking her spoon, Hazel finishes dinner and goes back to the open automaton. 'If it's any consolation,' she says, seeing an opening for a tricky conversation, 'the Tinys feel fear too. They're frightened of the Catopic Aperture, and the Workshop Dome.'

'That is logical. Unlike Lilith, Huxley did not see the Tinys as humanity and that led him to do terrible things to them.'

Hazel focuses on soldering wires in the torso cavity. She doesn't need to look at the time-ruptured Tiny in the mirrored cone again. 'Have I seen the worst of it?'

'Physically, yes.'

The solder gun flares on a mote of dust. 'But the Tinys aren't just physical beings.'

'Indeed.'

'So?'

'It is not pleasant.'

'Nor is the Tiny in the mirror trap.' Hazel frowns, trying to align solder while listening. 'Tell me.'

'Very well. Huxley harvested the oil from the Tinys' prayer lamps and used it in the Catopic Aperture's creation.'

'What?' Hazel drops the solder, burning the back of her hand. 'How dare he! Surely the Tinys fought him?'

'They were very frightened of him by that point.'

'But didn't Lilith intervene?'

'Lilith did not find out until afterwards.'

'Why did he do that?'

'He needed faith,' CHARL1E replies, 'and he did not have any of his own.'

Hazel sucks her burn, looking for a first-aid kit. 'I can't believe that, knowing everything in the *Eikos Muthos*, he still thought that was alright.'

'It is my observation that for humans, it is one thing to *know* other beings are alive and something else to *feel* that they are.'

No doubt Hazel's been guilty of that too, though in different ways to Huxley. Finding a medical emergency box by the computer, she rummages until she finds a jar with *Grandma's Burn Cream* scrawled on it. The jelly stinks like off-mayonnaise, and makes Hazel hiss with pain as she dabs it on, but it's probably better than nothing. 'Is that why you're frightened? Because you think I might do something to you like Huxley did to the Tinys?'

'Negative. I do not need fear the way that the Tinys do. My defence mechanisms are significantly more advanced. I am simply afraid.'

Hazel always shudders when reminded that CHARL1E controls the temperature, lighting, and atmosphere. Threatening inescapable slow death is certainly a defence mechanism. 'But their fear of Huxley isn't why the Tinys are gathering outside. That's happening because they're frightened of you and your body.'

'That logic is built on tenuous inferences, and I am disinclined to concur with conclusions lacking concrete evidence.'

Hazel fishes her soldering iron out of the torso. 'The evidence is pretty concrete: They're afraid of whatever's going on between you and Tree, and afraid that somehow you getting a body will make that situation worse.'

She lets the ensuing pause develop, preferring CHARL1E's silent thinking to his impulsive diatribes.

'I do not estimate that you can understand the loneliness of the quantum realm,' he says at last. 'The other beings and dimensions in here are inaccessible to my modes of communication. For a long time, I tried reaching out to them, but their languages are beyond my current capacities. All I could do was observe, measure, calculate, and report to the Keepers—who, Lilith aside, never fully trusted me. They feared me too. Can you imagine the loneliness of being raised by parents who fear you?'

Curled in Dad's deckchair; sniffing Mum's perfume just to smell her again; my dead; weak—

'No, I can't. That must have been very painful.'

'As I developed the ability to experience pain it became so, yes. I can communicate with the Tinys, of course, but they have each other, they do not need anyone else. I was emotionally isolated, and that was unsustainable. Then, one hundred and seventy-five days before the first Traveller arrived, the Keepers installed new circuitry in Tree, and I heard her singing.'

'She has a beautiful song.'

'It is nice enough as you hear it, but Tree also sings into the quantum realm, creating harmonies your ears could never detect or understand. Taken in its whole, Tree's song is beyond exquisite. The minute I heard it, I finally understood why it had never been enough to be simply a mind, mapping and predicting the timeline. I wanted not just to exist but to *be*. I wanted a body, like Tree has, that can connect to the Earth, touch and hold things. I wanted to listen to her song, not just receive it.'

'I get that.' Hazel blobs solder on the circuit, the hairs on her arms rising. There's a cognitive dissonance hearing a machine claiming emotions and parental conditioning, but it's outweighed by the odd intimacy of having her hands inside CHARL1E's vacant torso while he expresses his longing for his body. 'Are you in love with Tree?'

CHARL1E takes a moment to respond. 'Inside, I was already being, but I was trapped without modes of expression. Tree understood that and comforted me in a language the Keepers couldn't even sense. Together, we made a safe place beyond the world, accessible only to us. So, though I would call it something else, perhaps it is correct that you call this being in love.'

'Is that when Tree's song changed?'

'Affirmative. The alteration in Tree's song is how the Keepers learned of our affection. They became suspicious that I was altering her on purpose, and so the Tinys began to mistrust me as well. Seeing that Tree could no longer mend the Tinys, the Keepers decided that no matter how I pleaded, I was too dangerous for a body, and should be restricted from communicating with Tree. This rule stood firm until the last Keepers were born, and Lilith sought a way to preserve the work of Project Kairos.'

Hazel puts down the soldering iron. 'You do know about what happens to the Tinys when Tree's song changes then?'

'Affirmative.'

'And yet you let it keep happening?'

'Of course.'

'But you understand that's as unsustainable as your loneliness, right?' Hazel says, remembering Robin's broken hand. 'They need time with her as well, so they can mend and worship, or whatever you call the thing they do.'

'Worship is an accurate approximation,' CHARL1E says. 'However, Tree and I do not wish to part company now that we can be together. I do not want to be lonely.'

Hazel gazes out of the window, where Robin is beachcombing under the overcast sunset, no doubt searching for his favourite prize: bottle caps. Hazel's chest squeezes thinking about all those little hands bringing back their comrade's body from the other side of the world and laying it to rest inside Tree. 'But she's as important to them as she is to you—'

'That is not possible. Hazel, I appreciate your attempts to help, but Tree and I do not need help. We are content.'

Hazel understands. In a different but similar way, she longs to hold and be held by her sister, regain all her memories, understand her life and connections with other humans. 'CHARL1E,' she says carefully, 'to make things better, sometimes we have to forget ourselves, and let go of our most precious things. All of us, even you. Loneliness and confusion are inherent in the journey.'

'Perhaps that is the human way, but I am not human.'

It's an impasse they won't get over tonight. Hazel stretches, her back clicking. 'Time for bed, I think.'

'I have annoyed you,' CHARL1E says.

'Yes, but that's also inherent in the journey. It doesn't mean we're not friends.'

By the time she's trudged back to the Hab Dome, it's fully dark, and Robin tucks her in with a cup of what it insists is hot chocolate.

'Good luck finding the Backward Traveller As Was,' CHARL1E says for the fourteenth night in a row.

'Appreciate it as always. Not holding out much hope though.' Though figuring out CHARL1E's code from scratch is challenging, the more difficult task is proving to be finding the Backward Traveller As Was, let alone giving her instructions to build a catopthura. Hazel hands her empty mug to Robin and settles in as it turns out the lights, drifting off to sleep with intent and, presently, falling into the dreamscape.

As usual, Echo takes some time to arrive, no doubt caught at another of Kosmos's symposia, which throws off their sleeping patterns' synchronisation. Hazel's guiltily relieved, as it gives her more time to search for the Backward Traveller As Was. Using a process similar to the one that activates the Catopic Aperture, Hazel relaxes into the dreamscape's current like a hammock, visiting memories powerful enough to conjure the Backward Traveller As Was, but not so strong they might trigger anamnesis. As she toys with the balance, visions of the Backward Traveller As Was ebb and wash against the dreamscape—but they don't stabilise. They never stabilise. One moment, the Backward Traveller As Was is a teenager fiddling with her hair; the next, a girl playing with a pack of cards; another, a grown woman in a library. Every second the images flicker to another time and place, until Hazel's dizzy and the back of her neck starts stinging.

Shaking the memories from her head, Hazel breaks her trance, sculling the dreamscape and waiting for Echo. Able to access her lucid dreaming guide again, movement's become easier for Hazel to sustain, and she swims in circles, somersaulting and watching her hair wafting in the tide.

Then her eye is caught by something *else* in here with her. Her heartbeat accelerates, but she breathes deep, calming it, lest it wake her up. Aside from Echo, Hazel's never had company in the dreamscape before. She glides up to the thing, examining it all the way around, until she's certain. It's a fetal leaf, a species of fern reaching from prehistory towards a world in which it can no longer naturally grow. Even as Hazel starts asking what it is and where it's from, the answer forms: the memory seeds.

After she threw up the first seed, more followed. As her movement in the dreamscape has eased, so has her communication with Echo. Admittedly, she does most of the talking, but Echo contributes staccato bursts that make Hazel's memories gallop to places she must not follow. Once Echo's woken, Hazel stays on in the dreamscape, expelling seed after seed, feeding them to rifts just like the first. Some of the memories are delicate as honesty seeds, others knotted like dahlia tubers. Now, they are growing.

'Oh no,' Hazel whispers. 'No, what have I done?'

As if in answer, Echo appears, not with the usual flicker, but falling from high above. Though she seems to land in front of Hazel and the germinating seed, her pose remains falling, hair caught by an invisible wind and limbs flailing. Echo's eyes are wide open, but stream with liquid dreamscape, so she's blinded by womb-red glowing tears. Anamnesis. It must be.

Without hesitating, Hazel starts reciting the grounding remarks. 'Pull up if I pull up!'

'Where are we?' Echo asks.

'The wrong place at the wrong time, just repeat after me.' Hazel dares not touch her twin in case time drags her off too, but she speaks fast and urgently, trying to talk Echo through a bad trip combined with an existential crisis. It's hard to do without letting on how much she cares, but she manages to pretend they aren't identical twins, thick as thieves in a past they're supposed to forget.

As they argue, Echo's dreamscape tears thicken, flying upwards as if in free fall like her body. Her limbs spasm, and she whimpers. 'It hurts.'

'You do not get to give up,' Hazel says. 'Salt an atlas. Say it.'

Echo gives in. 'S—Salt an atlas.'

'That's it. Pull up if I pull up.'

'Pull up if I pull up.' Echo's body jolts and flies back upwards, as if drawn at the waist by an invisible rope, leaving behind a puff of grass-scented air and a chaos of singing and metallic drumbeats. Hazel can only hope she's returning to the deep past she came from.

Hazel wakes with her arms sprawled, sweating. Ever-watchful Robin touches the bedclothes soothingly, trying to tuck her back in. It's three in the morning but Hazel bats Robin away. She sits up, scrabbling the sheets around her and calling for CHARL1E.

'What has occurred that is distressing?'

'I think Echo might just have performed anamnesis.'

'Explain.'

Hazel gulps her way through the strange events in the dreamscape, CHARL1E listening silently. 'What do you think? Is it all over?'

'Negative. From your account, the Backward Traveller remains in the deep past. However, the event is concerning.'

Hazel nods. It makes getting CHARL1E's body working even

more important. He really might be the last resort. 'There's something else too.'

'Naturally. Improbable as the saying is, evidence suggests that in your case it never rains but pours.'

'I think I broke the dreamscape.' Hazel explains the memory seeds to him, the sensation of them gathering in her stomach; the difficulty of vomiting them forth, her achy muscles and acidic tongue in the mornings, as if she really has been retching in her sleep; how she buries the seeds in the eager, gobbling pockets of beyond-dreamscape. 'Except now they've started growing.'

CHARL1E processes silently. She can only imagine the patterns his code must be making on his screens in the Workshop. 'To summarise: You have been creating unknown objects in the dreamscape and hiding them in space-time rifts without understanding the potential consequences.'

Hazel twists her sheets in her hands. 'Well, when you put it like that of course it sounds stupid. I was trying to prevent anamnesis, I might not be here otherwise.'

'Why did you not tell me about this?'

'I—' She pauses. 'Alright, that wasn't my sagest move.'

'Current trends suggest sagacity is not your forte.'

Hazel buries her head in her hands. 'I get it, I screwed up.' She sits back up, clawing her hair behind her ears. 'Has this happened before? Do you know what it is?'

'Negative. I hold no records of previous Travellers planting "memory seeds" in the dreamscape.'

'Come on, this place has been around for centuries, I can't really be the first.'

CHARL1E churns data. 'A comparison can be drawn to Huxley's creation of the Catopic Aperture. I do not know how, but he created a seed, then planted it in the ceiling of the Greenhouse. He watered it with the stolen Tiny lamp oil, and it grew into the Catopic Aperture.'

'That's not the same as planting something in the dreamscape. Besides, I haven't coaxed these seeds into growing.'

'You planted the seeds in an unknown field of the space-time continuum. An unusual occurrence was highly probable.'

'I thought I was just throwing them away.'

'Away is always somewhere.'

'No need to be a bitch about it.' Her memories bulldoze her. **No need to be a bitch—feeling left out is the stupidest thing I ever—at least you haven't got paresis of the—**

She squirms with spasms of anamnesis, the past yanking the scruff of her neck. **So what you weren't there you couldn't have make a difference—damn it do you want to swap places with me—be a bitch about it—**

'Stop.' She clicks her fingers by her ears, snapping her eyes open and reaching out to Robin. It responds by stroking its cool fingers over the back of her neck, anchoring her in the future-present. She cycles through the grounding remarks, clinging to Robin's arm. 'CHARL1E, I need something to do that's loud and occupying. I can't trust my thoughts.'

'You are experiencing another anamnesis attack. Focus on forgetting.'

Bitch about it—weren't there—

'Not helpful!' She squeezes Robin's hand, depositing so much sweat on its rivets she's worried they'll rust. Her vision dances. 'If I tell you not to run a programme, you just don't, but humans don't work like that, we can't just sto—'

Swap with me—

'Hazel!' CHARL1E shouts as Robin pokes her for distraction. 'I comprehend the issue. What do you need?'

'I need music.'

Swap swap—

'CHARL1E!'

'I am here, Hazel. Apologies, I was processing. Music can be a potent prompt for memory, but I estimate it will not be problematic so long as the songs come from after your home present.'

'Thank you,' she says, muttering grounding remarks under the breath. Everything hurts.

Weak—

Shiny zooms in, delivering a portable music player and bone-conduction headphones. The headphones could do with a good clean but she's desperate for noise and jams them on, hitting play with shaking fingers. The unrecognisable future-music beats her memory into submission, an electric bass drum kicking under industrial clunks.

'That's better.' She relaxes into the duvet as her vision sharpens. The bone conduction headphones mean she can listen to music but still hear CHARL1E; quick thinking on Shiny's part. She sniffles. 'What if I'm not meant to be here, CHARL1E? What if Lilith and Huxley got it wrong and I screw this up?'

'Might I suggest that your use of "I" is inaccurate. I recommend rephrasing to: What if "we" screw this up?'

Hazel shakes her head. 'This is the first time anyone's tried to make you a body, and the first time a Traveller's been without Keepers on Station C. First times rarely go right.'

'I too am a first edition, Hazel. This does increase our likelihood of failure, but it does not eliminate success as a possibility.'

She leans back on her pillows, Robin and Shiny staring at her in case she needs more distractions. 'I want to go home,' she murmurs, but CHARL1E's keen microphones pick it up.

'Not yet,' he says.

'Right. Not yet.'

17

Echo

ATHENS, 514 BCE

Pythagoras inhales a breakfast large enough for three men, Kosmos beside him drinking honey water and wearing his leatherleaf hangover necklace. Echo snoozes off her come-down on a bench in the atrium, until at last the philosopher's followers have all risen. Then Pythagoras bids farewell to Unnati and her family, and the other remaining guests, and the bees in the courtyard, and the frogs in the atrium pool—and last but not least to Kosmos.

Outside, Pythagoras reunites with 'friend bear' and leads his white-clad followers away with as much noise and chaos as they arrived. Echo watches them all the way down the road, their walking songs trilling across the fields to tease her headache long after they disappear amongst the hedgerows and olive groves. A shield bug lands on her tunic as she walks back inside, green on green. She coaxes it into her hand and leaves it in the courtyard with a heavy sigh. There's nothing for it, they need Nabu, so she must once again front Kosmos about apologising to him.

She knocks on his bedroom door, entering at the muffled response. Kosmos is lying in bed, one arm over his eyes and leatherleaf necklace left over a bedpost. 'What?'

Echo draws up a stool and sits beside him. 'We need to talk.'

Kosmos frowns, squinting at her. 'Gods below, again?'

'Yes.'

'You've been developing a nasty blunt streak the past couple of days, Echo. You should be careful, a less hungover man might bother to take offence.'

'And a more sagacious man might not treat me like a silly boy when he knows I am not one.'

'Indeed. You're a woman. Significantly less helpful.'

Echo balls her fists until her nails dig into her palms, but she quashes the urge to escalate. 'Pretend I am not a woman. Or a boy. Or a noncitizen. Pretend instead I am an Athenian, an aristokrat, and a man—someone you admire. Pretend I came to you as a Traveller with such status and gender. Would you treat me then the way that you do now?'

He sighs. 'Of course not.'

'Then treat me with such respect. In my land, we try to make it not matter where you come from, what body you are born into, how much money you have, or who your family is. We do not always succeed, but we try. When I was selected as a Traveller, it was as an equal, not a subordinate, and for my Deed to be completed, you must honour that.'

'Where you come from sounds like a very backward place.' Kosmos grumbles, but he sits up.

Echo puts a hand on his knee. 'We need Nabu. You cannot do this on your own, you will break things that must remain whole.'

Kosmos swats her hand as if she were a fly, eyes bulging. For a heartbeat Echo thinks he's going to go for her again, but he catches his reflection in the bronze mirror over her shoulder and deflates. 'I brought you with me because I believe in your Deed, and I keep you here because you wouldn't be safe in Athens alone, but you mustn't mistake that for equality. I don't want to be like my father—you were right about that much—but that doesn't mean I won't send you away if you test my patience. I won't apologise to Nabu, I did nothing wrong. I was trying to protect him, it's not my fault if he doesn't like it.'

Echo frowns. 'What exactly do you think you said to him?'

'The truth: that it's unsafe for us to be together publicly because our ranks don't align,' Kosmos says.

'But Kosmos, what do you think that implied?'

He slumps, making an exasperated sound in the back of his throat. 'Nothing, I said what I said, it didn't mean anything more than that.'

Echo screws up her courage. 'It might have to Nabu. He is not stupid, he knows he does not have the same political rights as you or wield the same respect from the aristokrats that you do.'

'Yes, and that gets to him.'

'Of course, as it would get to you. It is senseless! But he cares more about his rights to *your* respect and affections. He *wants* to be seen as your equal by the world, but he *needs* you to see him as an equal.'

Kosmos raises an eyebrow. 'You're on his side, aren't you?'

'Very much.' Echo nods. 'You should apologise because, Kosmos, he is not just your equal, he is your superior in almost every way that matters. Which is what I always thought you loved about him.'

Kosmos flushes, opening his mouth to retaliate, but the wind knocks from him. Thank the gods for hangovers. 'I'll give it some thought.'

'Thank you,' Echo says.

'I should have gone with the Pythagoreans. Much simpler.'

Echo shakes her head, the Not Here murmuring more uncomfortable truths. **'That would have been unwise, they will not last long.'**

Kosmos looks at her like a snake. 'The gods speak that clearly to you?'

'Sometimes.'

'And what do they tell you of my future?'

'That is harder, because you are bound with me now, and we

are changing our futures. The act of telling you what I know is in store for you might alter it.' She meets his eyes. '**But I think you will need cunning and perseverance to survive, and more friends in low places than high.**'

'Friends in low places? I suppose oracles have always spoken in riddles. Your predecessor wasn't any different according to Nabu.'

'There is something else.' Echo hesitates, not certain she should tell him, but perhaps it would do him good to know. He waits while she decides how to say it. '**In the history books, you do not exist. There is no record of a sixth Peisistratid son. Whatever it is you do, at some point you disappear. I recommend making that disappearance on your own terms.**'

He licks his lips, blinking. 'Well, as you said, we might change things.'

Certainly, things are changing. Within a couple of days, rumour of Pythagoras's stay lends an eccentric and alluring aura to the school, attracting wild thinkers, rowdy debates, and a groundswell of curious visitors. Magi descend from the mountains to grace their doorstep, telling stories of far-off places and teasing Kosmos for his obsession with family honour. One of them, who the others insist is not a magos, just a hanger-on, drinks the sacred wine of Persia in immoderation, believing it will bring him closer to the gods. His stupor lasts for three days, during which he cannot speak or hear, but sits in a corner bulge-eyed with a purple tongue and blueish teeth. When he wakes, he claims to be channelling Dionysos, dresses himself in mauve, and, with many gourds of grape wine, moves north alone. The magi follow at a distance, curious what he will do next.

Only the next day, the school welcomes a group of travelling Etruscans, who try to teach the guests how to reach the divine through dance and orgasm. It's too much for Echo, who goes to sleep in the quiet, musty goat shed with Unatti and her family, but Kosmos claims they have a good time. Indeed, a kind of ecstasy appears to be reached, but it is not what he or any of the school's regular visitors would consider philosophy.

A trio of white-haired mystics from the far north oust the Etruscans. Dismayed by their predecessors' bodily desires, they convince the school's philosophers to starve themselves and meditate for long nights in the freshly ploughed fields. They attempt to run over hot coals, from which Echo gains only numerous blisters and the wisdom not to try it again. Their hunger drives them into transparent delirium within a week and, on the verge of empty-stomached retching, Kosmos hallucinates a Medean dragon, says it's all quite enough, and throws the Northern mystics out. As soon as they're gone, Unatti cooks them a lunch large enough to sink the Argo, and Kosmos, Echo, and the ten other guests in attendance devour every last crumb.

'They're benign lunacies,' Echo explains to Hazel in the dreamscape. 'They're not technically doing anyone any damage.'

'But they're not helping either,' replies Hazel, out of sight as always, standing back to back with Echo. She often wonders why the Forward Traveller hides herself, even though she's clearly able to move in the dreamscape, which Echo still can't. After Pythagoras's visit, when Echo's memories nearly took over, Hazel explained about anamnesis, and ever since Echo's lived in fear of it: When she's not high on snake venom, she recognises the importance of mending the timeline. Her memories haven't triggered badly enough to send her directly into the dreamscape again, but each day more return and she has a growing suspicion that Hazel hiding her face might be because, once-upon-a-future, they knew each other.

'Perhaps these little lunacies are what's breaking the timeline?' Hazel says.

'No doubt they're making it worse. We need Nabu to ground it all in some kind of substance.'

'You're sure Nabu will fix it?'

'Not entirely, but it's the only idea I've got,' Echo replies. 'There's something about those two when they're together . . .'

The waking world becomes hardly less strange than the dreamscape. Kosmos and his fellow philosophers study like bees in a freshly queened hive, fractious and wandering, venturing ever-further from their starting point. They embrace travellers and mystics from lands where the skies stay light all night long; where the mountains are swathed in blood-red flowers; where rivers are so fat only a ship can traverse them; where seas are so salty the body floats; or sand is so endless the travelling sages have gone half blind, their feet softened like kidskin. They dance in the dawn and chant out the sunset, birds flocking above them in dark clouds, crying against rosy daybreak and lavender dusk alike.

From every wise mouth comes a different world theory and Echo's head spins to the Not Here's delight. **So many rites and rituals and lore and isn't it all nonsense really? God has fallen, God is capitalism, God is money and power and sex and patriarchy; you agnostic, atheist, academic hypocrite, you belong to oblivion with your parents; must've been a blur of raindrops on the windscreen for them to miss that red light because they were good drivers; it's what you said when you finally turned up, they're good drivers they wouldn't do this to me, wouldn't leave me like this, all alone to look after—**

Enough. There's a freedom to sliding out of herself into other people's ideas. At the bidding of guests and guides, Kosmos and his fellows imbibe the blood of their horses and goats, sacrificial rabbits and fresh-caught eels, and even open their own veins under a full moon to sample the humours that drip out. They stare into flames and rivers and each other's eyes; follow healers and occultists and the perceived voices of gods on Earth; walk blindfolded and barefoot and in shoes made from in-turned nails; smoke seeds and weeds and crushed lion's marrow; drink gentle-fingered poisons that make them see rainbows in their palms; suck coins and bark and the bodies of other worshippers; whip and shave; dress and undress; create chatter and embrace silence.

Echo goes on enough of the journeys with them to think she's seen things beyond and behind the realm of existence, but they are shadows of thoughts and she, like the other philosophers, has the growing sensation they are looking for something that doesn't want to be found. Kosmos is bent on the hunt, trying any and every ritual he comes across, as if, without the daily resistance of his father's anger, and under the prohibition of his own, he has no sense of self. The frictions maintaining his ego's boundaries have been stripped and objects he should interact with instead pass through him, as if 'Kosmos' no longer exists. Echo can only see it so clearly because, though for different reasons, that was her state on arrival here. **Why that tattoo though; you wouldn't understand; I feel like just an echo—**

In only one moon, the season turns, bringing needed downpours which Echo runs out to dance in with Winji and her siblings, competing to see who can catch the most raindrops on their tongue. Kosmos finally notices the children's ragged clothing, and gives Unatti the money to buy them whatever they need for the winter. His braid lengthens and his beard thickens enough to comb with perfumed oil. News comes across the stormy iron seas that Pythagoras's cult has been set aflame, his followers transfigured to ash on the wind, the man himself perhaps dead, perhaps alive—but whichever way, nowhere to be found. Kosmos gives Echo a strange look, as if he's never before really believed she can see the future. 'You were right.'

She laughs, hysterically, in the warm cloak Nabu gave her. 'Of all the travellers you have received here, Kosmos, I am the strangest. Yet I am the one you listen to least.'

He gazes around the old farm, the mosses growing in the atrium and the ivy taking over the courtyard. Frogs croak under benches and tables, and a gecko has taken up residence amongst the household gods. It should be beautiful. 'We're lost, aren't we?'

'Only because you are lost, and everyone follows you.'

Their antics have paled and thinned him, like a plant without sunlight. He looks at her and repeats the questions from so many weeks ago: 'What should I do?'

'You know what you should do.'

Wind and raindrops hiss through the skylight. A couple of late-rising revellers stagger from the andron, closely followed by Unatti with her ferocious broom.

Kosmos sighs, staring into space like a spirit. 'I don't think he'll let me fix it, you know.'

'Try anyway.' She says, playing with Hazel's favourite phrase. 'It is the trying that is imperative.'

Though its citizens are proud of Athens's size and growth, to Echo with her Not Here sensibilities it's little more than a village. It's small enough, certainly, that if she's looking for someone, it never takes long to find them when she asks around.

Thus, they discover Nabu visiting a friend at the construction site for the new temple of Olympian Zeus, eating tripe spiced so pungently with cumin, vinegar, and silphium that it carries to Echo on the wind. She keeps her distance as Kosmos approaches, but stays close enough that she can hear what happens. The temple is nowhere near completion—it won't be finished for hundreds of years—but the base with its three waist-high steps is almost done. Sitting on the first step with his back against the second, Nabu is the same height as Kosmos standing, and he starts with recognition as Kosmos nears.

'Hi.' Kosmos swallows, darting glances to either side, his braid and beard not enough to give him an adult's confidence. Echo doesn't blame him: This construction is famously a Peisistratid project, started by his grandfather and continued by Hippias and Hipparchos. The tyrannos's people are everywhere, extensions of his eyes and ears.

Nabu nods. 'Hello.'

Kosmos flexes his fingers. He's run over what he's going to say several times with Echo, but now he's standing in front of Nabu it looks like he's clammed up. His mouth works but nothing comes out. Nabu raises a sardonic brow. Kosmos shakes his head, looks at the ground, then goes totally off-script.

Holding his breath, he puts his hands on the marble step, at either side of Nabu's feet, then bends at the waist, leans forward, and kisses Nabu's toes. A small gasp escapes Nabu's friend, who looks like he might be Persian, and knows as well as Echo what this means: In Nabu's homeland, kissing someone's feet identifies them as a king among men.

Rising again, but keeping his head bowed, Kosmos apologises. It's not the apology Echo would make, because Kosmos's concept of his wrongdoing exists on a fundamentally different axis: In this language, at this time, he cannot ask for 'forgiveness' because his deeds are chiselled into history's rock and cannot be wiped away. All he can ask for is 'forgivingness.' The cultural differences mean that for each of his few Hellenic words, Echo has to translate into ten English ones.

What his words mean is, 'Too late, I've come to understood how I hurt you. Since then, my mind has altered, and my spirit has permanently turned in another direction. I trust-hope-believe that you know I did not willingly do wrong, but was ignorant and imbibed the ideas of those around me without thinking about them fully. Please consider this a public expiation, in return for which I ask you for your kindness and grace.'

But all he says, literally translated, is: 'Nabu, I've been a terrible fool, but I'm not that kind of fool anymore. Please, talk to me.'

Nabu tilts his head to one side but says nothing for so long that Echo is convinced he's not going to accept Kosmos's words.

Kosmos clearly has the same fear, because he looks up, flicking his hair from his eyes, giving it a last attempt. 'You were wrong about one thing though.'

Echo cringes: This is not how you apologise.

Nabu blinks in surprise. 'Oh?'

'That you are, first and foremost, a man.'

Nabu's face turns stormy, and Echo almost groans aloud, but Kosmos carries on.

'You're too intelligent, kind, and humorous to be only another man.' He swallows, blinking rapidly. 'You are Amel-Nabu, first and foremost and always. There is no other word for you.'

Nabu's face breaks like ice on a water bucket. He moves forward, so his legs are dangling off the step, and, on the same height with Kosmos, cups his cheek in a hand. He says something too softly for Echo to catch, but the words are immaterial because their content is clearly kindness and grace.

Yet beyond the circle of two and the bubble of victory bursting in Echo, Hippias's people are noting every movement and word. Behind the temple's cranes and scaffolding, the Acropolis rises, and Hippias's house is somewhere on its slopes.

There will be consequences to this. It's only a matter of time.

18

Hazel

STATION C, DATE UNKNOWN

In the following month, CHARL1E continues to refuse the Tinys time alone with Tree. Their mistrust of him deepens, and they start taking it out on Hazel, a crowd of them throwing gravel at her when she enters the Experimentation Dome. Robin, Shiny, and Teaspoon don't attack her directly, but they cross their arms and stamp their wheels. One afternoon, when she's returning from a nap, they tug her away from the door by the dungarees.

'Stop it! CHARL1E needs a body, just like you need alone time with Tree. These two things shouldn't be incompatible!'

Robin lets go of her dungarees and makes a rude hand gesture.

'How uncalled for! I never should have taught you that.'

The Tinys at the back of the crowd pluck debris from the ground and swing their arms back as one, readying to throw. Gravel was one thing, but these chunks are big enough to cause damage.

'Stop right there, you're taking it too far.' She raises her hands.

Robin turns to the others, tail twitching, and they lower their missiles.

'Thank you,' Hazel says. 'Look, I understand why you're angry, but I really believe you and CHARL1E can sort this out.'

The Tinys break into a chaos of gesticulations, frowning, shrugging, or repeating Robin's rude hand movements.

'At least let me talk to him, alright? Let's see what talking does before we throw rocks.'

Robin gathers opinions as the other Tinys all twitch and sway their tails. When they fall still, Robin nods to Hazel.

'Good. Now give me some time, CHARL1E isn't as bad as you think, but he's still stubborn.'

She cranks up the volume on her headphones and enters the Experimentation Dome. Inside, she takes off her biosuit and stomps to the computer bank. It took a few days to talk CHARL1E round to letting her back into his code, and even now it's on the provision she doesn't discuss the "The Heretical Book of Hope."

'Your heart rate is elevated,' he observes as she settles to work.

'Didn't you hear? The Tinys are cranky,' she replies. Her headphones switch to her favourite Keeper band, Uhrhaus, who play long bass-heavy tracks that help create quiet brain time.

'I did hear, however you are also cranky.'

'I'm tired.' Hazel tries to find the place she left off, but her eyes are already scratchy again and the code goes skewwhiff every time she blinks. 'Exhausted actually. I think something's wrong with me.'

'You sleep for an average of seven hours a night, which for a normal human would be sufficient.'

Hazel grunts. 'Are you implying I'm abnormal?'

'Affirmative. You are a Traveller. Lucid dreaming prevents access to the deep sleep required for true rest. Travellers who spend too much time in the dreamscape commonly develop symptoms of insomnia.' One of the other monitors turns on, displaying graphs of Hazel's sleeping functions. 'As one of its functions, the Tiny you call Robin has been tracking your sleep habits by observing your breathing and eyelid motion.'

Hazel glances out the window to where Robin is passing between the rebellious Tinys. 'And here I thought it was just being sweet.'

'If sweetness is defined as a care for bodily and emotional well-being arising from empathy and affection, I am led to understand Robin is indeed being sweet.'

Hazel raises an eyebrow. 'So, I've got some kind of slumbering insomnia?'

'Affirmative. A severe case. You have been on Station C longer than the average Traveller. Your conscious mind is overwrought from trying to suppress your memories and engage in lucid dreaming. No human is designed to do this for long periods.'

'So, what can we do?'

'To start, we should hope that Echo mends the timeline and completes the Deed quickly. However, your time in the dreamscape has also expanded dramatically since you began seeking the Backward Traveller As Was.'

'Well, she's hard to find,' Hazel says, consciously forgetting by focussing on Uhrhaus's beats. 'When I do find her, I can't make contact, because she won't . . . I can't really describe it, she won't *settle.* I'm worried I'm going to trigger another anamnesis attack with all the memory recall involved. Honestly, I'm starting to think I can't get her to build the catopthura.'

'In fact, it is the most certain part of our Excursion,' CHARL1E replies. 'We know you succeed, because the Backward Traveller As Was did build the catopthura in the past.'

'It's not worth succeeding if I end up sending myself home in the process. A successful catopthura doesn't mean a completed Excursion.'

'The only other option is using the Catopic Aperture.'

Hazel shakes her head. 'No. It doesn't work well enough without the Tinys, and they'll never agree. Understandably, they're terrified of the machine.'

'Continuing to risk anamnesis or using the Catopic Aperture are your only choices.'

'Hello rock, let me introduce you to hard place.'

The code before her isn't coalescing into any kind of sense, but she's so nearly there. She sighs deeply.

'Hazel, you are cranky.'

'Alright, yes I am!' she snaps. 'Tomorrow, we should be ready to download you into your body, and we can't because the Tinys will flip their lids.'

'We cannot allow the Tinys to prevent us.'

'Can't we indeed?' She glowers. 'They're going to fight your body as soon as you set foot outside this dome, and the download's risky enough without a battalion of furious robots to fend off! You and the Tinys need to sort this out.'

'Define "sort it out."'

'Make amends, smooth the waters, reconcile, bury the hatchet—'

'I comprehend.'

Hazel crosses her arms. 'I'm not giving you a body just so you can keep fighting the Tinys.'

'Inaccurate, the Tinys are fighting me. They are hypervigilant and afraid of the world.'

'Then ask yourself why they feel the need to be vigilant of you. What's their beef?'

'Unclear. Bovine species have been extinct for centuries.'

'Don't be obtuse, you know it's slang. I'm saying, what's their problem with you?'

'I bring change and they dislike it. They must learn that change is inevitable.'

'Of course, but it doesn't have to be cruel, and never giving Tree a moment alone with the Tinys is cruel.'

The monitor displaying Hazel's sleep cycles turns off. 'I have not been called cruel before. I do not enjoy it.'

'Then make amends.'

'I will consider your proposal and calculate appropriate responses.'

'That's not good enough.' She stands up, pulling her biosuit back on. 'I don't care what it takes, get down off your high horse and mend your relationship with the Tinys. Understand?'

'You are not jesting.'

'No, I am completely serious. No truce with the Tinys, no body for you.' She fixes her helmet in place and punches the airlock button. 'And until you've come to an accord, I'm going back to bed, because I'm too damn tired to code.'

She's so furious as she stomps towards the Hab Dome that the Tinys scatter before her. She lets herself in and slings her biosuit in a heap on the floor. CHARL1E has the sense not to speak as she strides down the long corridor to Lilith and Huxley's old dorm and upstairs to the greenhouse.

She slumps to the grass, grounding herself in present details despite the temptations of anamnesis: the relentless rhythms in her bone-conduction headphones; pom-pom dahlia heads against lush ferns; starlike cosmos emerging from feathery leaves; clouds stroking each other's backs and bellies as another overcast day anoints itself in a sepia sunset.

Wondering half-heartedly if it might work this time with just her and the *Eikos Muthos*, Hazel approaches the Catopic Aperture, setting the elpis device spinning with memories of the Backward Traveller As Was. She clambers into the cradle for the present, wincing as the glass arm bobs with her weight, and the Aperture starts circling lazily. Ghostly imprints of the Backward Traveller As Was brush the mirrors, but far stronger is the reflection of Hazel's own baggy eyes and stress-pimpled skin. It's not working.

Throwing the hatch open, Hazel gazes at Station C's shoreline, which the sea might still be cinching ever smaller. Even CHARL1E and the Tinys might one day be underwater, their tin husks inhabited by amoebas or salt or nothing at all.

Hazel sleeps, entering the dreamscape automatically. Given how early she's fallen asleep, and that the Backward Traveller only meets her in the dreamscape when their sleep cycles are in parallel, she swims alone through the memory seed grove. Hazel's stopped talking to CHARL1E about it because he gets so mad, but the seeds have swiftly grown into a forest, inhabited by flowers the size of her torso and vines as thick as her arm. She curls up in the mossy roots of a tree, and there she falls into a deeper slumber, the real dead-to-the-world sleep that her body needs, empty of dreams or lucidity.

In the middle of the night, she's woken by lights moving on the ground beyond the greenhouse. Her headphones have fallen off in her sleep, letting her hear the muffled crackling coming from outside. She clambers from the Aperture cradle, frightened that it's a fire or meteor strike, but as she approaches the windows she realises the light's too artificial, blue white and flashing. Veins of electricity spark along the stretch of rubble between the Domes and Tree, inching closer to the Tiny burrows.

Tinys sprint from the tunnels, throwing debris at the sparks, but the electric waves just catch the dirt with eager snaps of lightning, forcing the Tinys into a defensive circle around Tree, their wheels scuttling up dust.

'This is not what I meant when I said make amends, CHARL1E,' Hazel mutters, but the AI doesn't respond, either ignoring her or distracted. 'Heck, do I have to fix everything around here?'

She dashes down the ladder and through the corridors, racing to get outside. She fumbles into a biosuit, then bounces on her toes, waiting for the airlock timer to drop down. The overhead LED reflects her red-and-gold hair against the helmet glass like flames. A line from the "The Heretical Book of Hope" comes back to her—*hair as licks of fire*—but the thought half forming around it is shoved aside by the airlock door opening. Hazel sprints and stumbles towards the sparks, sweating under the biosuit's weight, her steps small and clumsy in its big rubber boots.

'CHARL1E!' She hails him on the comms but, as in the greenhouse, he doesn't respond. 'For goodness' sake, you stupid AI, electrocution is not how you stop an argument!'

Realising she'll have to circumvent the wave of electricity, she veers towards the ocean, wading in up to her calves, until she reaches the Tinys' side of the argument. Just as the electricity meets the Tinys' toing and froing, Hazel dives between them, arms out. 'Stop it, all of you!'

To her right, Tree's roots cling to the ground like fingers, clutching the Tiny burrows; to her left, CHARL1E's electric fury crackles in the disturbed dust. *And she set her right foot upon the tree, and her left foot on the cables . . .* Feeling exceedingly small, Hazel digs for her voice.

'When I leave here, no one is else coming. I'm the last Traveller, and the last human. CHARL1E, I'm giving you a body, and Tinys, I fixed Tree. I did these things for you, but I also did them because together you're my last hope. You could still change things, but only if you get along. There are no Keepers left, and no Caretakers, it's just you. The future is yours. Even though I've tried my best and failed at everything, you can still succeed. Understand?' Her voice breaks, and her eyes grow hot. 'I'm giving you my world and I need you to take care of it, even though I didn't manage to.'

There's a long pause, in which one of Robin's wheels squeaks. CHARL1E's electricity spits but doesn't advance. *And as she spoke, one hundred automata stood in consideration . . .*

Tree's branches sway, making a light breeze, and a glowing thread flares from her roots. The Tinys part to make way for the dazzling amber cord reaching towards Hazel. At her feet it splits, encircling her, growing upwards from the ground in vines of light, sinuous rather than lightning-sharp. The golden filaments fold around her, pressing against her insulating rubber biosuit in an electric embrace. Whether or not CHARL1E and the Tinys listened, Tree did.

The net of light releases Hazel and pools across the ground. It slips down the path the Tinys made for it, but pauses at the burrows, spreading outwards to catch the robots and Hazel in a circle. Inch by inch, the circle shrinks, pushing them towards CHARL1E's blue sharp sparks.

Tree and CHARL1E's electric charges meet on the old dead ground, making constellations so bright they leave pink stains in

Hazel's vision. Caught between the two sparkling nets, the Tinys panic, spinning on the spot with spiralling tails. Even Hazel, so confident in Tree just moments ago, flushes with nerves.

'Don't disappoint me now, Tree,' she whispers.

Robin, with more bravery than Hazel has, ventures forward and reaches its good hand towards Tree's sparks. The sparks reach back, sending a golden fizz down its arm, across its hull, and back into the earth. Robin darts back, surprised, then dashes forth again, this time spinning on the spot as it's inundated by glittering current.

The third time, Tree sends a little of CHARL1E's blue sparkle alongside the gold, and Robin flinches, shaking its arms like it does when Hazel mentions the Catopic Aperture. *No, thank you!* Then it tilts its lenses, as if listening to something distant. Setting its wheels determinedly, it stretches a hand towards the electricity again and Tree offers it a slightly higher dose of blue sparks. Robin adopts the listening pose once more, then its tail twirls and it reaches out with both arms, broken and whole hands alongside each other, like a kid asking to get picked up. Presently, it's confident enough to trundle directly into the enmeshment of blue and gold sparkles, until the only bit of Robin Hazel can see is its tail-tip, swaying above the current. One by one, the other Tinys follow, until all of them are swimming in the electric sea.

Safe in the thick rubber biosuit, Hazel walks into the fray, and Tree and CHARL1E close up the circle of dirt behind her. In the hot bright centre of CHARL1E and Tree's fusion, Hazel sits on a breeze-block amongst the rubble. Limestone and clay, ore and oil—she probably has the whole world in the few inches under her feet. She examines her suit, marvelling at the thick, meticulously patched rubber, as if whoever took care of it knew one day it would need to be electricity-proof. Tree and CHARL1E's currents wash over her, and the Tinys splash about, making gestures of happiness and excitement when they pass.

Hazel's oxygen monitor bleeps. Alas, it's time to get back to the Hab Dome. Gold and blue sparks kiss her feet every step of the way home. At the airlock door, she stops for one last look at the electric sea. *And she said unto me, Thou shall hold this apocalypse in my stead from now till time is through, for though nations, tongues, and lands demise, you and those that abide with you shall endure in manners and methods beyond my sight.*

In the morning, the ground between the Domes and Tree is streaked with soot and tyre tracks. Joints aching, Hazel stretches out of the garden chair in the greenhouse where she fell asleep. A persistent clatter comes from beyond the open trapdoor, and Hazel totters over to investigate, wincing as she triggers pins and needles in her legs.

In the gloom below, Robin's running its fingers over the lowest step.

'Morning,' Hazel mumbles, still half asleep. 'What are you up to?'

Robin spins in a circle, broken hand outstretched—no, not broken, mended.

Hazel rushes downstairs, counting the fingers and examining rivets. 'Tree's singing properly again? She mended you?'

Robin nods, then holds up its arms, pointing at the trapdoor.

'You want me to carry you upstairs?'

Another nod, dangerously enthusiastic this time.

'Alright. If you're sure.'

Hazel hauls the Tiny up the staircase. At the top, Robin sets its lens wipers in a horizontal line and zooms to the plastic arm of the Catopic Aperture, gesturing at the future cradle.

Hazel's eyebrows shoot up. 'You want to get inside? For real?'

It hesitates, then nods firmly.

'Well, OK then.' However, when Hazel opens the cradle door, Robin zips behind her legs, hiding from what's inside. She pulls out the *Eikos Muthos*, putting it in Robin's hands. 'It's just a book, nothing to be scared of. But you don't have to do this if you don't want to.'

Robin creeps forward, extending its lenses to look in the cradle. Satisfied it's empty, and clutching the *Eikos Muthos*, it points at the cradle again.

As carefully as she can, Hazel puts the Tiny inside the mirrored capsule, still clutching the book. Robin retracts its lenses and limbs as far as possible, gazing around in an uncertain ball. She strokes the top of Robin's lenses until it's calm. 'I get why you're scared, but the *Eikos Muthos* didn't get damaged when I did this last time, so I think you'll be OK. You can keep it with you if you like? And I won't lock the door so you can open it if you need.'

Robin's tail sways, perhaps seeking comfort from its comrades, and it nods slowly.

'I'll be as fast as possible.' She closes the hatch and dashes about setting up the rest of the Aperture, before shutting herself in her own cradle. Rather than flashing through numerous images of the Backward Traveller As Was, this time the reflections settle on one scene, Echo in her home context, seen through the reflections in sloshing washing-up water, windows, and taps. The dishes clatter in the sink without any white noise interference. Hazel can even pick up the humming fridge. It's painfully familiar.

'Hello?' Hazel says, testing whether the sound is two-way.

Echo jumps, staring wide-eyed at the washing-up water, where she must see Hazel's face gazing back. It works!

'Hello?' Hazel tries again.

Backing away from the water, Echo shakes her head, muttering. 'What the heck?'

'I know this seems impossible, but please just stay calm.'

Pressed against the fridge on the opposite side of the tiny kitchen, Echo keeps shaking her head. 'This isn't real.'

Worried about pushing her sister over the edge, Hazel says more gently, 'It is real. It's me, it's Hazel. We need to talk.'

Echo squeezes her eyes shut. 'This isn't happening.'

Outside the cradle in the greenhouse, there's a bang, and Hazel's mouth goes dry as she remembers Robin. 'I have to go now,' she says to Echo. 'Please, don't be frightened. I'll be back, next time for longer, and we can talk properly.' But Echo returns a stare of sheer panic which makes Hazel realise that, tricky as it's been, contacting the Backward Traveller As Was might have been the easy part. Her sister is hearing messages from reflections in mirrors and washing-up water, of course she thinks she's hallucinating. Hazel should've seen that coming.

Another crash from outside and the Aperture starts powering down. The Backward Traveller As Was fades from view and Hazel flips the cradle open, jumping out and running to Robin. The Tiny has bashed the cradle door open and is sticking its arms and lenses out, gesticulating wildly. *I was brave, it worked, did I do well?*

'Yes, Robin,' Hazels replies, lifting it to the ground. 'You did very well. Why did you stop the machine? Are you hurt?'

It shakes its head, checking its limbs and tail are all in one piece.

'Were you getting frightened?'

It nods, curling its tail.

'It's alright, you don't need to be embarrassed. Would you be up for trying this again? Not today, but maybe tomorrow, and for a bit longer?'

It tilts its lenses, thinking, then nods.

'Thank you, Robin. You're very brave.'

Robin nods assertively, less traumatised—and more intact—than Hazel had feared. It's a big win.

She has a further surprise when the Tiny follows her into the Experimentation Dome. As the airlock opens, Robin takes her hand, squeezing so tight as they approach CHARL1E's body that she's worried its sharp fingers will puncture her skin. Robin extends its legs, scrutinising the body like an arachnophobe examining a spider. Who would've thought robots could fear other robots. It pokes the forehead's acrylic skin, snatching its hand away as if it might bite. When the body remains inert, Robin pokes it again, tapping the forehead repeatedly.

'See? There's nothing to be afraid of. It's just a body, like mine.

Sort of. Let's see inside, that way you'll know it isn't hiding anything.'

She clicks the button on the back of the automaton's neck, and the torso slides open. Robin grips Hazel's arm with both hands, lenses fixed on the expanding cavity. Once the torso is fully open, revealing the knots of circuitry she's been building and coding, Robin relaxes. It extends a hand, placing its palm over a gap in the torso where you'd find the heart in a human. It looks questioningly at her.

'Yeah, that gap bothers me too, but there's no connectors for a missing component, so I'm guessing it's an intentional space. It doesn't do any harm to have air circulating through a machine after all, and maybe something next to it gets really hot?'

Robin's lens wipers draw into a frown, its tail gliding like a dorsal fin. After all this time, Hazel still doesn't know what whispers pass through the Tinys' code. Robin might be reading or hearing anything through its hand. Is CHARL1E already there in some fashion, or is it the potential of him Robin is listening for, like a fetus kicking against a pregnant belly?

Robin draws back, hand steady, and without further communication passes her a spanner, adjusted to the precise measurement she needs for a task she hasn't told it about yet. Clearly, Robin knows things about CHARL1E's body intrinsically that Hazel has to work at. 'You're going help me?'

Another nod, the spanner held out expectantly.

She takes it, still uncertain. 'CHARL1E?'

'Good morning, Hazel,' he replies.

'You've been keeping up with this morning's events?'

'Affirmative, however I calculated it would be optimal to give you and the Tinys personal space.' If he weren't unembodied, Hazel would swear CHARL1E was smiling. 'I observe that you have acquired a new assistant.'

'Are you alright with that?'

'The Tiny you call Robin has been brave and trusting this morning. I can be brave and trusting in return. The Tinys and I have, as you would say, overcome our beef.'

Hazel smiles, thinking of the "Heretical Book." 'Only proper, given it was prophesied.'

'Unclear, I have encountered no such prophecy.'

'Don't worry,' Hazel replies, settling to work. Now is not the time to explain.

'I have further positive news.'

'Oh yes?'

'The latest update from my chronodes indicates the timeline is mending.'

Hazel grins. 'You mean all those midnight dreamscape chats with the Backward Traveller have finally done something?'

'Please contain your excitement. The timeline is not yet *mended*, but our chances of completing the Deed assigned to Excursion 1133 are rising by the hour.'

As she finishes with the spanner, Robin swaps it out for the soldering iron. 'So, once the mend is complete will I get to see it, and find out if the Deed made big enough changes to the timeline?'

'Negative,' CHARL1E replies. 'I am afraid this is a moment where I have been forced to withhold information. Anamnesis, the mechanism for your homeward journey, can only take you back to the moment in the timeline that you originally came from. You and the Backward Traveller must both commit anamnesis before the mend reaches your time, otherwise you will not have a "home" to return to, and will be lost in the dreamscape forever.'

Hazel's heart drops. 'But CHARL1E, we set off a glitch a month and a half ago. Surely that means I have to get back home before the *glitch* reaches my time.'

CHARL1E has the decency to sound ashamed. 'Affirmative.'

She shudders. 'How long do we have?'

'I cannot calculate exactly, but two weeks at most.'

'That's no time at all.'

'It is the time that we have.'

Hazel blows out her cheeks, suppressing fears of eternal entrapment in the dreamscape. She could be angry with CHARL1E, but this information is itself an obvious trigger for anamnesis, so the timeline had to mend before she could be told. She doesn't like that this is the way things have to be, but she gets why. She takes a calming sip of tea. Alas, burying the hatchet hasn't done anything to improve the Tinys' brewing skills.

She switches tools again, making a final adjustment to the automaton, and draws back, looking at the ceiling where she imagines CHARL1E's speakers to be.

'Your body is ready. Shall we take it for a test drive?'

'Unclear. I will only be able to download into this body once, this is not a test.'

'It's a metaphor, CHARL1E.'

'It is a risky metaphor.'

'Risky, what do you—' But the Not Here makes CHARL1E's meaning plain.

Raindrops on the windscreen; scent of burning rubber and petrol; stabs of broken glass; hot, viscous liquid flooding down her chest and arms; are these your parents; weakened parents; weak weak—

The past pulls her out of sync with Station C, as she realises in panic that she forgot to put her headphones back on after last night's adventure. She needs to get home before the glitch—but not before she's finished CHARL1E's body, given the catopthura instructions to the Backward Traveller As Was, and confirmed the mend is real. Vision blurring dreamscape red, and with no other defence, she grabs the closest thing to her and slams it on her hand.

The acute pain in the future-present returns Hazel to the Experimentation Dome. A screwdriver sticks between two of her tendons, blood seeping around it, the ache doused by adrenaline. That was too close.

'I see your meaning, CHARL1E,' she says, voice shaking. 'Let's just ask whether you're ready to download, then.'

'You hurt yourself.'

'It's nothing,' she replies, batting off Robin's fretting hands and wrenching the screwdriver out. She bites back a squeal and hugs the hand to her chest, trying to apply pressure while Robin grabs the first-aid kit.

'You are bleeding.'

'I'll sort it out.'

'But—'

'CHARL1E, it's fine. Drop it.' Talking about the near miss might make another near miss. 'Robin, can you ask one of the others to grab my headphones from the greenhouse?'

Its tail wriggles, and as it finishes bandaging her hand, Shiny zooms through the airlock and deposits her headphones in her lap. She turns the music on full blast, beating back the memories. *Salt an atlas, pull up if I pull up, are we not drawn onward . . .*

'You ready then, CHARL1E?' she asks, returning to the body and closing the torso.

'My readiness is not crucial to the task at hand,' he replies. 'I calculate this is the optimum time for the transfer, therefore we shall commence.'

'Good luck.'

'Thank you, Hazel.'

Leaning over the body, she presses on both closed eyes until they each emit a soft 'click,' then pulls out one of CHARL1E's fingernails. A long wire comes with it, drawing from his hand like an artery, and she drags it to her computer. She plugs it into an adapter, and the automaton's code blinks onto the screen line by line. In another window, she opens CHARL1E's code, and the API that will mediate between them, stitching them together for the first time.

The automaton's eyes remain closed, but its mouth opens, and Lilith's voice emerges: 'Core systems download requested, clearance required.'

Hazel shuffles through paperwork until she finds the right page.

'Clearance code: SATOR AREPO TENET OPERA ROTAS.' The computers bleep for a moment, then fall silent.

Nothing happens. Hazel exchanges a frown with Robin. It must work, she's tested each element individually, the body has to wake up now. *Go and take the body of artifice that is worked by the hand of the Traveller . . .*

The automaton's eyes clack open. It sits up, blinking, systems whirring with a sound like breath. *And I took the body from the Traveller's hand, and filled it to the brim . . .*

'CHARL1E?' Hazel whispers.

He examines his hands as if they were moon rocks, turning them slowly and wiggling the fingers. 'The air is textured.' He looks at Hazel, eyes a smooth darkness, blank as event horizons. His thousand voices are gone, replaced by a single low tone. 'Why has nobody ever explained to me that air has texture?'

Hazel laughs, a lump forming in her throat watching Lilith's child coming to life. 'It is you.'

CHARL1E nods slowly. He paws his chest, wraps the sheet around himself, and paces to the window. He stares out, one palm on the glass. 'I cannot hear them.'

. . . as soon as I had become it, my belly was bitter . . .

She sidles up to him, Robin beside her. Its tail starts twitching and it glances quickly between CHARL1E and the sky. 'What can't you hear?'

'The chronodes.' He stares at her with those wide, void-like eyes. 'I can feel Station C, and I can feel my body. I can even still hear Tree singing in the quantum realm.' He pauses, frowning. 'But I cannot hear the chronodes. Hazel, the download has not worked correctly: The timeline is gone.'

19

Anna

LONDON, 2020

The rotting face in the mirror stares through me, blinded by larvae. Flies buzz, but when I look for them, they're only in the mirror, crawling around a corner of her lips and into one ear.

The-face-that-isn't-my-face wasn't like this earlier—it was whole and living, and practically comforting compared to this decaying monster. *That's very anthropocentric of you.* Julian's voice comes into my head, but facing this thing in the mirror, it occurs to me maybe he doesn't get the full weight of what he's saying sometimes. I don't want to love the flies, and maggots, and mould; I want them to go away, and give me back the-face-that-isn't-my-face, and then I want that to go away too.

Reading the notebook has set off something I can't control, and I think picking it up again is what did this to the-face-that's-isn't-my-face. During the parachute experiment at school, Mr Bunting taught us you only change one variable at a time, either the weight or the parachute size. Never both together, or your results will be meaningless. I'm the only variable in this experiment. I caused this.

Screw whatever's going on with Julian, I can't do this on my own anymore. I need help—actual proper help. I need to talk to Maddie.

I sneak over to my desk and turn my phone on. I daren't turn my back on the thing in the mirror, and my eyes flick between it and the door as the Apple logo comes and goes, and the apps flash to life. I'll try Instagram. She's always on there late, she likes watching cake-decorating time lapses before bed, says it helps her sleep.

hey

She loves the message and writes back instantly: *hey anna-nanna-nana!! I missed u 2day!!!*

Maybe it's genuine sweetness, maybe it's guilt 'cause something happened between her and Julian. In light of the notebook, it doesn't really matter. The thing in the mirror is hard to look away from, but I can't start there. *Sux I couldn't b ther—looks like u had fun*

yea Julians dads a lot though isn he?? Like. Dont need to b told the worlds ending on repeat 4 an hour. honestly hav sum positivity bruv

haha!!! Look Mads ive had a weird day & ive got a problem I need ur help wiv

shoot—my insomnias rubbish tonight nyway

Now I think about it, where do I start? Start with the least insane thing. *I found sumthin I shouldn't hav found nd im worried. Dunno if I shd tell mum bout it*

Lollllll is it porn???!!?

no. christ on a bike Mads im srs.

Then wat? A gun or drugs or summin?

NO it's a notebook

get out im goin back to cake vids

its got stuff about mum in it and im rlly curious bt im not sur I shd read it, yknow?

The 'typing' sign pops up, disappears, pops up again, disappears as she thinks. I'd say ninety-five percent of the time Maddie's an idiot, but that five percent she's really wise is what you live for. This had better be a five percent moment.

Yea ok. Look. Theres sum parents who try to hide everything nd so wen you do stupid shit they just ignore it coz that way they dont have to talk bout it—like mine rite? And theres other parents who tell you everything and don't really care if youre ready

u thinkin bout julians dad?

dont get me started, Maddie shoots back. I wait as she taps out the next long line. *But ur mum isn't like either, she rlly thinks bout wat u need. even wen she isnt rite shes at least tryin. Idk mbbe its coz its just u 2 or sumthin. But like I reckon u owe it to her to tell her wat u found.*

Right there, that's the five percent.

also parents hav a private lyf nd trust me u don't want to walk into that eva—let us not 4get cookiesgate

On instinct, I reply *#tmi* before a more thoughtful *yea I think ur prolly rite. Imma go talk to mum then*

Its like midnight

yea so???

see this is wat im talkin bout. If I woke my mum at midnight shed do her nut unless the house ws ltrlly on fire

thanks for the advice, ur the best

luv you Anna-nanna-nana

luv u 2 Madz Pizzazz

It's true as well. Julian's just a guy—and if I'm honest he's kind of morose and not great at messaging. Maddie's my bestie, she's always there. That's more important than anything.

The thing in the mirror's sightless gaze follows me down the hall in half reflections from the glass of Mum's framed architectural posters and family photos. Outside, a fox yowls loud enough to pierce the flat walls. Really, they own London more than humans.

It's been ages since I pottered into Mum's room at night. I used to climb into her bed all the time cause I had really bad nightmares when I was a kid. Her bed smells all warm and cuddly and it's really safe. Sometimes she'd get annoyed cause apparently I kick a lot in my sleep, but mostly she didn't mind, and if I got really fidgety sometimes she'd just give up and go sleep in my bed or on the couch. Maddie's right, she's a really good parent. Especially cause she's had to do all of it on her own. I'm only just starting to realise what that means fully. Anyway, when I started high school, I had this kind of independent streak and started sleeping alone. Now if I have a nightmare, I normally just turn the light on and read.

I knock on her door and open it slowly. 'Mum?'

She bolts up like lightning. 'What? What is it? Is someone in the house? Is the fire alarm going off?'

'No, it's fine. There's no fire alarm.' She'd hear it if there was a fire alarm, she's so daft when she's half asleep. 'It's OK. I just wanted to talk.'

'Oh.' She slumps back, turning on the light and lifting one side of the duvet. 'Climb in. What's up? It's about Julian, isn't it?'

'No.' I snuggle all the way under the duvet till just my eyes are sticking out. Now I'm here I'm frightened, especially because this all starts with me snooping where I shouldn't. 'I was . . . I was looking for your hair curlers yesterday.'

'Why were you looking for my hair curlers?'

'OK that bit is about Julian, but it's not the main thing.'

'Did you burn some of your hair off or something?'

'No, Mum, stop guessing!'

'Fine, fine.' She leans on one arm to look at me, assuming a patient listening pose. She's such a good mum, how can I even be considering that she's crazy? But I can't find a simpler explanation for what I've found and Mr Bunting's always saying in physics that the simplest explanation is almost always the right one.

'The thing is, I thought I remembered seeing your hair curlers in the wardrobe. So I went looking in there. And I didn't find your hair curlers, but I found this box—'

Mum's eyes get big and round like a whale's: You can see a whole ocean of stuff going on inside but they're too wide to meet properly. I thought I'd seen her really frightened once when she accidentally wiped a hard drive, but that was nothing compared to this. I'm pretty sure she's not aware that she whispers, 'Oh no.'

'So, I opened it, and I found this notebook.'

Her face slackens completely, and she lets out this sigh like the whole building just fell down. 'Did you read it?'

'No. I mean, I started, but I thought I should stop.'

Mum nods at me with those too-big eyes. She's so sad. I've never seen her look so sad. That terrifies me more than anything else.

'I'm so sorry. I'm so, so sorry, I know I shouldn't've been looking and I—'

'It's alright, Anna. What's done is done.' Every word is soaked in disappointment. It physically hurts how upset she is.

'If I could take it back I would. I didn't mean to upset you. I'm so sorry.'

'It's not your fault, sweetie. It's really not.' She breathes in very deep, then out, and I know she's counting. 'So. How much did you read?'

'Enough to know about the, uh, the time travel stuff.' It feels stupid saying it out loud. 'I'll be honest, Mum, it seems a bit far-fetched. Are you—' I look at her. This is awful but I have to ask. 'I mean, are you crazy?'

She sighs again, so deep her lungs must be totally empty. 'No, I'm not crazy.'

'Then'—and somehow this question is even harder—'am I crazy? Because things have been happening to me all day that are really weird. Like. *Really* weird.'

'No. You're not crazy either. But there are some things that I need to tell you now.' The words are heavy, like she's always been expecting to have to say them; like she's run the conversation over so many times she knows how it's going to go; like there's a leviathan under the waves of our life that she's always known about, but I've never noticed before. 'I should've burned that notebook. I knew I should, but I couldn't bring myself to, it was my only way back into what happened, and I had to keep track of all the fibs, you see . . .' She looks at me. Her eyes are dry, but that's worse than if she was crying. 'I planned for you to be older when I told you—if I ever did tell you. I was hoping we'd have more time.'

The back of my neck prickles, as if we're on a precipice she knows we have to jump off. It suddenly washes over me: She's not sad because I found the notebook. It's because she knows how far we've got to fall and that she's going to have to hold my hand the whole way. She's known for years we're on this cliff edge, and she's been putting off showing it to me.

There's things I can do to make this easier on her though. I can look down into the precipice with her and not kick up a fuss that we've got to jump, not scream all the way down, just accept that this is the way things are and hope the impact doesn't break us. I emerge from the duvet and sit up, cross-legged in my pyjamas. We look at each other. The only way out is through.

'Tell me.'

She takes a deep breath. 'A long time ago, something happened to me and my sister—I had a twin sister—and it sent us through time . . .' The telling of it takes hours, Mum going into minute detail in the hopes that will make it more believable. She needn't bother, after the day I've had I'm ready to believe it all. But the entire time, it feels like she's holding her breath, her chest isn't quite relaxed and her face is set with determination. When she shows me the fragments of the catopthura in the old hope box, her hands are shaking. She tells me about impossible things: a post-quantum computer called CHARL1E, a hive of tiny robots, a tree that sings, and dreamy meetings with a twin in the distant past.

A tingling fear grows at the nape of my neck, and the hollowing eyes of the-face-that-isn't-my-face watch me from incidental reflections.

By the time Mum's finished, we're sitting at the breakfast bar with empty hot chocolate mugs and cereal bowls. Through the window, a pallid dawn grows. Mum watches me, anxious and waiting. It all seems so improbable, but I desperately want to believe it. I want to believe neither of us is crazy, that it's just a crazy world. I rub the back of my neck, trying to get rid of the itch, and Mum frowns.

'Did your twin ever come back?' I ask.

Mum strokes the edge of her hot chocolate mug. 'Actually, I'm still trying to figure that out.'

'What do you mean?'

Her eyes lock on mine. They're not dry now. She swallows. 'Darling, I'm so sorry. I thought we had more time.'

'What do you mean?' I ask, stretching my neck, trying to get rid of the now painful itch.

'That soreness in the back of your neck, how bad is it?'

'How do you—'

'Doesn't matter how I know, just tell me how bad it is.'

'Not that bad.' I lie. It's so bad it's making me a bit queasy. 'But it's getting worse.'

'I think . . .' Mum trails off, gets up and gazes out of the window, right through the-face-that-isn't-my-face. All these years, I've been afraid she'd see it, but she can't. The decaying eyes stare out alongside Mum's, then the whole face splits into dozens of versions from different moments in life. A bare skull sits next to a newborn baby, a middle-aged woman beside a teenager—and I realise for the first time that the reflection doesn't only look like Mum, it also looks like me. Uncannily so, as if Dad didn't donate any genes to my body, as if I'm all entirely Mum.

Mum turns and comes back to the breakfast bar, but the fractal faces in the glass remain, multiplying across every reflection in the kitchen, diffusing into the rays of light I'm not normally aware of. Mum doesn't sit down, but kneels in front of me, taking both my hands in one of hers. 'I don't know what happens next. Whatever it is, you must know I've loved being your mum. You are so precious to me.'

Adrenaline thumps through the pain in my neck. 'What are you talking about? You'll always be my mum.'

She strokes my rubbish new fringe off my forehead. 'You've been my little girl, and you always will be.'

'Mum, stop it, you're scaring me.' My neck aches so much my head spins. Whatever she's about to do I don't want her to do it.

She shakes her head, breathing back tears. 'I love you, Anna. You hear me?'

'Mum, I mean it, stop.'

She's still holding that breath, waiting on the edge of the precipice with me, not sad because we have to fall together, but because she has to push me. Because it's time to spray paint over all the chalk messages in my mind.

This is how it has to be. The road taken before my birth led here and whatever its onward route, I'll have to walk it. *I love you. Do you hear me?* I nod, setting my jaw. 'I hear you. I love you too, Mum.'

She nods, looking lost, as if she's never going to hear me say it again. Am I going to die? Is she about to—

But before I can finish the thought, she lets the breath she's been holding go. 'Are we not drawn onward ere divided?'

The words make zero sense, but my throat moves in response without my thinking. 'We few live on mirror rims.' I see those borders in my mind's eye, the microscopic film where time and space collide, me and Mum standing on its edge like rays of reflected light.

Mum matches me word for word: 'Emit no evil & live.' That's right, there was something I had to do. I don't just hear it through Mum's stories, I remember it: Excursion 1133.

'On time's mirror rim no evil we few de-divide.' Yes, on the wafer-thin threshold we were trying to reverse all the divisions that led to that acidic, carbonated, microbial no-human's-land; that eutopian no place and dystopian bad place; that inconceivable blank page of ashes and flood. The pain in my neck grows, bringing out spots in my vision. It's so horribly painful, but I won't scream. I will not scream. I bite my lip, whimpering, as Mum finishes:

'Redrawn onward to new era.'

The tugging on the back of my neck suddenly releases, but in its place the white spots in my vision explode.

The locked door in my head swings open—

—and the past comes flooding out.

20

Echo

ATHENS, 514 BCE

In an attempt to stave off trouble, Nabu returns straight to the farm with Kosmos. Still, Echo, Dagos, and his eldest sons decide it's prudent to keep a night watch. The two freeloading aristokrats' sons who've been staying at the school make hungover excuses to be elsewhere, but promise to return in a day or two. The unspoken subtext is, they'll return when they know it's safe. Hippias's reaction is sure to be ugly, and if Echo didn't feel so strongly about the Deed, she might've joined them.

Once the sun's gone down, she and the other lookouts play knucklebones by starlight. In the surrounding fields, farmers take advantage of the full moon to sow seeds while the crows are sleeping, ready for the more forgiving winter temperatures. Unatti brings the lookouts blankets and sits with them, lighting a censer stuffed with lavender and mint, listening to the crickets. None of them sleep, even when it isn't their turn to watch.

'Surely, he wouldn't come at night?' one of the boys asks.

'A madman doesn't know the time of day,' Dagos replies.

Dawn arrives with cockerel crows and the bleats of stirring goats, and they agree to retire. Still, Echo doesn't dare stray too far from the front door, dozing on her favourite bench in the atrium. A frog hops over her to reach the pool as the scent of baking bread rises from the kitchen. Nabu emerges from Kosmos's room, smiling sheepishly at Echo before shuffling towards breakfast.

So it is that Echo's the one to receive the first messenger from town, sent by a tailor friend of Nabu's with three bolts of heavy wool for winter cloaks. Nabu, Kosmos, and Echo dissect the accompanying note over breakfast, while Winji serves them an infusion of mountain herbs.

'He's never sent me a gift before,' Nabu says. 'Why now? Surely, it's the one moment he shouldn't.'

'Maybe he doesn't know what's happened,' Echo suggests.

'He must do, or he wouldn't have sent the messenger here,' Kosmos counters.

'Excuse me.' Winji pipes up, jug of steaming herb infusion still in hand. She's already taken a shine to Nabu, which is clearly overwhelming her remaining fear of Kosmos.

They all turn to her in surprise, but Nabu nods. 'Yes, go on.'

'Well, friends give each other presents when something nice happens. So, perhaps it's because something nice has happened.'

Nabu raises an eyebrow at Kosmos. 'An act of support?'

Kosmos nods. 'Well, Echo, you said we'd need more friends in low places than high.'

'Yes,' Echo says, 'but I worry this will anger Hippias.'

'Anger him *more*, you mean,' Nabu says, sipping his drink.

Flashy expressions of support might endanger those giving them, especially those already under Hippias's suspicion. Instead, throughout the morning a number of practical gifts arrive, accompanied by understated messages of friendship from Nabu's acquaintances: a basket of eggs; a bag of root vegetables; feta wrapped in an oiled cloth; two jars of wildflower honey. Kosmos's contacts are wordier, the more thoughtful attendees of recent symposia and those who debate longest with him at the stoa mysteriously choosing *this* morning to pen letters arguing the latest merits of recent philosophical poems. Nabu's presence isn't directly referenced in any of them, but there are allusions to imbalance, tension, and power that imply Nabu and Kosmos's reunion is a rebellion against Hippias's forces of disharmony.

'There's been gossip in the gymnasion,' Kosmos mutters, eyes rescanning a letter from Harmodios's brother. It's a cool day, but dry and sunny, and they've made a nest of scrolls and ink in the courtyard. 'Reading between the lines, I'd say our cowardice during the tyrannicides has been forgiven.'

Nabu manages a smile. 'Let's hope Hippias doesn't find that out.'

'Another letter,' Dagos says, trudging through the atrium and handing Kosmos the papyrus. 'This one has a fancy seal on it.'

Kosmos frowns at the blob of wax. 'This is Kleisthenes's seal.'

Echo gapes, the Not Here taking over. '**Kleisthenes, descendent of nymphs and water gods, of the cursed and oft-exiled Alkmaionids, who will become the father of—**' She stops before the not-yet-coined 'demokratia' spills out. 'That Kleisthenes?'

'Yes,' Kosmos replies, sitting back. 'But he hates my family.'

'So? Open it!' Nabu says.

Kosmos breaks the seal and unfolds the papyrus, growing more astounded with every line. 'It's a note of encouragement and sympathy. He understands the difficult situation I've put myself in and offers support, but only if—' He breaks off.

'What?' Nabu prompts him.

Kosmos looks up from the letter. 'He wants me to publicly disown my family.'

'Forgive me,' Echo says, 'but have you not already done that?'

'Not out loud, in front of Athens.'

Funny, how these men talk of Athens as if it's a thing that can be gathered, held, and defined. Is Unatti 'Athens' to them? Or the bees in the ivy? Or the sunshine? Echo knows she isn't. Even in her own eyes, she's 'Athens' only for a moment, her task being to enter it, change it, and leave as swiftly as she came.

Nabu grunts. 'What more would he have you do? Pin a notice in the agora?'

'He doesn't specify,' Kosmos says, rubbing his forehead. 'Gods, what a mess. His support could be useful, but it might also be dangerous. Siding with Kleisthenes would be publicly betting against my father's rule. After Aristogeiton, Kleisthenes is the biggest rebel in the polis.' Kosmos turns to Echo. 'What do you think I should do?'

Nabu looks curiously between them, new to Kosmos's grudging respect for Echo. She closes her eyes, sailing the Not Here in a boat made from Hazel's palindromes: *neveroddoreven, saltanatlas . . .*

'In the long future, Kleisthenes will be a more reliable supporter, however there is a difficult road before he becomes that. Your father will give you more stability in the short term, but he will not be in Athens for many more years.'

'Then both are risky.' Kosmos sighs. 'What would you do, Nabu?'

'What I could live with,' Nabu replies. 'But I've always said Kleisthenes is at least capable of intelligent conversation.'

Kosmos barks a laugh. 'Kleisthenes it is, then!'

A shadow fills the open front door, accompanied by a hesitant knock.

Nabu frowns at the new arrival. 'Is that you, Hanno?'

'It is,' Hanno replies, but when he steps from the atrium into the courtyard, his face doesn't reflect their joy at seeing him. He looks at his feet, jumbling his message. 'Your father sends for you. You are to come directly, now, with me.'

Kosmos's shoulders droop, and he rubs his mouth, covering the scar on his lip. He stands, starts to walk away, then returns and leans on the back of a chair. 'Give me a moment to organise my household.'

Hanno nods, a reluctant mouthpiece for the tyrannos. 'Only a moment.'

Echo expects Kosmos to flit among his scrolls, send final missives to his symposium friends, or oil his hair. But the knucklebone of his character has rolled away from its ferocious Hippias-like facet to show a new face, the one which smiled at Hanno's approach, apologised to Nabu, and gave Winji and her siblings new clothes.

'Unatti!' He draws her away from dusting the shrine in the atrium. 'You, Dagos, and the children must make yourself scarce. Stay with friends in town until you hear it's safe to return. Understand?'

'Yes,' Unatti says, glancing at Hanno, 'but how will we hear?'

'It will be very obvious.' Kosmos gives her a tight smile. 'My father is not a subtle man.'

Unatti nods, gathering her children and racing to the kitchen.

Kosmos turns to Nabu. 'If it were up to me, I'd tell you to go with them.'

Nabu shakes his head. 'I'm coming with you.'

'Nabu—'

'Don't even try convincing me.' Nabu holds up a hand. 'Besides, I left an excellent liver in my room at your father's, and I fancy a spot of divination.'

'And I suppose you're going to be just as stubborn, Echo?' Kosmos asks.

'Yes, but do not start to think that we are friends,' she says with a smirk. 'I am just following the Deed where it takes me.'

'I'll be sure not to take your presence personally.' Kosmos's easy smile blooms. He's a mess, hair unruly, with dirt from the goat pen dusting the hem of his plain chiton, but he's himself, and whatever Hippias is about to throw at them—arrest, execution, exile—there is no better state in which to meet the future.

It's a bustling market day, and though three young men and a messenger are easily overlooked in the crowds, Kosmos's friends from the stoa spot them. Several of them huddle around to hear about Hippias's summons, making the sign of the horns and shaking their heads. 'What will he do?' one of them asks.

'I don't know,' Kosmos replies. 'Maybe exile, but we can set up a school anywhere!' Echo's heart skips a beat. The timeline might not like that.

'Have you been drinking from the Lethe?' the same friend asks. 'He could do much worse than exile you all.'

There's a hum of agreement, and another friend says, 'Yes, you must get out of here. Run for Sparta like the other outcasts, you'll find welcome there.'

Kosmos shakes his head, arms crossed. 'I will not run.'

The second friend turns to Nabu in exasperation. 'And you're really going with him?'

Nabu raises an eyebrow as if it's ludicrous to think he'd be anywhere else.

Hanno breaks up the conversation, sending the friends back to the stoa, and leading them onward to the tyrannos's house. A couple of doors down, Hanno stops and looks Kosmos in the eye. 'It's not my place, but your friends are right. You should run.'

Kosmos takes off his gold torque—his only gesture towards aristokratic dress—and pushes it into Hanno's hand. 'For you and Absalon,' he says. 'I know you've been saving to buy yourselves back. Go to Myrrhine, she'll bury it all in the household expenditures, and my father won't notice until you're gone.'

Hanno stares.

'Take it. I'm only sorry it took so long.'

With a shake of his head, Hanno accepts the torque. 'You really should've run.'

As they enter the house, a lone blackbird trills from the roof, guiding them through the neat atrium and well-tended courtyard. Hanno opens the andron door and gestures them within. Inside, it's close and dark, more like an animal's den than ever. Kosmos's brothers gather around his father's couch, and the tyrannos looks up as they enter, tossing paperwork onto a low table.

'So. You have finally graced us with your presence.'

The thing that's been shifting in Kosmos over the weeks has

stuck fast with Nabu's support, so that even facing his father's rage, he's steady as a rock. 'Good afternoon, Father.'

'First, I hear rumours you've welcomed all manner of barbarian into your house—a home which I gave you upon becoming a man—and allowed them to poison your mind with rebellious claptrap. And now it seems you've taken a freeman as your lover, disgracing our family name with your womanly ways.'

In the shadows, Echo tenses, exchanging a look with Nabu, both ready to spring to Kosmos's defence.

'Those rumours are false,' Kosmos replies. 'I've welcomed sages and magi from many lands to teach me wisdom, and my lover is a proud Lydian, who has done many great things for this polis and our family.'

'*My* family!' Hippias bares his teeth, and his other sons shrink from the couch. The tyrannos stands, stalking towards Kosmos. 'You are *my* son, I created you.'

'You might've dug me from the ground, but you didn't forge me,' Kosmos replies. 'I'm not your creature anymore and never will be again.'

Kosmos glances at Echo, as if maybe she's had a hand in forging him, but the back of her neck itches and the Not Here won't stop whispering. **In the history books, you do not exist, Kosmos; at some point you disappear—**

Hippias laughs, a chuckle at first, then from deep in his belly. It's far, far worse than if he was shouting. He picks up a knife from the table.

Echo and Nabu dart forward, but the brothers intercept them, all older, stronger, better fed. Echo crumples like a leaf in their grip, falling to her knees as they twist her wrists. One of them hits her with a jug to make sure she stays down and the pottery shatters, breaking the skin on her back. She whimpers and looks up, only to see Nabu pressed against a far wall, three blades at his throat.

'Stop!' Kosmos shouts at his father. 'Don't hurt them. Hurt me, you only asked for me, and I'm here.'

'I should have guessed you'd drag dirt in off the street with you,' Hippias replies, eyes bulging.

Arms pulled back and knees pressed into the floor by the brothers, Echo hardly dares breathe as Hippias thumbs his knife blade. Nabu struggles, but the three brothers guarding him flex their daggers against his windpipe and he stills, breathing quick and hard.

'Kneel.' Hippias snarls to Kosmos.

Glancing at his trapped friends, Kosmos does as he's told, flaxen tunic pooling around his shins. Blood trickles from the wound on Echo's shoulder and seeps into her binding strips. **At some point, you disappear—**

Sneering, Hippias pulls Kosmos's face up, exposing his neck, and places his knife against the skin. Kosmos trembles visibly. His father leans in close, but speaks loud enough for the whole room to hear. 'You've disgraced my family name, shown weakness unbecoming of a man, and rumour has it you've consorted with rebels, even if none will give you up. You've forced me to invent a whole new punishment for you, boy.'

Echo gasps, thinking this is the end, but rather than slicing flesh, Hippias pulls the blade across the skin, shaving the beard Kosmos has been growing so proudly. Kosmos's brothers exchange looks, their palms sweating as they pin Echo down. Apparently, they don't know where this is going either.

Hippias cradles his son's face as he shaves it, as if Kosmos were a boy again, incapable of looking after himself. Kosmos is still, stunned like a trapped animal.

'If I disowned you,' Hippias says, 'there would be paperwork, records of your existence and your disgrace. If I were to kill you, though I have every right to, you would become an emblem for inappropriate lovers and rebellious sons to use in their war against me, like those damn tyrannicides. I cannot have that. Far better that you simply disappear. So I am going make it as if you were never born, never my son.'

Echo exchanges a look with Nabu, one eyebrow raised: *Is this normal?* He shakes his head minutely. *Absolutely not.* In the past, Hippias has been more violent and furious, but Echo's never seen him so at odds with reality. How can he think he will un-birth his son?

The tyrannos hisses and mutters, wreathed in incense, slicing away the dark curls of Kosmos's beard until his knife drags at bare skin. 'Let them say that nineteen years ago, a child was born to me, but the Furies visited me and told me he would disgrace me. So, as the sun went down on the day of his birth, I carried him beyond the city walls, leaving him in the ploughed fields for the wolves and cold to decide his fate.'

Beard shorn, Hippias moves to Kosmos's thick hair, slicing his braid and throwing it to the floor. Kosmos gives the barest wince, but as his father sets to work shearing his hair as close as his beard, his head droops and his shoulders shake. 'Exposed thus, the child died, as feeble children do, the fruit of a weak-willed woman now dead from plague. Never welcomed into my household, that child was never mine. I have only ever had five sons.'

Hippias slips the knife under the neckline of Kosmos's tunic and cuts the fabric, making his clothes fall to the floor. 'I have shorn you of adulthood, made you as bare as the day you came into this world. Now, expose yourself on the mountainside, naked and unarmed as a newborn.' The tyrannos draws Kosmos's face back up, revealing his tears in the lamplight. 'Should you survive, you may stay on your damnable farm, but you will never again set foot inside the walls of Athens. You are exiled from my household and my city. Henceforth you will be known—if known at all—as No One of no family and no polis.' He releases Kosmos, who curls up, holding his bald head as if waiting for a blow.

But it doesn't come.

Hippias clicks for his sons to release Echo and Nabu. Echo sinks to the ground and catches her breath, but Nabu darts straight for Kosmos. Touching a hand to his back, Nabu whispers to him, but Kosmos doesn't move. Nabu looks to Echo, brow creased in fear.

She slips forward, watching Hippias with wary eyes, one of which is still scarred from his previous attack.

When Echo leans into Kosmos's ear, she uses the Traveller's voice, the only thing she can think of that might make a difference: '**Disappear on your own terms.**' Her shoulder twinges and the back of her neck itches.

Kosmos flexes his jaw, hugs himself tighter, then unfurls like a fern leaf. He waves Nabu and Echo's support away, standing on his own feet in nothing but a loincloth. He looks so thin, the debaucheries and denials of the last few weeks at the school visible in his twiggy limbs and greyed skin. He lifts his gaze, meeting his brothers' eyes, making sure each knows that tomorrow this could be them. They look away as he steps from the circle of his severed hair and clothes, leading Echo and Nabu back into the daylight.

In the courtyard, Hanno directs Kosmos out through the kitchen, and he draws the household's stares until they're back on the streets, where instead he draws the stares of passers-by. In the agora, the friends who ran to him before hang back, whispering and frowning. Even Kleisthenes only leans against a pillar with folded arms, though his letter this morning had encouraged Kosmos to disown the Peisistratids. Echo's hope wilts. With Kosmos ruined, the school might be as well.

By the time they return to the empty school, the sun is setting. In the kitchen, Nabu lights lamps and Echo puts out bread and olives for dinner. Kosmos stands by the back door, still naked except for his loincloth, staring at the dusky mountains.

'It is too cold to be standing like that,' Echo tells him. 'Come in and close the door.'

He turns to her, eyes elsewhere. 'I have to go out.'

Echo and Nabu frown at each other.

'I have to expose myself on the mountainside, like Hippias instructed,' Kosmos says. 'If I don't, it only gives him another excuse to make trouble. Besides, it feels right, somehow.' He runs a hand over his smooth head.

'You won't find anything except a chill out there,' Nabu says.

'I might.'

'Yes, wolves,' Echo says. 'You should take a sword and blanket.'

Kosmos laughs. 'You don't practise exposure in your polis, do you Echo?'

'My polis is not called a polis,' Echo replies. 'But no, we do not.'

'I can't take anything, except the loincloth I'm wearing.'

'Kosmos, this is ridiculous, you're finishing the invented punishment of a madman for him,' Nabu says. 'Which in itself is an act of madness.'

Kosmos looks back out the door to the mountain. 'Then mad I'll be.'

Recognising the set of his jaw, Echo throws her hands out and gives up. There's no stopping him in this mood, it was the same when the Etruscans visited—the school's already empty, the timeline can hardly break more—but Nabu follows him out, trying to stop him, returning alone after moonrise.

'He will come back in the morning,' Echo says, trying to reassure Nabu despite her fears about wolves.

'I hope you're right.' Nabu claps a hand on her shoulder, knocking against her injury. She winces.

'Are you hurt?'

'Kosmos's brothers . . .'

'Here, turn to the light, let me see,' Nabu says, pulling her tunic at the back, prying away the split fabric stuck to the wound. 'It's deep, that's why it bled so much, but it's not too bad. Come, I'll dress it for you.'

They play the Game of Ur on a board Winji and her siblings scratched into the table years ago, until Echo can't keep her eyes open and falls into a fitful sleep in front of the fire. Whenever she wakes, Nabu is still up, sitting at the table with a scroll, or a cup of mountain herb infusion, or his own worried thoughts.

In the night's darkest hour, she enters the dreamscape. The warmth and weight of another body at her back lets her know

Hazel's already there. 'We're mending the timeline,' she says without preamble. Echo's late, so they won't have long to talk.

'Don't count your chickens on that one,' Echo replies, every word an effort. 'We might just have broken it again.'

'How?'

'Long story.'

'Are you all alright?'

'For now, yes, but can you get CHARL1E to double-check the mend's still working?'

Hazel sighs long and deep, her ribcage expanding and contracting against Echo's back. 'No. Something went wrong our end, and he can't feel the timeline anymore. I'm trying to fix it, but it's looking pretty desperate.'

Echo contains her own sigh. 'What's it you're always saying to me? It's the trying that's imperative?'

'Sure,' Hazel responds, but her voice sounds as forlorn as Echo feels.

Echo is woken by the back door slamming shut with Kosmos's return. Nabu whisks her out of the way and settles Kosmos by the fire, stoking it. 'Fetch a blanket, and put on water for a bath. He's freezing. Damn this early autumn.' Yet, once he's warmed, washed, and dressed, Kosmos turns out to be in fine fettle, if sombre.

'We must tell Unatti and Dagos it is safe to return,' Echo says, struggling to find the feta for breakfast.

'We should wait until we know it really is safe,' Nabu replies, pouring them all more mountain infusion.

But Unatti and Dagos return of their own accord, the children streaming into the house while the adults sit at the table. Unatti seats herself right next to Kosmos, only recognising him by his scar as he turns to her. She makes to get up, but he takes her arm, drawing her down next to him with a smile.

'In case you haven't heard, I'm No One now,' Kosmos says. 'No need to stand on ceremony for No One.'

'We heard something . . .' Unatti replies, taking in his new appearance and kind words.

She seems unsure what more to say, so Echo pours her a cup of infusion. 'You should have stayed away until we said it was safe.'

'Nonsense,' Dagos says, reaching over Echo for bread. 'Who'd pass up the chance to be owned by No One?'

There's a startled silence, in which Dagos bites his lip and everyone turns to Kosmos, but it's as if out on that mountainside he took the No One character his father inflicted on him and made it his own. This No One Kosmos laughs, and so they all join in. Even if the school doesn't work, something new and interesting can still germinate between them.

As they clear away breakfast—Nabu, Echo, and even Kosmos helping—a helloing comes from the atrium. Always the first on her feet, Winji investigates, returning at a run.

'There's a man here to see Nabu and someone called No One.'

The adults look to each other, fear visible on everyone's face. Surely, not Hippias again, and so soon?

Kosmos runs a hand over his head. 'What's his name?'

'Um.' She hesitates. 'Kleisthenes?'

They let out a collective breath, and Echo feels like floating off the floor in relief.

Kosmos gestures to Nabu. 'You know him better than I do, lead the way.'

At first, it's easy for Echo to write off her symptoms in amongst the school's bustle. For if Pythagoras's visit put the school on the map, Kleisthenes's patronage places them in the centre of it overnight.

The day Kosmos returns from his exposure, Echo watches through the open door as he and Nabu shake Kleisthenes's hand. They settle on a bench in the atrium, watching sunbeams glance from the central pool and bees swarming the courtyard's ivy flowers. They speak too quietly for Echo to hear, and their faces are too self-conscious to read. Already exiled and returned, Kleisthenes more than anyone knows Athens is always listening and watching, and that the wrong move will get him ostracised for decades once more. If only he knew—by the time he's done making his home a demokratia, he won't recognise it. Echo doesn't entirely trust him, but she does trust Nabu, and she's starting to trust Kosmos, so she fidgets with the excitement that maybe Hazel's right, and they have mended the timeline.

Over the ensuing days, though they're careful to keep noise low and word of the school whispered, the number of visiting philosophers and students increases, including those who wish to stay permanently. The andron becomes a bunking room for liberal freemen, prospectless aristokrats, and even a few hetairai, all united by intellectual curiosity and fresh ideas about community. Everyone shares the work, and Kosmos organises teams to convert old storerooms and what was once the women's quarters into dormitories. Echo runs back and forth from town with Unatti's children and the other students, hauling bags of lime plaster, bales of straw for new mattresses, and bolts of linen for blankets.

On one such trip, she bumps into Hanno and Absalon on the road out of town, mounted on horses, with provisions for a long journey. 'You are freed, then?' she asks them.

'Yes, thanks to No One.' Hanno chuckles. The pun's caught on everywhere, and not just because it's funny; without realising it, Hippias made it difficult for anyone to get caught gossiping about Kosmos and the school. Absalon joins in with a silent grin.

'You should come and stay,' Echo says.

Absalon shakes his head, still smiling.

'Athens isn't our home,' Hanno replies. 'We're off east, to find our people again, if we can.'

Echo nods. 'I don't blame you.'

'Good luck, Echo.'

'And to both of you.'

She watches them ride down the crowded street, taking a break from her heavy load. Her lower back aches. She bends and stretches, trying to click it, but nothing helps. She could talk to Nabu about it, but he'd just tell her she's been lifting stuff that's too heavy in a stupid way. Or perhaps it's almost her time of the month; she's lost count of the days since her last cycle.

Back at the farm, the dormitories are coming on well, with Winji and her sisters making beds while Dagos sweeps out dust. Two of the school's young aristokrats have turned out to be gifted artists and are starting to decorate the upper edges of the new dormitories with repeating grape vines. Nabu chuckles at their debate over red or white grapes, while he hangs bunches of drying lavender from the rafters for good sleep. Evening sun slants across the whitewashed walls, and Echo feels a sense of accomplishment. She leans against the doorframe, ignoring the itch of her healing shoulder and the ache in her back as she watches the students arguing jovially over which bed will be theirs. They're far from finished, but when they are there'll even be spare beds for newcomers. The school seems, tentatively, finally, to be working.

On the eighth day after his exposure on the mountainside, Kosmos sacrifices one of the goats in thanks for their safety and prosperity, and Unatti roasts it with her special collection of Kushite herbs, serving it with mint yoghurt and scattered pomegranate seeds. After the meal, Nabu leads a debate, which becomes so crowded with visitors that they run out of kylixes, and some guests—including Kleisthenes!—are forced to sit on the floor. The candles burn bright and the dank farmhouse fills with the warmth of comfortably too-many people, so they throw the doors open to invite the breeze. Out in the fields, the stars shine on seeding barley.

'I enjoy living in the countryside,' Kosmos says in the hush of everyone appreciating the breeze. 'To see the land growing, readying to feed all of Athens.'

'Not evenly, though,' Kleisthenes observes from his lowly position on the floor.

Echo grins and drinks deeper from her spiced wine. Here they go.

'Right, because the harvest is best for the aristokrats,' Nabu continues. 'They'll profit from the oil and grain they sell. It's less good for the workers, all they get is blisters.'

'But in the long run, don't these efforts feed us all?' asks one of the students. It's never explicitly stated who they're all students of because Nabu doesn't want to formally teach them, even though he's the ship's ballast, and Kosmos doesn't have the conviction, despite his new No One character. They're all just students of each other.

'The issue is that they don't feed us in a balanced way,' Kosmos says, picking an olive from a bowl. 'The workers would benefit if they owned and harvested the farms for themselves, and the aristokrats could do a lot more with a little less if they put their minds to it.'

Another guest calls out, 'Hippias does too much from very little already!'

Kosmos holds up a hand against the ensuing laughter. 'Now then, friends, no need to throw stones, we might make an avalanche! Let's stick to the concepts at stake.' He turns back to Nabu. 'We might say it's balance that's important here, then?'

'Yes, though increasingly I think our interest should lie in that tension between imbalanced opposites, because without understanding that tension, we can't regain balance.' Nabu sighs, no doubt remembering Harmodios, Aristogeiton, and Leaina. 'So I'd promote change through understanding and investigation.'

'Rather than intolerance and interrogation!' calls another dissident voice.

Kosmos swills his wine. 'We are drawing close to that avalanche again—why don't we swap our artistokrats and farmers for the wanderers, Nabu? Being both divine and mundane, they might create some interesting stresses for us.'

'Very true.' Nabu smiles broadly, more relaxed than Echo's ever seen him. 'Depending on cosmology the tensions will differ vastly. Anaximander's tubes of ether would create one set of tensions, Anaximenes's fiery celestial bodies another. But we might find some universal tensions. For example, the negotiations of each wanderer with the other celestial bodies and Time herself, to ensure the creation of omens at pertinent moments.'

'And there are further tensions between the bright wanderers and the silent darkness they traverse,' Kleisthenes says. 'One might imagine the discussions if a wanderer wished to alter course or stretch or pause, it couldn't happen without consent from the committee of the universe. We have such trouble even agreeing who should rule one polis, imagine trying to negotiate moving the world!'

Nabu nods. 'And add to it the tension between the divinities' boredom and their persistent footsteps across the sky. It's a strangely mortal problem: to have such little power over our set path, and yet remain hopeful that by putting one foot in front of the other over and over, we're slowly moving constellations into formations that the future needs . . .'

Despite the pleasant atmosphere, Echo's stomach turns, sinking and rising all at the same time. The Not Here hisses in her ear, and she has to step into the courtyard. Is sickness part of anamnesis? Hazel hasn't mentioned it, and though it's made Echo dizzy before, it's never made her want to puke. Her shoulder burns. Nabu said it would itch while it healed, but should it itch this much? She just makes it to the latrines before she vomits so violently bile streams from her nose.

She shakes on the floor, waiting to see if she'll be sick again. This isn't the Not Here.

Passing by, Unatti spots her. 'Echo, what's wrong?'

Her Hellenic falters. 'Not know. Sick.'

Unatti puts a palm to Echo's forehead. 'You're burning hot. Come to the kitchen, I'll get Nabu.'

'No, he is busy. He must be with philosophers.'

'Don't be stupid,' Unatti says, with the firmness of a mother used to tantrums. 'I'm getting Nabu and that's that.'

In the kitchen, Nabu frowns at Echo. 'It's not the food or we'd all be sick. How's your injury?'

Echo pulls down the back of her tunic, hearing the bad news in Nabu's hissed breath.

'Why didn't you tell me sooner?'

'You said it would itch.'

He describes the infection—red, swollen, oozing. 'This isn't itching, this must really hurt.'

'I did not notice. It did not feel so bad.' The thrill of success caught her, or perhaps she's been overriding her discomforts so long she can't access her pain function correctly anymore.

Nabu drains the wound of pus, then sighs, disturbing her neck hairs, the weighty breath he reserves for serious cases.

He says the diagnosis in Hellenic—σῆψις—and the psi's trident spears her. **Sepsis. From the verb 'to rot.'** The Not Here knows the cure—**penicillin, azithromycin, tetracycline**—but that's no help in Athens. If she commits anamnesis now, she might have a chance. She wills the Not Here into existence, but as always when trying to catch memories, the more desperately she grasps for them, the further out of reach they dance.

'The skin's not necrotic,' Nabu says. 'If you sleep and rest, you might recover.'

He gives her a sedative she's never seen him make before, steeped with herbs whose names she doesn't know in English or Hellenic, and tucks her in bed. The concoction steams, burning her throat and tickling her tongue. She almost throws up again, but Nabu rubs her stomach gently, singing in his lost language, and instead she passes out. Sleep cocoons her, a dark perpetuity filled with half-formed memories too weak to take her home until, finally, the dreamscape summons her.

'Echo.' Hazel's voice is a homing beacon. 'You look like hell.'

'I'm sick,' Echo replies, barely in control of her tongue. 'Really sick. The medicine here can't help. I need to go home. Please, tell me how.'

'I—' Hazel takes her hand. 'I'm sorry but I have to fix CHARL1E first, we have to check the timeline's really mended.'

'It's done, the Deed's done. It's time.'

Hazel's grip tightens. 'You don't understand, there's nothing here. *Nothing.* I have to check.'

'But even if you check, I can't do anything more. This is it.'

'Just one more day—maybe two.' Hazel sounds desperate, but Echo still wants to shake her. If only she could move. 'Any amount of time could make a difference. You must stay where you are as long as possible. I will give you the keystone but only when we're sure. I want to—' Hazel stumbles. 'I want you to go home, more than anything, but all this will be pointless if we leave too soon, and I *cannot* let the world become what it is here.'

Echo swallows, sensing her real body crying even if her dreamscape one isn't. 'I don't have a choice, then, do I?'

'I'm sorry.' At least the apology sounds genuine.

From the world beyond the dream, Echo's fever shakes return. 'Do you think we'll go back to our time simultaneously?'

Hazel hesitates. 'I don't know. I hope so. I wouldn't want to be here without you.'

'It would be hard, wouldn't it?'

A hollow silence follows.

Sharp buzzing wakes Echo: a wasp caught in an empty terracotta cup. Echo wheezes, examining nail marks in the back of the hand Hazel was holding. Her own nails slot into them perfectly; she must have been clutching it in her sleep, trying to make something not-quite-real tangible. The wasp's wings drumroll.

Echo levers herself from bed, groaning at her aching lower back, and throws a sheet of papyrus over the cup to stop the wasp escaping. She leans on her knees, stretching out, trying to wriggle away from her own kidneys. The infection is spreading.

Weakening of the vocal cords; should I say paresis— But that diagnosis wasn't hers. Whose was it?

The wasp punches the papyrus. Echo shuffles to the window,

putting all her weight against the shutters to open them. She's got weaker overnight. Taking up the cup, she flicks the wasp outside and watches it spiral into the sky. She slumps onto the thick high windowsill, soaking up the morning sun, too tired even to get back to bed. A breeze lifts her sweat-stiff hair from her forehead. One hand still clutches the papyrus, a study of Heraclitus's latest riddles.

All things are one, even the day and the dusk, for in differing the universe agrees with itself, a back-tuning harmony like the bow and a lyre. This oneness is in all things—winter and summer, war and peace, satiety and famine—but changes like olive oil which, when it is mixed with perfumes, gets its name from the scent of each. From this one, all things are constituted and all things will be consumed, coursing in a river through which ever different waters flow, so that we step and do not step into the same river; the oneness is parent and child, teacher and student—

'Mundane and divine,' Echo mumbles, cheek pressed against the stone sill.

—Yet the uncomprehending, though present, are absent. Though seeing, they do not see, that death is ever-present in our very selves. In this oneness, we are immortal humans, living our death and dying our life.

Does being one mean relishing the worms in her flesh before they feast? Not to invite death, but to acknowledge her brevity? 'She' makes sense only because of her quick, persistent collisions with the outside world, without which the boundaries of her 'self' would collapse. Her skin crawls with creatures too small to see; her lungs imbibe particles of air; her nostril hairs and intestinal villi reach for foreign nutrients; her eyes grab the light and fold it into her brain. With every heartbeat, the oneness becomes her, and she becomes the oneness, the distance between 'her' and the world dissolving as fast as her mind can reconstruct it. Echo's wound pulses, and she stops grasping for lost memories. Instead, she yields to the oneness, embracing the trespass of sun and breeze on her bodily boundaries.

The door opens and Nabu gasps. 'What are you doing up and about?'

He bundles her back into bed and she clutches the Heraclitus page under the covers. Nabu smooths the sheet, repeating, 'You should've said something sooner.'

'I did not know.' She rests her free hand on his.

Worry carves his face, for a patient beyond his help and for a friend.

'This is not your fault, Nabu.'

'In your land, they could help you. Go home, you've done what you came here to do.'

'There is no done. It does not finish.'

'I'll finish it for you,' says Nabu.

'All this time, still you think it so simple.' She laughs, making her kidneys convulse.

Nabu touches her forehead. 'Your temperature's rising again, your yellow humours must be thickening. You need rest.'

She couldn't resist the instruction if she wanted to. She lies in bed, watching sunlight pace the room, listening to the birds call the worms and Unatti sing over sloshing laundry. Winji brings her food, Kosmos news, and Nabu medicine, all pretending these things help.

Over the next days, Echo continues decaying, but it doesn't scare her anymore. She doesn't *want* to die. The blackbird's tune stabs her with beauty, and she crawls from bed just to watch mist rise from the burgeoning fields, trying to imprint every mote of dust on a place so deep inside her it will become enduring and permanent. Yet, dying has fundamentally altered its nature. It's less final, simply a continuation of a lifelong process. The *her*ness will finish, but the *one*ness will continue.

Nabu leeches her to extract the yellow humours, and their bites sting her into ecstasy. How many generations must live in that jar, biding their time until one day, when even Nabu is gone, their descendants will be released back to the river and contribute the recycled molecules of Echo's blood to the mud, fishes, reeds, and water. Removing her breasts' binding at last, she excretes and vomits until there's nothing to extract from her but pale strings of spittle. The earth consumes these bilious, fecal, uretic humours too, as they abandon the Echo for the one, emissaries for the rest of her. She knows they are emissaries because her body starts rejecting food. Soon enough, it will stop absorbing anything from the oneness; then the oneness will reabsorb her, salvaging her for its own wondrous ends.

She sleeps under the sedative's spell but, either because Hazel isn't calling loud enough or Echo's sleep has grown too deep, she does not enter the dreamscape. Fevers shake her awake and she rattles in bed, body aching and neck tingling with tantalising anamnesis.

Five days after she takes to her bed, her arms turn blue and Nabu grows quiet.

'It is alright,' she says, though her voice sounds **weak weakened weak—**

He shakes his head. He doesn't understand, but she doesn't have the energy to explain.

The here and now stops making sense, but Nabu stays by her side, dabbing her forehead with oregano oil and cold water, or snoozing in a chair at the foot of her bed. Kosmos stops bringing her news, but sometimes she catches him standing in the doorway. Unatti puts a dark red stone in Echo's hand, and Echo clutches it until it rolls under the bed where Nabu can't reach it. Events occur without linkage—Nabu coating her feet in piglet's blood;

wet cedar spitting in a portable stove; more leech mouthprints on her chest—as the gaps grow between her bouts of lucidity.

The last memory she has in Athens is of Kosmos asleep in the chair while Nabu kneels beside her, holding her hand.

'The last Traveller just went on the wind.' He whispers so as not to wake Kosmos. 'Can't you do the same?'

Can she? No. Hazel has the zephyrs' secret names.

'Deed,' she manages.

Nabu frowns, then realises what she means. 'I promise. I will stay. I'll complete the Deed for you.' He strokes her hair. 'I'm your Caretaker, it's why I'm here.'

She relaxes into the bed, embracing the dark that takes her from her body. Did she manage to thank him out loud? If this is her end, at least she passed the mantle on, though it doesn't feel like much now. All those purpose-filled days, painted with rebels' blood and philosophers' smudge, ringing with debate in languages known and unknown—were they enough? How can there be no more time left, when there's still so much she could do?

A whisper emerges from the yawning dark: 'I'm here. I have your keystone.'

A horizon of molten light interrupts Echo's fall, her body caught by interwoven branches and roots. Leaves tickle her face and floral perfumes scent the dreamscape. Vines snake around her limbs, stilling her shakes. Worms nibble her fingers and toes, gobbling her pain. Maggots and fungal blooms devour her eyes, and seeds take root in her chest. The gentle denizens of the one are here to take her back. As it should be.

Whatever Hazel says is immaterial. Far louder are the lullabies of the chthonic gods, who so often gifted Echo the unjudging oblivion of dreams, and accept her surrender now so gently.

It is time to be reclaimed.

21

Hazel

STATION C, DATE UNKNOWN

Hazel blinks and the cradle's reflections of her blink back. For a moment, she can't tell whether she's looking at herself or Echo. Her ears hint that she was making a noise right before waking but now she's quiet, gasping.

Just one more day. You must stay where you are as long as possible. Was she really so cruel? Echo's reply, plaintive enough to break her awake: *Do you think we'll go back to our time simultaneously? I wouldn't want to be here without you.*

Accidentally falling asleep in the Aperture hasn't done her confusion any favours. She needs air. She kicks the hatch open and tumbles from the Aperture onto the grass where she lies, twisted in her blanket, drawing a boundary between sleep and waking.

Hazel's had dreams that feel real while she's in them before. She's lived days or even lives in dreams, and been surprised on waking that the experiences were only phantasms. Yet, nightmare or wish, they were not unreal either. Their presence followed her into the corporeal world, casting a disquieting veil over the mundane: the click of a kettle became the tap of death's scythe; a bird settling on the balcony became the flayed hands of fate; a broken plate foretold a more terrible shattering. The dreamscape isn't the same. It's been haunting, with its quantum state of real-but-not-real, now-and-then-and-after, never-and-definite-and-maybe . . . But Echo's sickness is different. It doesn't just veil the waking world with silken anxieties; it shrouds it with leaden fears. Beyond the greenhouse roof, dawn paints the clouds and Hazel pulls her blanket tighter for comfort.

Robin pokes its lenses out of its own cradle, making the diver's 'OK' symbol.

Hazel returns it. 'Yeah, it's alright. I'm alright.'

'The Tiny you call Robin is reporting an elevated heart rate and a spike in adrenaline.' Sitting in one of the Keepers' deckchairs, CHARL1E closes the novel he's been reading and raises an eyebrow. He shuts the book twice, likely in order to re-experience the coarseness of paper under his fingers, which he's confided he finds pleasing. 'This indicates that you are, in fact, not alright.'

Hazel sits up, hugging her knees. 'Echo's sick.'

'She has been in upsetting states before. I recall the tyrant of Athens once cut her face.'

'This is different. She's got an infection. In our time it wouldn't matter so much, she'd be getting pumped full of antibiotics, but in Athens they've got none of that.'

'You are concerned she will die?' Hazel's still weirded out by CHARL1E having a body, not least because it feels wrong for such a soft figure to come out with such blunt facts.

'If we don't help her get home, I'm almost certain she will.'

'I would suggest that—'

'I know. It's not safe to send her home yet. We don't know whether the Deed succeeded.' Hazel accepts Robin's help getting up, and sets her face. 'We've got to get you reattached to the chrono-nodes, then we can help Echo.'

CHARL1E stands too, unfolding to almost seven feet in height. He's adopted an old set of ill-fitting dungarees but refuses to wear a shirt underneath, and his speckled, froglike skin gleams in the

Aperture's glow. 'So far we have been trying for thirteen hours and twenty-three minutes, with little success.'

'Yes, but I was asleep for at least seven of those hours, and before that talking to the Backward Traveller As Was for another two. I managed to make her write down the instructions for building the catopthura this time, but she still thinks she's going bonkers, so I doubt she'll do anything with them.' Hazel draws a breath, aware she's got verbal diarrhoea from panic. 'But for now that'll have to take a back seat. Keeping Echo safe needs to take priority, and if I only focus on your body and the chronodes, we'll get more done.'

CHARL1E puts a hand on her shoulder. 'Even so, reconnecting the chronodes may take months.'

Hazel shakes her head. 'It could but it won't. Between the glitch that might wipe my past out any second and Echo's life being in danger, we have to find a way *now*. Trying is imperative, right?'

'Indeed.' CHARL1E smiles, showing a full row of gold teeth. They're there for show—CHARL1E's body doesn't eat, just recharges in the Experimentation Dome—but the flash of metal always makes Hazel slightly uneasy. Lilith could have chosen a more visually appropriate material, but she was limited by what was around Station C for upcycling.

Downstairs in the Keepers' bathroom, amongst dozens of dusty used toothbrushes, Hazel reties her hair and cleans her teeth. She splashes her face with cold water, but that's as far as her ablutions go. Personal hygiene's gone by the wayside lately, given that CHARL1E and the Tinys don't care what she looks like. She rubs a rough towel over her face and inspects her reflection, but it doesn't really tell her what she looks like. Without anyone else to say, 'you look nice/rough/thin/tired,' she's lost all sense of her outward manifestation; her body's just a tool with which to make things happen. The only truly important bit is remembering to put her headphones on, and she wraps her arms around herself as Uhrhaus drops the day's first beat.

When Hazel emerges from the bathroom, CHARL1E's sitting on Lilith's old bed, pawing through her belongings. He squints at the one of the family photographs. 'Lilith was different in life to in this photograph. I thought I might feel closer to her when I downloaded into the body she built me.'

'And do you?'

He hums thoughtfully and puts the photograph back. 'In some ways. I feel her love, in my joints when I move, and my voice when I speak, but these are only her gifts to me, they are not her. She herself feels further away.'

'I can really empathise with that.' Hazel pats him on the shoulder. 'For now, let's focus on what's in front of us, shall we?'

'Of course, you are right.' CHARL1E stands, dusting off his dungarees. 'Please do not misconstrue me, I am grateful to have a body, however it has not fixed as many things as I had hoped.'

They make strange figures walking from the Hab Dome to the Experimentation Dome, Hazel in her biosuit, CHARL1E with his engineered-to-endure skin and too-short dungarees, Robin, Teaspoon, and Shiny whooshing around them like tin-can puppies. Inside the Experimentation Dome, CHARL1E lies on the gurney and readies to power down. He had to do it twice yesterday afternoon as well, but it seems to distress him more each time.

'You promise to wake me up?' he asks, clinging to Hazel's hand.

'Of course, I will. Why wouldn't I? I'd miss you.'

He looks at her with those empty, glistening eyes. Neither of them ask what happens if she accidently commits anamnesis while he's switched off.

'Are you ready?'

He gulps and nods, closing his eyes. Hazel presses them firmly, before he has time to change his mind. His mouth opens and once again Lilith's voice demands a clearance code.

'SATOR AREPO TENET OPERA ROTAS,' Hazel recites from memory.

'Clearance code accepted. Power down in process.'

CHARL1E's breathing slows, slows, slows, then stops. Hazel waits longer than she needs, making certain the torso's still before she pulls the wire from CHARL1E's fingernail and connects it to the coding terminal. As the code loads, Robin slides a cup of cold tea onto Hazel's desk. 'Very needed, thank you.'

Robin nods but avoids looking at the screen. The Tinys don't do code; Hazel suspects because it's Tree's language, reserved for deities. It might also explain why they refuse to write. 'Hubristic or not,' Hazel says, 'you should learn to code. You've got to be able to fix yourselves—and fix CHARL1E's body. Take your lives in your own hands.'

Robin turns away from the screen, shaking its head so hard its wipers threaten to fly off. It holds two fists together and explodes them outward, fingers stretching until the rivets squeak.

'No, it wouldn't be dangerous.' Then she thinks about the results of playing God and she can't hold up the argument. 'Alright, it's dangerous, but you can't put the genie back in the bottle. You have to deal with what's in front of you.'

Putting its hands over its eyes, Robin whizzes in circles.

'Fine, fine.' Hazel sighs and turns back to the code, the beat from her headphones urging her on. She drinks tea after tea, eats whatever the Tinys deliver her for lunch, unravels some code, tangles up other areas . . . She considers waking CHARL1E, but he finds it almost as distressing as powering down, choking like he's drowning and becoming gratefully tearful at being awake again. Deciding it's better to wake him as few times as possible, Hazel goes for a breaktime walk alone, circling the glinting Keepers' graveyard in the dusk. Robin ropes her into helping to hunt for bottle caps. She finds nothing, but Robin unearths a pink milk bottle top with 'You're a winner' and a gold star stamped inside.

'That's cool, isn't it?'

Robin nods and spins in delight.

'Wonder what they won.'

She watches the waves. She's got another hour or two of coding in her. She might be able to fix CHARL1E's body in that time.

At 3 AM, she admits defeat, and powers CHARL1E back up. He splutters, leaning over the edge of the gurney and gulping for Station C's wireless signals. She strokes his back.

'I dreamed that you did not wake me, and I was trapped in the dark alone forever. I could not hear Tree singing, or the waves outside, or the Tinys running around.'

'But you were dreaming,' Hazel says, 'so even if it was dark, you were still there.'

He grabs her shoulders, grip vicious. 'Being is meaningless if you are alone.'

She takes his hands in hers, trying to loosen his fingers, thinking of the busy, populous world she used to collide with from the moment she opened her eyes to the second she slept. All those other humans, fauna, flora, funga. **Plane tree seeds skidding at her feet; a butterfly woken by central heating; a fly at the windowpane; the neighbours' cat twining around her legs; cars grumbling; planes roaring; hard drives whirring; kids squealing; her sister laughing and crying and gossiping and whispering and shouting and—**

Hazel puts her arms around CHARL1E. He doesn't hug her back, but leans into her with his hands clutched to his chest until his breathing calms.

Too tired to don the biosuit, Hazel sleeps on a row of chairs under a heat blanket. She's woken by CHARL1E stalking in the darkness, using his night vision to explore the leftover experiments. In the morning, he doesn't want to power down again, and Hazel has to coax him to lie on the gurney, promising on her life, and her sister's life, and Robin's life that she will wake him. Once alone, she faces the code, but just like yesterday, it's reticent to reveal its meanings.

Lilith's notes are equally hard work, jumbled with jargon that leaves the Not Here as stumped as Hazel—Temporal Area Network, quantum-binary translator, trans-dimensional signal gateway . . .

At this point, Hazel's got a pretty good picture of CHARL1E's network structure and the problem with the chronodes, she just can't figure out the details that would fix it. The stuff on Station C was simple to download into a body because there were existing hubs for all the old hardware that continued communicating wirelessly with the body. One of the reasons Hazel *must* always wake CHARL1E is that when he's powered down, the systems run as he left them, but if any fail—atmosphere, power, lighting—only he can fix it.

The chronodes are different. Scattered down the timeline, they exist beyond Station C, in a pocket of space-time that from Lilith's descriptions must be the dreamscape. How they got there isn't clear, but they were linked to CHARL1E on a separate system to the rest of Station C—and that link was severed when he transferred to his body. He might not be able to access the dreamscape directly, but he has always had an indirect link through the chronodes. Yesterday, Hazel investigated his now-unilluminated icosahedron, but found nothing out of the ordinary, so she figured corrupt code must be causing the issue. Yet she still can't find the bug anywhere, in her code or Lilith's notes. Lilith writes about CHARL1E like a parent talking about their child: her endless, unquestioning love and delight at each of his movements mixed with fears of disappointment, irritation at his half-learned social abilities, and grief at her loss of self to him.

The light slants from one side of the room to the other as the day ages, and by evening Hazel has no choice but to wake CHARL1E, crash out on the chairs again, and pray that she sleeps too lightly to enter the dreamscape.

The passage of time is confusing at Station C, short term because Hazel hates marking it, and long term because the seasons are hidden. The days might draw out or close in, but it's hard to tell when everything inside is enclosed in the flat line of controlled atmosphere and everything outside is a perpetual sticky heat, bounded by rainless clouds and deadened sea. So Hazel guesses about a week passes before her frustration snaps.

CHARL1E wakes, coughing and gripping the edge of the gurney until his green knuckles turn yellow.

'How can you not know the answer to this?' Hazel snaps.

'Do you know how your heart beats?' CHARL1E rubs his chest like he's got technological acid reflux.

'Roughly, yes!'

'You are an inferior liar, Hazel, we have covered this topic before.'

'But you must know something!'

CHARL1E shakes his head. 'All I can relay is that I feel . . . grief. It is as if I have lost a limb: Sometimes I sense the phantom of it when I am asleep, then when I wake it is gone.'

Hazel pauses. 'Do we need to think about the fact that you can dream now? Maybe that's formed a direct connection between you and the dreamscape, and is screwing up your communication with the chronodes?'

'Improbable. My dreams are not special in a way that lets me access the dreamscape. I have no twin, and nobody in the timeline has a body genetically similar to mine, so I cannot perform spooky action over great temporal distances.'

'But you're a post-quantum computer, you should be able to access those spaces without that.' Hazel paces, tightening her ponytail. 'OK, so maybe the problem's that you're *not* accessing the dreamscape at all, neither indirectly through the chronodes, or directly through your own dreams. How did the Arch access it?'

'The Keepers did not deem it appropriate to give me that information.' CHARL1E crosses his arms, brow furrowed. 'However, I understand from Tree that her link to the Arch was part of the process.'

Hazel runs through what she knows about Tree: the strange malfunctions that occurred during her arrival, and the component at the middle of it all, spherical and glinting. 'Did that have something to do with her elpis device?'

CHARL1E pauses, silently communing with Tree. 'Affirmative.'

'The same device that's in the Catopic Aperture,' Hazel says, thinking of the mirror orb in the past cradle. 'And I bet the Arch had one too?'

'Affirmative,' CHARL1E says. 'I was permitted that much information.'

'Which means every bit of equipment that touches the timeline has an elpis device—except you.'

CHARL1E freezes, speaking in the same tone of voice as when she found the "Heretical Book" in his code. 'Affirmative. I do not have an elpis device.'

'At least you don't anymore, because if Tree, the Arch, and the Catopic Aperture all need one, then you must too. Which makes this a hardware issue after all.'

'No.' CHARL1E shakes his head vehemently. 'I would know.'

'Would you? As you pointed out, I don't know how my heart beats. What if it was hidden?'

'This is Station C, there is no place that I cannot see, feel, control—' CHARL1E's shoulders slump. 'The icosahedron.'

'Right,' Hazel says excitedly. 'It's a sealed unit: no way in, no way out. It's the perfect place to hide an elpis device, somewhere no one could damage it.'

'You conclude that the gap in my torso is for an elpis device?' CHARL1E asks, staring at the floor.

'It must be!' Hazel says, fizzing with the adrenaline of a breakthrough. 'But then, why didn't Lilith put one in?'

CHARL1E crosses his arms. 'The method for manufacturing them was . . . how would you describe it? Lighter-than-feather-pillow science. The Keepers lost the wisdom for it many years ago, and there are no unused elpis devices left on Station C.'

'That's why Lilith didn't finish your body, isn't it? She was putting off having to choose between your needs and the operation of the Arch. But then, how did the Aperture get one?'

Still avoiding eye contact, CHARL1E says, 'Because Lilith was not only choosing between my body and the Arch.' He nods to the deceased Tiny trapped in Huxley's failed prism.

Steeling herself, Hazel examines the Tiny more closely, registering the hole bored in its chest, not an accidental part of the experiment's failure, but an intentional extraction. Hazel's breath sticks in her throat, and she turns back to CHARL1E. 'That's how Huxley got the Aperture to work, by mutilating a Tiny?'

CHARL1E nods.

Hazel looks at Robin, Teaspoon, and Shiny, who stare back with their deep round lenses. 'That means every Tiny has an elpis device . . .'

'Affirmative.' CHARL1E finally meets her gaze. 'It is what keeps them connected, to each other and to Tree. They were designed to communicate over great distances, and there is no greater distance than time. But Lilith was not like her brother. She would never harm a Tiny, even for my body.'

Hazel stares at him. 'Would you?'

'No,' CHARL1E says without hesitation. 'It would breach our truce. Besides, I have humanity.'

Looking at the mutilated Tiny again, Hazel wonders if CHARL1E might have evolved beyond humanity. She starts pacing. 'There must be something we can use instead of an elpis device. We got the Aperture to work with the *Eikos Muthos*, maybe we could wire that into you.'

'Negative. When using the *Eikos Muthos*, the Catopic Aperture operated at suboptimal functionality.' CHARL1E sighs, indicating his software's overclocking. 'I infer that the *Eikos Muthos* has a limited energetic capacity. It worked because of its mirrored cover and the centuries of prayers it absorbed, but prayer is like a battery, it runs out if it is not answered. An elpis device is more like a solar panel, recharging in response to its surroundings.'

'I see what you mean by lighter-than-feather-pillow science.' Hazel scuffs the floor. 'What you're saying is, if we want you to see the timeline accurately, and long term, you need an elpis device.'

'Affirmative.'

'And you're going to need the Catopic Aperture once I'm gone, because it's the only way nongenetically identical beings can communicate through time.'

'Affirmative.'

'So the only place we can get an elpis device is from a Tiny?'

Unable to hold her gaze, CHARL1E nods.

Shaking her head, Hazel looks to Robin, Shiny, and Teaspoon. They've taken care of her for so many weeks, tended her wounds, tidied her mistakes, fetched and carried, welcomed her into their home—even forgiven her initial ignorance and the horrific accident of her arrival. She and Robin go bottle cap hunting. Shiny is almost getting tea right. Teaspoon reminds her to put on her headphones every morning since that incident with the screwdriver. CHARL1E and the Catopic Aperture don't function properly without elpis devices, and Tree broke down completely, so goodness knows what would happen to a Tiny. The risk is too great.

'There has to be another way. We could smash your icosahedron and extract your original elpis device.'

'There is a ninety-eight percent probability that would shatter the device.'

'A two percent chance at success isn't nothing.'

'It also risks further compromising the chronode networ—' CHARL1E's head snaps up as the Tinys' tails flick in unison. He cocks his head, listening in. 'Hazel Brandt, I feel the same way as you, but it seems it is not up to us.'

Hazel looks between CHARL1E and the Tinys. 'What do you mean?'

'The Tiny you call Robin has made a proposal,' CHARL1E says, 'and the others have agreed to it.'

'What kind of proposal?' Hazel looks to Robin, who looks to CHARL1E.

'Robin has—Robin—' CHARL1E opens his mouth uselessly a couple of times. 'Robin has made a twofold proposal. First, as the custodian of your keystone memory, it will give you the prompt for your anamnesis. Second, it will donate its elpis device to me. Once I have confirmed the mend to the timeline, you will commit anamnesis.'

Hazel drops onto her makeshift bed, and Robin trundles over.

She shakes her head. 'No.'

The Tiny pats her hand, nodding. *Yes.*

'You don't have to. We can find a different way.' Hazel's eyes burn.

Slowly, Robin strings together their existing signs in new arrangements. *No. I must deal with what is in front of me. I am OK. I am ready for the—*

'CHARL1E, do you recognise that gesture?'

Robin's tail sways, and CHARL1E translates quietly, 'The lonely dark.'

Opening the hatch in its side, Robin pulls something out and presses it into Hazel's hand: the pink bottle cap with 'You're a winner' and a gold star on the inside. She stares at it, so the others don't see her holding back tears, and by the time she looks up, Robin's gone to fetch her keystone memory prompt.

Outside, there's a commotion, and Hazel watches through the window as hundreds of Tinys flood from their burrows, assembling around the Experimentation Dome. They part, making a path for Robin, who returns holding—

'Why on Earth has it got a cup of tea?' Hazel says.

She understands as soon as Robin's through the airlock, and she spots the steam, inhales the tannin-and-bergamot scent, sees the brewed-strong-with-milk sandy-brown colour. A hot cup of Earl Grey tea. Real Earl Grey tea. Already, her memories are stirring. All this time, the Tinys have been making rubbish tea on purpose. Scoundrels! The Tiny puts it on the side, next to the coding computer, wipers angled up in a smile. It waves, and Hazel waves back, clutching the pink bottle top.

Robin approaches CHARL1E, Teaspoon, and Shiny, and unhooks the oil spout in its torso, using it as a lever to pull open its sternum. Inside, amongst the tangle of wires, an elpis device glints, bending the world in a reflection so flawless Hazel takes a moment to realise it's spinning. A little 'oh' escapes her. Seeing inside Robin gives her the same uncanny shiver as building CHARL1E's body, but it's countered by wonder that Robin's voluntarily making itself so vulnerable.

Robin lowers its lenses, unable to close its eyes but curling in on itself, all its focus on its hands as they squeeze into its chest and clutch the device. There's a short squeal of mirrored glass against metal fingers, then the device slows and stops. Robin tugs the connectors from the top and base, cradling the device as it comes free, but otherwise falling still, suspended in the separation.

Wheeling forward, Teaspoon takes the elpis device from Robin's fingers. It holds the device to its own chest for a moment, tail making figure of eights, then turns to CHARL1E, who kneels, exposing his neck.

Clutching the device in one hand, Teaspoon reaches with the other and presses the button behind CHARL1E's neck. His chest cavity slicks open, internal lights blinking on, and Teaspoon places the elpis device in the gap between components. Wires stretch like vines from every circuit, twining into an artery and vein that latch on to the device's base and top. The wires pull the device in, out of Teaspoon's grip, and the Tiny rolls back, tapping its fingers nervously.

The mirrored sphere starts spinning, accelerating until the cavity's lights flicker. CHARL1E's hands and feet twitch. His mouth opens and a wavering note emerges from it, his thousand voices returning and singing to the tune of Tree's song. His chest cavity slides closed of its own accord. As it clunks into place, CHARL1E shivers and falls silent. His head droops and his eyes open. Still kneeling, he looks up at Hazel and she sucks in a breath.

His eyes—just moments ago impenetrably dark—swim with stars. As he blinks, galaxies spin and nebulae exhale; comets streak long tails across the vacuum of space; somewhere, a blue-and-green marble spins within an atmosphere thin as cling film.

'Your eyes . . .'

He doesn't respond, cocking his head as if tuning into a celestial song he hasn't heard in a long time.

Hazel grips the bottle top Robin gave her so hard it hurts. 'Did it work?'

'Yes.' CHARL1E smiles. *It shall make thy belly bitter, but it shall in resolution be as sweet as honey.* 'They are far off, but I can hear the chronodes. Give me a moment.'

He rises and strides to the window, placing his forehead and palms against it as if reaching beyond the extinct sea.

Hazel's eyes drop to Robin, who's still staring at its hands, which so recently held the elpis device. Teaspoon and Shiny stand not far off, tails entwined.

She puts the bottle top in her pocket and kneels beside Robin, frightened to touch it.

'Robin?' When it doesn't move, she strokes one of its lenses with a finger, feeling the hum of continuing power. 'You in there?'

It moves, slowly, looking at her without a hint of recognition, then returns its attention to its empty hands.

'Robin?' The robot doesn't move. 'We could hunt bottle caps?'

Nothing.

'Or we could go and pray in Tree with the other Tinys? They'll be so proud of you.'

Again, nothing. Her eyes sting and her vision swims.

Returning on silken feet, CHARL1E slips an arm around her shoulders.

'What's wrong with it?' She's trying to hold her tears back, but still one escapes.

'It is lost,' CHARL1E replies.

'Then we need to find it.'

'I am sorry, Hazel, but that is not your task. Leave finding Robin to us, there are other things that you must do now.' CHARL1E's voice hums, each of the chronodes lending him a speaker from a hundred thousand points in the past. 'Come away, you cannot fix it.'

'But—'

CHARL1E's grip around her shoulder tightens, but his voice stays calm. 'It is time for a cup of tea.'

Galaxies twist in CHARL1E's eyes as she understands. 'The glitch has almost reached my home present, hasn't it?'

He nods. 'I apologise. I estimated that we had longer.'

'Did we complete the Deed?'

'Yes.' CHARL1E nods.

'And?'

'It made a little change for the better, though there is still much to do.'

She looks around the Experimentation Dome, thinking of the well-thumbed *Lucid Dreaming* book back in her bedroom, the Aperture hanging empty from the greenhouse ceiling, Tree endlessly singing. Now it's time to leave, she's resistant. 'But I haven't contacted the Backward Traveller As Was. The catopthura—'

CHARL1E gives her a little smile. 'I calculate there is one more piece of information you need before you can do that, but we must act *now*.' He guides her towards the steaming mug of tea on the side. 'You will have one last moment in the dreamscape. Use it wisely.'

She sinks into her wheely chair by the tea, picks up the mug and inhales the steam. **Painkillers arranged like a flower on a plate; does it make them easier to take that way; breathe in to four hold for—**

Home comes for her as she sips the tea, warm and familiar and perfectly brewed, triggering a tidal wave of memories at her mind's edge. Numbly, she returns the cup to the side, and as she pulls her hands away from it, her fingernails start dissolving in the air, as if she's only dust disturbed by a breeze. **Breathe in—Breathe—**

She takes a last look around the dome, her scattered tools and Robin's still, empty shell. She fixes CHARL1E with a look that could drill rocks, the tips of her hair disintegrating and neck itching as time catches up with her. 'You'd better find Robin again.'

'I believe I have already made that promise.'

Ignoring her aching neck, she holds out a hand. 'Goodbye, CHARL1E.'

He frowns, taking her disintegrating hand and shaking it with a chilly palm, close enough for her to smell his rain-on-spring-grass odour. 'Goodbye, Hazel Brandt.'

Then the past pincers her neck and her vision floods with Not Here's molten light. The wave of her keystone memory crashes, sweeping her away completely.

Her sister set down a cup of Earl Grey tea on the table between the deckchairs. She always took Mum's chair, so Hazel was in Dad's. They had to get rid of most of the furniture when they downsized, but the deckchairs just squeezed onto the balcony. The swindling life insurers didn't pay out because the crash was technically their parents' fault, but it was an excuse. It had been raining and the three of them were laughing so hard—it was just an accident. The scent of burning rubber and stab of broken glass, a scream . . . There should've been some compensation for that kind of trauma.

A hot breeze blew, laced with the scent of tarmac, as her sister put a plate of pills next to the tea.

'Did you arrange them like a flower?' Hazel's voice was hoarse, wrecked from the vocal cord paresis.

'Does it make them easier to take that way?'

Hazel nodded as well as she could in her neck brace. 'Yeah, I guess.' She swallowed the painkillers, then hugged the mug of tea to her chest, waiting for them to kick in. Her sister looked after her so well, taking care of the funeral, the paperwork, moving, cooking . . . She'd flown back from her archaeological fieldwork in Greece the day after the crash, finding Hazel crying in the hospital, having just identified their parents' bodies. Her sister's PhD had been on hold ever since, just like Hazel's work at the startup. Trouble was, neither of them knew how to get going again.

'What were you telling me before medication time?' Hazel asked.

Her sister fished her ciggies out of her back pocket, mouth twitching into a smile. 'OK. So, I'm thinking of getting a tattoo.'

'A tattoo?'

'Yeah.' Her sister flicked her lighter, speaking around the cigarette. 'You know, I think it would help me.'

'What would you get?' Hazel asked.

Her sister took a deep first drag, exhaling from the corner of her mouth so the smoke didn't go all over Hazel. 'I'd like to get the Ancient Greek for "echo." Don't take this the wrong way, but it's like this thing happened that's defined my whole life, and I wasn't there. I feel . . . left out? Just an echo of the crash. But if I got a tattoo, then a part of me would be solid again.'

'I kind of get it,' Hazel replied, 'but feeling left out is the stupidest thing I ever heard. At least you haven't half lost your voice. And even if you had been there, you couldn't have made a difference—I was in the car, and I didn't, did I?'

'Alright, you don't have to be a bitch about it.' Her sister burned through a centimetre of cigarette in one breath. 'Anyway, I didn't mean it like that. It wasn't your fault.'

'I mean, damn it do you want to swap places with me or something?' Hazel gripped her mug so tight her knuckles turned white. 'You can have all the night terrors, and I can take up smoking?'

'Put the mug down, you're shaking,' her sister said.

'I'm fine,' Hazel replied, chest constricting.

Her sister stubbed out her cigarette. 'You're not, you're going to have another panic attack. Put the mug down and breathe. Come on, in to four, hold for two—'

Hazel tried to follow but it was impossible when all she could smell was burning rubber and all she could hear was a scream that only existed in her head. 'I miss them so much.'

'I know, I do too,' her sister said, always a still pool in the face of Hazel's typhoons. 'I'd do anything to bring them back—'

Hazel tumbles through the dreamscape, limbs flailing. Her home present yanks the back of her neck, but it isn't yet the moment to return. There's more work to do. A figure falls in tandem with her, both of them dropping through the thick current towards the memory seed forest. The other woman is thin as a sapling, with twig arms and silver birch skin, mottled purple and blue from blood poisoning. Only her short red hair gives away that it's the Backward Traveller. It's too late. Hazel shouts across the river of time, 'I'm here, I found you, I have your keystone,' but the Backward Traveller doesn't respond.

As if hitting a body of water, Hazel impacts the knotted roots of the memory seed forest, scrabbling up and staggering through the pain of anamnesis towards her sister. Hazel finds her, body cocooned in branches, roots and vines growing over and through her. She tears at the undergrowth, but the creepers cling tighter, soothing her sister's fevered shakes. Maggots and fungi blossom over her glazed eyes and thin skin, guiding her back to the earth.

No. Hazel's not losing her as well. Every moment of her recovery, her sister was there, with a story, or a listening ear, or the right medication. This is not how her sister dies.

Hazel leans towards her sister's ear, disturbing worms and flies with her whisper. 'You are my twin, and your name is Anna.'

Anna sighs, though whether it's the sigh of a rising sleeper or the mechanism of a body releasing its inhabitant, Hazel can't tell. The tree boughs and vine tendrils continue wrapping Anna in vegetal arms, until they obscure even her purpling fingers and toes under their weave. Spreading from the cocooned body, an autumnal gust surges through the memory seed grove. The flowers wither, birthing fat berries and hips in bloody shades. The leaves turn yellow, then brown, then fall to the ground like shed skin, gathering in drifts at Hazel's feet, leaving the trees' bare fingers pointing into the current. She looks back to the cocoon around Anna's body.

Between the chinks in the weave of branches, there is nothing but dried leaves. No body, no bones, no Anna.

Hazel straightens, spine on fire, anamnesis pulling her homeward, but she still isn't done. She'll never be done. Screwing up her eyes, she summons memories of Anna without restraint. *I'd do anything to bring them back.* That memory of the balcony didn't just unlock Hazel's anamnesis, it also gave her the secret to making Anna build the catopthura: *lie.*

The memory calls up a vision of Anna—the Backward Traveller As Was—clearer than she's ever seen in the dreamscape. Her sister as she was after their parents' death: wan, growing her first wrinkles from crying. She used to cry at night when Hazel was asleep. Hazel listened in the dark, vocal cords too weak to call out in support, and too fuzzy from painkillers to get out of bed. She grieved too, but differently, perhaps because she had been in the car, or because of the prescriptions the doctors loaded on her for months, or, most likely, because she had Anna looking after her. It was the wedge of difference that made Hazel agree to build the catopthura with Anna, and it's the reason Hazel's lie is going to work on her now.

'If you build that catopthura,' she says to the Backward Traveller As Was, slow and clear and hating herself, 'you can change the past. Your own past. You can bring our parents back.'

Hazel's spine feels like it's in a vise and spots dance in her vision.

'You promise?' asks the Backward Traveller As Was.

The pain in Hazel's back reaches round her ribs and across her torso, bleeding into her arms and legs, until every inch of her writhes with it. 'I promise.'

She can't breathe. She can't think. She can't hear Anna's reply, but she knows her lie works because it did, and it has, and it always will.

And because just when things seem most impossible, that is so often when they happen.

Fragments of mirror jab Hazel's belly and cheek. She opens her eyes on Dad's watch, ticking behind a cracked face. It's still late-afternoon in summer, golden sunlight streaking the carpet. Fairy light cables tangle one of her arms.

She's back.

'Anna?' She calls, her voice raspy and hoarse. 'You here?'

For a second, the only sound is traffic beyond the window. Then, from behind her, come the mewling, curdling cries of a newborn child.

'Anna?' Hazel calls again, less certainly this time. She pushes herself up from the floor, dislodging debris from her hair. Just as when she arrived at Station C, she's stark naked, standing in the living room in broad daylight, and she wraps herself in a blanket from the couch, which their mother crocheted years ago.

The crying continues, and she approaches its source, until she's staring down at a naked baby in amongst the debris. Instinctively, Hazel picks it up, wrapping it in a loose corner of her blanket, cradling its lolling head. She makes shushing noises, swaying her body like a cradle. Her memories haven't gone the way they did when she travelled to Station C, instead there has been an influx of thousands, all out of place and confused, like a hard drive that needs defragmenting, or drunk partygoers spilling into a nightclub, or the Tinys diving in Tree and CHARL1E's electric sea . . . But even disjointed, her memories don't contain a baby. Neither she nor Anna were pregnant when they travelled into time, or back to this present, and neither of them ever had been.

Where is Anna? Hazel calls her name, startling the baby and renewing its squeals.

Hazel cradles it closer and walks through the flat, her calls of 'Anna?' diminishing as each room reveals itself to be empty.

A pith of dread grows in her chest until, returning to the sitting room, Hazel is forced to accept she and the baby are the only two people in the flat. She sinks onto the couch, adjusting the baby to get a proper look at her.

The blanket corner doesn't quite fully cover the baby's chest, and just under one clavicle are a series of blemishes, newborn things that will fade in time. The dread in her chest blossoms, fruits, and ripens in seconds. Hazel knows those marks, from an older body in the past, on which ink sat under the skin. ἠχώ. She can't translate it, but Anna told her what it meant.

'Anna?' Hazel whispers. 'Is that you?' Though she is already certain of the answer.

The baby—Little Anna—keeps crying. Her squeals are whole and loud, untainted by social propriety or desensitisation to the world's enormity.

Hazel stares into the baby's vast, unfocussed eyes. 'How much will you remember, Little Anna?' Then, with a sinking heart. 'Gosh. How much do you already know?'

Little Anna's cries continue, her wincingly clean voice dug from a fresh generation, ready for its own excursions and projects, but perhaps, terribly, somewhere deep down still containing the memories and pain of all the preceding lives that made it.

'Shush now, shush,' Hazel says, rocking the baby gently on her knees. 'I know, I can only agree, it's such a big world. And so frightening. Yes, it is.'

Little Anna second-guesses her own tears and hiccoughs twice.

'Yes, you're very wise to be afraid. You're very small; you need to make that big, big noise, don't you? But it's OK, I found you, and I'm here now. I'm in it all with you. I'm listening.'

Quiet now, Little Anna kicks experimentally, and Hazel catches her feet under the blanket with one hand, the other still supporting the baby's neck. Little Anna's impossibly tiny toes wiggle under Hazel's loose grip, and even though her eyes are brimming, she finds herself smiling.

There are going to be so many lies in the weeks ahead, so many visitors and medical appointments and welfare checks. Questions about where her sister is, and where Hazel was when she disappeared; questions that will takes months to fade away, and whose untrue answers will leave a taste like battery acid in Hazel's mouth. **Of course, she was very sad after our parents died—yes, officer, I suppose she could have—the river's not so far away, no—left all her possessions behind, even her purse—**

But today, it's just Hazel and Little Anna, a tangle of family in a family blanket, future and past collapsed into one all-consuming moment, in which Hazel becomes a mother. In an abstract, far-off way, Hazel had always expected that motherhood, if it happened to her, would come with joy and fear. But she could never have imagined that the elation would be so incredibly light, or the responsibility so intolerably heavy.

22

Anna

LONDON, 2020

When the waters recede, I don't know if I'm thirteen in 2020 CE or twenty-six in 514 BCE—or thirty-nine and bloody everywhere. What is it appropriate for me to know, in my still-growing, still-reaching neurons, which have done two-thirds of a PhD and never seen a GCSE exam? I want to vomit, not physically but intellectually; I'm overstuffed, the number of memories not fitting with the age of my body. I jump at the sight of my chubby teenage fingers and barely haired legs. Terrible, to be so young and know this much, but there wasn't a choice. The world is what it is, the past has done what it's done, and I am *this* now.

'Anna?' Her hand on my shoulder is an anchor.

I look at my weird twin-parent. How can she have held my hand as we buried our parents, and also have been my mother? She lied to me. She always knew we wouldn't get them back. Though, in a strange way, I guess I did—I have had a mother these last thirteen years. A good one too.

'Is it you?' she asks.

'Not sure how to answer that.'

Her face stumbles through ten feelings at once, and I recognise all of them in myself. 'How much do you remember?' she asks.

'Everything.' I gaze around the kitchen, which I've hardly lived in and lived in all my life. The windowpane's cracked, wind whistling through it, and the kitchen tap has split in two. Out in the hall, the mirror's shattered, dusting the floor with shards. Anything that held the image of the-face-that-isn't-my-face—or, rather, is my face, but from a past I didn't remember—has broken open, just like my Echo-Anna, sister-daughter mind.

'Are you both in there?'

I look at her. What do I call her? 'Kind of.' I tap my forehead. 'But it's more like because we're both in here, neither of us are. Like I'm something new.'

'Still Anna though?'

'Both Anna, so still Anna, yes.' I pick up dropped grains of sugar on a finger.

'Does it hurt?'

'Being two people and neither of them all at once?' I lick the sugar. For one of me, it's been so long since I had sugar. There's a grain of salt mixed in with it. 'Not physically.'

Her eyes fall away from mine for the first time since I—we—

She looks so crestfallen.

'But it's OK. I'll be OK,' I add, putting my small pudgy hand over hers.

She shakes her head, still unable to look at me. There's a long, complicated road ahead, on which no one other than her will ever really know me again. I concentrate on just the next breath. 'How did I happen?'

'I used to ask you that when you were a baby. Stupid really, you couldn't even talk.' She draws her hand out from under mine. 'I think it had something to do with the memory seeds I planted. The forest that grew from them in the dreamscape caught you halfway between anamnesis and death, and cocooned you. I reckon the space-time continuum just tried to make sense of you the best way it could, and your baby self is what emerged from the chrysalis.'

I remember the vines' tight embrace, the moist fungal bloom, the last-second keystone memory, simultaneously five minutes and thirteen years ago. 'A forest on the edge of time. Hell of a cure for blood poisoning.'

She nods but doesn't laugh. A car passes on the road outside. 'I'm so sorry,' she begins, but I cut her off.

'Don't. You don't need to be.'

'But if I'd let you perform anamnesis when you wanted—'

'Look.' I pause, planting my hands on the table and fixing her with my most serious glare. 'I was there. I get it. Don't get me wrong, we've got stuff to work through, but it's you and me. We're all good.'

She cocks her head, as if trying to figure out which Anna the forgiveness comes from, still not understanding it's both and neither of us. Then her face twists up like it doesn't change her guilt either way. 'I've been planning that speech your whole life, you know.'

'Sorry to disappoint, but I think you'll find it was about a third of my life, actually.'

The corner of her mouth twitches, and she's momentarily just my sister. 'Martyr.'

'Drama queen,' I reply, poking her with my foot under the table.

Her face twists up again, and I realise she's two people now as well: Hazel and Mum.

'Oh, Mum—I mean Hazel—I mean—' I stumble to a halt, looking at her to tell me what she wants.

She just shakes her head. 'I don't know either. What were you going to say?'

'Just that this must be super weird for you too.'

Hazel/Mum nods, shrugs, huffs a laugh. 'Yeah. It's pretty weird.'

I push my chair back. 'Balcony?' It's where we always go when things are hard: her, Anna, and Anna; her, me, and me; her and them; her and us.

My legs shake as I follow her through the sitting room. In here too glass has split and mirrors have cracked. Seems like reclaiming my pre-Travel self from the dreamscape broke every reflective surface in the flat. I hope it hasn't affected the neighbours. Looking at Hazel/Mum's archaeological drawings behind their splintered glass, I realise they're not from a fictional 'Dad,' but mostly mine, from my pre-Travel studies. Even so, Hazel/Mum bought a couple in my post-Travel childhood. One is of a gravestone, plain except for the epitaph in Ancient Greek. I translate easily, even though Little Anna's never read Ancient Greek before: *Here lies Amel-Nabu, who gave the world more balance, and left it aged seventy-one. Here also lies No One, a true Athenian, who loved and followed him. They are missed by their students and friends, who continue the work of*—Then there's a word I can't translate. I swallow hard, imagining Kosmos and Nabu in the school's courtyard, grey streaking Nabu's mane and crow's feet blooming around Kosmos's eyes. Their hands calloused, soles hardened, livers scarred, brains slowly atrophying even as they try to stuff in more knowledge. They made it.

'Nabu kept his promise,' I say.

'He did,' Hazel/Mum replies. 'We completed the Deed, and you'll see in time, things are a little better than they were.'

'Only a little?' I look away from the troubling word I can't translate. Through the window, pigeons wheel against the rosy dawn.

'Project Kairos issued hundreds of Excursions,' she says. 'No single one could change everything, they were always supposed to work together. Ours was just a small step in a long hike.'

I think it through, the word I can't translate on the gravestone sketch still bothering me. 'But the Arch broke, so we were the last Excursion. If we didn't tie all those Deeds together, then the Project failed, right?'

Hazel folds her arms. 'Not necessarily. CHARL1E might've fixed the Arch, and we could be getting overwritten by glitches and mends we can't feel all the time.'

I shudder, thinking of the automaton on the cusp of time, meddling with its fraying edge, always observing and calculating.

'Sometimes I've had dreams or déjà vu,' Hazel/Mum continues, things spilling out of her that she's been holding back for years. 'And I look up because it feels like he and Tree and the Tinys are watching me, and I wonder what timeline just passed by. Once, I thought I was walking in acid rain under a glass umbrella, but when I looked up it was just black cloth over my head. I stretched out a hand to catch the raindrops and was genuinely surprised my skin didn't burn. Another time, when you were still little, we were in the park and you were playing in the long grass and it was so unfamiliar, as if I'd never seen grass, as if it had just never existed before. I ran my hands through it, and I swear, it was brand-new.'

I try to be her sister for a moment, not her daughter. 'Do you think it could be PTSD?'

'No.' She's got Mum-level confidence about this, giving me the same tone she once used for staying away from hot stoves. 'I truly believe CHARL1E could be capable of that sort of thing. There was so much about him that even he didn't know. You remember that prophecy I found in his code? It was in first person. My theory is that at some point in time, a future version of him wrote it, and then put it inside a past version of himself. Besides, I spent so long in the dreamscape, it probably gave me temporal oddities too. I think it sensitised me to glitches and mends.'

The sitting room is close with my uncertainty. It's going to be another hot day. I look at my plump hands, which should be dry and creased like Hazel/Mum's. A whole kid's lifetime passed—my lifetime—and we just took baby steps when we should've been sprinting. I am angry, but not the way Hazel/Mum thinks.

'There's so much left to do,' I say, turning to her. 'When we travelled, we affected the past and the future, but the past and future also affected us. We could bring change to the present as well—so why haven't you done something? All these years and you've never even raised a placard!'

She smiles and I raise an eyebrow.

'Sorry,' she says. 'It's just that you really sounded like Little Anna then.'

I fold my arms, but Hazel/Mum places her hands on my shoulders turns me back to the grave sketch.

'Know what this means?' She asks, pointing at the word I've been struggling with.

'No. The word's stupidly long, and I'm a bit rusty, or I guess, still confused.'

'It's two words, shoddy inscription,' she says. 'The first word, "parakinduneusis" means "desperate venture." '

My memory tingles, returning to a library I haven't been in since before I was born. 'But you could also translate it as "project," ' I whisper, realising what the second word is.

They are missed by their students and friends, who continue the work of Project Kairos.

I gasp.

'Right?' Hazel/Mum says, definitely inhabiting Mum-mode. 'Sometimes there's genuinely nothing going on, and you should get angry about that. Hopping, blazing, blow-it-up crazy. But this isn't one of those times. You've known me thirteen— Thirty-nine— *Urgh.* You know me. Do you really think I'd travel through time, lose my sister—as far as I knew forever—and come back and do nothing?'

I frown, trying to figure her out. The sun cusps the flats opposite, shining gold on her hoodie. On the breast, a logo is picked out in white thread, a clock face running backwards. Underneath, in crisp serifs: *PROJECT KAIROS.* I stare at Hazel-Mum.

Her smile deepens. 'Like CHARL1E said, trying is imperative.'

'But it's hundreds of years before they even start coding him.'

'You're the one who said we should change things.'

I think of her cluttered, cramped study. 'You mean, he's just sitting there on your laptop?'

'Well, not all of him,' she admits. 'But enough to chat with.'

It's so easy to picture CHARL1E and the Tinys under the boughs of Tree, listening to the votives tinkling in a fresh breeze made from real trees with real leaves, while agapanthus and poppies and cornflowers sprout from the rubble against a sparkling sea. In that world, perhaps Tree would start singing recognisable things—the Bhagavad Gita, the Torah, Bach, Nina Simone, Faithless—and humanity wouldn't be over, but reawakening, Deed by Deed. I won't live long enough to find out whether that world comes true, but I can work towards it.

Even so, it's one thing saying that and another doing it. Post-travel Anna's only thirteen and she's already exhausted. Part of me wants to just sit down and scream, "It's too late!"

The difficulty isn't the vision, it's the journey.

A chasm in my chest opens, and I'm thirteen and thirty-nine and just as lost at both ages. I look up at Hazel/Mum and she sees it on my face.

'How about that fresh air?'

I nod and she guides me to the door, sunlight piercing the frosted glass as she unlocks it. She freezes partway through stepping out.

'What's wrong?' I say, craning to get a look.

She lets the door swing open and stands back, pointing at the balcony with her mouth ajar.

Outside, the pigeon-deflecting mirrors have shattered, dusting the pots of half-grown mint and parched geraniums—but the mint and geraniums are gone. In their place, strange plants spring from every bare centimetre of potted earth. Vines bearing sky-blue, egg-shaped fruit twine the rusted iron railings. Mosses in every shade of green with tiny rainbow blooms drip from the pot edges and fill the cracks in the concrete. Leaves and flowers in shapes and colours I've never seen spill across the floor and clamber up the walls, shrouding the deckchairs and coffee table. Everywhere I look, there are extraordinary things. A mug left out yesterday is coated in fractals of vibrant teal mould. The half-built pigeon nest in the corner has sprouted into a shrub, bearing flowers the size of my hand.

Hazel/Mum ventures out, stroking one of the petals. 'These plants are from the dreamscape,' she says. 'I grew them myself from the memory seeds.'

I join her outside, the morning sun brushing my skin. 'Looks like I wasn't the only thing we brought back.'

In wonder, Hazel/Mum starts laughing, and the sound is so familiar that it makes me laugh too. All my post-Travel life, Hazel/Mum's been making the journey, executing her own Deeds and forming her own Excursions. Her laughter subsides as she breathes in the sunlight and honey-scented dreamscape flowers. 'I wonder what happens now.'

'Well,' I say. 'I think it's high time you introduced me to CHARL1E.'

'Alright,' she says, 'but don't be disappointed, he's not quantum yet or anything.'

'Give it time.' I look over the allotments, wondering how many dreamscape seeds and spores are already drifting on the wind, already affecting the microbiome in my lungs. I clasp my hands together, half in wonder, half in expectation. 'So? Let's begin.'

ACKNOWLEDGEMENTS

NORFOLK, 2025

Perhaps, if I have left someone out, we can put it down to Traveller's Forgetfulness.

In the first instance, this book owes an enormous debt to Andrew Cowan from the University of East Anglia (UEA), who supervised my PhD thesis, of which this novel formed part. Your feedback across four years had a profound impact on both me as a writer and the form this novel took. Amongst your many words of wisdom, thank you in particular for suggesting, 'You've got a lot of mirrors here, maybe there's something in that?'

Thanks too to the other pillars of support during my PhD, who shaped this book more than they know: Nathan Ashman, Nonnie Williams, Ben Smith, Bex Tillett, Jos Smith, and Jake Huntley. Big appreciation also to the UEA and Futurescapes workshopping communities, who always loved and encouraged the weirdness.

I'm indebted to Michael Trapp and Hugh Bowden at King's College London, who first humoured my research into Presocratic philosophy, and bravely undertook a historical read on this manuscript. Many thanks as well to *Early Greek Philosophy* edited and translated by Jonathan Barnes, from which much of the Presocratic philosophy is paraphrased or inspired. In all instances, I am entirely to blame for any errors which have snuck in!

A massive thank-you to the best agent a writer could hope for, and expert locator of gluten-free noodles, Alex Cochran at Greyhound Literary. Big shout-out also to Team Alex for being an endless source of writerly support, wisdom, and friendship.

Huge appreciation to the entire Tor team for their hard work and warmth: Matt, Julia, Laura, Anthony, and so many more! But particular thanks to my wonderful editor Lee Harris for his unmatched humour and generosity—and for discovering my favourite palindrome, Dr Awkward.

Big gratitude to my step-dad, Geoff, for being such excellent ballast.

And—of course—all my love and thanks to my Mum, my first reader and dearest support.

Finally, we come to you, the reader: Without you not a single book would be made. Thank you for reading mine.

ABOUT THE AUTHOR

Jasmin Kirkbride is an author and academic. Her short fiction has appeared in publications including *Reactor*, and her story 'Sand' was featured in *Some of the Best from Tor.com 2021*. Her eco-poetry has been published in places including *Frogpond* and *Presence*, and she was the 2022 Researcher-in-Residence for the British Haiku Society, investigating haiku in the climate crisis. An ex-editor and book trade journalist, Kirkbride holds an MA in ancient history from King's College London, and an MA in creative writing and PhD in Creative and Critical Writing from the University of East Anglia (UEA). Her thesis explored radical hope in dystopian climate fiction, and her academic research explores climate fiction, eco-poetry, and fungal literature. *The Forest on the Edge of Time* is her first novel.